PLAYBILL

THE HANGAR THEATRE

Saturday April 21, 2012

THE UNINTENDED

WALLY WIGGINS

The Players

Junito Cubero (Aldo Sanchez, and the Guard/Officer)
Junito has been in the local acting scene for about 12 years now, with over 27 productions under his belt. He was last seen in Steady Rain a 2 man show where he played "Denny" for the Reader's Theatre in December of 2011.

Michael Donato (Barney Rifkin)
Michael's recent appearances include "Sir Toby Belch" in the Ithaca Shakespeare Company's production of Twelfth Night, "John Murphy" in the short film Ward 11 produced through Ithaca College, and "Norman" in Arabian Nights for AWI.

Carolina Osorio Gil (Lucie Alverz)
Carolina most recently portrayed "Iphigenia" in Caridad Svich's Iphigenia. Favorite roles include "Mustardseed" in Midsummer Night's Dream, "Borachio" in The Tempest, "God" in Poona, and "The Cat" in References to Salvador Dali Make Me Hot.

Lance Milne (District Attorney, Gary Samson)
Lance originally hails from Rochester, NY and arrived in Ithaca by way of NYC. He's performed in films, theater productions, commercials and industrials, TV pilots, workshops and seminars, comedy groups, haunted tours, and projects at NYU, IC, Cornell and RIT.

David Romm (Toro Santoros)
David first played the Hangar in the 1970's, part of Hangar Playfair. Decades later he studied at the Ithaca Actors Workshop and has since appeared in many local Plays and films. He is a member of the Comedy FLOPS.

Judy Rossiter (The Judge)
Judge, Ithaca City Court, Elected, 1995 to 2000; Re-elected 2001 to 2010; 2011 to 2020 Judge, Ithaca City Court, Appointed by Mayor of Ithaca, 1994 to 1995.

Katie Spallone (Marguax McBride)
In addition to performing and teaching at the Actor's Workshop of Ithaca since 2006, Katie performed leading roles with the Babes in Arms Women's Theatre Collective, Third Floor Productions, the Firehouse Theatre and in several independent films. She was last seen as "Beth" in Orange Flower Water and as "Becca" in The Workshop's 10th anniversary production of Rabbit Hole at Risley Theatre.

Nick Saldivar - Director
Nick's work has garnered the recognition of the Kennedy Center's American College Theatre Festival, where he was a finalist for the directing initiative. Directing credits include, *The Trojan Women 2.0* and *ORAL* (Best of the Festival List by the Orlando Sentinel) at the Orlando Fringe, Baby with the Bathwater at the Surfside Playhouse. Nick is also the Literary Manager at the Hangar Theatre.

A special thank you to:
The Hangar Theatre, Americana Winery, La Tourelle Resort and Spa, Scott, Leslie, Ashley, Frances, Loret, Stephanie, Janice, Dave, Donna, Suzy, Jacob, Tony, Meryl, Jonni, Jessica, Marcus, Cindy, Alek, Nick and all the great performers.

TO THE CLAN:

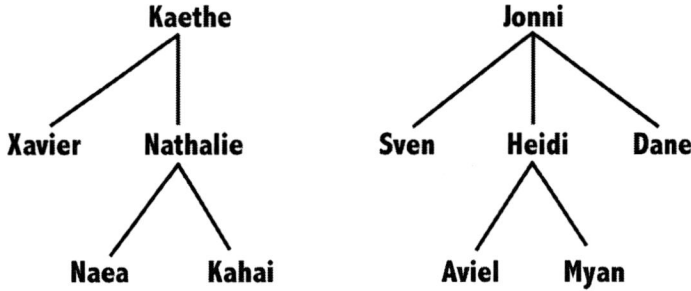

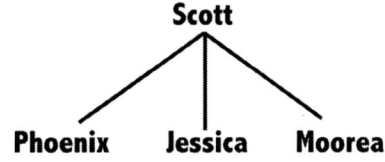

CHAPTER ONE

For over eight months Margaux and Lucie had been bunkmates at the Richford Hills State Prison for Women in Westchester County, twenty-five miles from New York City. They became inseparable friends, despite the multiple differences between them. Margaux was a New York City attorney convicted of grand larceny for stealing a quarter of a million dollars from the estate of Katrina Shauffler. Lucie was born and raised in a small village in Mexico, south of Laredo, Texas. She thought sooner or later she would get married, have kids, and get fat just like most of her girlfriends. But then she met Harold. Army guys stationed in Laredo like him would come to her village on three-day leaves to get drunk on cheap tequila and get laid. They succeeded in doing both most of the time. The local girls were hoping for a ticket out of Mexico.

Harold was quiet and respectful, different from the others who were just looking for a good time. He courted her for about a month and then he told her his hitch in the army would be up in a few weeks and as soon as he was discharged he would come back because he had a serious question to ask her. She said, "Why don't you just ask me now?" He laughed and told her he had to clear up some things back home first. In less than a month he returned and asked her to marry him, and then he handed her a plane ticket to New York and gave her a brand new suitcase packed with beautiful clothes, and shoes to match.

After her plane landed at JFK, when she picked her bag off the carousel, a security guard asked her to come with him to an examining room. He then commanded her to open the suitcase. Over $5,000 worth of cocaine was packed into the hollow heels of the new shoes, and there was a false bottom in the suitcase containing hundreds of small glassine envelopes of cocaine with a street value of over $40,000. She tried to call Harold but his cell phone had been disconnected and she never heard from him again.

The lawyer who was assigned to defend her recommended that she accept the district attorney's offer to plead guilty to a lesser charge. He claimed he was surprised when the judge sentenced her to fifteen months in state prison. She accepted her fate and was grateful that she wasn't serving her time in a Mexican jail. *In fact,* she mused, *the food and lodging here*

To Bill & Debbie
Two of my dearest friends
(May it always be so!)

[signature]

4/21/12

If I ever had a
brother I would
want him to
be sort of
like Bill

THE UNINTENDED
A PENWORKS PUBLISHERS BOOK

All rights reserved
Copyright 2011 Wally Wiggins
Edited by Beth H. Evans
Cover Photo and Interior Layout by Mark Costa
Proofread by Storm Somers and Peter Katz

No part of this book may be reproduced
or transmitted in any form or by any means, electronic or
mechanical, including photocopying, recording, or by any
information storage and retrieval system, without permission
in writing from the publisher.
Printed in USA

For information address:
    PenWorks Publishers, Inc.
    395 McDuffy Hollow Rd.
    Van Etten, NY 14889
    PenWorksPublishers.com

ISBN 978-0-9768575-7-0

Library of Congress Control
Number: 2010941726

10 9 8 7 6 5 4 3 2 1

are better than back home. I miss my freedom, but I'm learning the ways of the world.

Meeting and befriending Margaux at the prison was a turning point in Lucie's life. Margaux became her mentor and they developed a loving relationship that exceeded the joys that either of them had ever experienced from a prior friendship. They shared secrets, intimacies and dreams.

During the time they served together, there were two rival factions battling for control of trafficking contraband of every kind into the prison, from cosmetics to crack cocaine. Within a few months after her incarceration, Margaux, the most highly educated prisoner in the facility, and her lieutenant, Lucie, became the leaders of the *Hawks*. Rosie O'Rourke, with ten years left to serve, was the unchallenged captain of the *Bitches*.

Shortly before "lights out" on the evening before Margaux's scheduled release, Rosie caught Margaux alone in the locker room. Consumed with hate, and jealous of Margaux's beauty and imminent release, Rosie sidled up behind Margaux and spoke her name, softly. When Margaux turned to see who it was, Rosie threw 190 pounds of muscle behind her fist into Margaux's face.

"Just a little going away present, shyster," Rosie said.

Margaux staggered to her feet, feigned being disoriented by the blow, picked up a five pound barbell from the wooden bench beside her locker and struck Rosie across the bridge of her nose with the piece of iron.

In keeping with the code among the prisoners neither Rosie nor Margaux reported the incident.

Lucie bartered for some cosmetics to disguise Margaux's injury, and now they waited silently for the call that would allow Margaux's release from prison.

The loudspeaker blared, "McBride. Come to the front desk."

Both women immediately stood up and embraced. Margaux McBride, dressed in high-fashion, executive-tailored, boardroom black; Lucie Alvarez, wearing baggy orange fatigues and sneakers. As tears streamed down their cheeks, Lucie released Margaux and pushed her forward. "I'll see you in a couple of weeks. Get the hell out of here," she sobbed.

Margaux walked slowly up to the desk and signed out. An officer accompanied her down the long corridor leading to the rear exit of the Richford Hills State Prison for Women.

Margaux passed through the final gate, stepped into a patch of sunlight, and breathed deeply of the fresh September air. She took a few steps toward the black town car that was parked at the curb. A swarm of tabloid photojournalists assaulted her, with cameras flashing. One year as a prisoner had not diminished Margaux McBride's media allure. In fact the photographers all agreed that her classic beauty had been enhanced since they had last seen her in handcuffs on the day she was sentenced to prison. She came face to face with the woman who had dubbed her the "Barrister Beauty" during her trial. *Incredibly attractive and Arrogant with a capital A,"* she had written in the *Post*.

"What next, Margaux?" the columnist asked. Margaux stopped, smiled weakly, looked at the woman and said, "I'm not sure, Helena. I made a horrible mistake. I deeply regret what I did. There's nothing more I can say at this time."

From the back of the crowd a man's voice demanded, "How are you planning to pay back the $250,000 you stole, Margaux?"

You son of a bitch, Margaux muttered to herself. Ignoring the questioner, she waved and said "It's great to see you guys again." Then she slipped quickly into the town car her attorney had provided for her. It sped down the long driveway and disappeared.

 Dan Simpson of the *Enquirer* said, "Borrr-ing. I liked her better when she was a rattlesnake."

"Where to, Miss?" the driver asked when they exited the prison grounds.

"Attorney Barnard Rifkin's office. It's in Manhattan, East 45th Street between Third and Lex."

On the trip into Manhattan, Margaux tried to relax in the luxurious back seat of the limo. She opened the window and breathed in the heady fragrance of freedom, but the odor of the prison lingered in her clothing and she couldn't erase the image of Lucie from her mind.

At that moment, Lucie was seated in her cell, staring at the wall. "*Dios*, how I'm going to miss her. I love her so," she moaned.

Margaux was ushered into the Rifkin Law office as soon as she arrived. When she stepped forward to receive Barney's embrace, he said, "I can't believe it. You look more gorgeous than when—"

"Than when they locked me up?"

"Yeah, I guess that's what I was thinking," he said. "But it's true, you know. I'm not just saying it to make you feel good."

"You never told me anything that made me feel good," Margaux said, sitting down in the chair opposite Barney's desk and glancing around the office. "It doesn't look as if anything has changed much in a year. How about you, Barney? Is there anything new in your life?"

"Not really. I'm still trying to prevent the district attorney from putting innocent people in jail."

"What went wrong in my case, Barney?" she asked.

Does she want the truth or sympathy? he wondered. "It was a difficult case," he answered, looking away from her.

"Look at me, Barney; I want you to level with me. You're one of the best criminal lawyers in the city. How come you let those twelve jerks convict me?"

He turned back to her. "It was a tough case, Margaux, and, and—"

"Never mind, Barn. Just tell me—how much money do I have left?" Margaux demanded.

Barney opened a file envelope on his desk, removed a single sheet of paper and handed it to Margaux. "That memo tells the whole story. The amount you left with me when you went to jail and every penny I've paid out for you while you've been gone. Your condo maintenance fee, taxes and insurance are all paid up until the end of the year. The tenants moved out last month. They left the place spotless." He pulled a set of keys from the file and pushed them across the desk.

Margaux put the keys in her purse and glanced at the memo. "So I've got a little over fifty thousand left. That won't last long in this city. And then, as you know, there's another small problem. The parole board has given me two years to pay back the money they claim I stole. Got any ideas, Barney?"

"I don't know, Margaux" he shrugged. "The appellate division won't entertain a motion to restore your license to practice law for another four years."

"Okay, so I'll sell my body."

"How much?" Barney asked with a straight face. They both laughed, but Barney couldn't be sure whether or not she was joking.

After Margaux left Attorney Rifkin's office he eased himself back into his old fashioned leather swivel chair.

How much? He pondered the question, reflecting upon everything he knew about Margaux McBride.

The story really began when Margaux was called Maggie Doyle, he thought....

Maggie had been the product of a coupling between her mother, a strikingly attractive "townie", and several members in good standing of the Upsilon Psi Gamma fraternity, including the scholarly president of the Class of 1970 at Iroquois College in upstate New York.

Having consumed a number of the fraternity's specialty called a *Pink Russian,* that looked and tasted like a strawberry malted but contained four ounces of vodka in each drink, the seventeen year-old young woman thought the idea of having sex with three handsome young college men at their graduation party would be a "hoot". However, the consequences were unintended. The problem was that when Maggie's grandmother learned that her daughter was pregnant and took her to a lawyer to make the putative father pay for medical expenses and for support of the child, the daughter demanded to speak to the lawyer privately. When she explained to the attorney that there were three possible fathers and she only knew the name of one of them, and she couldn't really be certain about him, the attorney said his fee for trying to figure it all out would be $5,000, and he couldn't guarantee success. He explained that he would be required to try to obtain a court order directing every member of the fraternity to submit a sample of his blood, and since by the time the two women had come to see him, the culprits had left town, some of them for good, the situation was impossible. "In fact," he said, "on second thought I'm afraid I'll need a retainer of $10,000."

He suggested that they check with the Department of Social Services and let them figure it out.

At a very early age, Maggie moved in with her grandmother, an alcoholic who let her do whatever she wanted. Incredibly, through it all, her ambition and her father's genes guided her life, enabling her to graduate in the top of her high school class. The Department of Social Services wisely sponsored her first two years at the local community college and she went on to graduate from law school. She married a U.S. Army officer and Maggie Doyle became Mrs. Margaux McBride. Her husband was killed in the line of duty less than a year after their marriage. After passing the New York bar exam, the attractive young widow was hired by a small, prestigious law firm in Manhattan where she got mixed up with Frank Dunn, the senior partner, in a scam to steal a quarter of a million dollars from an estate that the law firm represented.

Barney leaned forward, reopened Margaux's file, and removed the transcript of the trial in which Margaux was charged with grand larceny. He had defended her on the theory that it was Frank Dunn, and not Margaux, who planned and executed the theft from the Shauffler estate and that she got caught in the trap of innocently following orders from her boss who had also become her lover.

He leafed through the transcript until he found the remarks of the judge who sentenced her to Richford Hills State Prison. He read it over and thought, *This says it all.*

Ms. McBride, as you know, I have had the benefit of a comprehensive pre-sentence investigation report; I have heard Mr. Rifkin's very moving plea on your behalf, and finally, I have listened to your own words which described so eloquently the dilemma you faced as a young attorney who fell in love with the senior partner of the law firm that hired you upon graduation from law school.

It became painfully clear to me, as the evidence was examined during the trial, that an invidious crime was committed against Mrs. Shauffler's estate. Under the terms of Mrs. Shauffler's will she created a $250,000 trust for the benefit of the Irving Shauffler School for young, disadvantaged boys. When you participated in the theft of those funds, you stole the dreams and aspirations of scores of youngsters.

The jury found you guilty of the charges against you. I am unable to say they were mistaken in their judgment, for if it had been my decision to make, I would have found you guilty as well. However, today we are only concerned with what punishment you should receive for your participation in the scheme that defrauded the Shauffler trust of a quarter of a million dollars.

Barney remembered at that point Margaux had nodded her head sadly, and wiped away her tears with the back of her hand. Judge Masson had hesitated then and looked away from her notes. She stared out the window a few moments and then continued:

For a first offender in a non-violent crime, probation and restitution are generally the appropriate penalties, and when I came to court today, I was prepared to give you the benefit of the doubt. However, after listening to the words which I know you chose with great care when you made your final plea to the Court, Ms. McBride, I decided that you are a consummate liar and an absolute disgrace to the legal profession. It is abundantly clear to me that you participated in a breach of trust, Ms. McBride. Perhaps if in your final plea to me you had said, 'I'm sorry, fellow members of the judiciary, for disgracing the honorable profession of the law, and I promise the Court that I will faithfully restore the stolen funds so that Mrs. Shauffler's most generous gift will be applied exactly as she wished....'

Barney recalled that before continuing, Judge Masson pushed her notes aside and looked directly at Margaux.

But instead you brazenly denied culpability as the tears rolled down your cheeks.

I am ashamed that you are a lawyer and I am ashamed that you are a woman.

It is the decision of this court that the defendant, Margaux McBride, be sentenced to one to three years in state prison and that she pay restitution to the estate of Katrina Shauffler in the amount of $250,000 with interest. Bail is hereby revoked. Remand the prisoner to county jail. Court is adjourned.

Barney remembered Margaux's reaction to the judge's sentence. She had gripped the counsel table with both hands while the blood drained from her face.

"What the fuck did she say?" she gasped.

On the day after she was released from prison, Margaux's picture appeared on the front pages of the tabloids under banner headlines:

BARRISTER BEAUTY COMES HOME...
DISBARRED, DISGRACED AND DISTRAUGHT...
FEMME FATALE ADMITS CRIME DOES NOT PAY...

Barney bought copies of all of them. They were spread out on his desk when his old friend and client Dimitri Santoros came into his office. Barney was representing Dimitri's son Nick, who had been arrested for selling drugs. Dimitri, known as Toro to his friends, picked up one of the newspapers.

"Geez, what a dish! Who is this broad, anyway? The name rings a bell," he said, shaking his head.

"Be careful what you say, Toro, she's one of my esteemed clients," Barney laughed.

Toro put down the paper and looked up at Barney. "Are you shittin' me? Man, she is outrageous. What'd she do? Shoot her old man?"

"I can't tell you anything more than you can read in the newspaper because she's my client; but she might be for sale." Barney left him while he retrieved the son's file. Toro picked up the paper again and began to read the story. He read all the papers, slowly, carefully. When Barney returned to his office he was still reading, moving his finger from word to word along each line of newsprint. "What's the price?" he asked, without looking up from the paper.

"What are you talking about?"

Toro held up the newspaper with Margaux's picture on the front page. "You said she's for sale. I might be in the market," he replied, grim-faced.

"I was only kidding, buddy."

"I'm not. I want you should introduce me to her. I've got some health problems. I'm not sure how serious—maybe early stages of lung cancer." Barney thought about the situation for a minute.

"She's down on her luck a bit at the moment, Toro. Actually she's an attorney—very bright. She can't practice law right now, but I've got to tell you, Toro, she's a high class lady."

"So what am I, low class? Like it says in the paper, she just got out of jail, and you say she needs money—is that right? Lemme tell you somethin', Rifkin, money don't know what class it is. How much?"

Barney leaned back in his chair, "I'd say right now she needs about a quarter of a million dollars."

Toro didn't flinch. "So introduce me, like next week. I'll take you and her to lunch, but after the appetizer you disappear, see?"

"But—" Barney stammered.

"No buts. You're my lawyer, ain't you? Twenty years you been my fuckin' lawyer."

"Sure I am, but I'm not your pimp."

"Yeah you are." Toro stood up, fished a bill out of his wallet and threw it down on the desk. Barney stared at it for a moment. It had Grover Cleveland's picture on it. He picked up the thousand-dollar bill and put it in his pocket. "You're paying for lunch too, right?" Barney said.

"What's up?" Margaux asked, when she responded to Barney's invitation to meet at his office to discuss a possible job opportunity for her. He told her he had a client by the name of Dimitri Santoros who was looking for someone with a legal background to become his personal assistant.

"Sounds perfect. What kind of business?" Margaux asked.

"He's semi-retired now. It's a matter of managing his investment portfolio, and you know...."

"What's he willing to pay?" she demanded.

"I'd say the going rate for a job like that would probably be around seventy-five thousand."

Margaux did not let her disappointment show. Before serving time at Richford Hills, she had been earning over $200,000 a year as a practicing attorney. But now, having lost her license to practice law, and being a convicted felon, she had become *persona non grata*. Her notoriety was such that every prospective employer knew that she would be coming with unsavory baggage.

She had begun the process of trying to find employment that paid at least $100,000 a year, but she had been humbled by her inability to find a job as a professional and she was desperate.

"How old is he?" she asked.

"I'm not sure...early seventies I would guess."

"What's his health?"

"Actually he has confided in me that he may have early stages of lung cancer, but you'd never know it."

Margaux stood up and paced the room. Neither of them said a word.

Finally Barney said, "If you play your cards right, I think he might help you pay your $250,000 fine. But he's not what you'd call a philanthropist or a wilting petunia. I'm sure he'd be expecting...companionship. However, he tells me that the last time he checked, his accountant told him he was a multi-millionaire."

"Margaux shrugged her shoulders and removed a copy of *Pattern's Jury Charges* from the bookshelf in Barney's office. When she found the life expectancy chart, she asked, "How old did you say he is?"

"Around seventy-one or seventy-two, I'd say."

Margaux ran her finger down the chart. "If he's in good health he's got a life expectancy of about twelve years or so," she said absently. She put the book back in its place, walked over to the window and stared down at the traffic moving along Lexington Avenue. She turned back to Barney. "But you say you think he's got lung cancer? What stage is it?"

"That I don't know," Barney answered, returning his attention to the legal documents on his desk.

"Exactly what did you mean by that remark about his expecting 'companionship'? I'm not the nurse's aide type, you know. There's no way I'd cut his toenails and change his diapers," Margaux said.

"You certainly don't need to tell *me* that," Barney laughed. "I was just trying to avoid the uncomfortable details that are none of my business. It's reasonable to assume that he is probably interested in the benefits of marriage without necessarily becoming entangled in the burdens of matrimony. How's that?"

"That's what I thought you said. Hey, Barney, one way or the other, I need a six figure salary. I'm a big girl. I know how to play the game. When and where am I supposed to meet with him?"

"Tomorrow. One o'clock for lunch at the Algonquin Hotel."

"I'll be there. Thanks, Barney."

Margaux spent the rest of the day on her computer learning as much as she could about Dimitri Santoros. She was able to confirm that he was a widower with two grown children, and that he was indeed reported to be a multi-millionaire. She decided that was all she needed to know for the present.

CHAPTER TWO

The facts about Dimitri Santoros' life that couldn't be found on the Internet were much more interesting:

A generation before the New York State government went into the lottery business, "Toro" Santoros ran numbers in Brooklyn. He lived on Flatbush Avenue, not far from the Brooklyn Bridge. While his friends were playing stickball in the streets and rolling dice for baseball cards, Toro was making more money than his old man who worked driving a garbage truck and referred to himself as a sanitation engineer. Toro gave half of what he earned to his mother who desperately needed the money to feed her eight children. She never asked where it was coming from. Toro was not the only kid in Brooklyn who was running numbers, but he was different from most of them because instead of buying dude clothes, messing with girls, doing dope and gambling, he put his money in the bank until he had enough to buy his own garbage truck. His father was his first employee. Between the two of them, they ran the truck 24/7, picking up garbage on a daily basis from dozens of restaurants that were constantly plagued by overflowing trash cans that the city would only pick up once a week.

By the time he was twenty-five he was running twenty trucks around the clock. And then the Teamsters Union representatives visited his office. Instead of fighting them, Toro made a deal to pay the drivers and loaders the increased wages they demanded, but reserved the right to hire and fire. They agreed upon a ten-year contract with small raises each year. Within one month after the deal was done, Toro invested in a piece of equipment that no one in Brooklyn had ever heard of before. It was called a "dumpster" and with his specially-equipped trucks he was able to cut his workforce by fifty percent. The union screamed and called in their lawyers. A strike was threatened, but with the advent of the dumpsters, Toro's business had grown so much that the total number of employees had more than doubled and peace was restored. In the following years, he expanded into the Bronx and Manhattan and his considerable fortune was made.

In 1975, Toro Santoros married Maria Sarkos. Despite Maria's fervent prayers, they remained childless for more than ten years. Then for reasons known only to science, chance, or one's deity of choice, their son Nicholas was born and three years later Maria gave birth to their daughter,

Xenia. In 1999, Maria was diagnosed with multiple sclerosis. Her physical condition deteriorated rapidly. Toro devoted his life to her care until she died.

Toro's son, Nick, was sixteen years old when his father found him in his room, snorting cocaine. Toro smacked him full in the face. Blood spurted from the boy's nose as he fell to the floor, barely conscious. His father turned, left the room and never looked back.

The next morning Nick was gone.

Toro was devastated by the loss of his son. After his wife died he had devoted himself to protecting his daughter Xenia and had allowed Nick to drift pretty much on his own. He realized his mistake too late. After Nick left, Toro became even more protective of Xenia. She attended parochial school, and as she began to mature, he planned every moment of her life.

Although Toro learned of Nick's whereabouts from time to time, it was more than three years before they made contact with each other again. Barney Rifkin succeeded in getting the felony charges against Nick reduced and he copped a plea. He was sentenced to a year in county jail. It was while Nick was serving time on the drug charge that Xenia, who had just turned seventeen and was attending private school, sought permission to spend the weekend with her father. He invited her into his den when she arrived. She sat down in the chair across from his desk.

"You look wonderful, darling. Tell me everything that's happened since I saw you last month."

Xenia burst into tears.

"Now, now, little one. Stop the crying. You know I can't stand to see you cry. Tell me the problem, my sweetheart. Whatever it is it can't be worth those tears. Did you fail that geometry exam you were worried about?"

"I'm p-p-pregnant," she wailed.

"No, no, NO!" he roared, slamming his fist on the desk. Xenia turned her head away and instinctively threw up her hands to protect herself from the blow she knew was inevitable. When it didn't come she stifled her sobs as best she could and looked back at him. He was no longer scowling or stern. He just looked old and sad and it made her start to cry all over again.

When the well of tears finally ran dry, he said, "So tell me Xenia, who is the father?"

"Vittorio," she mumbled.

"Vittorio…Vittorio…Vittorio who?"

"Vittorio Del Renzo."

"What does he do—this Vittorio?"

"I-I-I don't know exactly what he does."

"Where did you meet him?"

"At a party."

"How old is he?"

"Twenty-five, I think?"

"You think? Where does he live?"

"I'm not sure. In Brooklyn somewhere."

"This is wonderful. He knows you well enough to make you pregnant, but you don't know how old he is, what work he does, or where he lives!"

"I'm sorry, Daddy. I'm so very sorry."

They sat in silence. Finally Xenia spoke, barely above a whisper. "Vito has offered to pay for an abortion...."

Toro's hands came crashing down on the desktop again. "There will be no abortion in my family. I will not allow some butcher to kill you or my first grandchild."

"I love him, Daddy."

"You love him." Toro sneered. "What do you know about love? I'll kill him."

"NO! NO!" Xenia screamed. "If you hurt him, I swear to God I'll kill myself and my baby!"

"Now, now, Xenia. I ain't gonna hurt your lover-boy. All I wanna know is: if you're gonna have a baby, you gotta have a husband, at least until after the baby is born."

"I think he's already married," Xenia whimpered, and started crying again.

"Then he's gonna get unmarried. Fast. Or you're gonna marry someone else. My first grandchild ain't gonna be a bastard! Period! End of discussion! You tell Lover-Boy I wanna see him here tomorrow night, six o'clock sharp. If he don't wanna come voluntarily, I'll send an escort to pick him up. One way or the other, he'll be here at six o'clock tomorrow."

"He will be here, Daddy. I just want you to understand one thing. If you do anything bad to him, I'll kill myself and my baby."

"You said that already. I heard you the first time."

Xenia stood up and walked out of the room, closing the door softly behind her. Toro's shoulders sagged as he leaned back in his chair.

"Papa, this is Vittorio. Vittorio Del Renzo. Vito, this is my father."

Toro remained seated in his chair, unsmiling.

"Leave us alone, Xenia. Your friend and I have things to talk about." Xenia started to protest, then realized it would be foolish to begin a battle she couldn't win.

Toro never stood up from his chair. Neither man offered to shake hands. Vittorio remained standing.

"Okay, okay. Sit down, Lover-Boy."

Vito continued to stand. "I am Vittorio."

"Maybe to my daughter Xenia, but to me, you're Lover-Boy. Now sit down."

Vito didn't move a muscle.

"I am Vittorio Del Renzo," he said again.

"You're Italian?" Toro asked, barely moving his lips.

"I am Sicilian. My family comes from Sicily."

"I know where Sicilians come from." Toro spit out the words. "Now sit down...."

Vittorio suppressed a smile. Toro passed gas.

"Xenia tells me you're the father of my grandchild."

"That is true," Vittorio said.

"She tells me you're married."

"That is also true," Vittorio replied.

"How long have you been married?"

"Five years."

"Do you have kids?"

"I have a stepson."

"How old is he?"

"Five years."

"Where do you live?"

"I live in Brooklyn. My wife and my stepson live in Sicily."

"Why?" Toro asked.

"She is a pig. I come from a small village in Sicily. Her father is a big man there. He runs the district. He made me marry his daughter. I am not the father of her child. He killed the father of her child. You want me to marry your daughter, *signor* Santoros? It cost you ten thousand dollars."

Toro stared at the handsome young man. "You want my daughter to drop the charges of statutory rape, *signor* Del Renzo, it'll cost you twenty thousand dollars."

Ten days later Xenia Santoros and Vittorio Del Renzo were joined in marriage by Monseignor Antonio Mastinardi in a private ceremony held at the home of the bride. On behalf of the Immaculate Conception Church of Brooklyn, Monseignor Mastinardi accepted a most generous contribution to its building fund from the father of the bride. A healthy nine pound boy was born "prematurely" to the newlyweds seven months later. He was christened Dimitri Santoros Del Renzo. Eventually the legal problem of Vittorio's marriage to Xenia—while he was still married to Mary Renato, who lived with her son in her grandmother's home in Sicily—got resolved. It was just a matter of time and money.

Luigi Calfano changed his name to Vittorio Del Renzo in order to conceal his criminal history when he shipped out on a freighter from Palermo, Sicily, one dark night in June, 2000. Ten days later, shortly after midnight, when the ship was a quarter of a mile from Hoboken, New Jersey, he jumped ship and swam ashore with all his clothing, a cell phone and a stash of cocaine tightly packed in a waterproof bag. He made a pre-arranged call to his cousin Enrico on his cell phone. Enrico picked him up and took him to his apartment where he exchanged the cocaine he had carried from Palermo for a forged passport and a green card. There was always room for one more enterprising young man in America.

Luis Ramiriz was the son of one of the "boat people" from Cuba. His mother had been imprisoned in Cuba for killing the woman who had stolen her boyfriend. When Castro played the joke of the decade on President Carter in 1980 by opening up the prison gates in Havana and allowing thousands of criminals to join an army of undesirables to "escape" to the United States, Juanita Ramiriz took her ten-year old child with her aboard the celebrated ship, *Mariel*.

When they arrived in Miami, Florida with a U.S. Coast Guard escort, Juanita quickly resumed her regular trade as a prostitute. Her son Luis was a handsome youngster who attended public school. He excelled in his studies, became proficient in English and by the time he reached age eighteen he had become skilled as a jewel thief.

Young women found him attractive and innocently provided information that enabled Luis to gain access to their friends' homes. He left no clues when he separated his victims from their property, and since in almost every instance the losses were covered by insurance and the police were overworked with more serious crimes to solve, his misdeeds went mostly unpunished.

Vittotio had been an auto mechanic in Palermo with the ability to render stolen vehicles unrecognizable and unidentifiable. His special skills were in demand in the New York City market which served the needs of unscrupulous used car dealers throughout the country. Ramiriz and Del Renzo became friends.

Vittorio Del Renzo considered that Toro Santoros's offer to supervise the maintenance of his multi-million dollar truck and equipment inventory with a salary of $60,000 not only gave him the opportunity to become legitimate, but within a few years at most, his young wife would inherit fifty percent of a multi-million dollar estate. It was, as they say, an offer he couldn't refuse.

CHAPTER THREE

The lunch at the Algonquin proceeded according to plan. Margaux was radiant. Toro was gracious, solicitous and amusing. Over coffee and dessert, they negotiated the terms of her employment. After paying the bill Toro said, "I know how expensive this town can be." Then he wrote a check for $8,000 and handed it to her. "I thought maybe it would help if I paid your first month's salary in advance."

"That's very thoughtful of you, Mr. Santoros," Margaux said, slipping the check into her purse.

As they strolled out of the dining room with her arm tucked in his, Toro exulted in the admiring glances of every male they passed.

A few weeks after Margaux started working for Toro, he stopped into her office and said, "Perhaps you could join me at Sardi's for dinner on Saturday evening."

"I have an engagement this weekend," Margaux lied, "but perhaps next Saturday, Mr. Santoros...It's almost my birthday," she lied again.

"You got a date, and maybe by that time you could ditch the 'Mr. Santoros' business except in the office. My friends call me Toro. I'll pick you up at seven o'clock."

As Margaux was preparing herself for their date at Sardi's she thought about where her relationship with Toro might lead. She had been pleasantly surprised to discover that he really did need an assistant with legal experience. His financial records *were* in disorder; but there was no doubt about his generosity, the magnitude of his fortune or his desire for female "companionship." In terms of her own need for male companionship, she had not been with a man for over a year. Toro Santoros would not be the man of her choice, but his assets would. *The last time I did it for love, and look where that got me,* she mused *This time....*

They were escorted to a table for two with Demi Moore and her husband seated at the adjoining table and Larry King and a spectacular-looking Asian woman across the aisle. At the end of the meal, when the waiter arrived with an enormous birthday cake, everyone in the room sang Happy Birthday to her.

After dessert Toro reached in his pocket and placed an exquisitely wrapped present in front of her. When she opened it, she stared dumbfounded at the Cartier diamond watch. She had seen that very same watch advertised in *Vanity Fair* magazine, priced at $50,000.

When she squealed with wonder, everyone around them glanced over at their table. She held up her arm for everyone to see, and the jewels sent rays of color in every direction around the room. When she kissed Toro, everyone applauded. The tourists among them assumed that the distinguished older man must be a Hollywood producer and the strikingly beautiful young woman an up-and-coming movie star.

Although Margaux became Toro's regular social companion, she drew the line at the bedroom door. The ever-increasing value of his gifts to her ensured the continuation of their platonic friendship, but after testing the waters, Toro got the message that sex and a very large diamond on the fourth finger of her left hand were inextricably intertwined. Before considering the possibility of marriage, however, Toro sought counsel from Barney Rifkin.

"So what am I getting into if she agrees to marry me?" Toro asked.

"What are you getting into?" Barney was about to make a locker-room response but he realized that Toro was taking the marriage thing very seriously. He shifted gears quickly. "There's no question but that you'll need a foolproof prenuptial agreement. You've got millions of dollars involved here, Toro. Without an agreement she'd be entitled to one third of everything you own upon your death."

"Upon my death, what do I care?"

Barney stared at him. Toro was moving his lips, talking to himself.... "one-third of everything would be about two million bucks," he mumbled softly. He looked back up at Barney.

"You're my lawyer, not hers, right?"

"That's right, but Margaux's an attorney as well. She was one of the best young lawyers around when she was practicing, and she's plenty capable of taking care of herself."

Toro had clearly given up on the idea of an intimate relationship without a legal commitment. Margaux knew he was prepared to make a proposal, and that ultimately it would just be a a question of money.

How much should I demand? she wondered as she drew a hot bath, preparing for their date to see a revival of the Broadway musical *Cats*. Just before she eased down into the steaming bubbles, she stood in front of her full-length mirror and appraised herself. She swirled her luxurious, unretouched black, naturally soft-curled hair and knew that she looked exactly like the top TV models in the Clairol commercials. Her emerald eyes sparkled: a gift from her maternal grandmother who emigrated from Dublin to seek her fortune in America just before the stock market crash of 1929. Her prominent cheekbones and exquisite alabaster complexion were contributions from her Scandinavian father who never learned that his one night stand with a "townie" at his college graduation party produced a seven and a half pound baby girl.

She turned ninety degrees to verify that her belly was still flat and her buns firm, thanks to her hard work at the gym. "And whom do I thank for these magnificent tits?" she said aloud, cupping them with her hands and turning from side to side, admiring them in the mirror. *First, of course, I must thank Dr. Richard Carter, the creative surgeon, and then my former lover, Frank Dunn, who paid for them.* She smiled. *I guess I just lucked out with these long legs.* She tested the bath water with her toe. *Perfect. I always do my best thinking when I'm in my bathtub with heaps of bubbles,* she said to herself, as she slipped deep into the tub.

She poured herself a martini from the pitcher of them she had made in anticipation of her long, languid bath ritual. She plucked the onion out of the glass, popped it into her mouth and sucked on it. She closed her eyes and lay back in the tub and relaxed. When the water began to cool, she opened the hot water tap. *Okay, so now we address the critical issues,* she thought, after rinsing off the bubbles and sitting upright in the tub.

She knew Toro had two major concerns. First, the possibility of his being cuckolded, which his male Greek ego feared the most, and second, the price she was demanding for becoming his wife. Barney told her Toro thought it was outrageous, but he was willing to negotiate.

As she saw the situation, she was in the prime of her life and although she recognized that she was "damaged goods" because of her past difficulties, she knew she was still an exceptionally attractive woman. She also knew that with each passing year, her value as a consort would diminish, and she had no other prospects on the horizon. Finally she had to take into consideration the fact that she wouldn't be able to get her license to practice law reinstated until 2010, and in order to get off probation, she would have to demand $250,000 plus interest up front from Toro so she could pay restitution to the Shauffler estate for the money she had embezzled.

Toro is insisting that the agreement provide that if I am unfaithful to him at any time during the first five years of marriage I will forfeit all property rights, alimony, and any interest in his estate when he dies. I can't deal with that!

She acknowledged that Toro was not stupid, but she hated his near-illiteracy and his inability to discuss anything other than his business interests and sports. As far as she could tell he had never read a book from cover to cover in his life. The Catholic Church dictated his social views, and his political opinions were gleaned from conservative television commentators like Rush Limbaugh.

To Margaux, the idea of having sex solely with Toro for five years or until he died was unacceptable, but he insisted it was a non-negotiable condition of the agreement. Her own view of sex was that the only reason to copulate was for pleasure. *The reality of the situation here is, I want the money; I need the money, but I'll be damned if I will give up sex, except with Toro Santoros, for five years at this time of my life. But how can I get the money without paying the price? I realize it's not a novel problem. Women have been trading pussy for security since the caveman days.* She poured herself another martini. *C'mon, Margaux, put that big brain of yours to work. There has to be a way to solve this problem.* And then she almost leaped out of the tub when the idea struck her. She wrapped herself in a big Turkish towel and hurried into her den and pulled *Black's Law Dictionary* off the shelf. She quickly flipped through the pages until she found the legal definition of adultery:

"Voluntary sexual intercourse of a married person with a person other than the offender's husband or wife."

"GOTCHA," she exclaimed out loud. *It's so simple and so logical and so foolproof. I'll give Toro all the assurance he needs that I won't commit adultery…and I won't. I'll just fake the orgasms like millions of other married women all over the world do, and when Lucie is released from prison I'll be able to have my cake and eat it too.* She laughed out loud at her own naughty play on words.

I learned in Richford Hills that a woman can tease and please another woman as well if not better than most men, except for those rare moments in life when one is truly in love, and my chances of ever going there again are one in a million.

When Margaux visited Barney Rifkin's office to pick up Toro's latest offer, he said, "Toro tells me this is his final offer, and I believe him, Margaux. I never thought he would come anywhere near meeting your demands, but obviously you've got what he wants and I guess he can afford it. Take the agreement home and study it. He's agreed that his estate will pay you one quarter of his total assets at the time of his death, but he won't budge on the requirement that if you are unfaithful to him at anytime during the first five years of marriage, you lose everything. Certainly you can understand why your offer of three years is unacceptable. What the hell, Margaux, all he's asking is that you honor your marriage vows for at least five years."

Margaux took the twelve-page contract from him and scanned it quickly. "Price, price, that's all I hear from you guys. The fact is, I've agreed to drastically compromise my rights as a surviving spouse in consideration for a lump sum payment if things don't work out after three years of marriage." She sat down and silently studied the latest proposal. Barney waited patiently for her response.

"The funny thing is, Barney, I really like Toro. He's cute. He's old world. Although he can only read and write English one word at a time, you know, he's very bright and he can be a very charming man, but he's freaking forty years older than me. These are the best years of my life, Barney, don't you understand that?" Barney started to speak, but she interrupted him. "Yeah, yeah, I know. I don't have to sign it." Margaux decided to gamble. "Forget it, Barney. I'll commit to four years of marriage before a payout unless he dies in the interim, but the money stays the same." She crossed out the new dollar numbers that Toro had offered, inserted her original demand of one third of his estate, changed the five years to four, initialed the changes and signed the agreement. "My offer is good for twenty-four hours. If he doesn't sign it just the way it is, to hell with him. I'm through negotiating." She stomped out of the office without another word.

Barney was certain Toro would never go for it, but he was mistaken.

"My doc only gives me a couple of years to live...three or four, max," Toro said. "I needed that extra year from her. What the hell do I care about the money after that?"

I suppose I gotta wear one of them monkey suits if we're gonna get hitched in Saint Patrick's Cathedral. Am I right, darling?"

"Absolutely," Margaux smiled, "but don't worry about it. I'm making all the arrangements and I'd be happy to take care of that for you as well."

"You don't understand, sweetheart. You can't just pick up one of them off the rack at Macy's. Everything I wear is hand tailored. They don't manufacture ready-mades in my size. My chest is 52, my gut is 60, my arms are 30 and my neck is bigger than an NFL linebacker's. It's size twenty-two and a half. Would you believe it?"

"I believe it," she said with a touch of sadness.

Six weeks later they were married in Saint Patrick's Cathedral, followed by a lavish reception party at the Waldorf, where Tony Terini and his Orchestra played music from the fifties and sixties until dawn.

People magazine estimated that the cost of the party, including the engraved gifts for the 200 guests, was over $100,000.

When they returned home from their honeymoon in Aruba, Margaux became a lady of leisure. It was Toro's opinion that a woman's place was in the home with a maid and a cook who prepared dinner five nights a week. Margaux didn't quarrel with the arrangement. Five or six times a month she suffered through the sex charade with Toro.

She went to the gym three times a week and worked with her personal trainer. She had taken lessons in tennis and golf and had become reasonably proficient in both sports. With regret, she had turned down numerous offers from a number of men her own age to dally in the dunes in Southhampton, but she decided that the penalty for adultery prescribed in their prenuptial agreement significantly outweighed the transient pleasure of an illicit sexual adventure. Besides, in that department, as soon as Lucie was released from prison in a little over a month, the whole sex problem would be solved.

CHAPTER FOUR

The doorbell rang. Gary said, "Get that, will you, honey? I've got to keep my eye on these popovers. I'm sure it's Pete and Louise."

When Melinda opened the door, Pierre DeLisle said, "Oh my God, Lindy, you look like a movie star! How old are you now—sweet sixteen?"

"Hi, Uncle Pete. Come in. Poppi is in the kitchen making something special for you."

"Look at you, Sweetie," Louise said. "How did your father manage to pry you out of your blue jeans?"

"It was my idea. I thought I'd shock him on his birthday."

Gary came into the hallway, wiping his hands on a dish towel.

No one ever described Gary as handsome; his facial features were angular, with deep-set brown eyes. You'd call him lanky, relaxed, and casual...a tight end, not a linebacker, or perhaps on the basketball court you would automatically think of him as a defensive guard. When you first met him, it didn't matter whether you were a man or a woman, you immediately thought that you would like to have him as a friend. While some thought him a little too self-assured, when they picked their friends it would be rare if they didn't include him as a member of the first team.

"Okay, guys, come on out on the terrace. It's party time," Gary said, putting his arm around Melinda and Louise and leading them toward the rear yard that sat high above Roslyn harbor on Long Island.

They all gathered around the picnic table where Pierre had piled up the gaily wrapped presents. When Gary started to pour the drinks, Pierre held up his hand.

"Hold on, hold on, birthday boy, you have to open *this* present now."

"But can't we have a drink first?" Gary asked.

"No we can't, dammit," Pierre insisted. "C'mon man, get cracking."

Gary ripped off the fancy paper, revealing a case of Dom Perignon champagne.

"Hooray! Break out the champagne glasses, Lindy. We're really going to have a party."

"One for me too, right, Poppi?"

"Absolutely!" Pierre declared. "In that fancy dress and high heels, you certainly look old enough to drink." Melinda laughed and skipped away to the kitchen. Pierre sidled over to Gary and slung an arm over his shoulder.

"I'm sorry you look so much older than you are, partner," he said. "It's amazing. I was sure you were going to be forty-five instead of thirty-five."

"I understand that, Mr. DeLisle. Of course if I were forty-five, that would make you sixty-five."

When the expensive sparkling wine was poured and the toasts made, Pierre said, "Okay, partner, open the others," indicating an exquisitely wrapped large flat box, with a card from Louise.

Gary carefully removed the wrapping. "Lordy, Louise, it's gorgeous." It was a water color painting that Louise had made of Gary skippering his sailboat in a heavy wind, with Melinda leaning far out on the gunwale, handling the jib. Her long auburn hair was flying in the sea spray. Gary was standing at the helm, stripped to the waist, gazing up at the full sail while Melinda was wild with the excitement of the moment.

Gary picked up Louise as if she were a ballerina. "I love you, I love you," he chanted. "It's so freaking beautiful, Louise—however can I thank you?"

"You can start by putting me back down on terra firma," she said shyly. "I'm a landlubber, you know." They all joined in the laughter and Pierre poured another round of champagne. Gary sat back in his chair, continuing to gaze at the painting with awe and admiration. Then Pierre handed Gary a box about eighteen inches square, roughly wrapped but securely fastened in every direction with Scotch tape.

"I wrapped it myself," he said proudly.

"As if I couldn't guess," Gary chided him, ducking under the right uppercut Pierre swung at him.

When he opened the present, a hand-tooled leather portfolio was revealed. Embossed in gold on its face was the legend, "Samson & DeLisle Productions. October 8, 1999."

"I don't get it," Gary said, looking over at Pierre who took the ledger from him and opened it up.

"This is our financial report audited right up to today. There!" Pierre said, pointing to the bottom line-item, highlighted in gold leaf:

PARTNER'S SHARE-GARY SAMSON...$1,013,412. 26

Gary stared at the inscription uncomprehendingly. Pierre was grinning from ear to ear. "Don't you remember?"

"Remember what?" Gary asked, in a daze.

"Don't tell me you've forgotten when you were in my office the first day we met. You were just a wise-ass kid. You said you had two long-range objectives, one of which was to become a millionaire by the time you were thirty-five. Well, you made it, partner." Pierre punched Gary on the arm, beaming. "I've been keeping my eye on the balance sheet for the past nine months, and…well, there it is."

Gary grabbed the half-full bottle of champagne, shook it up and squirted it at Pierre. Pierre jumped back, but Gary ran after him screaming, "You are a crazy son of a B, and…and I love you."

"Hey stupid, you're wasting that expensive champagne," Pierre yelled.

"It's okay, I can afford it," Gary said, laughing hysterically.

Melinda and Louise went into the kitchen and brought out the food Gary had prepared. The two men continued to drink and congratulate each other. Pierre leaned back and said, "Do you remember the other crazy idea you told me about ten years ago, Gary?"

"To make a movie, you mean?" Gary laughed.

"That's it, but you said it had to be good enough to win an Academy Award, right?"

"Absolutely. If you were able to make me a million dollars in ten years, I ought to be able to win us an Academy Award for Best Dreamer."

"Why don't we give it a try?" Pierre said.

"You're joking, right?"

"Hell no, I'm willing to gamble. Are you?" Pierre asked.

"I know you're only messing with my head, partner, but of course I am. It's only money. I didn't want to be a millionaire so I could count it every day. You're talking about giving me a chance to realize my dream. Just talking about it makes me dizzy. But we can't make a serious film with a couple of million dollars."

"I believe I can leverage what we've got into enough money to do it. What do you say, kiddo?" Pierre asked, opening another bottle of champagne.

Gary started to speak, hesitated, and then stared thoughtfully at Pierre. "Are you sure this idea didn't pop out of that bottle you're holding in your hand? If you wake up in the morning with the wicked hangover I know you're headed for, you aren't going to call me up with amnesia, are you?"

"I think we can do it, Gair. Honest." Pierre said, holding out his hand to Gary.

"You haven't been wrong yet, old man. Let's go for broke."

Melinda and Louise were sitting silently in the shadows, listening to the conversation. Melinda was enthralled. Louise appeared to be sick to her stomach. Gary glanced over at his daughter. "And there'll be a bit part for you, Lindy."

"Do you mean it, Poppi, I'm really going to be in a movie?"

"You betcha, Baby."

Louise gasped for air. "Oh dear," she said.

Melinda Joy was the name Lindy and Gary chose to be Lindy's stage name for the part she played as the star's daughter in the ninety-minute film produced by Samson & DeLisle. It was a small part, but the critics praised her performance.

The movie was declared to be an artistic triumph, but it was a financial disaster.

During the year it took to produce the movie, Samson and DeLisle's TV commercial film business deteriorated because no one was watching the store. Pierre and Gary lost their fortune when their movie, *The Bridge*, failed at the box office, but they went back to doing what they did best. At one point, their attorney suggested that they might consider filing for bankruptcy. Gary was unwilling to discuss it.

"I know that I'm the one who's primarily responsible for this financial disaster, Pierre," he said, "and the way I see it, the people we owe the money to trusted us and although we tried our best it wasn't good enough. I'm unwilling to walk away from our obligations to them. I don't care how long it takes me, but I'm going to pay each and every one of our creditors what we owe. You must do whatever you think is best for you and Louise. I understand that, and will love you guys no less whatever you decide."

"Hey man," Pierre said, "we're partners. Just like being married. We'll do it together."

Six years later they celebrated their exit from insolvency quietly at Pierre's home in Scarsdale. Pierre and Gary drank a toast to their friendship, their partnership and their future. As Gary was leaving, Pierre put his arm around him, and in a voice that was choked with two parts emotion and one part liquor, he said, "I love you, man. Now, by God, we'll climb to the top of the mountain once more. I'm sixty-two years old. Most men my age are thinking about retirement, but I've just been born again. This time, partner, you and me, we're going to make it big. There's time, my friend. I mean, you're only forty-two-years old."

"Hey, buddy, there's plenty of time. Tomorrow is the first day of the rest of our lives. Damn, I wish I had thought of that line first." They both laughed and Gary called out to Louise in the kitchen, "Goodnight, sweetheart, I'm leaving before you ask me to help with the dishes."

Gary's reputation continued to expand and there were those who claimed he was the Steven Spielberg of the thirty-second TV commercial.

Melinda had been tutored through her junior and senior years in high school while she was performing in the film Samson and Delisle had produced. She enrolled at Ithaca College in upstate New York where she majored in drama and played the lead at the Hangar Theater in Ithaca in *Dance of the Mantis* during the summer before her senior year. A Hollywood agent who was a graduate of the college had brought her daughter to visit the college campus, along with Cornell University, which is also located in Ithaca. While they were there, they caught Melinda's performance. At the time, a major Hollywood studio was casting the film, *Jazz*—a heart-warming story about a New Orleans musician and his daughter who survived the devastation of Hurricane Katrina and helped to restore Bourbon Street to its former grandeur. As a result of the rave reviews Melinda had earned for her performance in the movie produced by Samson and Delisle, and the Hollywood agent's personal recommendation, Melinda was given an audition and was cast in a starring role. The movie was included in the first round of Academy Award nominations for best musical score and Melinda was chosen in a *TIME* magazine survey as one of the most talented of Hollywood's new young starlets.

CHAPTER FIVE

Gary was heading home from a film shoot in Chicago. He had been seated alone in a bar at the airport when Margaux Santoros entered the lounge. He thought she must be a celebrity, probably an actress whose name he couldn't remember, because he was certain he had seen her picture in the press. He couldn't believe his good fortune when she stopped at his table.

"Excuse me, sir, is this seat taken?" she asked.

Gary glanced around the room. There were several unoccupied chairs available. "No, I've been saving it for *you*," he quipped, glancing briefly at the large diamond ring on the fourth finger of her left hand, overshadowing what he thought—but couldn't be certain—was a slim gold wedding band.

She smiled and slipped into the booth across from him. She removed a paperback from her large handbag and placed it on the table. Then she gazed around the room, searching for a waitress. There weren't any in sight. She sighed and picked up her book.

"The service here leaves much to be desired," Gary said. "May I get you a drink?"

She looked up from her book, hesitated briefly and then said, "That would be lovely, thank you. I think I'm ready for a Gray Goose vodka martini with an onion. A double, please."

As soon as he was out of sight she removed her wedding ring and slipped it into her purse.

When he returned with the drink he placed it on the table with a flourish and eased his tall, lean frame onto the bench seat opposite her. She opened her purse and held out a large bill.

"No, no. It's my pleasure. Cheers," he said, holding his drink aloft. "My name is Gary Samson. Who might you be?" he asked, trying desperately to remember where he had seen her before.

"I'm Margaux."

"Margo who? From where?"

"I run a little parlor on the corner of Main Street and Oak Avenue. Just knock three times and say that Margaux sent you."

"I can tell you that Margo sent me the moment I saw her."

She raised her eyebrows and cocked her head, indicating appreciation for the compliment and the quick wit. "The truth is, I'm from Brooklyn. Thank you for the drink, by the way."

"*De nada.*"

"How about you? Where are you headed?" she asked.

"I live on Long Island. Small village. Sea Cliff. I don't suppose by any stroke of magnificent good fortune you are on Delta Flight 563 to JFK leaving at, let me see…" He pulled a packet of crumpled papers out of his pocket, searching for his ticket.

"8:17," Margaux said.

"Right, leaving at 8:17…*Karma,* that's what I call it. So, is Brooklyn your home base?" Gary looked carefully again at her left hand. He was pleasantly surprised to discover that he must have been mistaken. There was no wedding band branding her.

"To my home…and Shirah." Margaux raised her glass.

"Shirah? Is that a daughter?"

"Actually, it's the name of my Siamese cat."

They chatted amiably for a while and Gary insisted they have another round of drinks. "A toast to Shirah," he said, raising his glass. He checked his watch. "When we finish these drinks we'd better head down to the gate. Perhaps we can arrange some compatible seating—that is, if you think you can put up with me for another two hours."

"To be honest, I was looking forward to finishing my book on this flight."

"What are you reading?"

"*Without Reservations*. It's quite good. It's sort of a travel book, but it's much more than that. It's about a single woman traveling alone through western Europe. I'm really enjoying it."

"Who wrote it?" Gary asked. Margaux picked up the book in her lap and glanced at the cover. "Alice Steinbach."

"Never heard of her."

"I hadn't either, but I learned that she's a Nobel Prize winner. That tells you something."

"Well, think about the situation this way. You only have this one opportunity in a lifetime to continue our conversation, but your book will still be there when I'm long gone."

"True, but can you guarantee that the conversation will be as entertaining as my book? Besides, I'm programmed to fall asleep on airplanes. I might just doze off in the middle of a sentence, but if that doesn't bother you, I'm game."

Gary paid the bill, and they walked casually down to the departure gate. When they arrived, there was a long line of passengers, and a flashing sign that said that their flight had been cancelled.

"Oh, no," Margaux sighed. "What now?"

"I happen to know this is the last flight out of Chicago to New York tonight, so it looks like we're stuck here. Damn! Have you eaten yet?"

"No, and I'm starving!"

"Okay, so you'll come to dinner with me. Let's go."

"Wait a minute. Aren't the airlines supposed to pay for dinner and put us up for the night when they cancel a flight like this?"

"You're absolutely right. All you have to do is stand in line here for a couple of hours while everyone gets their travel plans straightened out, and then they'll bus us to the nearest Motel 6 and give us a dinner chit worth ten dollars. I think I have a better idea."

"Like what?"

"Like we'll grab a cab and I'll take you to the John Thomas Steakhouse in downtown Chicago, where they serve the best aged prime beef you've ever tasted, and then we'll go to the Palmer House where a buddy of mine is the manager, get a good night's sleep and head back home bright and early in the morning."

Margaux looked at the long line, which had not moved perceptibly during their conversation, felt her stomach rumble, and thought about eating dinner alone in a motel restaurant. She was aware that there was an element of risk in accepting a total stranger's invitation to dinner, but....

"Okay, you're on," she said.

"Great. Let's go," said Gary, picking up their bags and guiding her away from the throng that had become more and more agitated by the slow process of servicing the tangled mass of unhappy travelers.

The restaurant was both chic and homey. The food was spectacular and the conversation was interesting. Neither of them offered any pertinent information about their respective lives, but as the dinner was coming to a close, Gary told her an amusing story about the time he was chased by a cow when he was six years old. When his hand accidentally brushed hers, she experienced a shiver of excitement. They sat without speaking for a bit. Finally, Gary broke the silence. "Why is it," he said wistfully, "every time I meet a woman—I swear it never fails—every time I meet a beautiful woman with brains, she's either married or engaged."

Margaux raised her left hand and smiled. "Camouflage. It was my grandmother's engagement ring. It usually keeps the riffraff from hitting on me. I'm rather glad it didn't put you off."

"Nah, engagement rings don't bother me, but wedding bands are a no-no."

"Exactly what does that mean?" she asked.

"Well, since all my intentions are dishonorable, I make it a practice not to mess with married women."

"You don't see a wedding band on my finger, do you?" she said, waving her left hand in the air, and smiling as she thought about the gold band in her purse.

Gary hailed a cab and told the driver to take them to the Palmer House Hotel. When they arrived, Gary's friend Scott, the general manager, was behind the desk.

"Hey, big guy, aren't you supposed to be on your way back to New York? What's up—did you forget your toothbrush?"

When Gary explained their plight, the manager informed them they were fully booked, and offered to call the Hyatt. But then he said, "Wait a minute. Look, I've got a two-bedroom suite in the tower. Ordinarily it carries a hefty price tag, but we're not likely to sell it at this late hour, and..." He checked the computer screen at the front desk, "I see that it's not booked for the next two days, so it's a gift to you with my compliments. You don't have to register, but you *must* be out by 10:00 a.m. on the day after tomorrow because we have guests checking in at noon and we've got to give the housekeeping staff time to get in and get it ready before they arrive."

"Hey, that's first class," Gary said. "We really appreciate it."

"Wait a minute. Don't I get a say in these arrangements?" Margaux demanded, with a touch of cool in her voice.

"I'm sorry. David, this is Margo...uh, Margo...."

"I don't mean to be a problem here, but I want my own room which I intend to pay for, if you don't mind, gentlemen."

"My apologies, Ms....uh...Margo, I assumed that you and Gary...." His face reddened. "But it's easily solved," he said quickly. "The suite has separate entrances for each bedroom. Now what shall I send up to your rooms besides a Jack Daniels on the rocks for Gary and...for you, Margo?"

"I would love a cosmopolitan, if that's possible."

"So be it," the manager said, ringing for the porter to take their luggage.

The penthouse suite was the only hotel accommodation on the twenty-fourth floor. When they stepped out of the elevator directly into the suite, the porter pulled aside the drapes, offering a spectacular view of downtown Chicago, ablaze with lights.

"Now, what do you think of that?" Gary demanded.

"It's absolutely breathtaking."

When Margaux returned to the living room after calling Toro from the privacy of her bedroom and explaining that her flight had been cancelled, she overheard Gary explaining the situation to Melinda. When he ended the call by saying, "Bye, Lindy Love," Margaux raised her eyebrows and asked, "Who is Lindy? You didn't tell me you were married! I thought—"

Gary laughed. "I'm not married. Melinda is my daughter. She lives with me." As they stood looking out over the city, without speaking, each deep in his own thoughts about how the evening might end, room service arrived with their drinks and a cheese platter, compliments of the manager.

They continued to talk, but the carefree intimacy was gone. Margaux seemed preoccupied, self-searching. Several times she started to say something and then either lost her train of thought or decided not to share it with Gary. When the clock on the mantel in the parlor struck midnight, Gary said, "I guess we'd better call it a day. The flight to New York leaves at 7:20 in the morning. In order to get to the airport when we're supposed to, we'll have to be up ready to go by five-thirty, quarter to six. I'd better call the front desk and ask for a wake-up call."

Margaux stood up and stepped close to him.

"Which bedroom are we sleeping in—yours or mine?" she asked.

Gary forgot about the wakeup call. It was past one o'clock in the morning when they finally fell asleep, wrapped in each other's arms. Margaux slept fitfully in the strange bed with the strange man. She kept looking at the digital bedside clock: 3:05…3:30…3:47….She glanced over at Gary, who continued to sleep peacefully. *Not fair,* she decided, and lightly twisted the curly brown and gray hairs on his chest between her fingers. Then she tugged on a few hairs below his tight muscular belly. She smiled when he gave a start and turned onto his side, with his back to her. She caressed his bare back and his buns, and he still didn't wake up, but when she slid her hand further down and squeezed ever so gently, he sat up immediately. "What the—" he cried. When he remembered where he was and why, he grabbed a handful of her luxurious ebony hair. "You little wench, I could…."

"You could what?" she teased.

He threw the covers off the bed.

"What does it look like to you?" he answered proudly.

"It looks marvelous," she said, laughing.

When they were sated, she lay curled around him with her head snuggled on his shoulder.

Margaux was awakened when the sun splashed across the bed. She looked at the bedside clock and screamed, "Oh my God, It's seven-thirty!" She jumped up and threw the curtains wide open. "Whatever happened to the wakeup call? Oh, Lord, the plane left fifteen minutes ago. What am I going to do?"

"Whaa?" Gary demanded, still half asleep. Margaux ignored him and rushed into the bathroom. Gary lay back on the bed, heard the toilet flush and then the shower splashing against Margaux's body.

I can't believe it, he thought. *I'm just lying here thinking about her standing in the shower and I want to make love to her again. I am bewitched, bothered and bewildered, or besotted, or I don't know exactly what but I'm not complaining!*

He sat up on the edge of the bed when she returned to the bedroom wrapped in a bath towel. Gary convinced her there was no sense in rushing out to the airport until they called and found out when the next flight to New York was scheduled to depart and whether there were any seats available. Margaux sat down at the desk in the living room and began to call the airlines. Gary fell back asleep.

When he awoke all the curtains were drawn in the bedroom. He studied the hand-carved bed posts and the burgundy velvet canopy. The events of the previous evening and the intimate adventure that followed in the early morning hours quickly flashed through his mind, but when he reached out to caress her, he discovered that he was alone in the king-sized bed. He got up, pulled the drapes aside and looked out at the wind-scuffed waters of Lake Michigan; then he shut the blackout curtain, throwing the room back into total darkness. When he cautiously opened the bedroom door and peered into the parlor, Margaux had her back to him. He tiptoed up to her and planted a kiss on the back of her neck. She swirled around, startled.

"Gary!" she cried. She was wearing a negligee, open in the front from top to bottom.

"Good morning, pretty lady," he said, and was about to take her into his arms just as the elevator doors opened. Margaux screamed and pulled the silk peignoir across her chest. The young man in the elevator mumbled "excuse me," and immediately closed the doors. When Margaux realized Gary was totally nude, she burst out laughing and exclaimed, "Oo la la, *monsieur*, where are your manners? I am totally embarrassed and blushing profusely at what I see. I am a fair young maiden, unaccustomed to such happenings."

Gary reached out and took her hand. "Let me lead you back to the bedroom so I can cover myself in darkness."

"But kind sir, I hardly know you and I am afraid of the dark."

"Actually, my pretty lady, my thought is to open wide the drapes and let the morning sun caress your lovely body as we make love—as soon as I have my first cup of coffee, that is, and then I shall describe our itinerary for the day."

"I have already arranged that, sir. I choose not to refuse your kind offer of a dalliance in the sunshine, if that is your wish. However, since we have already missed the 7:20 flight I have arranged for a chariot to take us to the airport so we can catch the 11:57 flying carpet back to New York."

"Ah, but pretty lady," Gary replied, sipping on his cup of steaming java that Margaux had brewed, "I propose a far different plan for your consideration."

Margaux glanced briefly at his pride which had risen to the occasion, and said, "Being a woman I can multi-task, but my preference is to do first things first."

She took him by the elbow and guided him back to the bedroom.

When the frenzy had settled, Gary lay back with Margaux's head snuggled in the hollow of his shoulder again. *My God*, he thought, *the woman is deliciously insatiable.*

They were still comfortably ensconced in bed when he finished describing his alternate plan to her. She told him that it sounded marvelous, but that it was impossible.

"I told you I must, absolutely *must* be on that flight to New York. How could I possibly explain to…Shirah why I was spending another whole day in Chicago?"

"I'm sure your cat will understand, don't you think?"

"He's all alone with no one to feed him."

"I guarantee he won't starve to death. But can't you call a neighbor and ask them to feed the darn cat?"

"My neighbor doesn't have a key to my place. Let me think, I'll figure something out.... Okay, I'll make a deal with you." She let her fingers walk across his bare chest and then head south. When he immediately began to respond to her, she sat up and exclaimed, "Oh, oh, I didn't mean to do that…well, I guess I did mean to do it but I didn't expect such a quick response. Look, I enjoyed last night more than you can imagine, and I really don't want to return home right away. I'm willing to stay with you and take the last plane back to New York—you know, the flight we were scheduled to take last night—but only on one condition."

"And that is?" Gary asked, performing the finger-walking trick on Margaux. "Wait now," she whispered, steering his fingers in a different direction. "You haven't listened to the terms of the contract yet."

"I don't care. I accept them sight unseen, or unheard, or whatever." He smiled.

"Done deal!" she replied, and put his hand back on her belly.

"So what have I got myself into?" he said, chuckling.

"You have just agreed to pay me $25,000 for the day," she replied with a straight face. Gary quickly removed his hand that was only inches from its destination, as if he had accidentally put it into an open flame. He sat up in the bed and stared at her. "You're kidding, right? I mean, please tell me it's just a joke, I mean...."

Margaux couldn't contain her laughter. When she was able to speak again, she said, "My dear Gary, I must tell you that I would give anything to have a picture of your reaction. First of all you turned absolutely ashen, as if you were a French Legionnaire standing up against the wall in Morocco and you had just heard the firing squad leader say, *Ready, aim, fire!* She pushed him back down on the bed and climbed on top of him.

"This one is on the house," she said.

The condition she had imposed in exchange for her agreement to spend the day with him was that after they stepped off the plane in New York, they would never see each other again. He had to promise that he would never attempt to talk to her or ever try to find her; that they would both put the twenty-four hour interlude in their memory books to be savored forever.

"Suppose I agree to pay the $25,000," he asked, "Then what?"

Margaux started to speak, hesitated, and then, running her tongue over her upper lip, she said, "Okay, here's a new offer. If you're willing to put two million dollars into my account at the Chase Manhattan bank, I'll marry you. How's that?"

"If I had two million dollars, I'd consider it."

"That's what I thought. So let's get this memorable day underway," she said, pulling him up out of bed.

"Hey, wait a minute, we have some unfinished business here," he complained.

"Later, darling. You already know what I can do in the bedroom, so if this is going to be a day we're to cherish all our lives, we can't spend the whole time on a mattress."

Yeah we can, he thought.

Margaux checked the massive antique clock in the lobby. "9:47," she mused. "We have seven hours to do whatever we want before we head back to the airport."

"You know what I want," Gary said, sullenly.

"Now, now, little boy, don't sulk. If you promise to eat your spinach, I promise you a scrumptious dessert."

"Why can't we have the dessert first? Why can't we have five desserts?"

"Because I want you to grow up big and strong, so you must eat your vegetables. Besides, you had two desserts last night and another one early this morning. Now there are other muscles we must exercise, so we are going to take a nice, long walk to Lake Michigan. But first, I must tell you, I'm starved to death."

They decided to have breakfast in the beautiful Lockwood Restaurant at the hotel. During the meal, Gary regaled her with the history of the place.

"As I recall, Potter Palmer, the man who built this hotel, arrived in Chicago when he was twenty-six years old."

"My goodness," Margaux said, "How long ago was that?"

"In the middle of the eighteen-hundreds. As I remember it, at the time there were only 38,000 residents in all of Chicago. Now there are over three million."

"You mean he built this enormous hotel when there were only 38,000 people living here? That sounds crazy."

"No, no. It only had 255 rooms when it opened in 1871."

"However do you remember all this trivia?"

"I can't help myself. I have an IQ off the charts. I'm classified as a genius, I'm afraid."

"I'm impressed," she conceded. "What else do you know about this gorgeous hotel?"

"Well, it started with 255 rooms, like I said. Now there are over 1,600 rooms and after it was built, guess what?"

"It burned down in the Great Chicago Fire. Am I right?" Margaux asked.

"I don't know, but it might have, because I remember the hotel opened about the same time Mrs. O'Leary's cow kicked over the lantern that started the whole catastrophe. Or so they say."

"Of course, that's the male version of what happened. The truth is, it was a bull."

"I think you're full of bull," Gary countered.

"Actually I *was* gored a few times last night."

"Stop complaining."

"Who's complaining?"

"Do you want to be enlightened about this hotel or do you just want to exchange witticisms?" he demanded.

"Both. So tell me, what was the significant historical fact you wanted to share with me?"

"What I wanted to tell you is that when Potter Palmer finished building this hotel, he gave it to his wife Bertha for her birthday, and that's a fact."

"And then she burned it down for the insurance money? Is that what happened?"

"Shut up. I don't want to talk to you any more."

"Oh my, darling," she said, "I think I could fall in love with you." And then she leaned close to him and stuck her tongue in his ear.

As Margaux was waiting in the lobby while Gary was settling the bill for breakfast, she picked up a brochure from the concierge desk. She glanced at the photos and was about to throw it away when she noticed a picture of the original hotel with the caption, "Happy birthday, Bertha." She scanned the article: *Potter Palmer, the man who built this hotel, arrived in Chicago when he was twenty-six years old...38,000 residents in all of Chicago. Now there are over three million...when Potter Palmer finished building this hotel, he gave it to his wife Bertha for her birthday....*

When they were leaving the hotel, arm in arm, she handed the brochure to Gary. "IQ off the charts—genius—What a colossal fraud you are!" she said.

"Only when it doesn't involve matters of the heart...or money. Let's get started on this $25,000 day," he answered.

It was a glorious end of summer day in Chicago when they entered Grant Park, adjacent to the hotel. They were overwhelmed by the range of facilities and events taking place in the park. They began with the Lake Shore Trail, had lunch beside the Buckingham Fountain—one of the largest in the world—and ended up in the controversial Millennium Park that opened in 2004 at a cost of 475 million dollars. They visited Lurie Garden and the Boeing Galleries, and finally headed back to the hotel.

After they picked up their luggage at the terminal in New York's LaGuardia Airport, Gary asked Margaux to meet him again as soon as possible. She immediately replied, "It mustn't happen, Gary, you promised."

"I had my fingers crossed, so it doesn't count," he said, but she didn't smile.

"I mustn't see you again." She started to move quickly away from him. He reached out and pulled her close to him. "You can't just walk away, Margo. You—"

She turned her head aside, but not before Gary saw a tear slide down her cheek. She put her head against his chest. "I don't regret what we did," she wept, "and I'll remember it always, but it can't happen again." She broke away from him and quickly lost herself in the crowd.

"Where to, Miss?" the cabbie asked.

"Freemont Avenue, Brooklyn. Number 756," Margaux replied. She settled back in the taxi and thought about having to leave Gary and face Toro.

I have a boring, fat, old jerk of a husband who can't get it up most of the time. I'm also playing with fire. Last night was a mistake. It could be a 2,000,000 mistake if I'm not careful. But God, it was spectacular. The problem is, I've only been away from him for fifteen minutes and already I know I want to see him again.

Melinda picked Gary up at the airport hotel when he arrived back from his trip to Chicago. "Hey, Sport, how did it go in the Windy City? Did they like the pitch?" she asked.

"I'm never certain until the film is in the can, but they all seemed pretty excited about what I showed them. I think it's solid," Gary replied.

"You guys are really doing all right these days, eh?" Melinda asked as she pulled onto the expressway and headed home. Gary enjoyed watching Melinda skillfully weave in and out of the traffic in her new Lexus SC hardtop convertible. It was a spectacular, warm, summer night, and with her long ash-blond hair flying wild, she looked every inch the celebrity that she was.

"As far as money is concerned, I don't have a clue. That's your Uncle Pete's bailiwick, you know, but I've got more work than I can handle. How goes it with *your* new project?"

Before answering, Melinda zoomed past a slow-moving ten-wheeler. The truck driver honked his horn when she waved at him on the way by. "I'm leaving for the coast the day after tomorrow, but I've got you all to myself until then. What time can you get away from the office tomorrow? Maybe we could catch a sunset sail. What do you say, Poppi?"

"I'll leave the office around 3:30, beat the traffic heading out of the city and have the old *Emily Mae* off the mooring by five o'clock."

"Aye, aye, skipper."

CHAPTER SIX

Gary asked a friend of his who worked for the airlines to track down Margo's last name. "That's illegal, Gary. I'm sorry, but I can't do it."

"I'm not a terrorist, for Christ sake, Chuck. You know I'd do it for you."

His friend called back a few hours later and told Gary that there wasn't anyone on his plane by the name of Margo. He said, "Maybe if you could come up with a last name or a seat number, I could help you locate her. There were 217 passengers on that flight, you know."

"Damn! I threw away my ticket stub and I can't remember my seat number. But I'm pretty sure it was twenty-something, and I had the middle seat. There was a guy sitting on the aisle, and she had the window seat. Surely that should narrow it down. I know it's a lot of trouble and all, but it's really important."

"If I do come up with the right answer and someone finds out I'm the one who broke into the computer, I'll be fired, and maybe arrested, but if you tell me, swear to God, it's a matter of life or death...."

"No, it's not. It's a matter of the heart that could change the direction of my life—for better or for worse. I won't be able to tell which until I find her."

"Why the hell didn't you tell me that in the first place? I thought you wanted to return a book you borrowed, or something. If I had known you had the hots for her—sure, I'll find out who she is."

"That's kind of a crude way to put it, but I guess you're right, Chuck. Maybe that's all it is.... On the other hand it could be a lot more than that. I thought at least I knew her first name, but I guess all I know is that she's gorgeous, she's got a body that's out of sight and a great sense of humor, and she lives in Brooklyn. So you see, my friend, you're my only chance. My destiny is in your hands."

"All right, already, you've convinced me. I'll call you back."

When three days had passed with no word from his airline friend, Gary had given up hope, but he couldn't get Margaux out of his mind. Then one day he came home and there was a message on his answering machine. "It's Chuck here. Her name might be Margaux McBride. Margaux is spelled *M-a-r-g-a-u-x*."

Gary immediately turned on his laptop, and went to Intelius.com search directory. Margaux McBride was not one of the names listed. He went to the Brooklyn/Manhattan telephone directory. There were many McBrides listed, but no one by the name of Margaux. He started making calls, realizing his chances of finding her by random calls were very slim. After a dozen unsuccessful calls, he gave up. *There's got to be a better way,* he decided. A few days later, out of the blue, he recalled seeing a sticker on her gym bag—*EVOLUTION SPORTS CLUB.* He found such a club listed in Brooklyn but when he called there he learned that although there was no member by the name of Margaux McBride, the unusual spelling of the first name was the same as a member named Margaux Santoros, but they wouldn't give him any further information. Since many of the young women members traveled alone after dark, the gym tenaciously guarded its clients' privacy. After a few weeks of fruitless effort, when he was about to abandon the project as hopeless, he lucked out.

When the telephone rang in Margaux and Toro's home, it was the cook's weekend off and Toro and Margaux were eating microwave dinners in front of their fifty-inch flat-screen TV.

"I'll get it," Toro said, struggling to ease his five-foot five overweight body out of his Barcalounger. He patted Margaux affectionately as he passed by. When he picked up the phone and said, "Hello," Gary asked for Margaux Santoros, and Toro said, "Who's this?" Gary hesitated briefly, and then answered, "Mr. Palmer House." Toro checked his caller I.D. and wrote down the number on the scratch pad. "What do you want her for? She don't want to buy nothin', if you're sellin' somethin'."

"No, sir, I was—"

"Who is it, honey?" Margaux asked.

Toro covered the mouthpiece with his hand. "Some guy by the name of Palmer House. Do you know him?"

"I don't think so," and then it struck her. *Chicago. The Palmer House. Gary Samson. Oh God.*

"She says she don't know you." He slammed down the phone. "Assholes. Ain't there some way to stop them creeps from callin'?"

They watched a movie. When it ended, Margaux sighed and went upstairs. She was putting on her nightgown when she heard Toro's heavy footsteps slowly coming down the hallway toward her separate bedroom. She quickly turned out the light, slipped into bed and buried her head under the pillow. He opened the bedroom door cautiously and poked his head in.

"Margaux," he said softly. Margaux held her breath.

"Margaux?" Toro raised his voice slightly. She kept her eyes tightly shut and crossed her fingers.

"Shit," he mumbled, and closed the door.

Margaux rolled over on her side and thought about Chicago and the Palmer House. When she finally fell asleep, she dreamed about Gary.

Toro lay awake for an hour, staring at the ceiling.

Early the following evening, just as Margaux was about to make a call, the phone rang. She picked it up.

"Hello," she said.

"May I speak with Margaux?"

"Who is this?" she demanded.

"Palmer House."

"Gary," Margaux whispered, "How did you get my number? Where are you?"

"Like I told you, I'm a genius. I'm at home," Gary said, "and I've got this stupendous idea."

Margaux glanced at her husband, seated on the opposite side of the living room. He had stopped watching TV and was staring at her.

"We're not interested," she said.

"Wait a minute," Gary said. "Call me as soon as you can at 516-272-7871."

Margaux hung up the phone. Toro went back to watching TV.

Margaux repeated the number to herself several times as she walked into the kitchen and wrote the number down in her recipe book. Toro ambled into the kitchen. "Who was that?" he asked. She told him it was a lady who wanted to know if they were interested in switching to AT&T.

"So, what's for dinner?" he asked. "Not another one of them frozen garbage things, I hope." Everything important in Toro's life led directly to his stomach.

Margaux's head was spinning. "I've got an idea.... Honey, why don't you pop down to the deli and pick up some lettuce, tomatoes, goat cheese and fresh garlic? I'll make you moussaka and bake you an apple pie."

Toro's eyes glazed over.

"Also, we don't have any red wine left, so you better stop at Northside Liquor and pick up a case."

"Sounds great to me," Toro replied. Before he put on his coat he checked the caller ID and compared the number with the one he had noted the night before. It was the same. He shoved the note in his pocket and left the house. As soon as Margaux heard his car pull out of the driveway she dialed the number Gary had given her. When he came on the line, she said, "Are you crazy, Gary? I told you I don't want to see you again. I'm really sorry, but—"

"Oh, how nice it is to hear your voice again," Gary said. "Could I please speak to the sweet and lovely Margaux...spelled *M-a-r-g-a-u-x*...Santoros?"

"How did you find out my name?" Margaux gasped.

"I told you I was a genius," Gary laughed. Margaux tried to stay angry, but she couldn't. "Gary," she said, "You don't understand. What is it about my request not to contact me that you didn't understand?"

"It's very simple. I miss you and I want to see you again. Doesn't it please you to know that I can't get you out of my mind?"

Margaux suppressed a smile and melted back into the overstuffed chair. She felt that tingling of excitement and sighed, "Yes, of course it pleases me, but—"

"No buts. You're making this too complicated. When can I see you?" She didn't answer. But she didn't hang up.

"Margaux?"

"It's too complicated," she finally said.

"Why don't we just meet for lunch and uncomplicate it?"

"I'm afraid to meet you again. I rationalized our night in Chicago because it was all just a wonderful, spontaneous accident. It wasn't planned, it just happened. But if I meet you for lunch, that would be an intentional act. There's a big difference."

"Sure, I understand that, so why don't we accidentally meet at one o'clock tomorrow at the Simply Red Cafe? Do you know the place? It's just a block north of the entrance to the Brooklyn Bridge on the Brooklyn side of the river. It's a two-story building painted entirely red—fire engine red. You can't miss it."

Thoughts were tumbling through Margaux's mind. *Toro is planning to meet his buddies at Yankee Stadium in the Bronx to watch his beloved New York Yankees tomorrow. It's a double-header game. He always leaves home at noon and won't get back until after six o'clock.*

When she didn't immediately respond, Gary said, "Are you still on the line?"

"I'm thinking," she replied, hesitantly.

"I'll be sitting at a table for two in the corner near the bar, wearing a red carnation in my lapel, just so you don't pick up the wrong guy."

"You're a nut case, Samson. I've got to hang up and get back to the kitchen."

"So, are we going to have an accident tomorrow at one o'clock?"

"I...I don't know. I'll have to think about it."

"You can't leave me hanging like that, you—"

Margaux hung up the phone.

When Toro returned with the wine and groceries, he brought them into the kitchen where Margaux was busily preparing dinner. The heat in the kitchen, the aroma of his favorite meal, the sight of Margaux, her face slightly flushed, wearing tight mini-shorts and a low-cut halter that exposed most of her lush torso, aroused his multiple appetites. "I'll kill the son of a bitch that tries to steal her. I bought and paid for her. She's mine," he muttered under his breath.

"What did you say?" Margaux asked as she slipped the apple pie into the oven.

"I was...just saying a little prayer," he answered.

"To whom, for what?" she asked, not really caring what his answer might be.

"I was praying that maybe after this scrumptious dinner you're preparing, you might invite me into your bedroom tonight." Margaux started to offer an excuse, and then she thought that pleasing Toro tonight might ease her conscience when she pleased Gary the next day.

"Why not?" she said, brightly. "But it mustn't be an all night affair like the last time. I've got a big day tomorrow."

"Shopping, I suppose."

"As a matter of fact that's true. How did you guess?"

"I just figured it was either tennis, the gym with that wimp trainer of yours or shopping with Lucie. I got two tickets to the Yankees game tomorrow but I don't suppose there's any way of talking you into going to the game with me?"

"'Fraid not, Toro. Lucie asked me to help her find a dress for her friend's wedding. Besides, you know I hate baseball." Margaux knew Lucie would cover for her.

As soon as Margaux heard Toro singing in the shower—the prelude to their lovemaking, such as it was—she raced down to the kitchen, retrieved Gary's telephone number and called him. As soon as he picked up, she said, "I'll be there tomorrow at one." Then she hung up the phone, raced back up the stairs, slipped off her nightgown and waited for her husband.

Gary sat in the Simply Red Cafe, awaiting Margaux's arrival. He was trying to analyze his feelings for her.

She's very attractive, but I'm not a stranger to beautiful women, he said to himself. *Why do us guys pass by the plain Janes with the brains? Because, most of the time we're not looking for a* mate, *we're looking for a* playmate. *So, what is there about Margaux that I find so appealing? It's true that she's one of the most exciting bed partners I've ever met, but I'm old enough to know that's not enough to sustain a relationship....*

At that moment he saw Margaux striding elegantly toward his table. He stood up, grinning. "Hey there, pretty woman," he said, kissing her on each cheek and the palm of her extended hand. "I was just thinking about you."

After lunch at the cafe, Gary suggested that they take a ride out onto Long Island so he could show her his home in Sea Cliff. Margaux glanced at her watch. "I'd love to, but I must be back home by five-thirty at the latest."

"Why? I don't get it."

"You're not supposed to," she laughed.

"Okay, Let's go. Beggars can't be choosers."

As Toro was approaching the entrance to the Brooklyn Bridge, intending to take the East River Parkway up to Yankee Stadium to watch the Yankees play a double header, his brand new baby blue Cadillac conked out and wouldn't restart. He called AAA, and sat fuming. He cursed General Motors in Brooklynese and Greek. It was almost two o'clock when the car was finally running again.

As soon as he paid the bill, he raced out of the service station hoping to make the best of a bad situation. When he stopped at a red light he spied Margaux and Gary driving by in Gary's dark green Jaguar convertible with the top down. Toro pulled around the car in front of him and ran two red lights. He managed to get Gary's license plate number just before he heard the siren. The NYPD patrol car with flashing lights was right on his tail. By the time the cop finished writing up a half-dozen tickets Toro had forgotten some of the numbers and their sequence. He bagged the ball game and went straight home to wait for Margaux. He called Lucie's number but he only got her answering machine. It didn't matter; he knew Lucie wouldn't tell him the truth, anyway.

When Gary and Margaux arrived at Gary's home in Sea Cliff, he rounded up one of Melinda's bikinis for Margaux and they strolled, hand in hand, out to the end of Gary's dock.

"I'm definitely *into* the swimming," Margaux said, "but I'm afraid I'm mostly *out of* this bikini. How old did you say your daughter was?" she laughed, tugging on the skimpy top.

"You don't hear me complaining, do you?" Gary grinned. When she joined him in the water, he dove under and untied the top of her bikini and swam away with it.

"Come back here, you thief!" she screamed. Gary climbed up on the dock, tied the bikini to the lanyard and raised it to the top of the flagpole where it waved sensuously in the afternoon breeze. When she swam back to the dock she asked him to stop acting like a jerk and give her back her top or a towel to cover up. He ignored the request and said, "I'm going to invite the neighbors over for cocktails. What do you say?"

"I don't care," she said, as she brazenly scrambled up the ladder and posed topless on the dock. "I don't live in the neighborhood."

Gary picked up a beach towel and brought it to her, but when she reached for it, he dropped it and took her in his arms. She did not resist.

Two martinis later he invited her up to his master bedroom.

"I'm sorry, Gary—I can't."

"You can't or you won't?" he asked, with a frown.

She hesitated a moment and then said, "If you put it that way, I guess the answer is, I won't."

"I don't get it. What did I do? You're not pissed at me because I stole your bikini top, I hope?"

"Of course not, and I'm willing to pleasure *you*, but we can't, you know...make love."

"But what about the Palmer House?"

"I will savor every moment of that night and day as long as I live, but that was different."

"How so?"

"The Palmer House was an adventure. I know I should have refused to meet you for lunch and I should have refused to come here to your home, but...."

"But what?"

"If you must know, I wanted to see you again. I knew that sooner or later I would have to face this moment between us, but I was hoping for some sort of miracle, I guess."

"Like what?"

"I don't know. You can't imagine how much I want us to make love again, like in Chicago, but I can't and I wanted to believe that we could enjoy each other just the way we have all day...until the moment you invited me to bed."

"But I'm a healthy forty-six year old male animal. I don't see how you can expect me to—"

Margaux interrupted him. "I am acutely aware of the fact that you are a vigorous male," she said, glancing at the bulge in his bathing trunks, "and the thought of it takes my breath away and I want to cry, but it's impossible." She checked her watch. "Oh God," she exclaimed. "I'm already late. I've got to go home immediately."

She hurried back into the house and got dressed.

In the car, driving back to Brooklyn, Gary sulked most of the way. Finally he said, "I don't get it. You're over twenty-one. You told me you're not married. What's the story here?" She didn't answer him. Neither of them spoke during the balance of the trip to Brooklyn.

When they arrived at the parking garage where she had left her BMW, she refused to tell him where she lived. He attempted to embrace her, but she hopped out of the car and scrambled away.

When Margaux hadn't returned home by five o'clock, Toro went into his den and poured himself a hefty Scotch on the rocks. He slumped down in the chair behind his desk. He could feel his heart thumping in his chest and for a few seconds he had difficulty breathing. He had been having problems with shortness of breath on exertion, and was anxiously awaiting the results of a number of tests his old friend and family physician Sam Newman had put him through. But he was frightened by this onset of a breathing problem while he was only sitting quietly in his chair. He remained calm until his breathing returned to normal and then swiveled his chair around and fumbled with the dial on his wall safe. When he removed his prenuptial agreement from the safe, he held the document up close to his face so that he could read the fine legal print. He flipped the pages until he reached the heading: Termination of Marriage: Spousal Support and Equitable Distribution.

He read it aloud to himself, slowly moving his finger along each word as he spoke. "When the parties have completed four years of cohabitation during which the wife agrees to fulfill all her conjugal obligations, the husband shall place the sum of two million dollars ($2,000,000) in trust for the benefit of the wife, payable to the wife upon the husband's death. In the event that the net estate of the husband shall exceed 6,000,000 (including said $2,000,000 held in trust), at the time of his death, the wife shall be paid one third of any amount in excess of $6,000,000. Said payment shall constitute full settlement and satisfaction of all spousal claims against the husband or his estate, for the wife's support and for equitable distribution.

In the event the husband shall abandon the wife or otherwise terminate their marital relationship in less than four years from the date of marriage, the husband shall pay to the wife the sum of five thousand dollars ($5,000) for each week they have resided together as husband and wife.

In the event the husband shall predecease the wife prior to the time the parties shall have been married for a period of four years, the estate of the husband shall pay to the wife the sum of $2,000,000 in full settlement of all spousal claims of the wife.

HOWEVER, in the event the wife shall commit adultery at any time during the first four years of the marriage of the parties, the wife shall be paid $100 in full settlement of all claims against Dimitri Santoros or his estate."

He put the agreement aside. "Fucking lawyer gobbledygook," he said, but the words "In the event the husband shall predecease the wife..." kept reverberating in his mind. If she was cheating on him he had to prove it before his death or before their fourth anniversary on January 13, 2010.

He tried to think back over the past few months to recall signs of Margaux's discontent; to find a starting point of her infidelity if that's what it was, but absolutely nothing came to mind.

For the first year I watched her like a hawk. I didn't see nothin'. I mean, to be honest, from the moment I first seen her, I wanted her. I wanted to fuck her brains out. I didn't care what it cost. And then I began to love her. Not like with Maria, God rest her soul, but better than I thought it could ever be at my age...I didn't like living alone. I wanted a good looking woman, shit, I don't know what I wanted, but I got more than I bargained for.

I didn't pay much attention this past year. Everything was almost perfect. I didn't like the separate bedroom crap, but she let me call the shots most of the time. Now this Jaguar son of a bitch shows up and I'm suspicious of everything. I don't trust her no more. The question is, how long's it been goin' on?

Toro heard the garage door mechanism squeal when Margaux arrived home. He had parked his car around the block so she wouldn't know he was home. He was waiting for her in the kitchen with the shades drawn when she came in from the garage. She burst through the kitchen door and screamed when she saw a man sitting in the shadows.

"It's only me, Sweetheart. Can I help you carry in all the packages from your shopping trip with Lucie?"

Margaux caught a glimpse of her image in the hall mirror. Her hair was wild and still damp. Her nose was sunburned. She had expected to have plenty of time to shower and change before Toro came home from the ball game, but....

"I didn't go shopping with Lucie. She cancelled out on me. I went to the club and took a swim in the pool."

"Who was there?" he asked.

"No one I knew. Actually, the place was deserted. Must be everyone's on the Cape or out in the Hamptons. How come we don't have a place in the Hamptons?" she complained. "We never do anything except sit here in Brooklyn and sweat. Every night I get all dressed up for you when you come home and then we spend the night watching frigging television. Sports and junk. I'm fed up with it." She turned and started to leave the room.

"Where do you think you're going?" Toro growled.

"Up to take a shower and get dressed and I'm not cooking dinner. We're going out to dinner in the most expensive restaurant in Manhattan, or I'm going alone." She started to march out of the kitchen. Toro grabbed her arm.

"You ain't going nowhere, baby, until you tell me where you been this afternoon."

"Let go of my arm. You're hurting me."

"Where were you, God damn it? I know you weren't at the club. You're lying through your teeth. You was riding with some guy in a green convertible."

"You're out of your mind."

"I saw you with my own eyes!"

"Prove it," she hissed. She managed to jerk her arm free and ran up to her bedroom and locked the door.

He followed her and pounded on the door. "I'll break down the God damn door if you don't open it, bitch."

"I just dialed 911. The operator is listening to this conversation. Yell a little louder, Toro. Tell me again how you're going to break down my bedroom door and beat the shit out of me. Say it again, Toro, so the operator can get it on tape. Yes, Operator, I do want to press charges for assault and, and—" Toro stopped pounding on the door.

"For Chrissake Margaux, hang up the phone, you know I wouldn't hurt you."

"You already did. I've got the bruises on my arm to prove it. Hold on Operator, please, I'll give you my name and address in a minute. How far do you want to take this, Toro?"

"Hang up the phone, Margaux. We'll talk."

Margaux continued to hold down the button on the phone. There was no connection, but she said, loudly, "My name is Margaux Santoros. I live at 756 Freemont Avenue, Brooklyn. If you don't hear from me in thirty minutes, send an officer to my home. But be careful. My husband is armed."

During the next twenty minutes, they negotiated a deal through the locked bedroom door. Margaux agreed not to press charges for assault, and Toro agreed to drop the subject of her afternoon at the country club. However, the next day Margaux had a professional photographer take photos of her bruised arm and Toro called Barney Rifkin.

"Rifkin? It's Toro."

"What's up, man? How are you doing? How's the missus?"

"That's what I want to talk to you about. You drew up that nuptial agreement thing. You remember?"

"Sure. I don't remember the details, but what's the problem?" the attorney asked.

"The agreement says if we're still married after four years, I gotta put two million bucks in the bank for her which she can't touch until I die, but if she commits adultery before four years or before I kick off, she doesn't get shit. My doc says I got a serious medical problem and I ain't got too much time left. I think she's fuckin' around with some guy I seen her driving around with. She says she ain't, but I don't believe her. When I accused her, she said 'prove it'. She's no dope, you know."

"I told you that before I introduced you to her. But that's the point. In my opinion there's no way she would run the risk of losing two million dollars before you have to ante up the money. He's probably just some jerk she knows, like an insurance salesman or something."

"He don't look like no insurance salesman to me, drivin' around in a Jaguar convertible in the middle of the afternoon. What would she need an insurance salesman for, anyway?"

Barney shook his head and smiled, while Toro talked on and on about his marital problems. Barney thought, *How can a guy who is smart enough to stash five or six million in the bank be so stupid when it comes to pussy?*

"Hey, Barney, are you listening to me?" Toro demanded. "I'm asking you what I should do. I don't want her collecting no two million bucks from me after she's been screwin' around with some insurance asshole." Barney couldn't help but laugh, but he didn't cover the mouthpiece in time.

"Hey, Mr. Big Shot Attorney," Toro growled. "This ain't no laughin' matter, and if you think it is, I'll find another lawyer. So you been my lawyer for twenty years and I've paid you big, big, bucks, thousands and thousands…so now when there's somethin' really serious, you think it's a big fuckin' joke…well, let me tell you somethin', Rifkin…."

"Toro, Toro," Barney interrupted. "I wasn't laughing at *you*, I was laughing at the situation. We've all been in it. When it comes to sex, us guys get led around by our dicks. Do you remember that time when your wife Maria, God bless her, caught you shacked up in the penthouse at the Waldorf, and you tried to convince her that the lady who was locked in the bathroom was a seamstress who was fitting you for a new suit?"

"Don't mention my wife's name, may she rest in peace, when we're talkin' about Margaux, the whore," Toro cursed.

"Wait a minute, Toro, calm down. I'm just trying to tell you that screaming at me doesn't solve anything. You need to find out who the guy is. It could be a totally innocent situation. Let me give you a number to call. The guy's name is Sanchez. He's a retired NYPD investigator. Just tell him I told you to call. He'll treat you right."

CHAPTER SEVEN

Aldo Sanchez had begun his career as a foot patrolman in Harlem at age eighteen, but for the last half of his career with the force, he had worked in the detective division. After thirty years with the NYPD, he had retired with a gold watch and a modest pension on the one hand and an amicable divorce on the other. Totally free of professional and marital obligations, he had intended to spend his time traveling to exotic destinations and going to ball games. But he soon realized that he didn't have enough money to do the things he had been dreaming about.

After a gloomy, rainy day watching soap operas and game shows, he checked with a couple of the private detective agencies he had come across over the years to see what might be available on a part-time basis. He discovered that, unless he was licensed as an investigator, no one was interested in hiring him. He also learned that since he was an ex-cop, all the government wanted from him to set up shop on his own was a fee of $400, proof that he had been a police officer for at least twenty years, and the ability to pass a simple examination.

After he obtained his license, he called his friend Barney Rifkin, and learned that Barney was representing a wife in a messy divorce action, but she couldn't afford to pay the $10,000 retainer that his regular investigator demanded to do the job. Sanchez eagerly agreed to take on the case for the amount she could afford, hired a receptionist/secretary and hung out a sign.

He had been working as a private investigator for only two months when Toro called his office.

"Confidential Investigations. This is Brenda speaking."

"Yeah," Toro replied. "I want to speak to Mr. Sanchez."

"Of course, sir,"

"Sanchez, here."

"Yeah, Sanchez, my lawyer Barney Rifkin told me to call you. I need the name of a guy what owns a certain car. I think I got most of the letters and numbers on the license plate. I only seen it drivin' by, see, and maybe I ain't put 'em down right, like maybe not exactly the way they go together, see what I mean?"

"Well," Sanchez replied, "if Barney recommended you to me, I'll do my very best. If you aren't certain of the numbers and their sequence, it makes it a lot more difficult, but not impossible. It may take some time. If you give me everything you've got, we'll go to work on it right away. What are the numbers?"

"6807CRQ, or something close to that," Toro said.

"What state and year?"

"New York State, 2007."

"Do you know anything else, like the make of the car, color, whatever you can remember?"

"It was a dark green Jaguar convertible, I don't know the year, you know them foreign cars all look alike."

"How about the driver? I mean was he a kid, or an old man, you know—so we can sort of match up his date of birth?" Sanchez asked.

"Yeah, the son of a bitch looked like maybe he was in his mid-forties."

"Good, that's a help. How soon do you need this information?"

"As soon as possible. And what's the cost?"

"That depends on how complicated finding the answer may be," Sanchez said.

"What the hell does that mean?"

"Like I said. If all we've got is a routine inquiry, it won't cost you over five hundred bucks. If it's a stolen vehicle, switched plates, altered plates, you know—a criminally-oriented vehicle, it's a different kettle of fish."

"It ain't complicated," Toro said.

"Assuming you're right, I'll get back to you in a day or two. What's your name?"

"Dimitri Santoros."

"I'll send the information to you as soon as I can. Your address, please."

Toro hesitated and then gave him his home address.

"You got it," Sanchez said, and hung up the phone. He immediately dialed his old precinct, spoke briefly to the duty officer and was put through to one of his former colleagues.

"Hey, old buddy, how's it going?" Sanchez asked.

"Now, what do you want? For Christ's sake, you're supposed to be retired."

"This is an easy one, Willy, I just need a readout on the owner of a green Jaguar convertible registered in New York. I've got most of the license plate numbers. It's a hit and run or something."

"Okay, give me the info. Yeah, here I am up to my ass in homicide, making peanuts, while you're making big bucks and collecting on the pension fund what I'm paying for and is gonna be broke by the time I retire...."

"Like I always said, Willy, you sound just like one of them cops on *Law and Order*. Don't let anybody tell you otherwise."

"What a bunch of bullshit this is. You better be good to me, Sanchez, or I'll make you write a letter to the Motor Vehicle Bureau and maybe, just *maybe*, if you're lucky, in about three months, you might get an answer."

While they were talking, the officer had punched the information into the computer on the console behind him, and within minutes, three names flashed on the screen. Gary Samson was among them, with his present address and date of birth. One of the others was over sixty years old, and the third vehicle was red.

Sanchez smiled when his buddy gave him the data. He said, "Thanks Willy. I'll meet you at Gilhooley's when you get off work tonight. I'm buyin'. What time?"

"Well, now you're talking. I'm out of here at six o'clock sharp."

"You got it, old friend. See you then. Course, I might be a little late cause I'm gettin' paid a hundred fifty dollars an hour as an accident reconstruction expert. Did you know that, Willy?"

"Fuck off!" Willy hung up the phone.

Sanchez looked at his time sheet. *Let's see*, he mumbled to himself, *seventeen minutes; call it twenty, divided into $500 equals, ah, ah, twenty-five. So, that's twenty-five dollars a minute, which means I've been paid at the rate of sixty times twenty-five which is fifteen hundred dollars an hour. Holy Shit!*

When Toro picked up his mail two days later, there was a plain brown envelope marked confidential. It had a return address but no sender's name. He went into his den, poured himself a drink, tore open the envelope and stared at the name. Gary Samson. *So now what I'm gonna do? So now I'll find out who this son of a bitch is, and if they're doin' what I figure they're doin', I'll divorce the bitch and cut off the fucker's nuts.*

Margaux lay awake in her bedroom until long past midnight. She and Gary had met a number of times following their afternoon at Gary's home in Sea Cliff. On each occasion, it would end unhappily with Gary sulking when she refused his sexual advances. He would always promise not to ask of her what she said she couldn't do, and she would always tell him that if they couldn't just be friends it wasn't fair to either of them to continue seeing each other. She decided she must cut Gary totally out of her life. *I'm such a jerk*, she lamented. *If it were just sex, I've been there before and I know how to solve that problem, but the only screwing going on around here is in my head. He's got my head screwed up.* She wrapped the comforter around herself and groped about in the dark for the pack of cigarettes she had hidden away. *I can't even smoke anymore, because Gary hates it,* she grumbled, *and now that I'm trying to quit, I can't stand Toro's stinking cigar breath which never bothered me before.* She sat down on her chaise, lit a cigarette and inhaled, sucking the poison deep into her lungs, gratified by the instant nicotine kick. But as she gazed through the smoke at the view of the lights on the Brooklyn Bridge and the pale ethereal glow of the Statue of Liberty, far off in the distance, she felt an animal-like craving to have Gary hold her and love her again. She thought, *This is absolute madness. I am being consumed by this man. I want to touch him and hear him laugh and feel his back in the curve of my body as we sleep together. What am I going to do?* And then she began to cry, softly. *Sure as hell, we're going to get caught. It's crazy. Two million dollars. Has any woman in the world ever paid two million dollars to have her bones jumped? I must end it immediately…tomorrow…there's no other way.* She slipped off the chaise and dug down deep in the back corner of her dresser drawer and pulled out the thick manila folder buried among her fancy silk underclothes. She lay back down on her bed and turned on the reading lamp, flipping through the pages of the weighty document until she found what she was looking for.

> In the event the husband shall predecease the wife prior to the time the parties shall have been married for a period of four years, the estate of the husband shall pay to the wife the sum of $2,000,000 in full settlement of all spousal claims of the wife.
>
> HOWEVER, in the event the wife shall commit adultery at any time during the first four years of the marriage of the parties, the wife shall be paid $100 in full settlement of all claims against Dimitri Santoros or his estate.

She put the agreement down and stared at the ceiling. *Unless I do something, I'm going to lose either Gary or $2,000,000, or both.* The last thing she remembered before finally falling asleep were the words, In the event the husband shall predecease the wife prior to the time the parties shall have been married for a period of four years, the estate of the husband shall pay to the wife the sum of $2,000,000.

…predecease…PREDECEASE…Die Toro…Die Toro, Please die Toro, Oh God, what am I thinking?

When she finished her workout at the gym the next day she went to the public phone and called Gary's office number. As soon as his secretary confirmed that he was in, she immediately hung up the phone and dialed his home number. She didn't want to talk to him because she felt the usual craving for him whenever they conversed. She even felt a flutter in her stomach when she heard his recorded voice: "I'm sorry I missed your call, please leave me a message...."

"Gary," she said, speaking to the answering machine, "someone must have seen us that afternoon when we went to your place. You know I care for you—a lot, but if you have any feelings for me at all, I beg you never to contact me again. Maybe sometime soon in the future I'll be able to see you again, but *not now*. I don't expect you to wait for me because I have no way of knowing how long it might be. Please forgive and forget me, as I am going to try and forget you. This is not a game. It's my life."

That evening Margaux handed Toro a card with a phone number and advised him that since he was always complaining about telemarketers, she had paid for a new unlisted number.

When Gary first heard the message on his answering machine, he was angry. He listened to it several times and decided to call her bluff. He called her number, intending to duke it out with her. The phone rang a number of times before a female voice answered. It was a recording.

"The number you have reached, 273-0479, is no longer in service."

Gary threw the mobile phone across the room. "Oh, no you don't," he shouted.

Gary and Pierre DeLisle were scheduled to meet in Pierre's office. When Gary opened the door, Pierre was on the phone. While Gary waited for him to finish his telephone call, he glanced out the window at the bridge over the East River and smiled to himself. *This is where it all started—how many years ago? I can't believe it, over twenty years.* He saw the bridge's suspension cables glistening in the afternoon sun, just the way he remembered them from the first time he had come to Pierre's office. He pulled himself up out of the chair and ambled over to the sideboard to pour himself a glass of Pierre's famous lemonade. Then he stood gazing out over the river. *Nothing I can see out there has changed but everything in my life has,* he thought. *A lot of water has passed under that bridge. There she stands after all these years. She hasn't shed a single gray rivet, and here I am, my life more than half over, still struggling to understand what it's all about, still striving for success and fulfillment, still searching for...what? For someone to love besides Lindy, I guess. My darling Melinda, on her way to a successful career in film, Pete and me at the top of our game, and now I've found a woman who is rattling my cage. What is there about Margaux that's got me flamboozled?*

Pierre finally finished his call. "Sorry to keep you waiting, ole buddy, but it looks like we just picked up the InterState Airlines account. How about that?"

"That's stupendous. I get to work with all those first-class cabin flight attendants, right?"

"You got it. They want the shoot done in and around their home office in Phoenix."

"Ugh," Gary groaned. "I hate Phoenix."

"Tough shit, baby, 'cause that's where you're going tonight."

"Hey, partner, I run the artistic side of this business, and I'm telling you, Phoenix sucks."

"And I'm running the financial side, and I think Phoenix is beautiful because our new client thinks it's beautiful. So go home and pack 'cause you're meeting with ISA's marketing people tomorrow afternoon. It's big, Gair, it's very big for us."

"I hear you, Pete, and the truth is I think Phoenix is a great city, I just didn't want to be away from New York right now, and it sounds like this isn't going to be a one-night stand kind of thing."

You're right, Gair. I've got it budgeted for a week."

"If I'm lucky," Gary complained. "The problem is, Pete, when I'm the one who has to work with the marketing guys from these big companies like ISA, all of them are would-be Hollywood screen writers, directors, producers. I admit that usually they're pretty imaginative, but invariably they want us to produce an award-winning product on a peanut butter budget. Anyway," he sighed audibly, "what's the concept on this one?"

"They didn't tell me and I don't care. That's your department. I just collect the money, and there's no one in the business better than you who can pull A-plus rabbits out of C-plus hats."

Gary laughed. "I know when I'm being buttered up for the kill."

"Pick up all the info from MaryLou. She's got your ticket, a hotel reservation for you tonight at the airport—the works. The good news is that you leave at 7:20 tomorrow morning and arrive in Phoenix at 9:30."

"You're a riot, Pete. Like I'm not supposed to know there's a two hour time change; like I don't know it's a four hour flight and I'll be spending the weekend in steaming Phoenix instead of racing my beautiful little sailboat in the Larchmont Regatta, one of the highlights of the Sea Cliff Yacht Club sailing season. Damn it Pete, you're ruining my life for a couple of bucks."

Pierre stood up and slung his arm around Gary's shoulder. "Like I don't know I've got the best partner a fellow could ever have, but Gair, it's not nickels and dimes—if you pull this one off and we keep the account, we're talking a couple of million bucks."

Gary whistled, "Okay, okay. Look, I don't mind being bamboozled by a beautiful woman, but—"

"What beautiful woman?"

"I can't tell you yet."

"Why the hell not? You've always told me everything."

"Because I can't find her, God dammit. Never mind, it's too complicated, but when I return from Phoenix, I'm not coming back to work until I find her."

"That's okay as long as you remember that I'm going to be sixty-five in a few months, and I promised Louise that I would hand over my office keys to you on my birthday, and Samson and Delisle will be all yours. Then, not only will you manage the artistic side of the business that you do so well, but you will also be the chief financial officer and you'll discover it ain't a piece of cake, and you're going to miss your old nagging buddy Pete. But until then, I'm in charge of the money side of this outfit, and I'm ordering you to get your ass down to Phoenix, Arizona, and help me lock up the deal with ISA.

"I'm also ordering you and Lindy to come out to our house for a barbeque on my *sixty-fifth* just like we did for you on your *thirty-fifth*, ten years ago."

"Okay, okay, if you put it that way, I'm off to Arizona. Nothing and nobody can keep Lindy and me away from your party," Gary said.

CHAPTER EIGHT

Bridget Mulvaney was born on Valentine's day in Tempe, Arizona, east of Phoenix. She grew up in the Montecito Mobile Home Estates with her mother, Elizabeth, a devoted, caring single parent who gave her extraordinarily personable child as much love as any daughter could hope for. Bridget attended Arizona State University, majored in drama, and enjoyed some modest success performing in summer stock theater after graduation from the university. She finally settled for a well-paying job as a flight attendant with InterState Airlines.

On a trip from Phoenix to Los Angeles, she met and subsequently married Jeremy Tulane, a dynamic young entrepreneur who became the father of their two children. Tragically, Jeremy died following a minor surgical procedure that went awry, leaving his family with debt that greatly exceeded its assets. Bridget immediately returned to work with the airline, and for the first few months she was exhilarated by the daily interaction with her peers and the challenges of her job; but her long absences from home began to have a demonstrably negative impact on her children. Their grades and behavior in school deteriorated and after her midterm parent/teacher conference, Bridget knew she had to make some changes in their family situation. She was becoming distraught because she needed the income and the health benefits her job provided, but at the depth of her despair, the Goddess of Goodwill had touched her on the shoulder with her magic wand.

One of her first-class passengers, the vice president of ISA marketing, had been searching for a fresh face to portray the airline's new image in a series of TV commercials to be produced by Samson & DeLisle. By the time they had touched down in Phoenix, Bridget had enthusiastically agreed to audition for the job.

The evening before she was scheduled to meet with Gary Samson, she slipped out into her tiny garden after the children went to bed. It was a warm, sensuous Arizona night, with a dark, dark, blue-black sky, a mass of bright flashing stars, and an almost full moon rising.

"I am so incredibly lucky," she whispered. "It looks as if all of my problems may be solved."

Except one, her inner voice reminded her.

You're right—all but one, she sighed.

Bridget missed her husband desperately. Although she was constantly being propositioned by most of the pilots and many of her first-class passengers, she wasn't interested in one-night stands. She wanted a man with whom she could share her children and her life in every way, not just in the bedroom.

"No doubt about it," she said aloud, tilting her head back and looking up at the sky, "I'm incredibly fortunate, but—I need a freaking man, Mr. Moon!"

When Gary met with the InterState Airlines marketing team in Phoenix, he learned that the marketing and sales guys had already decided upon the artistic concept for the commercial. One of the senior members of the marketing team had actually written the script, and a vice president of the company had chosen the female lead from the ranks of their own flight attendants.

Gary called Pierre. "What the hell have you gotten me into down here?" he screamed. "Jesus Christ, Pete. I thought we had all the money we needed."

"A successful business always needs money to go on being successful. We always need money!" Pierre said.

"I realize that, but this is too much."

"Hold on, hold on, Gair, just take it easy and explain the situation nice and slow, so your old Uncle Pete can get his arms around the problem. First of all, what are they trying to do? What's the marketing concept?"

"Something about a flight attendant who has mesmerized a group of business executives. They take whatever flight she's on, regardless of its destination, and consequently their companies are opening up new branches all over the country, and ISA is flying into a slew of new destinations. It's a way to introduce all of ISA's new air routes."

Pierre gave a low chuckle. "That doesn't sound so awful, Gair. It could be sort of fun, don't you think?"

"Sure, if you want to sign up J-Lo, or how about Angelina Jolie, to play the role of the flight attendant who is so alluring that all the male passengers are willing to follow her to the ends of the earth. Do you think you could squeeze either of them into the budget?"

"Hey, man, we've got a roster of beauties who would pay *us* to get a part like that. Okay, so what's the problem?"

"The problem, partner, is that I'm not permitted to use a professional model to play the lead. A vice president of the company has already selected one of their flight attendants he's probably sleeping with for that role. C'mon, Pete, you've got to get me out of this nightmare. I know exactly what's going to happen. The show is going to bomb and I'll be blamed."

The line was silent for a minute and then Pierre said, "How about this: audition their candidate and then run her ass into the ground so she quits and then you bring in the professional you want and everyone lives happily ever after. I've seen you work magic on a number of professionals you didn't like. A cheerleader from Arizona ought to be a pushover. If you pull this baby off, there are four more in the wings. At a half million dollars a pop, we ain't talking peanuts, bro. By the way, how did you enjoy the suite we gave you at the airport last night so you wouldn't miss your 7:00 a.m. flight this morning?"

"I knew you wouldn't understand." Gary hung up and headed down to the hotel cocktail lounge, where he attempted to gain insight with an overdose of Jack Daniels that left him with a colossal hangover.

When Bridget Tulane was ushered into his makeshift office the next day, Gary was initially disdainful. She was attractive enough, but in a southern, small town, girl-next-door kind of way. Not exactly the superseductress the script called for. Gary glanced at her resumé.

"Have you ever done any modeling?" he asked.

"In fact, I have," she answered. "I helped pay my way through university, learning the standards." She got him laughing with her Marilyn Monroe routine (head tilted back, lips parted), The Pout (lips puckered, eyes lowered) and The Breathless (hand on side of head, fingertips in slightly open mouth, eyes heavy-lidded). For a finale, she put one hand up in the air and the other on her hip, thrust her pelvis a foot in front of the rest of her exquisite body and vamped across the room. She was bright, vibrant and vivacious, but at the same time you had the feeling you would enjoy her company having a milkshake at the local ice cream parlor as much as an extra-dry martini in the hotel cocktail lounge.

Gary excused himself and went unsteadily to the men's room where, groaning, he stared at his image in the mirror. There were multiple yellowish, purple bags under his eyes, and in the battle of the eyeballs the white team had clearly lost the battle to the red team which completed the picture of an unshaven derelict. He spruced up as best he could, and told Bridget that they would continue the audition the next day because unforeseen difficulties had surfaced and he had to study the situation an additional twenty-four hours before bringing in the cameraman and crew to prepare for the shoot.

As soon as she left, Gary headed for the nearest barbershop, ordered "the works," went back to his hotel and crashed for twelve hours. Early the next morning, approaching the task from a totally different perspective, he reworked the script they had given him, blocked the scenes and studied

Bridget's portfolio. He had decided she would be perfect for the role.

On the evening of the second night of the shoot, he took her to dinner. He found her to be a thoughtful, gracious southern belle, with a gentle spirit and a great sense of humor—a delightful woman overall.

After a week of their working together and spending almost every evening in each other's company, Gary subtly suggested a few times that they might do something a little more intimate, but Bridget always just smiled and changed the subject with an endearing comment or a gentle gesture.

On their last night together they went dancing at Papagayo's, a popular local night club, and both got a little giddy on champagne. They were each acutely aware of how their association had grown from professional respect to more than a casual friendship. Gary was trying hard to keep it cool and not embarrass himself by an invitation to take their friendship to a higher level that Bridget might not have any desire to pursue.

For her part, Bridget was smitten. It seemed to her that Gary possessed all of the characteristics in a man that she had been searching for since her husband's death. There was the added fact that he obviously took pleasure and pride in his role as a father, which was an added bonus from her perspective. She ached with desire when their bodies melded together on the dance floor, and it was impossible to ignore Gary's arousal, but somewhere deep in her sense of being a woman, she knew that if she accepted his lightly veiled invitations to share his bed, the emotional costs could be devastating.

When they parted, they promised to stay in touch. She meant it seriously, and hoped that he did as well.

Shortly after his flight took off, Gary ordered a vodka/orange juice, settled back in his deep, soft leather first-class seat, and began to compare Bridget and Margaux. They were both about the same age; maybe Margaux was a couple of years older.... They seemed to be exactly matched when it came to intelligence, personality, sense of humor, and over-all attractiveness; but Margaux was clearly more exciting. Bridget seemed to be more down-to-earth, and then of course there was the problem of Bridget's teen-age kids. There was also the sex thing. Margaux was dynamite and Bridget was an unknown. He stared blankly out the window. He had been a happy single parent and a very comfortable bachelor, living with Lindy for almost twenty years. But when she went off to college, his life changed significantly. They no longer sat across the table from each other every morning and evening, sharing the details of their lives. He missed helping her with her homework and rehearsing her lines for the Senior Play. And as she stepped into her increasingly successful adventures in Hollywood, his passion for his work was not enough to sustain him. He slid into a deep funk, rarely participating in the exotic social life available to him in the "city that never sleeps." Most nights when he wasn't working he would be at home, reading, tinkering in his wood-working shop, or tweaking a screenplay he had been writing for ten years. All that changed when he met Margaux…and then Bridget.

When Margaux awakened on a Tuesday, she looked out the window. It was raining.

"I can't do this anymore!" she hissed through clenched teeth. She had been depressed for several weeks, but she felt she was going over the edge when Toro sneaked into her bedroom at four o'clock in the morning and woke her up by caressing her sexually.

I'm counting the days until he dies. It's just like when I was in prison and counting the days until I would be released, except when I was in good old Richford Hills, my sentence was finite: 365 days. But now I swear the son of a bitch will probably outlive me. Two million dollars! I've sold the best years of my life for two million dollars….

"Die! Die! Die!" she sobbed, smashing her fist into her pillow.

At ten-thirty the following morning she picked up her cell phone and dialed her friend Lucie at work. They spoke on the phone almost every day and had lunch together at least once a week. When Lucie answered, Margaux told her she really needed to meet with her for lunch.

"What's the problem, Hon?" Lucie asked.

"I'll tell you everything over lunch," Margaux said.

As soon as they were seated and had given the waiter their drink orders, Margaux said, "I can't stand it anymore, Lucie. Toro is driving me crazy. What the hell am I going to do?"

"Give me a reason you didn't know about before you married him," Lucie said.

"He figures he owns me, like I'm his Barbie doll."

"That's what you are."

"Shut up a minute and listen to me, will you please? I don't mind his showing me off. I know I'm his trophy wife. He bought me. But that doesn't mean that he has the right to treat me like a piece of shit. As soon as the ball game on TV was over last night, the same as every night, he went to bed."

"That's lucky for you, right?" Lucie shrugged.

"Wrong! Between the time he goes to bed and eight o'clock in the morning, his bladder controls his life—like an alarm clock. Every night exactly at midnight and again exactly at four a.m., he has to relieve himself. I mean *every* night. Now, listen to me. We have two bathrooms on the second floor. The one down the hall is supposed to be his. It's got all his medications, shaving equipment and whatever. The other one is mine, right next to my bedroom and across the hall from his. So where does he go to pee at midnight and four in the morning? Naturally, in my private bathroom adjoining my bedroom. He slams around, coughs, hawks up phlegm, spits, lifts up the toilet seat and never puts it back down so on the rare occasion when I have to pee in the middle of the night, I end up falling into the toilet bowl...."

Lucie yelped.

"Don't you dare laugh, Lucie," Margaux said. "Okay, so it sounds hilarious...I mean I know it happens with almost all old guys, but all you need to do to make most of those guys happy is to let them empty their bladders, but not my Toro. I mean it's four o'clock in the morning, I'm sound asleep, but he's wide awake and while he's peeing he's got his thing in his hand, of course, so he decides he wants to put it somewhere...like you know where.

"Jesus, Lucie, how did I ever get myself into this mess? I'm so depressed. I can't stand the sight of him."

"Don't go there, Margaux. He just paid your quarter of a million dollar fine, and he gives you a salary of ten thousand dollars a month to show up in his office a couple of hours a week to keep his legal affairs in order. What more can you ask? Look at me. Although I feel lucky to have my job and I enjoy my work as a sales person in the home furnishings department at Macy's, I make ten bucks an hour and five percent commission. Like on the price of a lamp on sale for ninety-nine dollars...I make five extra bucks. I've got no sympathy for you, baby.

"Besides which, Toro adores you. I haven't got anyone."

"But you have the freedom to see whomever you please. Freedom to go out to dinner and go dancing whenever you want to—with people your own age. That's what I want—instead of sitting in front of the boob tube night after night watching the freaking Yankees smack a baseball around."

"Me and a few million other women I know would trade with you in a heartbeat."

"I know, I know, and I was coping with it okay until I met Gary. Now that's all I can think about. You'll understand once you meet him, Lucie. Please listen to me, Lucie-Love. These are the best years of my life. And if I tell Gary the truth about being married, I'm going to lose him. If I don't tell him the truth and he finds out I'm married, I'm going to lose him, and if Toro finds out about Gary and me before he dies, I'm going to lose two million bucks. I'm really serious about this. Lucie, are you paying attention to me?"

"I'm listening," Lucie shrugged.

"You remember I told you how I started screwing my Social Sci teacher in high school and how he got me into college where I started messing with my English Lit professor who helped get me into Law School? And then after I passed the New York Bar examination I went to work for Frank Dunn as a lawyer and then he fell in love with me and—"

"Margaux darling, you have told me this saga so many times I could vomit it back to you word for word. Where are you going with this conversation that you claim is so serious? Get to the frigging point, will you please?"

"Okay, okay. Here's the point. Every guy I ever knew, including the prestigious senior partner of the law firm, was always willing to tweak the truth whenever it served his interest. My high school teacher, my college professor and Frank Dunn were all married but it didn't stop them from jumping into bed with me whenever they could sneak away from their old ladies. And then, Frank Dunn, my lover and legal mentor, showed me how to steal a quarter of a million dollars from an eighty-year old widow so that I could live the elevated lifestyle he had introduced me to, so what happens? The son of a bitch gets himself murdered—by his wife no less—and I get put in the slammer because he wasn't around to admit the embezzlement was all his idea. And then—"

"For God's sake Margaux, I've heard all this a billion times."

"I'm getting there. The point is, that for the first time in my life I meet a straight arrow. He's kind and sensitive, and honest and gentle, but he's also strong and he cares about people, and he's a leader not a follower, and—"

Lucie had just taken a sip of her drink and blew it into her napkin. "You claim your beloved husband Toro is a straight arrow? C'mon, Baby, gimme a break. What's the big deal? I found a man just like that when I was twelve years old. I worshipped the ground he walked on. His name is Jesus."

"No, stupid. I don't mean Toro! I'm talking about Gary, the small fry football coach, the peewee hockey mentor, the—" Lucie had turned her head away and was signaling the waiter. "Christ, Lucie," Margaux complained, "I don't think you've heard a word I said."

"I've heard it all, *ad nauseum*, except the Gary part," Lucie said, ordering the waiter to bring them another drink.

"Alright wiseguy. Gary is the man I've been searching for all my life, and I love him. I want to change my life. I want to be a new person. I'm fed up with the lies and cheating, I want to live with Gary in the village of Sea Cliff, and have a baby and belong to the P.T.A. and be invited to the neighbor's barbeque and—"

"So what's stopping you, for God's sake? You told me he's crazy about you. I don't get it."

The waiter arrived with the new round of cocktails. As Margaux leaned forward to take her drink from him he stared down her low-cut, open-necked silk blouse. She never wore a bra except when she played tennis. The waiter was mesmerized by the sight of her firm nipples. When he smiled and winked at her, she unbuttoned the last button on her blouse. "Is this better, slimeball?" she muttered, as her breasts almost fell out on the table.

"Where was I?" she said, popping the onion into her mouth.

"You're impossible, Margaux. Just now you were mercilessly teasing the poor waiter, and then you blame him for responding," Lucie sighed. "Okay, continue—you're saying you are ready to join the choir in the Episcopal Church in Sea Cliff, I think...." Lucie smirked.

"Don't laugh at me, Lucie, I'm really serious. I want to go straight. I want Gary so badly I—"

"So stop moaning and groaning, and tell him."

"You know I can't do that."

"Why the hell not?"

"Because I had to cut him out of my life, that's why. I suppose you would just throw the $2,000,000 out the window."

"Maybe...who knows what I would do? I just wish I had such a choice! But knowing you as I do, I'll bet you ten to one if you give up your $2,000,000, within six months, maybe less, when the passion wears off and all of your darling Gary's warts, and yours as well, appear and—"

"What the hell is that supposed to mean, my warts?" Margaux hissed.

"Hold on, baby. Don't get testy with me. I'm the only real friend you've got in the whole world. Do you really want to know?"

Margaux hesitated. "Sure, but since you haven't even met him, why don't you start with Gary's warts, as you call them?"

"Why not?" Lucie smiled. "First of all, hot-shot Gary is a member of the male species, I believe, and that's the biggest wart of all, but moving on, I'd say it's reasonable to assume that when the honeymoon is over, you will discover that he picks his nose at the dinner table, or he farts in bed, or...."

"I get it, I get it, so what warts do you think I've got that could break up a marriage?"

"Let's talk about the weather," Lucie suggested.

"No, I really want to know."

"No you don't. All I'm saying is, $2,000,000 puts you on Easy Street for the rest of your life, if you guard it carefully. A roll in the hay is just that, a roll in the hay."

Margaux remained silent for a bit, mulling over what Lucie had said.

"Okay, how about this scenario: The name of the game is adultery during Toro's lifetime. I'm saying that the fact he saw me riding in a car with some guy in the middle of the afternoon is not adultery. I'm also saying I'm smarter than him and he's not going to catch me the next time. Right?"

"Hey, Hon, it's your two million bucks. It's your life. You're thirty-something and I'm twenty-something. I can get along without sex, no problem, but I can't get along without money."

Margaux slid out of the booth. "I don't want to talk about it anymore. Besides I'm due at the club in twenty minutes." She threw a twenty dollar bill down on the table and was gone.

After he returned from Phoenix, Gary didn't have an opportunity to resume his search for Margaux or consider whether his infatuation with Bridget should be taken seriously. But one Wednesday morning, when his afternoon appointment was cancelled, he pulled up the notes he had entered into his computer referencing his efforts to find Margaux and was reminded that she worked out every Wednesday afternoon at the Evolution Sports Club. He told his secretary he was leaving for the day, skipped lunch and headed out to Brooklyn.

He found a parking space within two blocks of the club, and checked his watch: 12:30. If he had guessed right, she should show up sometime after one o'clock. At 1:55, he was exhilarated when he saw her, head down, hurrying toward the front entrance. He stepped quickly into her path.

"Hello, pretty woman," he said.

"Gary," she gasped, barely moving her lips. "I'm certain I'm being followed. Please, don't give me away." As she passed by him, she said, "Call the club in ten minutes. I'll talk to you." She skipped up the stairs and entered the club. Gary walked casually away and entered the first pub he came to. He ordered a beer, borrowed a telephone book and dialed the number of the club on his cell phone. When Margaux came on the line, she whispered, "Meet me at the New York Public Library on Fifth Avenue next Wednesday at three o'clock." The line went dead.

CHAPTER NINE

Toro called Aldo Sanchez. "Sanchez? It's Toro Santoros. Remember me?"

"Of course, sir. How are you doing? You got that information okay, right?"

"Yeah. Say listen, Sanchez. I want you should get me a picture of the creep. I wanna see if it's the guy what I seen drivin' that Jag, and then I want to meet with you. When can you do that?"

Sanchez replied, "If all you want is an ID photo, I can probably get it in a couple of hours."

"So how 'bout I meet you at Louie's, that diner on Adams Street just as you come off the bridge into Brooklyn. Say, two o'clock?"

"Sure, I know the place. Okay, but you better give me a number to reach you just in case I can't get there right away."

"Hey, Sanchez, you heard me, right? I said I'd meet you at two o'clock at Louie's. You want my money or should I give it to somebody else?"

"I'll be there at two o'clock," Sanchez said.

Toro hung up the phone, leaned back in his chair and lit a cigar. He was in a turmoil. He knew that finding someone to marry him was no problem; that it was just a question of price. Women were for sale all over the world. Beautiful women. Any age, size, color or nationality. The truth was that he cared more about Margaux than he did about saving his estate $2,000,000. *What good is the fucking money when I'm dead?* he asked himself. He knew he could never again in his lifetime find a woman like Margaux.

Margaux is a classy broad. I don't want to divorce her, I just don't want her screwin' this guy Samson. So maybe the problem ain't Margaux. Maybe the problem is Samson. No Samson...no problem, but maybe he ain't the only one, and I ain't gonna spend the last days of my life livin' on death row for knockin' off the wrong guy....

Toro and Sanchez shook hands briefly and then settled into a booth in the back corner of the diner. Toro looked around the room warily, then he turned to Sanchez.

"Let me see it."

Sanchez handed him a sealed manila envelope. Toro's hand was shaking as he opened the envelope and withdrew a piece of paper. It was an invoice for $350. "Shit," he mumbled, then reached back into the envelope and withdrew an eight-by-ten enlargement of Gary Samson's driver's license. His facial features were strong but not without warmth. Toro sucked in his breath and muttered, "That's him, all right. He looks like a fuckin' movie actor, for Christ's sake."

He tossed the photo back on the table, but he continued to stare at it. He looked over at Sanchez and asked, "What does he do? Is he married? What's the story on him?"

Sanchez pursed his lips, shrugged his shoulders and said, "I don't know, sir. I just did what you asked me to do."

Toro glared at him, then thought about the situation for a moment, took out his wallet and threw four one-hundred dollar bills down on the table. Sanchez checked the bills, and pocketed them.

"You owe me fifty bucks," Toro said. Sanchez started to reach for his wallet. "Wait." Toro put his hand on Sanchez' arm. "I guess I can't just leave it there. I've got to know more. What's that gonna cost?"

"It depends, sir, on how much information you need, when you need it, and how detailed it has to be. Like I said before, I can work by the hour or by the day or by the job."

Toro thought a moment and then replied, "I think it better be by the job. That way, we both know where we stand."

Sanchez smiled. "No, sir, that way *you* can't lose. Only I can lose. I can see you didn't get to be driving around in that fifty thousand-dollar automobile by being at the bottom of your class."

"I *was* in the bottom of my class," Toro answered without a smile. "So, how much are we talkin' about here?"

"Well, from what you said, you'd like to know what kind of work he does, what his family situation is, and generally what kind of person he is. It would help me if I knew why you wanted the information. I mean, I would look for different things if you were interested in him as a business partner, or maybe it's a matrimonial problem. I could waste a lot of time getting the wrong kind of information if I don't know the reason you want it."

"I can understand that, Sanchez. Let's just say it's a family matter. Let's just say...what the hell, the truth is, I believe my wife's been messing with this shmuck and if she is, she ain't gonna get nothin' from me when I kick off. Like she'll lose big bucks, see, but what I really want to know is, why? I mean I want to know why she's messing with him, and for how long, and how often."

"Well, that's going to be difficult, sir, I mean, finding out how long they may have been involved and how often they may be seeing each other. I could only handle those matters on a time basis. You know, like if you were a surgeon doing a tonsillectomy, you'd know exactly what the situation is. But if you're doing heart surgery, you never know what you're going to run into, or how long it's going to take to solve the problem. See what I mean?"

"You ain't no surgeon, Sanchez, so let's take it one step at a time. First, get me all the background material—what he does, where he works, what his family situation is. And then…" He hesitated. "Who am I kidding? What do I care what he does or where he works? What I really want to know is, how long has he been fucking my wife! So what would that cost?"

Sanchez thought a moment, took out a little notebook and pen, made a number of calculations, closed the notebook and put it and the pen back in his pocket, and said, "We'll put your wife on surveillance for a week and then—"

Toro interrupted him. "I don't like the idea of having her followed. That's crummy. Why not follow him around?"

"Because *you* can give me all I need to know about your wife's habits, you see? And, of course, since you only want to know how often they meet and under what circumstances, they can't meet without her being there, right?" Sanchez laughed at his little joke. "I mean, it's just a matter of money. If you want us to tail Samson, we'll tail Samson. It's just harder and therefore, more expensive."

Toro didn't smile. "So follow my wife."

"When do you want us to begin?"

"Let me think. Me and her are going to Atlantic City this weekend, so how about starting next Wednesday?"

"What does she usually do on Wednesdays?" Sanchez asked.

"For one thing, she always goes to the gym on Wednesday afternoon."

"Great. We'll start next Wednesday as you suggested. Tell me where the gym is and we'll stake it out. If she shows, we wait and see when she leaves and where she goes. If she doesn't show, you can casually ask her, after you get our report, how the gym class went. If she says it went great and we know she didn't show up at the gym, we learned a lot without much expense. Or, if she leaves early and meets someone, we'll follow her and report back to you."

"Are you personally going to follow her?" Toro asked.

"That's up to you. I can if you want, but my assistant can do the job as well at half the price. She can probably do it better than me because she can follow your wife into places I couldn't, like the ladies' room, for instance. And you'll like this part: She's only seventy-five dollars an hour."

"I'll take her."

When Sanchez got back to his office, he asked his receptionist, Brenda, to join him in his private office.

When she was seated, she looked over at him expectantly.

"How would you like to do a little job for me, Brenda?" he asked.

"Sure thing , Mr. Sanchez, Whatever you want."

If I told her what I really wanted from her, she'd probably call 911, Sanchez said to himself.

"I've got a business proposition for you, but it's a little complicated, you know, sort of confidential between you and me. Is that okay with you?"

"Whatever you say, Mr. Sanchez. I know how to keep a secret."

"First of all, what am I paying you now?"

"Fifteen dollars an hour," Brenda said.

"Suppose I told you I'd like you to do a little moonlighting for me, and I could pay you twenty-five bucks an hour, tax free, under the table?"

Brenda leaned forward in her chair. She lowered her voice and said, "Mr. Sanchez, if you pay me twenty-five dollars an hour, I'll go under the table for you myself."

Sanchez laughed and said, "How about we meet for a drink after work and discuss this proposal?"

"Which proposal? Yours or mine?" she smiled. "You're the boss, Mr. Sanchez. Does the twenty-five dollars per hour begin when I meet you for that drink?"

"I'll have to think about that," Sanchez said, warily.

"Portal to portal?" Brenda asked, in her most sensuous, husky voice.

"Tell me, young lady, have you ever heard about the goose who laid the golden egg?"

Brenda put her finger to her cheek, pensively, smiled provocatively and answered, "I'm not sure, but I know quite a bit about ganders and gold."

"We can continue this conversation at Gilhooley's Bar at six o'clock," Sanchez said.

"Gilhooley's is not my kind of bar, Mr. Sanchez. Could I suggest The Golden Cocoon?" Brenda asked sweetly.

The drinks taste the same but they cost twice as much, he thought. "Okay, the Golden Cocoon it is," he said, wondering if he had won or lost the round.

Brenda Szmanski was 39 years old. She had had three husbands and had been divorced four times, having remarried husband number one. It was her favorite joke. Actually, Brenda was a very ambitious woman who had a knack for picking the wrong men. *Who else would be dumb enough to marry the same loser twice?* she asked herself when she finished paying for her most recent divorce only a few months before Sanchez invited her out for a drink after work.

Sanchez had noticed that after her most recent divorce Brenda appeared to him in a different light.

Brenda had been down the slippery slope many times. Now she was free again, but each time she gained her freedom in the past, she would immediately become overwhelmed with loneliness and jump at the first new opportunity to remarry.

As she sat in The Golden Cocoon, she thought about Aldo Sanchez and wondered what had happened that prompted Aldo to treat her as a woman instead of a fixture in his office. *It's true that since my divorce came through I've dressed a bit more like the real me instead of an office drone, and maybe I've teased him a wee bit by the way I walk away from him and lean over his desk so he gets a good look at my most attractive features…both of them,* she laughed to herself. *I don't know…I'm a few pounds overweight, but he's carrying a nice little pot belly himself.* She sat back in her chair, pulled her blouse down tight against her chest and looked forward to Aldo's arrival. She assumed they wouldn't stop at one drink, and if things went as she hoped, they might have dinner together. She wasn't about to let Aldo take her to bed in exchange for a beer or two at Hooligan's. This time, there would be a good many dinners at the best restaurants in Manhattan before she would consider allowing him entry to her bedroom.

It had been over a month since her divorce had become final, and she was convinced that Aldo was definitely a candidate for more than a casual friendship. When she saw him approaching, she felt her pulse quicken.

It had been a very warm day for the end of September, and the cool, dark interior of the cocktail lounge was a welcome relief from the mugginess which had hung heavily over the city all day. Sanchez nodded to the bartender and headed towards the corner booth at the back of the lounge where Brenda was waiting. When the waitress arrived, Sanchez ordered.

"A Mic light for me, and how about you, Brenda?"

"Chivas Regal, please," she answered.

"How would you like that, ma'am?" the waitress asked.

"With water on the side, if I may."

The girl made a note on her pad and disappeared. Sanchez was in good spirits. He was having more fun and making more money than he ever dreamed possible. And now, here he was, in the company of this very attractive young woman. He considered the possibilities unlimited as he turned to appraise her in the soft candlelight. There was no doubt about it. She was a very classy lady. Her long blond hair trailed down to her mid-back. Sanchez hadn't noticed before how long and how soft her hair actually was. As a matter of fact, he had not remembered ever seeing her with her hair worn long before, but he found it very appealing.

When the drinks were delivered, they raised their glasses, and Sanchez said, "Here's to A & B."

"What's 'A & B'?" Brenda asked.

"That's us, of course," Sanchez laughed. "Aldo and Brenda, Investigators."

Brenda smiled and said, "I'll drink to that."

She sipped the liquor tentatively and looked straight into Sanchez' eyes before tipping up the shot glass and returning it to the table, empty. Sanchez said admiringly, "I thought only men drank their liquor neat."

Brenda laughed. "I'm a purist."

"You're also a very attractive young woman. I love your hair today."

"Thank you very much, sir," Brenda said, bowing her head.

"Is that the true color of your hair?" Sanchez asked skeptically.

"Of course it's the true color," Brenda replied indignantly. "It says so right on the box."

Sanchez burst out laughing. He decided it was going to be a marvelous evening.

Three hours and three Chivas Regals later, Brenda looked as sedate and unruffled as if they had spent the time at a church social, whereas Sanchez, who had switched to drinking boilermakers, was having difficulty keeping Brenda and the situation in focus. He didn't realize that he was being seduced. On the other hand, Brenda, in her inimitable fashion, decided that she was in love and that within a few months she would become Mrs. Aldo Sanchez. She had made her decision shortly after the second Chivas Regal and confirmed it after the third.

She tried to think back over her numerous affairs and pick out the lovers who most nearly matched Sanchez' personality so that she could decide how best to pursue her objective. She drew a blank because he was, in fact, totally different from any other man she had ever known. She decided that she was brighter than him, but he was very clever and streetwise. As the hours passed and they continued to joke about their new relationship, the idea of marriage seemed more and more possible.

She noticed that Sanchez winced when the check arrived and she made a mental note to explore further his attitude toward money. She could not abide a stingy man. She had no interest in money except for what it could buy, and would not consider becoming involved with a man who could not enjoy being generous. She had to admit that the bar bill was a bit higher than she would have expected (the Chivas Regal drinks were fifteen dollars each) but considering the atmosphere and the live music, it was worth it. The test, she decided, was whether or not Sanchez was going to invite her to dinner and, if so, what kind of a restaurant he would choose.

Sanchez was shocked by the total bill. Seventy-eight dollars plus tip for a "drink after work" was not exactly what he had had in mind. However, Brenda had turned out to be absolutely everything he had hoped for. The effects of the alcohol had impaired his ability to separate fact from fancy. He knew there was no way he could spend the rest of the evening with Brenda without inviting her to dinner. He also had the impression that she would not be happy at Hal's Deli. Acknowledging that "he who hesitates is lost," he took the plunge.

"If you don't have anything special planned, I thought we might have dinner here. What do you say?"

"What a delightful idea, Aldo. Unfortunately, a girlfriend and I were planning to go to the late show to see that new Jack Nicholson film. Maybe if I gave her a call...Jeez, that's not a very nice thing to do. I think I better take a rain check."

Aldo was psyched. Somehow he had it in his head that if he didn't take her to dinner this very night, his world would disintegrate.

"Please, Brenda, at least give it a try. If she's a real friend I'm sure she'll understand."

Since the bit about the movie date with her girlfriend was a fictional ploy, she let Aldo persuade her to call her friend.

"Be back in a minute. Promise not to go away, now."

She excused herself, went to the ladies' room and called her friend who thought the scam was hilarious. Sanchez watched her as she crossed the room. Her walk was provocative. Sanchez muttered under his breath, "Sweet Jesus."

At two a.m., when Sanchez let himself into his duplex three blocks from the Brooklyn Bridge, he was $289.25 poorer than when he had left his office, but his spirits had soared off the Richter scale.

During their second dinner date, at Peter Luger's Steakhouse, one of the most renowned restaurants in New York, with a magnificent view of the Statue of Liberty, they were both dressed to the nines. Brenda had taken Sanchez to Brooks Brothers in Manhattan, chosen a suit, shirt and tie for him, and insisted that it must be tailored in time for their date on Saturday night. It would be their first real date and they were both treating it as if they were attending their high school senior prom. Sanchez bought Brenda an orchid corsage that she allowed him to pin on her gown, and smiled when he took a peek as he did so. What he observed sent him into orbit. She suggested that if they first discussed Brenda's assignment as an investigator during dinner, he would be able to deduct the cost of the dinner as an expense on his income tax form.

"That way," she said, "you can spend thirty percent more on drinks and dinner and it won't cost a penny."

"Have you ever eaten here before?" Sanchez asked, as he casually pointed out that Leslie Stahl and her husband were seated at the table on the side of the room with the best view of the Brooklyn Bridge. The only table Sanchez had been able to reserve had a view of the ladies' room but, he argued, it was more coveted than the table with the view of the men's room. Brenda pointed out that of course it all depended upon who was doing the viewing. When Brenda observed a gorgeous young woman headed toward the rest room, she grabbed Sanchez' hand. "Oh my God, Aldo, look over there," she whispered, "I'm sure that's Melinda Joy. She was in *Jazz*. This is incredible. Wait till I tell my girlfriends. I mean can you believe it, Aldo? I saw her father's picture in the Santoros file a couple of days ago, and now here I am having dinner in the same dining room with Melinda Joy. I can't believe it. I like his looks better than most of those smooth leading men in Hollywood. What I wouldn't do to become *his* leading lady."

"Ahhhhh," Sanchez groaned, as if his million dollar lottery ticket was only off by a single number.

"Oh, Aldo, I'm only teasing you. What do I care about that old Samson guy? If he's unmarried he's got to be gay. I'm not interested in Samson, I'm interested in Aldo Sanchez." Brenda leaned across the table. "He's my man."

Sanchez grinned. He could clearly see everything her gown was presumably designed to hide. He began to fantasize that he should pick her up, sling her over his shoulder, carry her out of the restaurant, and lay her gently down in a field of wildflowers. "Let's go," he said, and started to get up. Brenda pulled him back down.

"Oh, no you don't," she said. "We have dessert and an after-dinner drink coming. I'm not leaving. Remember, Aldo, this is a business meeting. You're supposed to be telling me about my new job where I'm going to earn twenty-five dollars an hour."

Sanchez sat back down and pouted for a bit. Brenda reached over and put her hand on top of his. Sanchez looked up at her sparkling eyes and sweet smile. He was hooked and he knew it. He sighed and slowly began to describe how he would be spending the next few evenings training her in the art of surveillance.

"Surveillance!" Brenda exclaimed. "You mean I'm going to follow somebody? Like I'm going to be a tail, right?"

Sanchez blushed slightly as he thought about her question.

"Who will I be surveilling? Is it a man or a woman? Is it dangerous? When do I start? What am I supposed to find out? What if the guy turns around and sees me and he's got a gun? Should I call the cops?"

"Slow down, slow down. If you're going to become a private investigator you must always go slowly, and think before you speak or act."

"Oh yes, I see, Aldo, it's just that I'm so excited, and so grateful to you for giving me this chance, but, please tell me everything," she pleaded.

"Okay. On Monday, we'll go over the file together. I didn't realize Samson's daughter is an actress. Are you sure about that?"

"Absolutely. It's been in all the movie magazines, and—" Melinda exited from the rest room and walked casually within a few feet of their table. They both stared at her. She had become accustomed to people ogling her after her most recent successful film, and smiled at them as she passed by.

"Oh, Aldo, I can see it clearly. She's the female image of her father, but she's so beautiful, I want to cry."

"I agree. But who cares? Any woman who's that beautiful must be impossible to live with. I'm not interested in Melinda Joy. Brenda Szmanski is my gal."

"You are so sweet, Aldo," Brenda cooed.

"We also have some pictures of Santoros' wife, whose name is Margaux, and your job will be to follow Mrs. Santoros. We're interested in Samson as well, but you'll only be following Margaux Santoros. She's scheduled to go to the Evolution Sports Club on 35th street at two o'clock next Wednesday afternoon. Do you know the place?"

"I've been there a couple of times."

"Good. What I want to find out is whether she comes in late or goes home early. And in any event you'll follow her when she leaves the club. She's supposed to be home by around five-thirty to start dinner for her hubby. There appears to be some doubt as to her undivided loyalty to him, and our job, or in this instance I should say, *your* job, is to find out if she's being unfaithful to her husband. Do you understand?"

"Is she a nice lady?"

"What's that got to do with it?" Sanchez asked.

"Oh, I don't know. If she's a nice lady and the only thing she's doing is trying to cover a "quickie" in the afternoon, I'd feel kinda bad about the whole thing."

Brenda sat anxiously behind the wheel of Sanchez' car, waiting for Margaux to arrive at the gym club. At 1:45 Margaux drove into the gym parking lot, and Brenda recognized her from the photos that Toro had given to Sanchez. She was wearing a sweat suit and carrying an overnight bag. At 2:06 Margaux came out of the club. She had changed into a high-fashion white linen suit. Brenda followed her to a parking garage on Fifth Avenue in Manhattan, near the New York Public Library, but lost her as she was entering the building.

Gary was seated on the ledge next to one of the big stone lions by the steps leading up to the library. He was worried that with the hundreds of people entering and leaving the building every hour, he would miss Margaux.

Since parting from Bridget in Phoenix, his ardor had cooled a bit. Bridget was warm and comfortable to be with, but Margaux was vibrant, volatile, mercurial and challenging. She could also be exasperating, but from the moment he spied her again at the gym club, Bridget dissolved into a pleasant memory.

When he saw her climbing the stairs, she looked radiant in the late summer sun. Her jet black, shoulder length hair was pulled back tight in a pony tail, held in place by a diamond-studded tie. She was wearing a black and white silk blouse, and black and silver open-toed high heels that enhanced the beauty of her legs and tight buttocks.

He followed her closely with his eyes, and then quickly ran up the steps, overtaking her. He grazed her arm with his elbow as he rushed past her, making certain she wouldn't lose sight of him. He stopped at the information desk and watched her out of the corner of his eye. She walked slowly by one of the displays and appeared to be reading what was posted there. Their eyes met. She smiled and moved down the hall, stopping at the elevators. As he walked past her, she said, "Third floor." He waited a few minutes, entered the other elevator and went up to the third floor. He followed her down the hallway to a deserted alcove and then enveloped her in his arms. They kissed, breathlessly, passionately, with a hunger so compelling he ached to take her there, standing up, against the wall. She pulled away from him, removed a notepad from her handbag, scribbled on the pad and passed the pad and pen to Gary.

"Hello darling," she wrote.

"I think I'm falling in love," he responded.

"Me too," she wrote.

Gary started to say something, but Margaux put her finger to her lips. She glanced down the hall and checked her watch. "I must go," she wrote, and started to leave.

Gary put his hand on her arm. "Please, Margaux, give me a place and time to meet and talk," he whispered.

Margaux reached out to him and caressed his hand. "Oh, Gary," she said breathlessly. Then she wrote down an address and handed the note to him. "Next Monday. Two-thirty," she said, and hurried away.

At first, Brenda panicked when she lost Margaux, but she decided she should go back to the garage and wait for her there. At four o'clock Margaux returned to her car, drove back to Brooklyn, went inside the gym, and came back out in twenty minutes wearing her sweat suit and carrying her overnight bag. Brenda followed her to her home, and then went to her own apartment and wrote up her report. The idea of invading Margaux's privacy no longer troubled Brenda's mind. It was just an exciting game that she was being paid to play.

When she delivered her report to Sanchez the next morning, he told her she had done a fine job and paid her $150. He edited the report, adding some details to make it appear more professional. Then he called Toro at his office and told him that since he was going to be in the vicinity of the Santoros home that afternoon, he would drop it into his mailbox. He also suggested that after he had read the report, perhaps they might meet and discuss its implications. Toro agreed.

When Margaux arrived home from her hairdresser on Thursday afternoon, she picked up the mail, sorted through it and was about to drop all of Toro's mail on the desk in his den when she noted the thin brown envelope that was scotch-taped so that it couldn't be opened without cutting the tape. There was a return address on the outside of the envelope, but the sender's name did not appear anywhere. It only took her a short while on her computer to learn that the address was for the office of Confidential Investigations. She needed to know what was in the report, but Toro was due to arrive home at any minute. She placed the mail carefully on his desk with the strange envelope on the bottom of the pile, then climbed the stairs to the second level of the two hundred year-old home he had purchased and restored before they were married. She got down on her knees and looked through the grille on the floor. Her plan might work, if she was lucky.

Margaux was in the kitchen making dinner when Toro came home from the office. He went directly to his den and poured himself a hefty Scotch on the rocks. Margaux came into his den carrying a glass of red wine. "Hi, Hon," she said brightly.

"I didn't hear you come in," she lied, leaning over and kissing him on his cheek. He mumbled something inaudible and upended his glass of Scotch. She asked, "How did it go today? Did you get that new contract? It would be a beautiful piece of business."

He looked over at her. *God damn, she's beautiful,* he thought. "Yeah," he said. "They shortened the term to three years, but they accepted everything else. You did a good job preparing that contract. I wouldn't have thought about putting in that gasoline surcharge. You were right, though, without it we could lose some big bucks if the price of gasoline keeps climbing." *And she's so God damn smart. Her input on that deal will save me thousands and thousands of dollars.*

He noticed the thin brown Scotch taped envelope on the bottom of his pile of mail. He wanted to get rid of her so he could see what it said. She continued to sit in her chair, smiling and sipping on her wine.

She picked up the bottle of Scotch. "Want another?" she said sweetly.

"Nah. I seen you drinking that red and that's what I want. But don't give me any of that California crap of yours. How about fetching a bottle of Masi Amarone? I know I've still got a bottle down in the cellar somewhere."

"I'll find it," she said. As she was leaving the room, out of the corner of her eye she saw him reach for the thin brown envelope.

When she was out of sight, Toro tried to open the report from Sanchez. He couldn't rip it open. Cursing, he began to search for a pair of scissors.

As soon as Margaux left the room she raced upstairs and lay prone in the room directly above Toro's den.

At the time the old home was built by one of the original Dutch settlers of the area that subsequently came to be known as Breuklen, later anglicized to Brooklyn, central heating hadn't been invented. The second story bedrooms were heated by the hot air rising from the fireplaces located on the first floor. She was able to look through the grille with a bird's-eye view of Toro's den below. She smiled when she saw him struggling to open the securely wrapped envelope. When he finally succeeded in removing the report from the envelope, he appeared to read it over several times, moving his finger along the page from word to word, shaking his head occasionally. He started to put the letter in his desk drawer, then changed his mind and slid it carefully under the blotter on the top of his desk. As soon as he stood up again, Margaux hurried down the back stairs, through the kitchen and down into the basement. She found the bottle of wine he wanted and raced back up to the kitchen. Toro was waiting there for her, peeking into the oven.

"I finally found the damn bottle," she said. There were smudges of dirt on her forehead, and cobwebs caught in her hair. "Here!" she offered the dust-covered bottle to Toro. "I've got to change and wash up. I'm a mess. Next time it's your turn to go down in that filthy basement. You promised to have it cleaned up months ago."

"You're right, I forgot about how bad it is. I'm sorry."

"It's no big deal, I just wanted to bitch a little. Did I ever tell you why women bitch?"

"No, lay it on me."

"Women bitch because they don't burp and they can't fart so if they didn't bitch they'd blow up."

Toro chuckled appreciatively. His spirits had lifted considerably when he read the report and there was no mention of Margaux meeting Samson.

"Do you know why women can't fart?" she asked.

Toro was enjoying the light intimate banter. "No, tell me, how come they can't?"

"Because they don't keep their mouths closed long enough to build up the necessary pressure to send it on its way."

Toro laughed until tears streamed down his cheeks.

"Keep your eye on the stew, okay?" she said as she hurried from the room. Before heading upstairs she sneaked into Toro's den, retrieved the report, quickly scanned its contents, returned it to its hiding place under the blotter and scooted upstairs. As she reached the second floor landing, she heard Toro go back to his den. She turned the water on full force in the shower and then glided silently back to the guest bedroom where she could again observe Toro's actions below. She saw him remove the report from under the blotter, read it again and then place it in his wall safe.

As Margaux took her shower she repeated and memorized what she had read in the report. Later she would write it all down for future reference.

At dinner, she said casually, "Did I tell you that I've signed up at the library for a course in philosophy? I've been thinking about it for some time. Actually, I went to the library yesterday for my first session. I don't look too fat for missing my Wednesday workout, do I?" She stood up, sucked in her tummy and stuck out her chest.

"I think you look great, honey, just great."

On Friday morning, the day after Toro received Sanchez' report, he sat in Sanchez' office. "Margaux told me all about this library thing," he said, relating everything Margaux had told him.

"Well," Sanchez said, "what you asked us to find out was whether your wife was telling you the truth about her daily activities. If she *is* telling you the whole truth, that should end the matter. But it seems to me that we have a very suspicious situation here. My opinion is that your wife is using the club as a cover-up for something she's not sharing with you."

"So what I'm supposed to do now, take the fucking philosophy course at the library?"

"My recommendation is that we continue the surveillance for another day. Hopefully she's telling you the truth and she did not go to the library to meet Samson."

"Why didn't you follow her into the library to see what she was doing?" Toro growled.

"To be fair, Mr. Santoros, you opted to get as much information for as little expense as possible. We did that. Now I believe it's time to set the trap."

"What do you mean, set the trap?" Toro demanded.

"Instead of us spending a lot of hours hoping to find convincing proof that your wife is or isn't cheating on you, we're going to bait a trap with an irresistible opportunity for your wife to meet this fellow Samson."

"I don't know what the hell you're talking about."

"What I'm saying is that you want to know for sure what your wife is up to. Although meeting a guy here and there from time to time may give you good reason to be suspicious, it don't prove adultery. You need proof, right?"

Toro didn't answer immediately. He looked around the cramped office. There were manila folders piled indiscriminately on Sanchez' desk, on the floor behind his chair, and stuffed into three partially open, battered file cabinets. He had the urge to grab Sanchez by the throat and scream at him, *No, asshole, I'm hoping you'll find proof she's* not *fucking this jerk. Don't you get it*? Instead, he just sat there, wishing he were somewhere else, wishing he had never heard of Samson, wishing the problem would go away, wishing he were younger and that he looked like Samson instead of the old, overweight, jealous husband that he was.

"So give it to me again—what's your idea?" he said, looking back at Sanchez who had remained silent, waiting for Toro to make the next move.

"Okay, here's the deal. If your wife and this guy are getting it on, and you have solid proof—that's the key word, *proof*—then you can get a divorce on the grounds of adultery."

"Yeah, but it ain't the money, it's—never mind, tell me what I'm supposed to do."

Sanchez got up and stepped over to a large blackboard. He picked up a piece of chalk and drew a big funnel with a box at the small end. "You see, if they take the bait, they enter the trap here," he said, drawing two stick figures walking into the large opening, "and they end up here in the box, where I'm waiting for them with my camera, and click, click, I've got the proof. We don't want to spend thousands and thousands of dollars following them around and end up with a bushel basket full of circumstantial evidence and no solid proof," Sanchez said, smiling triumphantly as he wiped the chalk off his hands and settled back into his chair. "Like I said, if they *are* lovers, we must give them the opportunity to be together without being concerned about being caught."

"Hey Sanchez, I'm not a fuckin' idiot. Never mind the funnels and the bait shit. Tell me what's gonna go down, huh?"

"There are all kinds of possible scenarios, but based upon what you've told me, here's what we're going to do. You're a Yankees fan like me, right?"

"Yeah, so what?"

"Just listen to me carefully."

On Saturday, Margaux drove into Manhattan to meet Lucie for lunch.

After they had settled comfortably into their favorite booth in the bar at the Algonquin and ordered their drinks, Lucie said, "Remember, we're going to flip a coin to see who pays for lunch. Furthermore, besides looking like Miss America, did you just swallow the proverbial canary?"

Margaux couldn't sit still. "I did, I did," she cried. "Remember I told you that when I met Gary on Wednesday at the library, I set up the meeting at your apartment for last Monday?"

"Of course I remember it. I said you were crazy, and I was crazier to let you do it. And I don't want to hear the gory details *and* you didn't change the sheets like you promised, soooo?"

"So, apparently my loving husband had me followed when I went to the club and then to the library, but thank God, they never saw Gary meet me there. Anyway, Toro bought my explanation as to what I was doing at the library, so now he and I are all lovey-dovey again."

"What brought that about?" Lucie asked.

"I let him lick my pussy and he figured he hit a home run, and that's what this is all about. Home runs." Margaux signaled the waiter for another round of drinks.

"Are you on something besides that one martini?" Lucie asked.

"Just listen to me. Toro came home from work last night, and he's all excited about flying up to Boston and then to Denver with a bunch of guys for a couple of days to watch a series of baseball games, which means I'll be free to spend the whole weekend with Gary. We've never been able to be together for more than a few hours, except for the first time I met him."

"You're playing with dynamite, kiddo," Lucie said.

"I know how to protect myself. I proved that last Monday. I'll lead those gumshoes around in circles until they're dizzy and then Gair and I will fly to the moon."

"If you really don't want to get caught, that's probably the only place you can go. Remember, sweetie, they're professionals. You spent time up the river because you thought you were smarter than the cops, but you weren't. Okay, so I suppose you want me to meet with Gary and pass along the good news. Am I right?" Lucie asked.

"You're reading my mind, dear friend. C'mon, I'll walk you back to Macy's and tell you what to say to him. Tell him it's his job to find us a hideaway and get us there and back undetected."

"You know, of course, that you're nuts, doing what you're doing. Christ Almighty…two million dollars, and your old man adores you, doesn't get drunk all the time and never beats up on you. Granted he's a little old for you and maybe a bit overweight…."

"A *bit* overweight did you say?" Margaux interrupted with a sneer. "He's five foot-five and weighs about 180 pounds."

"Wait a minute, baby. How much did he weigh when you married him? And he's not a bad looking guy, love. He has that beautiful head of silver hair and a lovely smile, and do you want to tell me how much lighter his wallet is since you met him? Starting with the quarter of a million dollar restitution he paid into court for you…."

"Yeah, yeah, and his teeth are like stars, right?"

"What's that supposed to mean? His teeth are like stars?"

"Like the stars, they come out at night. He's got more metal in his mouth than a dollar's worth of nickels. He's lucky if he has a half-dozen teeth that are real." Lucie tried not to laugh, but she had a picture in her mind of Toro with a mouth full of nickels.

It was a beautiful warm day in Manhattan as they strolled leisurely, arm in arm, from 44th and Fifth Avenue to 34th and Broadway, as if they didn't have a care in the world. Margaux accompanied her friend up to the furniture department and bought a leather desk set for Toro.

CHAPTER TEN

Gary told Margaux that he had found the perfect place to spend the weekend. He had rented a cabin in Vermont not too far from the New York border. He suggested picking her up at her home, but she told him the only way it could work would be if they met someplace along the way. They agreed to meet at the bus station in Mount Vernon at ten o'clock on Saturday morning.

He had given up trying to understand why she continued to be so secretive about her living arrangements and had finally accepted their affair on her terms. At one point he had asked her point-blank if she were married and all she said was that she was in a complex relationship and it was left at that.

Margaux drove Toro to La Guardia to catch the early shuttle to Boston. Sanchez tailed the car when they left their home in Brooklyn. He parked his own car discreetly in the airport parking garage a few spaces away from theirs and followed them into the American Airlines departure building, keeping Margaux in sight after Toro and his friends went through security.

Gary glanced at his watch as he pulled into the parking lot of the bus station in Mount Vernon. It was 11:05. When he looked up again, he saw her standing alone by her car with her overnight bag slung over her shoulder. She scurried over to his car, jumped quickly in beside him, and said, "Okay, let's get this show on the road, partner."

Sanchez had followed Margaux to Mount Vernon and watched her get out of her car, lean against it and check her watch. He was certain what would happen next. "Bingo," he whispered aloud when he recognized Samson from the photo he carried in his briefcase.

She was wearing blue jeans, a brown suede jacket and hiking boots. She threw her bag in the back, slipped into the soft leather bucket seat and then reached over with both hands and pulled his face down to hers. She kissed him hard on the lips, and then wiggled away from him when he tried to embrace her.

"Not now," she said, laughing. "It's only eleven in the morning. C'mon, let's get this rattletrap in gear. We've got places to go and things to do."

Gary took her hand and held it against his cheek. They drove in total silence as he maneuvered the Jag through the traffic. Margaux spoke first. "Do you really like me, darling?" she asked. Gary glanced over at her. She wasn't smiling.

"What kind of a dumb question is that? Of course I like you. What would I be doing here if I didn't like you—a lot?"

"I don't know. Men are different than women. I mean they're more casual about, you know...like this weekend."

"Excuse me, what did you say your name was?" he teased.

"I want you to be serious for a minute. How much do you like me? What do you like best about me?"

"I think the thing I like best is...." He hesitated.

She reached over and put her hand lightly on his arm. "Please tell me, love."

"The thing I like best is your belly button."

"My what?" she cried.

"Your belly button," he said. "I'm a belly button aficionado."

"Well," she said indignantly, "I'll have no more of that. I was wondering what you were doing skulking around down there and now I know. A Royal Naval spy, that's what you are."

"Okay, my love, you win the battle of quips again. Won't you ever let me come out on top?"

"Is that a complaint or an invitation?" she asked.

"See what I mean? I'm always left sputtering. I stand toe to toe with you for a while and then I run out of juice."

"That's O.K. lover, as long as you don't *lie down* toe to toe with me and run out of juice."

"I give up," he said, shaking his head.

It was a glorious day, with the sky a penetrating blue, interrupted by big, lazy, white puffs of cloud.

They continued north to Albany and then on to Vermont. They drove into the mountains, thick and lush with the reds and golds of autumn. They stopped for coffee, and then bought lots of food, including home baked bread and farm-fresh eggs, in an old fashioned country store.

When they got back into the car, Margaux asked how much longer it would take to reach their destination.

"I'd say about an hour or so. The roads begin to wind around a bit from here on."

Margaux curled up in the front seat with her head leaning on Gary's shoulder, halfway between waking and sleeping. She kept trying to push her feelings of guilt and fear away, to bury them beneath the sensuous feelings that washed over her as she felt the warmth of Gary's body beside her.

Sunlight and shadow danced across her face as they passed beneath the tall hemlocks and pines beside the road that followed a stream, twisting and turning in a seemingly never-ending quest for its destination. Margaux wanted to preserve the moments so that she would be able to savor them in the gray tomorrows that must follow. She had decided to tell Gary the whole truth about her marriage and how this weekend must be their last time together. She could tell that despite his humor and lighthearted banter, he was beginning to take their relationship seriously. *And me too*, she said to herself. *These next two days must be the end. The last time I faced a situation like this, I let my heart influence my decision and what did it get me? A year in state prison. I absolutely will not make the same mistake twice.* As she drifted off to sleep, she thought, *It's always about sex and money.*

Sanchez had had no difficulty keeping them in sight as they headed toward Albany. He was careful to allow cars to pass him from time to time so as not to arouse any suspicion. He followed them through Bennington and had a moment of concern when Gary turned onto a dirt road a mile or so after they had passed through the hamlet of Wilmington. He knew it would be much more difficult to keep them in sight without causing suspicion, because there weren't any other cars on the road to give him cover, but it had rained earlier in the day and Gary's tires were leaving distinct tread marks on the lonely dirt road, so he dropped back and followed the tire tracks. After about ten miles of winding road he spotted the car ahead, slowing down. He decided to stop and wait a bit. After he started up again he hadn't traveled very far when the car tracks turned into a long private drive. He could see a lake through the trees and the roof of a cottage snuggled down among a stand of hemlock and long-needled pine.

He continued past the private road several hundred yards and then parked in a secluded area.

"Wake up, Margaux, we're here." Gary leaned over and kissed her as she struggled to return to reality. The car was parked in front of a weathered cedar log cabin on Lake Somerset. The cabin blended into the forest that surrounded it in the afternoon sun.

"Oh, love," she cried. "It's beautiful!" She jumped out of the car and ran down to the edge of the lake, startling a family of mallards that motored out into the water in tight formation. She watched her reflection ripple in the wake of the ducks' departure as Gary came up beside her. They stood quietly together, looking out over the lake. After many minutes, he took her tightly in his arms and rocked her back and forth. "I so hoped you would love it as I do."

"I absolutely adore it."

She sat down on a grassy knoll beside the lake and pulled him down to her. She caressed him and felt the hardness of him rising to her own need to be fulfilled. She had never been so aggressive before in moments of love.

When her passion was sated, she pushed him away and ran, nude, down to the water's edge. Gary sat up and watched as she waded into the lake. "Oooh," she cried, "it's so c-c-cold" But then she dived under and began to swim furiously. When she finally took a breather, she treaded water and threw her arms up to the sky. "It's marvelous, absolutely marvelous—once you get in, that is. C'mon, lover, I'll race you across the lake."

"No way you're going to get me in that ice-water. My whatevers wouldn't thaw out for a week."

"Sissy."

"Sticks and stones, you know. Besides, here I am bleeding to death from brush burns on my knees and elbows and you just trash me like a vibrator with a dead battery." He pulled on his jeans, gathered up all the clothes and carried them up to the porch overlooking the lake.

He retrieved some towels and a blanket for Margaux, who was heading toward shore. He wrapped her up and carried her, shivering, up to the cabin. When she was dressed, she walked slowly back down beside the lake, pausing every so often to absorb the glory of her surroundings. She sat quietly at the end of the tiny dock and watched the sun melt into the treetops on the far side of the lake. Like a fairy tale cameo, a flock of Canadian geese flew through the sun's aura, and then swooped down to land in formation like a squadron of PBY seaplanes. The moment was so perfect she didn't dare move for fear she would fracture the delicate beauty that surrounded her. *If only one could experience the pleasure without the pain*, she thought. *Why must it always be so?* Then she heard Gary call to her. *Even the way he speaks my name brings me joy!* She could recall only one other man in her life who could bring a flush to her cheeks by just speaking her name.

Gary came out on the dock and lifted her up into his arms, holding her so close she could feel his heart beating against her breast. The fragrance of pine forest surrounded her as she tipped up her face to receive his kiss. *Oh, God, I think I'm truly falling in love...but I mustn't, I mustn't.*

As soon as the sun disappeared, a chill breeze whispered across the lake. Gary took off his jacket and wrapped it around her shoulders as they ambled back to the cabin. He had a fire going in the fireplace, and their drinks were set out on the coffee table with a platter of Dutch cheese, black bread and a sprig of colorful fall leaves next to her glass.

She said, "How will I ever be able to leave this fantasy and return to the real world?"

She lay back on the enormous overstuffed sofa in front of the fire and within minutes she fell asleep. When she woke up, she was snuggled in a goose-down comforter that Gary had thrown over her. She had no idea how long she had slept, but the moon was rising, and she was absolutely famished. She heard the car door slam shut, and when she glanced out the window, she saw Gary coming down the steps to the cabin carrying the groceries they had bought in Bennington.

As she watched him, she felt an animal craving to have him hold her and love her again. She thought, *How I wish that this day, this night, this place, this man could go on forever. I want to stay here and be loved and cared for. I want to touch him and hear him laugh.* She was sitting up in front of the fire when Gary burst in the door, yelling "Wake up, wake up, me beauty, you are about to embark on a gastronomical adventure, the likes of which would be the envy of Vatel."

"Of who?" she laughed.

"Vatel, you petty bourgeois ignoramus. The chef who killed himself while in the employ of the Prince of Condé because the fish course did not arrive on time."

"You've got to be kidding."

"Oh, no, my love, we masters of the culinary arts take our responsibilities more seriously than you could ever imagine." After emptying the contents of the shopping bag onto the kitchen counter, he reached for the carving knife hanging above the sink and tiptoed over to stand above her. "As a matter of fact," he said in a stage whisper, "If you do not judge this meal to be the most exquisite, exotic and erotic that has ever passed through thy sensuous lips, I shall skewer me innards with this here carving knife and leave you to clean up the bloody mess by yourself." Gary pressed the point of the knife against his stomach, looked heavenward and stuck out his tongue.

"Stop it, you idiot!" she cried, "If anyone is going to do you in, it will be me, in my own time. I'm not through with you, my fine fellow. I may choose to lie down with thee again beside the still waters, and perhaps one day you will walk through the valley of death, but not yet, my sweet. Not unless the fruit of thy loins is offered to another, and then, my love.... As a matter of fact—" Margaux grabbed the knife from him, tossed it away and pulled him down on the sofa beside her.

They stuffed themselves with the delicacies Gary had prepared, and a bottle of Chardonnay from the Finger Lakes region of upstate New York. After cleaning up the kitchen, he joined her out on the dock, carrying two tiny glasses of Drambouie. She declined, so he drank both of them and when he noticed her starting to nod off to sleep, he said, "Okay, Babe, I think it's time to call it a day. And what a day it has been."

They walked in the moonlight with their arms around each other, up the long path to the cabin. When they entered it, Gary switched on his portable CD player and the Mills Brothers' classic ballads oozed into the room like fresh maple syrup poured over homemade waffles. He stoked the fire in the fieldstone fireplace and lit the candles. A kiss lingered longer than either of them had intended, and their fatigue was soon forgotten. She pulled her sweater up over her head, stepped out of her jeans and unbuttoned his shirt, holding him tight to her so that he could feel the rising heat of her.

They began to dance nude in the bedroom to the sound of the mellow voices.

I'm gonna buy a paper doll....
You're nobody till somebody loves you....
Up the Lazy River....

Then Gary began to sing softly along with the recording.

You always hurt the one you love....

"Oh God," Margaux moaned, and started to cry. Gary picked her up and laid her down on the bed.

"Margaux, my darling, my darling, I have never, never, never—" he whispered.

"Just hold me," she sobbed.

He blew out the candles, crawled in beside her and held her ever so gently until she fell asleep in his arms.

Sanchez walked silently through the heavily wooded area beside the winding dirt road that led to the cottage. When he reached the clearing, he spotted the vehicle he had been following. He stood quietly, listening for signs of life, but the only sounds were those of the unseen wildlife surrounding him.

Keeping himself hidden, he crept closer until he reached a point behind a large oak and crouched silently until the flock of birds he had disturbed settled down. Reaching into his pocket for his note pad, he jotted down the license plate numbers, the time and date. He then took a picture of the car, zooming in on the license plate, and took a number of panoramic shots of the car and the cabin.

He crept closer and peered down toward the tiny dock at the water's edge, barely visible through the trees. He saw Margaux looking out across the lake. He attached his telescopic lens, moved closer and watched Margaux reach up and pull her companion's head down to her lips, locking him into an embrace, sliding her hands seductively down Samson's back and thrusting her body tight against his. He snapped the picture.

Gary awakened as the first rays of dawn spilled across the tiny lake. He studied Margaux, her jet black mane falling upon her bare shoulders. She was hugging her pillow like a favorite Teddy, her knees raised up in the fetal position. She looked so pure and vulnerable. *I've known her such a short time,* he thought, *but I feel as if I've been searching for her all my life.*

He covered her nakedness with the blanket, slipped out of bed quietly, hiked on his jeans and flannel shirt, and headed to the kitchen, where he built a fire in the old fashioned wood stove. He carried a pot of steaming coffee and a melon out to the front porch and set the table, overlooking the lake, for two.

"Rise and shine, lovely lady," he crooned, gently stroking her shoulder. She groaned and snuggled down deeper under the covers. "Oh, no you don't," he teased, pulling the blanket off her. "It's time to face the day with your favorite lover."

"No, no, no," she cried, grabbing the blanket back and burying her head under the pillow.

"Okay hotshot, the next step is the ice cube massage treatment." He went to the kitchen, dumped the tray of ice cubes into a bowl and returned to the bedroom, reached under the blanket with a handful of ice and began rubbing it on her belly. "You bastard," she shrieked. She sat up and took a swing at him, hitting him in the eye with her fist.

"Yow!" he yelled. "What the hell is the matter with you, you crazy bitch?"

She snatched up her clothes from the floor beside the bed and marched into the bathroom. "Don't you ever pull a dumb-ass trick like that with me, ever, ever again," she cursed, slamming the door behind her.

Gary felt his eye beginning to swell. Within a few minutes it was almost swollen shut. He picked up the scattered ice cubes, wrapped them in a dish towel and held them against his eye. He tried to open the bathroom door, but it was locked. "Open the God damn door and take a look at what you've done to my eye, for Christ sake!" he shouted.

"Poor baby," she answered. "Mommy will kiss it and make it better...but not now." She turned on the shower and spent the next half hour in the bathroom. Gary went out and sulked on the dock, trying to decide what to do next. He considered packing up the car and taking off. *It's a long walk back to Brooklyn,* he thought. *Serve her right, dammit.*

As the pain in his eye began to subside, his anger went with it. He even smiled when he returned to the cabin and looked in the mirror. He realized he was going to have one hell of a shiner. The problem was that when he thought about her in the shower he became aroused. *I'm just a horny jerk,* he said to himself. *What is it with this fucking woman?*

When Margaux finally emerged from the bathroom wearing a towel-turban and nothing more, Gary thought, *She looks more beautiful than I've ever seen her.* She walked slowly up to him. He stood perfectly still, but it took all his willpower to keep from reaching out and taking her in his arms. She stood on her tiptoes and gently kissed his eye…and then his cheek…and then his lips, pushing her warm tongue deep into his mouth. Gary forgot all about his eye when she pulled him down on the disheveled bed.

He had thrown two fishing poles in the trunk of the car, and that afternoon, on the way back to the city, when he spotted a stream winding down the mountain beside the highway he pulled into a little dirt road and parked the car. With the picnic basket in one hand and the poles in the other, he led the way up the stream until they reached a lovely little pond. They found a magnificent old apple tree hugging the bank and set up their menage. Margaux had organized the picnic supplies, including a bottle of Moncontour which Gary had remembered to bring. It was a lilting French wine, a Vouvray, that had been their favorite ever since they had discovered it on their first date at the Simply Red Cafe. Gary disappeared in search of bait, whooping with delight every time he turned over a boulder and found a big fat worm.

Margaux had filled a mason jar with Gray Goose vodka and orange juice back in the cabin. As Gary was puttering around with the fishing gear, she filled two paper cups with ice and the concoction and ambled down to where Gary had finally gotten things ready to begin their first fishing adventure.

She had accompanied Toro on one of his fishing trips with his friends and their wives at Sheepshead Bay in Brooklyn. It didn't seem to matter to any of them that they failed to catch anything worth discussing. They all consumed an enormous amount of booze and Greek food, told dirty jokes, argued about the Yankees, and laughed a lot. Today, with Gary, it was totally different. Gary made it an exciting and amusing game, and before she realized it, she was engrossed in the effort to make the first catch. They each had several nibbles that resulted in lost bait and no fish, but just as Margaux's attention began to wane, she felt a strike that almost tore the pole from her hands. She screamed as the whir of the reel feeding out line paid tribute to the strength and speed of the struggling fish. Gary was beside her instantly, helping her and guiding her gently in landing what turned out to be a beautiful brook trout. He made her remove the hook herself as the fish struggled to free itself from her grasp. Just as she managed to ease the barbed steel from the mouth of her catch and held it up in a triumphant gesture, the fish slipped through her grasp, landed in the stream and was gone.

"Oh, Gary!" cried Margaux, "He got away—that slippery son-of-a-bitch got away!"

Later, they lay back in the deep cool grass with the sound of rushing water beside them, staring up through the shadows of the leaves that twisted and turned in the gentle autumn wind. Margaux picked a blade of grass and traced it along the creases of Gary's forehead and the deep lines around the corners of his eyes. She brushed her lips across his brow as lightly as the fluttering wings of a butterfly, and then asked, "Tell me, love, where are you now? You seem so far away."

"I was just thinking, sweetheart."

"You've told me never to ask a question if I couldn't handle the answer, but I'm ready to gamble. What were you thinking?"

"Well, I just had this daydream. I actually saw this scene where I was walking along a dirt country lane like the one we've been traveling, and I came to a fork in the road. I was all alone, and I was lost, and everything around me seemed so unreal, and then I saw a sign posted by the side of the road. It said, *Paradise,* with an arrow pointing ahead. I smiled and started up the road. Everything was green and lush and it smelled of hemlock and pine, and then I came to a gate and there was an old man standing beside the gate. He was tall and his long silver hair framed a strong, beautiful face, bronzed by the sun. As I reached the gate and started to pass through, the old man stepped toward me and asked, 'What's your name, sir?' 'Samson', I said. 'Gary Samson.' And then he opened a big book and ran his finger down a long list of names. After a moment or two, he put his hand on my shoulder and said, 'I'm sorry, son, but you cannot enter paradise.' And I looked at him, and I thought of the past two days and I smiled and said, 'It's okay, old man, I've already been there.'"

Just before he dropped her off at a taxi stand on Flatbush Avenue in Brooklyn, Gary said, "We never got to talk about, you know, the things you promised to tell me."

"I know. Don't try to call me. Don't try to find me," she said, and she was gone.

CHAPTER ELEVEN

On Wednesday, when Margaux returned home after her workout at the gym, she picked up the mail in the foyer and went straight to Toro's bar in his den. She poured herself a gin and tonic and sat down at his desk to read her mail. Mixed among her magazines and catalogues was a large, thick, manila envelope addressed to Toro. It was marked 'PERSONAL & CONFIDENTIAL', with the same return address she recognized from the earlier investigator's report. This time, the envelope was stapled as well as Scotch-taped. She stared at it briefly and then took it into the kitchen and cut it open. It contained Sanchez's report that described how he had followed her to the bus station in Mount Vernon where she met Gary and rode with him up to the cabin in Vermont. There were telephoto, time-dated pictures of them when they stopped in Albany and again outside Bennington carrying groceries to their car. Another series of intimate photos began with their embrace on the dock and ended with an enlarged photograph of them taken in silhouette, dancing nude in the bedroom.

Margaux poured herself another drink and called Sanchez. Brenda passed the call through to him.

"Aldo Sanchez."

"Mr. Sanchez, my name is Elizabeth Raymond. I need to see you right away. How soon can I meet with you?"

Sanchez looked at his watch. "If you can come to my office right now I can see you. What kind of a problem have you got?"

"I don't want to discuss it on the phone, but I'll be in your office by six o'clock." Margaux hung up the phone. She stuffed the report in her purse and hurried out to her car.

When she entered Sanchez' small, cluttered cubicle, he stood up from behind his desk.

"Mrs. Raymond, I'm Aldo—" The photos he had taken of her flashed through his mind. "Excuse me, but aren't you Margaux Santoros?" he asked nervously.

She didn't answer him.

"Well, I...um. Please sit down, Mrs...ah...Raymond." He removed a stack of files from the only other chair in his tiny office.

"I assume I can speak with you in confidence?" Margaux asked, removing Sanchez's report from the envelope in her purse. She put the envelope on his desk and returned the report to her purse.

"I'm not sure about that," he replied, recognizing the envelope that had contained the report he had sent to Toro. He didn't want to speak with her until he understood the situation. "Why don't you tell me why you're here?"

"As you have probably guessed, I'm here to discuss your surveillance report," she replied.

"Dimitri shared it with you?" he asked cautiously.

"Actually not," Margaux replied quickly. "He hasn't seen it yet. You could say I intercepted it."

"It was addressed to Dimitri and marked 'PERSONAL & CONFIDENTIAL' in bold letters, as you can see," Sanchez said, pointing to the envelope.

"That's why I'm here. I love my husband very much. I made a horrible mistake. Your report will end my marriage. I beg you not to send it to him; I beg you to destroy it." She began to cry real tears.

"I don't see how I can possibly do that," Sanchez said. "I have a professional obligation to give that information to your husband."

Margaux dried her tears and stared at him until he averted his eyes, and then she leaned forward and said, "If Toro reads your report, not only will it cause the end of our marriage, but Toro is going to be seventy-seven years old on his next birthday and he's been diagnosed with lung cancer." She started to cry again.

Sanchez glanced back at her. He hunched his shoulders, fiddled with his pencil, looked down at his desk, drew a few doodles on his pad and said, "Shouldn't you have thought about that before you spent the weekend with Samson?"

"Of course I should. I'm so ashamed," she sobbed. "I don't want to hurt Toro. I love him. Please try and understand."

"It's not that I don't understand, Mrs. San...Mrs. Raymond, but how could I possibly take your husband's money and then not give him my report?"

"Because you will be giving him the gift of life. Put yourself in his position. He is praying your report will find that I have been faithful to him, in which case he will be a happy man until he dies, because I promise you I will never, never do such a stupid thing again. Please," she begged, "I don't care about myself, but my foolishness will hurt him so much, and with so little time left for him to live...." Tears were streaming down her cheeks, streaked blue with mascara. "Please, Mr. Sanchez, give me the chance to make it up to him and take care of him in every way for the rest of his life."

Sanchez started to speak, hesitated, and swiveled his chair around to look out the dirt-encrusted window at the auto body shop next door. Neither of them spoke for several minutes while he mulled the problem over in his mind.

When he turned back to her he said, "If I give your husband evidence of your adultery his estate won't have to pay you any money, right?"

Margaux was stunned. "I never even thought about that. I suppose that's true, but...but..." she stammered, "this has nothing to do with money, I swear to you. I'm only thinking of Toro. Please, please, Mr. Sanchez," Margaux sobbed.

Sanchez didn't say anything for several minutes. Finally he said, "I'm sorry Mrs. Santoros, I cannot violate my ethical duty to your husband. He trusted me and has paid me well to find proof of your adultery. I've done that. I have no choice—"

"No, no. You don't understand. He didn't want you to find proof of my adultery. He wanted to find proof of my fidelity. He's dying and wished above all else that I would remain faithful to him until he died."

"And you didn't," Sanchez sneered.

"That's true, but I didn't mean to do what I did. I love him, don't you see, but I'm still a young woman and I lost control."

"And you don't want to lose the money, right?"

"Oh God, Mr. Sanchez, the money means nothing to me. I have $10,000 in my own bank account. I'll give it all to you. I swear I don't care about the money, I care about Toro."

"How much will you get when he dies?"

"I don't know and I don't care."

"I care," Sanchez said.

"Look, Mr. Sanchez. I get paid $10,000 a month. I'll give you fifty percent of my salary every month until Toro dies, at which time I'll be out of a job, but I'll keep paying you $5,000 until I've paid you a total of $100,000. That's it. If we can't agree, my husband and you will be the losers. Not me. There are a lot of guys out there that will pay big bucks for me. What have you got going?"

Sanchez thought a moment. *She's probably right. The old man ain't going to pay me a hundred grand for proving his wife is cheating on him.*

"Will you put it in writing and sign it?"

"Of course," she replied. "I'll put the whole agreement in my own handwriting."

Sanchez slid the yellow legal pad across the desk-top and handed her his pen.

When Toro received Sanchez' report that Margaux was not involved in an adulterous affair with Gary Samson, he felt he had been reborn, even though the last report from his physician indicated that his prognosis was not good. The most difficult thing for him to understand was that except for his shortness of breath and the cough that he had had for years, his tobacco-induced lung cancer was causing him no pain or discomfort. His physician had advised him that the disease had probably metastasized elsewhere in his body, but the lesions there were not yet large enough to show up in the radiological studies.

"What about this chemotherapy crap I keep hearing about?" Toro asked.

Dr. Newman replied, "I didn't offer it to you, Toro, because it would just be a waste of money and make you miserable besides. When the pain comes, I can relieve it with medication. I'll do my best to make your life as comfortable as possible, but in the meantime, I suggest you take a trip to Greece or Rome or Paris. Invite that beautiful wife of yours to go on a cruise around the world. Enjoy the time that is left to you, Toro. You've told me that you have enough money to do whatever you want—so do it! My advice is to eat, drink and be merry."

"How much time have I really got?" Toro demanded.

"You refused to undergo the testing I prescribed so I don't really know, Toro. I can only guess."

"Yeah." Toro felt woozy. He put a hand on the table to steady himself. "So, give me your best guess. Give it to me straight."

"Maybe six months, a year; eighteen months, maximum."

Toro kept the bad news to himself. He didn't believe that sharing it with Margaux would change anything for the better. There were no further suspicious incidents, and for the most part, his life progressed uneventfully through the Christmas holidays and into the new year. However, when he returned to Dr. Newman's office in late January for his regular monthly checkup, the doctor renewed his advice to get away from the miserable winter in New York.

"Good Lord, Toro, rent a villa in the Caribbean or on the Riviera. Whoop it up a bit."

While they were at dinner that night, Toro reached over and put his hand over Margaux's. She grimaced. She could no longer stand him touching her. He looked at her and smiled.

"Doc Newman gave me the bad news today. He advised me to forget about the chemotherapy bullshit, it's too late for that, he says. He tells me what I should really do is take you on vacation, so I'm going to sign us up for a cruise in the South Pacific. What do you think about that?"

A few thoughts raced quickly through Margaux's mind. The good news was that if Toro didn't undergo treatment he might die sooner; the bad news was that the idea of spending twenty-four hours a day with him, cooped up on a ship with no escape.

"I always wanted to go to Hawaii, you know," Toro said. "My travel agent suggested this really great trip they got where we fly from New York to Hawaii, spend a week or so there soaking up the sun, and then get on a cruise ship and sail to Tahiti—You know, Tahiti, where they got all them hula dancing ladies like in *Mutiny on the Bounty* with Marlon Brando. Would you believe I saw it when it first come out with Clark Gable?" he laughed. "And then we go to this island they call Bora Bora. I heard of that, ain't you, Babe? Bora Bora? After that we hit Fiji, and then Samoa. What do you say?" Toro had a wide mischievous grin. "I'll get us the biggest stateroom they got on the boat and we'll dance under the stars like it says in the brochure. I'll take the kids along and stick them in the opposite end of the boat, but we could have maybe like a drink and dinner together once in a while."

Margaux thought a moment. "Actually, except for taking the kids along, it's not a bad idea, Toro. Of course I'll need a whole new wardrobe, you know—they dress up for dinner on those ships. You've put on some weight since our trip down the aisle at Saint Patrick's, so you'll have to get a new tuxedo and I'll need new gowns and dresses for afternoon cocktails. I'll buy some new bathing suits and deck robes and luggage, and I'll also have to get some—"

Toro interrupted her. "Yes my darling, you can have whatever you want. You can buy one of them big trunks like them ladies on TV have when they travel to Europe. You can fill it with whatever you want, because when I walk into that dining room where the captain's table is and I've got my baby on my arm, they'll all be looking at old Toro with the most beautiful woman on the ship at his side."

"And what about Nick's dud wife and that creep Vittorio? Are you going to invite them, too?"

"Well, sure, Carmen can be a little snotty and she's a gimme, gimme girl, but we don't need to pay no attention to them."

"Except for Xenia, they're all zeros, Toro. If it weren't for you they'd all be on welfare or in jail."

"Ah come on, Margaux, Nick's a dreamer, that's all."

"You're right about that; but all he dreams about is when he's going get his share of your money. He tells everybody he's vice president of your company, but he's nothing but an office boy."

"Hey, Margaux, you got a bad mouth. Stop with that shit. He's my son. He was my son before you was born. My kids are coming with us, and that's the end of it! Period! End of discussion!"

Margaux sighed. Most of the time she could wrap Toro around her finger, but when it came to his children, she had learned long ago not to argue with him. She got up, poured herself a cup of coffee and left the table. She turned on the big flat-screen TV, and was soon engrossed in the medical misfortunes of a patient suffering from shock in the emergency room at Manhattan Medical Center.

Carmen burst through the door of her home in Brooklyn. She rushed into the living room where Nick was watching the New York Giants battle the New England Patriots in the 2008 Superbowl game. He had $5,000 riding on the Giants. Instead of playing the point spread, he had gotten three-to-one odds favoring New England. Everyone told him he was crazy because with the Patriots' record going into the Superbowl, they all said it wasn't a question of who would win—the only real bets were on the fifteen point spread. But Nick had serious gambling debts and needed to win big.

There were less than two minutes left to play. The score was 14 to 10. The Giants were down by 4, but they had possession of the ball deep in their own territory. The young quarterback, Eli Manning, started the long march toward the Patriots' end zone. The New York crowd was going wild. Ninety percent of the spectators had money riding on the game. A guy who Nick knew from Brooklyn had box seats on the fifty yard line. He had bet $100,000 on the game.

"Guess what, Hon? Your old man's taking us on a cruise!" Carmen squealed.

"Not now, Carm. You got a choice: Go take a walk or sit down and shut up."

The Giants had reached midfield with less than a minute left. It was third down and three yards to go. Manning threw a pass, but the Patriots' defense was all over the receiver and blocked it.

Nick screamed, "Jesus Christ! You dumb son-of-a-bitch! Oh my God! I don't fucking believe it!" He threw his empty beer can across the room. The Giants were on their own forty-nine yard line, fourth down and three yards to go for a first down to keep the game alive. They gave the ball to Jacobs, their big fullback. If he didn't make it, the ball game would be over, Nick would be in very serious financial difficulty, and his father would cut off his balls.

Carmen came over to sit beside him on the couch. Nick's eyes were glued to the tiny screen. He pushed her away.

"What's the matter, honey? What did I do? Don't you love me, honey? Baby?"

Jacobs ran for the first down. The Giants had no timeouts left. There were twenty seconds left on the clock.

"Tell me you love me, sugar."

Manning couldn't get the pass off and he scrambled.

"GO! GO! GO!" Nick pounded the coffee table. Manning headed to the sidelines to stop the clock. There were ten seconds left in the game.

"I'll bet you can't guess where we're going?" Carmen cooed.

"If you don't shut up, I'll tell you where *you're* going."

"You're so cute when you get all excited, baby. But it's only a game, you know."

Nick couldn't tell Carmen that he had $5,000 riding on the game, because after the last time his father had to pay off his debts, the old man made him swear in blood that he would never gamble again.

"First we fly to Hawaii! What do you think of that, big boy?"

Nick's mouth was dry. He could hardly breathe. The old man would never bail him out a second time.

"Please, God! Please, God!" and then the ball was in the air. It looked as if there were a man open in the corner of the end zone, but the defensive cornerback raced across…too late! The ball floated into the arms of the Giants' receiver with two seconds left to play. His ten teammates swarmed on top of him.

Nick leaped up in the air, "EEEAAAHHHOOOO", he yelled at the top of his lungs, and then picked up his wife and swirled her around like a rag doll. When he finally settled down and grasped the fact that they had been invited to go on a cruise, he said, "It's about time he spread some of his money around instead of spending it all on the Bitch."

Carmen said, "He treats her like a queen, and we're his own flesh and blood and he treats us like dirt. But listen to this. He says we have to dress up for dinner every night and he gave Xenia and me each a thousand dollars to buy whatever we want. I think he's losing his marbles. The old guy is still living in the dark ages. I'm lucky if I can get a single evening gown for a grand. The Bitch was wearing an outfit last week that I saw advertised in *Vanity Fair* magazine. I think it was Gucci, or maybe Ralph Lauren. Thirty-five hundred for a blouse, a skirt and a pair of boots, and Zee told me he gave Margaux $5,000 to buy clothes for the trip, can you believe that?"

Nick lit a cigarette and switched the channel with the remote. He thought, *I hate the old man*. "I can't stand that bitch living up there in that mansion he bought after Mom died, and driving around in that brand new BMW, and here we are, with two kids, jammed into a three bedroom house in Flatbush driving a frigging three-year-old Subaru wagon that's falling apart."

"I know, I know, I hate that bitch too. Of course, if you would just stop pissing away our money at Aqueduct we could—"

"There you go again, God damn, it never frigging ends." He got up and went to the kitchen for another beer. The cupboard was bare. He kicked the refrigerator door shut. "Jesus Christ," he cursed.

"What's the matter, honey?" Carmen said.

"Nothin'." Nick grabbed his New York Giants football jacket and headed for the front door.

"Where are you going, now?" Carmen whined.

"I don't know. I'll tell you when I fucking get there."

As soon as he hit the street he pulled up the hood on his parka and lit up a joint. He sucked the warm air deep into his lungs and held it there for a few seconds and then let it escape slowly through his nose and mouth. He headed down the block in the direction of Chico's, the neighborhood bar. It had been snowing on and off all day. He turned his head away from the bitter cold wind that sliced down the street between the row houses.

When he stepped inside Chico's on Montgomery Street, his spirits were immediately lifted by the warmth of the bar and his first-of-the-day shot of tequila.

"Hey, Nick! What's up?" the self-appointed President of the Regulars, old Mike Taormina asked.

"Not much, Mike. Except, this weather is so shitty I think maybe I'll take my wife on a cruise. You know, like to Hawaii…Tahiti…Bora Bora… It's them islands where the women run around naked." He threw a fifty dollar bill on the bar. "Set 'em up for the boys," Nick said.

"You must have been on the Giants," Mike observed.

"You got that right, ole buddy. Five big ones. Anybody seen Vito?"

"Yeah, he was here watchin' the game. He just left a few minutes ago, but he said he'd be back in about a half an hour."

Nick ordered another shot of tequila and hitched himself up on a bar stool. When Vito showed up they went back to a corner booth away from the blare of the television.

"So what's new, Vittorio? How's my kid sister doin'?"

"She's okay, but did Carmen tell you what the old man leaked to Zee about the Bitch when he was drunk the other night?" Vito answered.

"You mean about the money she's gonna get? Yeah, Jesus, that pisses me off."

"I got an idea and I want to see what you think," Vito said, leaning closer to Nick.

"Shoot." Nick settled back in the booth.

"You heard about this here cruise we're going on with the old man and the Bitch, right?"

"Not bad, hey?"

"Yeah, but it got me to thinkin', you know? Maybe you and me could work a deal while we're soakin' up the sun. That money the Bitch is gonna get should be going to you and my old lady, you agree?"

"Absolutely. I mean it ain't right. Two million, so's my old man can get laid once a month. Shit, man, that's highway robbery."

"So we should do somethin' about it, right?" Vito said.

"Like what? I tried to ask him once what he was gonna do with his money, but he told me it was none of my fuckin' business. He said it was his fuckin' money, he earned it and he could do whatever he wanted with it. I can't talk to him, you know. I mean, me and Zee are his kids. I mean we're blood. Me and Zee are blood. She's just a goddam whore."

"He's pussy-whipped, kid. You and I know that. Now listen up. Zee talked to Toro's lawyer, Rifkin, and he says it's all locked up. The agreement your pop signed is legal, and there's no way it can be broken. That's what Zee told me." Vito stood up. "You want another shot?"

"Sure. And get a couple bags of chips."

When Vittorio returned to the booth with the drinks, he said, "Mike tells me you had five grand on the Giants. I thought you wasn't messin' with that shit no more." Vito threw the chips down on the table and eased back into the corner of the booth.

Nick ignored the question.

"Suppose," Vito continued, "Suppose I told you that if we each come up with twenty-five hundred bucks, I'll guarantee you'll get back a million."

"I knew you was a little whacko, brother," Nick leaned forward and whispered, "or are you planning to rob a bank, in which case I'll consider it."

"What I got in mind, there's no downside except maybe losin' a couple grand if it don't come off."

"Okay, let's have it. Talk is cheap."

Vito glanced around the room to make certain no one was within earshot, and lowered his voice. "I got this buddy, he's a little crazy, but he'll do anything if the price is right. I mean *anything*." Vito took a swallow of beer, licked his lips and continued. "So Zee found out that there's a thing in the agreement that if the Bitch gets caught fucking some guy, she gets nothin', *nada*, when Toro dies, in which case you and Zee get to split an extra two million bucks. Zee told you about that, right?"

"Yeah, so if you're thinking about hiring this guy to bump off Margaux, I might consider it."

"Shut up a minute and let me finish. So we're all going on this cruise together, including the Bitch. That's number one. Number two, this guy I was just telling you about…he's a real good lookin' dude. His name is Luis Ramiriz. He's Cuban, but he's legal and he's got class. Women go nuts over him. His deal is, he only messes with married women. He nails them to the mattress in their fancy homes while the hubby is at work, and when they goes to the shitter, he steals their jewelry. They never know what hit 'em until he's long gone. And then, see, they can't go to the police because they wouldn't be able to explain to their husbands what Luis was doing in their bedroom in the first place.

"All we got to do is get him together with the Bitch. We make sure they meet on this cruise. Then him and the Bitch, you know, champagne in the moonlight and all that crap, and then when he gets her so she's beggin' for it, he takes her to his stateroom where he's got like a camera hooked up like them DEA bastards use on drug busts. He turns it on just before they go in the bedroom, and bingo! We slip the film anonymous-like into Toro's room, he recognizes the Bitch, the leading lady in our little porno flick, and you and Zee split the big bucks and the Bitch gets *nada*. It would be the most expensive fuck a woman ever had in the history of the world. Whaddaya think of that?"

Nick sat silent, staring down at the tabletop.

"What say?" Vito demanded.

"Jeez, I don't know. She only married him for the bucks, that's for sure, but I don't think my old man's got much time left, and..."

"Hey, man, we're talking two million big ones here. We'd be doin' him a favor, for Christ's sake. He'd see what a cheatin' bitch she really is."

"If he ever found out we was involved, he'd disown me and Zee in a second. We'd be the ones that would end up with *nada*."

"How can he find out? It's got nothin' to do with us. We slip Luis some money to buy a ticket on the cruise and after that he's on his own. If he wins, we give him a bonus after Toro dies. If he doesn't score with the Bitch, we're out a couple of bucks and Luis gets a free vacation. Big deal. Whaddaya say?"

Nick raised his head and looked Vito straight in the eye. "Let me talk to Zee...see what she thinks."

"No! Jesus, Nick, you can't do that. My wife worships the old man. She don't understand business like us, see? And this is a straight business deal."

"Maybe you're right, man, let me think about it."

Gary pushed Margaux down into the deep recesses of his mind and made it through the holidays. He dated a few other women, but he found them to be too young and immature, or too old and set in their ways, or sexless, or searching for a permanent relationship, or, or, or....

By the middle of February, 2008, he decided he was through playing games with Margaux. Either she was going to move in with him or he was going to close the book on her. When he finally reached her she agreed to meet him at a restaurant she knew near the Bear Mountain Bridge at three o'clock on February twenty-third.

The day turned out to be overcast with on-and-off bursts of cold rain. Gary decided to give himself plenty of time in case traffic backed up because of the weather. He arrived at the restaurant an hour before they had agreed to meet and immediately ordered a double Grey Goose vodka martini in a rocks glass. When Margaux hadn't shown up by three-thirty, he signaled the waiter for a second drink. Shortly after four o'clock, as he finished off his third double martini, he saw her BMW convertible drive into the parking lot. She stepped out of the car, turned up the collar of her trench coat, hunched her shoulders into the rain, and walked purposefully toward the front door of the restaurant. She entered the darkened lounge, which was deserted except for the bartender and Gary, who was seated at the bar.

He stood up, unsteadily, grinning foolishly. "Hello, pretty woman," he said.

She looked at him quizzically. "You're drunk," she snapped, and turned to leave.

"Please, Margaux," he said softly. He reached out to take her arm. She stepped back.

"You promised," he pleaded.

She hesitated.

"Please," he said again.

She slid cautiously into the closest booth. Gary sat down across from her. The bartender came over to them. "What'll it be, Miss?"

"Coffee, thank you." Margaux unbuttoned her coat, shrugged it off her shoulders, and sat solemnly back in the booth.

Gary nodded and started to hold up his glass to the bartender. Margaux put her hand on his arm. He glanced at her stern face. "No more for me, Kit," he said, sheepishly. He leaned back in the booth and smiled at Margaux.

"Thank you for coming," he said, slowly and deliberately, trying not to slur his words. "Terribly important." She didn't say anything. "I've been lost since our weekend in Vermont," he continued. "When you wouldn't talk to me, I... I... sort of fell apart. I love you, Margaux."

Margaux turned away from him and stared out the window.

"You told me you felt the same way about me, and now you refuse to see me. I just don't get it."

She continued to stare out the window without speaking. "For God's sake, Margaux, talk to me," Gary pleaded.

She turned back to him. "Will you deposit $2,000,000 into my bank and marry me tomorrow?"

Gary laughed. "Sure, why not? You made the same offer to me in Chicago, remember?"

"It's easy to promise when you haven't got it, right?" she sighed. The bartender brought the coffee. She started to speak, then hesitated, fussed with the hot cup, took a sip, blew on it, took another sip. Gary sat silently, waiting for her to finish with the coffee routine. As she put the cup gently into the saucer and looked up at him, she said, "I'll bet you could raise it if you really wanted to. Like, you could sell your home in Sea Cliff, *and* your Jaguar *and* your boat...."

"Hold it, sweetheart," he said, holding his hand up in the air like a traffic cop. "I'll admit I've had a few drinks, but you're the one who's talking crazy."

"Don't you see, Gary, that's the whole *point*. The way it is now, you have nothing to lose. If you discover in a month or two that you aren't really in love with me, you can tell me that you're very sorry but things aren't working out, and you can walk away unscathed. I'd be just a small blip on your screen." Margaux sat quietly, waiting for Gary to respond. But he just sat looking at her, perplexed.

"Okay, how about this?" She stared straight into his bloodshot eyes. "We won't see each other for six months, possibly a year... but no more than two years. No contact of any kind, not even by telephone, but at the end of that time, we get married. Would you promise to do that?"

Gary was having some difficulty focusing his eyes on her. "I don't have a damn clue what you're talking about. All I want to know is, do you love me?"

"Do I love you? Do you mean at this very moment? When you are overflowing with martinis? Absolutely not! Did I love you in Vermont? Absolutely yes! Could I love you again tomorrow when you're sober? Probably, but I'm unwilling to take the chance, unless, as I said, you sweeten the pot and marry me now, or promise to marry me possibly within a year, but for certain by February 2010."

"You mean if I paid you a big bunch of money you would marry me right now?"

Margaux smiled for the first time. "In an instant!" she said. "The bottom line is, I can't put love in the bank! My heart aches when I think of the life we could have together. When I walk away from you, I'll cry for a week, and then as the months go by I'll lie in bed at night and remember our time together in the cabin, and cry all over again, and...." She reached over and put her hand over his. "Maybe in six months, surely no longer than a year and a half. Please, Gary, try to understand." He just stared at her and shook his head. They sat silently, each deep in thought. Finally, Margaux said, "I told you I'm married, right, Gary?"

"No, as a matter of fact, you denied it," he said solemnly. If you had told me, we would have had a pleasant drink together in the airport the day I met you, and that would have been the end of it. I told you, I never mess with other men's wives. I take that marriage business pretty seriously. Maybe that's the reason I've never remarried all these years." Gary put his elbows on the table with his chin in his hands and stared into Margaux's eyes. "So you've been cheating on your husband and me the whole time, is that it?"

"That's not exactly the way I'd put it."

"Okay, lay it on me. How would *you* describe it?" He leaned back in the booth and crossed his arms over his chest.

Margaux thought a moment before answering. "Perhaps you should withhold judgment until you are sober and then listen to my story," but, taking a deep breath and sighing, she continued. "Here goes...."

She told him about spending a year in state prison and confessed that she had married Toro Santoros, forty years her senior, who had paid her $250,000 fine and agreed that his estate would pay her $2,000,000 upon his death unless she was unfaithful to him during the first four years of their marriage.

"And now he's dying. He hasn't got much time left. In a year, maybe less, I'll have enough money to live very comfortably for the rest of my life, but I almost blew the whole thing with our Vermont adventure, and I can't let that happen again. Certainly you can understand that, can't you?" she pleaded.

"No, actually, I can't," Gary said sadly, shaking his head. As I see it, you already blew it right from the beginning with our wonderful night in the Palmer House in Chicago. You broke your agreement with your husband then and there, that first night in the Palmer House, and again at your friend Lucie's apartment, and then big time in Vermont. You lied to your husband and you lied to me, Margaux. Over and over, you lied to me."

"Be serious, here, Gary. Only you and I know about those things, and in case you weren't listening, I said $2,000,000. I mean—"

"Two million, ten million...it doesn't make any difference, Margaux, you've lied to me and broken the agreement with your husband." He reached out to her, putting his hand gently on her arm.

"Don't touch me," she hissed, twisting away from him and running out of the restaurant.

Gary watched her car kick up gravel as she sped out of the parking lot. He ordered another double martini.

When he finally decided it was time to go home, the bartender wouldn't let him drive.

In the morning, he had a vague recollection of grappling with the bartender who took his car keys and wouldn't give them back. After that it was all one big blur, ending up with his spending the night at a motel near the Bear Mountain Bridge.

CHAPTER TWELVE

When Gary arrived late at the office the next afternoon after his unsuccessful attempt to booze Margaux out of his life, his secretary took one look at him and said, "It must have been one heck of a good party, Mr. Samson. You look like—"

"Don't say a word, just get me some aspirin and a cup of coffee and please don't walk on the hardwood floors in your high heels." When she tiptoed into his office in her stocking feet with his coffee, she whispered that he had several calls from the bank that handled the Samson & DeLisle account. Ken Robertson, the corporate vice president at First Security, had asked to speak with Pierre, but when he learned that Pierre had retired, he insisted upon speaking with Gary.

When he called Robertson, the banker said, "We've got a problem, Gary. Where have you been?"

"I've been shooting in Texas and California for the past month …shooting film, that is. I just got back yesterday. What's up?"

"Samson & DeLisle's operating account is overdrawn by more than $100,000… $107,941.26 to be exact, and this is above your $250,000 regular line of credit with us. We have examiners coming in two weeks. I can hold these outstanding checks for ten days, but that's the best I can do, and if you don't make a deposit to cover them within that time, I'll have to dishonor them and demand payment of your $250,000 operating loan because of your default."

"I don't understand, Ken. I'm sure there's a simple explanation because business has never been better here. You know, Pierre has always handled the money part of the business—we probably just forgot to switch over an account before I left for the west coast."

"I figured as much. That's why I've held the checks," the banker said, "but it must get straightened out right away. My hands are tied."

Gary went to his bookkeeper and asked him to pull up the latest numbers. He learned that Pierre had recently withdrawn over $200,000 from the company's reserve account. It was his share of the company's accounts receivable on the books when he retired. They had been collected since that time, and he had the absolute right to withdraw his funds, but it left the company with no cash reserves.

Gary called his secretary into his office. He was sitting slumped in his chair. He raised his head slowly.

"Evelyn, see if you can reach Pete right away. I need to talk to him ASAP."

"I really don't know where he might be, Mr. Samson. If I had to guess I'd say he's probably at the hotel he's building on Isla di Oro."

"Hotel? I know he and Louise are building a vacation home somewhere in the Caribbean, but I never heard about a hotel. It looks as if everyone knows what's going on around here except me."

It took twenty-four hours for Gary's secretary to get a message through to Pierre. When she finally got him on the line and passed him through to Gary, Gary said, "Where the hell are you, man? What is this I hear about a hotel you're building?"

Pierre briefly described the situation and then Gary explained the cash flow problem that was created when Pierre withdrew his funds.

"You had every right to do that, Pete, it's my own fault. I just wasn't paying any attention to the numbers because I always counted on you for that. Robertson at the bank says if I don't come up with $100,000 in ten days, they're going to bounce the company's checks and call our operating loan. Our creditors will be scrambling to get paid and we'll be bankrupt."

"Damn it, Gary. I told you to watch the numbers."

"I know, I know, but I've been racing all over the country, doing what I do. We've got lots of money coming in as soon as I finish up a few projects. Apparently, it's just the cash flow that's the problem. Can you help me out a little? I only need sixty days, three months at the most."

"Ordinarily I'd be able to do that without a problem, but I very stupidly got myself into a similar jam down here on the Island, and I'm on the verge of bankruptcy myself. But I've got some time to solve my problem, so let's concentrate on your situation first. I'll come up to New York in the next couple of days and we'll see what we can do."

After they completed their call, Pierre called Melinda, explained that Gary needed some help and asked if she could fly east and meet with him in New York at the Algonquin Hotel.

"Please, Uncle Pierre, tell me—Poppi's not seriously ill or anything?"

"No, no, he's physically just fine. Apparently he's got some serious financial problems and he's emotionally distraught. I'll see you Thursday." Before she could ask any further questions he had disconnected the call.

On Friday morning, Gary was in his office nervously awaiting word from Pierre. A number of the company's creditors had called, wondering why they hadn't yet received the payments that Gary had promised them. Robertson, the banker, had actually stopped by Gary's office to remind him that time was running out.

What in God's name am I going to do if Pierre can't come through? he asked himself.

CHAPTER THIRTEEN

Pierre and Louise had discovered the island of Isla di Oro in 1964. It was just a spit of land twenty-six miles off the coast of Venezuela.

They were both dedicated scuba divers and had chartered a boat to take them from Aruba to Isla Di Oro. The dive master told them they would find the most spectacular coral reefs in the world at the tiny island. It was true. Over the years they had spent every winter vacation diving at different islands in the Caribbean, and although the island of Bonaire came close, the reefs at Isla di Oro were the best. They had often talked about building a vacation cottage on the island, but it never got beyond the dreaming stage.

On Pierre's sixtieth-fifth birthday, Louise had presented him with an envelope that he assumed was a gift certificate like the one she gave him every year on his birthday so that he could add to his collection of hand-carved masks.

"Of course I know what this is," he said, "and I've already got my eye on a Polynesian mask I saw in a shop on Second Avenue. Thank you, darling." He kissed her on the cheek and put the envelope aside without opening it.

"I think you should open it, dear. After all, it is your big sixty-fifth birthday and your retirement begins tomorrow, remember? While you were out, Gary called to congratulate you. He's back out on the Coast again, but he made a date with us for next week. He's bringing Lindy back home with him and he's planning a party just for the four of us. He says he hasn't forgotten the gold watch, either. Do you remember that, dear?"

"Of course I do," he smiled, picking up the envelope and removing its contents. It was a legal-looking document. It had the word DEED printed in bold letters on the yellowed parchment cover. Pierre's first agonized thought was that with Louise's penchant for careful planning she was giving him a deed to a burial plot on his birthday. But then he began to read it carefully. "Oh my God," he shouted. It was a deed to a fifty-acre parcel of land with 1,000 feet of powder-white sand beach on Isla di Oro. Louise had bought it in 1969 with $25,000 from an inheritance she had received from her grandfather and for reasons she couldn't explain, she had kept it a secret for over thirty years. Pierre was overwhelmed. Louise was such a steady, conservative, no-nonsense, no-frills kind of a lady that this single outrageous thing she had done astounded him. Besides, he told her, he was familiar with land values in the Caribbean and by now its value must have increased tremendously.

"But it's our secret, Pierre. And to make certain we aren't ever tempted to sell it, and since we don't have any children and we both love Lindy as if she were our own daughter, I want her to have it when we die, so it sort of only belongs to us during our lifetimes."

"How wonderfully wise you are, sweetheart," Pierre said, giving her a bear hug and a sloppy kiss.

"And that's not all." She shyly handed Pierre a scroll tied with a red ribbon. Pierre unrolled it gently. Louise had had an architect's rendering made from a sketch of their dream cottage that she had made many years earlier.

When the euphoria of the wonderful gift wore off, a discomforting factor crept into their conversations with respect to their future retirement on Isla di Oro. The heart of the problem was that Pierre and Louise each had a totally different concept of how their retirement should be planned and enjoyed. Louise had envisioned lounging on her private beach, sketching, reading, writing to her friends back home, doing her daily crossword puzzles and ending each week with the challenging New York Times Sunday puzzle. It didn't matter that the Sunday Times didn't usually arrive until several weeks after its date, and never on a Sunday.

Pierre, on the other hand, was a creator. Not artistically like Gary, but rather in the building of things—anything from a bookshelf to the guest apartment he built above their garage. His dream of retirement on Isla di Oro was to construct six to ten guest cottages that he would build himself. He envisioned himself and Louise operating them as a boutique resort for scuba divers and honeymooners and elderly guests who would appreciate the quiet beauty of the island with no modern conveniences except indoor plumbing and an ice maker for drinks at sundown.

Although Pierre's plan was a far cry from what Louise had in mind, she was content to follow his lead, as long as he promised that she wouldn't have to cook or clean or worry. At first she couldn't imagine how his ideas could possibly comport with her vision of their golden years on the Island of Gold. But she quickly got caught up in Pierre's enthusiasm and became excited by her role as interior designer, selecting the furniture, drapes, bedspreads and the multitude of amenities that even the most primitive accommodations required. Her studio in their home in Westchester soon became filled with fabric samples, color boards, floor tiles and enough catalogues to design and equip the interior of a major Caribbean resort.

Pierre was exhilarated by preparing the business plan, site plan, feasibility study and construction drawings. When he first conceived the project, he thought he could build the main house and the cottages for under a million dollars, but he had expanded the project to include a swimming pool, a small bar and restaurant, a desalinization facility to convert sea water into fresh water and a comprehensive sewage disposal system because everything was being built upon solid coral. The beautiful blanket of green adjacent to the beach was only skin deep. He also learned that it was essential that a sea wall be built to protect the buildings because although the island had never suffered any severe hurricane damage, their land was on the windward side. This was a marvelous feature for enjoying the cooling effects of the trade winds, but the locals warned them that on a few occasions in the past, storms had sent the sea crashing over their entire fifty acres of land. As long as there were no buildings on the site, no serious damage had occurred because within a few days, the sea would calm down and in a month or two the vegetation would resume its normal life cycle. Because of the cost of building such a protective sea wall, the land was not quite the bargain they had thought, although everyone agreed that after the wall was built, it would become a very valuable piece of real estate.

When Pierre was finally able to put all the numbers together he was shocked to see that, without furnishings or working capital the cost of his project would be over $2,000,000. When he added in the furniture and equipment he would need another $100,000 or more.

Although none of the U.S. banks were interested in providing any financing for a twelve-unit facility in the Caribbean, he contacted a private investor who was willing to talk to him.

"Where did you say you were planning to build?" he asked. "Did you say Aruba?"

"No," Pierre replied." I said it was twenty miles *from* Aruba. You see, the idea is that the guests will fly to Aruba or Curaçao, or Venezuela, and travel by boat to my island." The financier smiled knowingly and handed Pierre's beautiful photographs, renderings and feasibility study back to him.

"Beautiful beach," he said. "Let me know when it's built. I'd love to visit you. Good luck."

And so began Pierre's adventure as a developer/contractor/hotelier and banker in his sixty-sixth year.

They sold their house in Westchester for $675,000, and built their first guest cottage to live in during construction of the project. Pierre couldn't believe how expensive it turned out to be. He had carefully selected all of the construction materials in a building supply warehouse in Miami and had them shipped to the free port in Aruba. The first serious problem began when he tried to get the container shipped to his island. It was too big to be sent over on a small ship and there was no dock big enough on his island to accommodate a large ship. He finally arranged to have the materials off-loaded from the container in Aruba and reloaded onto a small Columbian tramp steamer that agreed to anchor off Isla di Oro and transfer the materials onto a number of small motor craft that Pierre had hired from the fishermen on the island. When the last piece of plywood and the last case of nails was piled up on his beach, Pierre threw a party for the islanders who had helped. A few hours after the end of the successful party, a freak storm sent the sea surging up on the beach, some of the lumber floated away and the rain drenched all of the unprotected building materials. When Pierre completed his inventory check in the days that followed, he found that in addition to the storm damage, a substantial number of items that had been transferred from the container in Aruba apparently didn't get loaded onto the steamer, and some additional items that got off-loaded from the steamer to the small craft didn't make it to the island. The total loss was over $100,000.

I'm a babe in the woods, he lamented. *How could I be so smart in business for forty years and be so dumb when it comes to building in the Caribbean? Okay, so I've paid my tuition; they won't ever fool me again....*

But they did. The final disaster occurred when he purchased the cinderblock for the project in the Dominican Republic. The deal had been brokered by a member of the Dominican government he had met in his travels. The fellow had arranged for the delivery of the blocks, fabricated in his country at a cost that was significantly less than buying them in Miami. Pierre had paid for the blocks and their transportation by a cashier's check delivered to the broker. In turn he had received a bill of lading confirming that the blocks had been loaded on the carrier, which was a World War II troop landing craft that could be driven right up onto Pierre's beach for offloading. He was advised to expect the delivery within twenty days. When the ship hadn't arrived in thirty days Pierre checked with the broker who said he would investigate the matter and get back to him. He called again and was assured that the craft had departed the from Dominican Republic several weeks earlier and should be arriving soon. The ship and the broker were never heard from again. Pierre soon realized that the crooks on Wall Street were amateurs compared to what he was contending with among some of the operators in the Caribbean.

After speaking with Melinda, Pierre climbed up the steep hill behind their home and guest cottages. They had named their place Orquedia, the Spanish word for orchid.

It took him about a half-hour to reach the top, where he had built a lean-to under a tree the locals called a Carawara.

A pair of wild goats occupied his lair when he was absent and he whisked away some of their droppings with a palm-frond broom he had made.

Isla di Oro, Island of Gold. A bit of irony there, he mused. *No gold, no natural resources whatsoever, except the sun the sea and the sand, plus Louise, me, thirty-nine other good souls, some lizards, a dozen or so iguanas and twenty-seven goats.*

By the time construction of their dream retirement home and six guest cottages was completed, the project had cost them twice what Pierre had budgeted. All of their savings were depleted, they needed $50,000 for furnishings and equipment, and they had no money left to pay for advertising their little hideaway guest cottages.

As Pierre sat gazing down on the beautiful little island, he thought, *on the other hand, except for the mess I've made of things, I'm healthier and stronger than I've been in years, and my darling, wonderful, loyal wife hasn't once said, "I told you so, you old fool."*

"Mr. Samson, you have a surprise visitor."

"Send him in," Gary replied, heading for his office door to welcome Pierre.

"It's not a him, it's a her, Mr. Samson."

"What the—" Gary blurted when Melinda and Pierre came bursting through the door.

Melinda rushed into Gary's arms. Pierre stood back, smiling.

"Lindy, darling...Pete...." Gary held out his hand to Pierre with one arm still around Melinda's shoulders. "What's the story here? It's so wonderful to see both of you but...Pete?"

"Maybe you could invite us to sit down and I can explain," Pierre said.

"Of course." Gary led Melinda to the conversation corner of Pierre's old office where he and Gary had met in 1986. "Now, please tell me what this is all about. No, wait a minute, would you like a glass of lemonade first, Pete?"

"You bet I would," Pierre replied, laughing.

"I'll get the drinks," Melinda said, jumping up and heading to the built-in bar. "You guys just go ahead and talk business."

"Why are you sitting there with that shit-eating grin on your face, Pete? Do you think I'm joking about the frigging mess I got myself into?"

"Calm down, Gary. The point is, I believe we've got both our problems solved. If you'll just sit down and relax, I'll tell you the whole plan."

Melinda returned with a pitcher of lemonade, an ice bucket and three glasses. Gary started to speak, but Melinda interrupted him.

"Like Uncle Pete said, Poppi, just sit back, relax and drink your lemonade." With a wide grin, she handed him a glass.

"What's so funny? You two are driving me crazy."

"Oh, Poppi, I do love you so." Melinda planted a noisy kiss on her father's cheek, sat down beside him on the red leather settee and slipped her arm through his. "Okay, Uncle Pete, lay it on him."

"I think I need a real drink," Gary said, starting to get up.

Melinda held him back. "Remember what you always told me, Poppi. No alcohol during business hours." Gary eased back down on the settee.

"In a nutshell, partner," Pierre began, "you probably don't remember, but on the day after I gave you that check for a million dollars on your thirty-fifth birthday eleven years ago, you and I had a big discussion about the cost of Lindy's college education. Do you remember that?"

"Sort of, but not really." Gary said.

"Lindy was seventeen, almost eighteen years old. You told me that you had calculated that tuition, books, room and board, the whole shebang for her college education, was going to cost as much as $200,000 for four years at an Ivy League school. You instructed me to get in touch with our lawyers and set up a trust to cover the cost before any money was invested in our film venture. You wrote out a check for that amount and told me I should be the trustee. That was in 1996."

He turned to Melinda. "Good Lord, Lindy, Can that be true? You're now, what, twenty-eight years old?"

"You got that right, Uncle Pete. Let me see, that makes you…?"

"Never mind, dear Lindy." Pierre stood up and walked over to the window overlooking the East River.

"Remember *The Bridge,* Gary? You know, Louise and I watched our movie for the umpteenth time not too long ago. We invited some new friends that we made on Isla Di Oro over to the house and showed it on DVD. It really is a beautiful film, Gary. And Lindy, I must say it's easy to tell why you've become a star. You're spectacular and you can thank your dad for giving you that chance. I don't say you might not have made it on your own, because there's no doubt about your talent as an actress, but I think his boost helped you get started."

Melinda smiled, picked up her father's hand and kissed it. "Thanks, Poppi. You is my man."

"Well, now, back to the saga," Pierre said. "As trustee, I put half the money in tax-free government bonds and the rest in blue chip stocks. Remember, now, this was back in 1996. A couple years later when you gave me Lindy's college bills to pay out of the trust, you weren't paying any attention to the money we were making, Gary, you left it all up to me; and I decided I would pay those bills out of your earnings and leave the trust alone, so I never took a dime out of the trust—I just let it sit there and grow, until 2006. Of course I kept my eye on things because I had to file a tax return for the trust every year, and when Bush got us into this stupid war in Iraq, I immediately decided to get out of the market, and by that time most of the stocks I had invested in had more than doubled in value, so with the accumulated interest on the bonds, the stock dividends and the capital gains on the stocks, when I cashed out in 2006, the principal of the trust had grown to a little over a half million dollars.

"In the meantime, Melinda had graduated from college and was doing very well for herself in Hollywood. The trust was set up so that if there was any money left after all the college expenses were paid, it was all to go to Lindy when she reached her thirtieth birthday.

"After you called me a few days ago, Gary, I checked the trust account and lo and behold, although the principal hasn't grown in the last two years because it's all been invested in safe, tax-free bonds, the accumulated interest has increased the value of the trust by an additional $50,000, so when she reaches thirty, I'll be able to terminate the trust and hand Lindy a check for…" Pierre reached in his pocket, pulled out an adding machine tape, studied it carefully and said, "$567,834.22."

Melinda jumped up, clapped her hands and danced around the room. Pierre pumped a raised fist in the air. When Melinda finally quieted down, he continued, "Now technically it all belongs to Lindy, but she has some ideas she wants to run by you."

"What do you think about this idea, Poppi? First of all, I owe you $200,000 plus interest for the money you loaned my trust to pay for my education. Next, Uncle Pete has explained to me that he made so many mistakes building his little hotel on Isla Di Oro that he doesn't have anything left to pay for marketing, so I've made a deal with him. I'm going to buy like a timeshare from him for $50,000 that will allow me to stay in one of his cottages whenever you or I want to for…how long, Uncle Pete?"

"Forever, kiddo."

"Forever, Poppi. For you and me. Now listen up, Poppi. We're going to make a TV commercial advertising Uncle Pete's hotel, and…" (Lindy took a dramatic pose) "I'm going to be the unpaid star in the commercial and you're going to be the unpaid creator, producer and director of the commercial.

"I've also decided to give Uncle Pete an extra $25,000 for doing such a spectacular job as trustee and you and me, Poppi, are going to split the balance. Like how much will be left, Uncle Pierre?"

"I figure about $300,000."

"Right," Lindy continued, "And I'm going to use my half to put down a deposit on a small house in Hollywood. How 'bout them apples, Poppi?"

Gary began to laugh uproariously, and then he began to cry, and then they were all laughing and hugging and crying and kissing, and Gary went to the bar, opened up a bottle of champagne, shook it up, and aimed it at Pierre and then at Melinda.

CHAPTER FOURTEEN

Toro marched aboard the cruise ship *Seadancer* like Caesar leading his troops into Greece.

On the day they sailed, he gave Margaux a large antique gold pendant and chain with an enormous two-carat diamond embedded on its face.

"So you gotta wear it every Saturday forever," Toro said when he fastened it around her neck.

"How come?" Margaux asked.

"Because we was married on Saturday, we're leavin' on this cruise on Saturday, I was born on a Saturday, and I'll probably die on a Saturday. Saturday is Toro day."

When he purchased it, he instructed the jeweler to engrave his initials and hers inside a heart on the back of the pendant. The jeweler who sold it to him refused to deface the rare piece, so Toro took it to another shop that had no such qualms. When he gave it to her, she thought the enormous diamond was fake and ostentatious, but when she learned that the diamond was real and all by itself was worth $25,000, she promised to wear it every Saturday night forever.

For Margaux, being with Toro on the ship 24/7 was like serving a prison sentence. Mentally, she marked off the days until he was expected to die.

She had demanded a two bedroom suite as a condition of her agreement to accompany him and his family on the cruise. She had her private bedroom at home because she claimed that Toro's snoring made it impossible for her to sleep, and she refused to spend a fortnight of sleepless nights on the cruise.

When they entered their deluxe suite, Margaux was impressed.

"Darling, it's fabulous," she said. The living room was spacious, with beautiful, polished mahogany floors, oriental throw rugs, plush leather furniture, exquisite accessories, and silk drapes. There was a fully stocked bar, enormous flat-screen television, opulent bedrooms, private baths—each with its own jacuzzi—and off the living room, a six by ten foot balcony.

After unpacking her wardrobe trunk the first day aboard, Margaux waited until Toro began his afternoon nap and then slipped out to meet his daughter, Zee, at a cozy bar on the lower level at the bow of the ship. The first time a large wave covered the glass on the forward wall of the bar, she gasped, believing the ship had started to sink. Zee laughed and told Margaux that she had actually screamed when she and Vito had first visited the bar.

Nick and Vito had checked out the casino and gone searching for Vito's friend, Luis Ramiriz, who had agreed to entice Margaux into his bed in exchange for a free vacation aboard the *Seadancer*.

Margaux and Zee were drinking cosmopolitans when Ramiriz entered the bar. He took the end stool and ordered a Dewars on the rocks. When the bar tender placed it in front of him, he held it up and said, "Here's to *you*, ladies." Zee smiled and raised her glass. Margaux, who had begun to feel the effects of her second cosmopolitan, ignored him at first, but by the time she was halfway through her third drink, they had all become great friends. When their little party was about to break up, Luis slid over and while seated next to Margaux, casually caressed her crossed knee. They agreed to resume the party on the following day at the same hour.

The day after the magnificent cruise ship had departed from Hawaii, Margaux and Toro were lying in the sun on the deck. As soon as he fell asleep, she immediately got up to take a walk around the ship. She strolled up to the uppermost deck. With more than fifteen hundred passengers on board it was difficult to find a secluded spot to just relax and do nothing except think about the decision she had made.

I realize it may have sounded cold and uncaring, but it isn't. Gary could have agreed to wait a year or two if he really loves me. Why couldn't he understand that I wasn't choosing money over our love?...Well, maybe I was, but how could I be sure our affair would lead to something permanent? Suppose I gave up $2,000,000 and I discovered later that Gary is an alcoholic, or going bankrupt, or was just playing the game of love?

The more she thought about it, the more convinced she became that she had made the right decision.

If Gary truly loves me, he'll wait. I'm not going to think about it any more.

As they approached the beautiful Polynesian island of Tahiti shortly after Margaux left Toro sleeping in a deck chair, a ship's officer gently awakened him and delivered a cable marked 'URGENT'.

"Say, what..." Toro grumbled.

"Excuse me, sir, I'm terribly sorry to disturb you, but this message is marked 'URGENT' and 'PERSONAL' and I thought you should have it right away."

"Where's Margaux?" Toro demanded.

"Margaux? Is that your daughter? The attractive young lady who was beside you earlier?" the officer asked.

"Margaux is my wife!"

"Yes sir, the man said, embarrassed by his blunder. "Shall I have her paged?"

"No. No need for that. I'm sure she'll be back shortly. I don't have my glasses. Would you mind reading the damn cable to me?"

"All right, sir," the officer said, opening the envelope and glancing quickly at the message. "It's from Dr. Newman and it says:

"*Dear Toro, I have the most wonderful news for you. I've had your films read by another doctor friend of mine who works at Sloane-Kettering and he believes your condition has been misdiagnosed. You don't have small cell carcinoma which is a terminal condition. You have adenocarcinoma, and I can now tell you that the lesion on your lung is treatable. If you behave yourself, there is no reason why you can't live to be a hundred.*

Regards, Your Friend, Dr. Samuel Newman."

"Holy shit!" Toro yelled. "I'll be a son of a bitch."

"What wonderful news. Congratulations, sir," the officer said.

"Wait till Margaux hears this. It'll blow her mind. Do you realize what those dumb assholes at the hospital did? They put me through hell for the past two months. I thought I was a dead duck and now the old Doc tells me I'm gonna live to be a hundred. Can you believe it? By God, I'll sue the bastards. I'll bet I'll get enough money for me and Margaux to go around the world in this old tub. Wait till she hears the news."

When Toro had issued the invitation to the family to join Margaux and him on the cruise, he told everybody that there was just one rule they must obey. He didn't care how they spent their time on the ship, but they must show up for drinks and dinner every night at the special table he had reserved. When dinner was over, they were free to do whatever they wanted. "But if you don't show up for dinner, I'll throw your ass overboard," he had said.

They all managed to tolerate each other between the before-dinner cocktail and the after-dinner brandy. Occasionally Nicky and Vito would show up late or not at all if they were on a hot run at the casino, but generally they hung around for a second brandy at the old man's expense and the three ladies would always go to the casino and play the slot machines or take in a show.

On the evening after Toro had received the cable from Dr. Newman, when cocktails were served he stood up and clinked on his wine glass.

"I have a serious announcement to make," he said, solemnly. "About two months ago I was diagnosed with lung cancer. The doctors told me that statistically I could live as little as two months but no longer than six months. I didn't tell anyone, not even Margaux, because I didn't want to spoil our trip...."

Margaux could barely keep from screaming out loud for joy.

Xenia started to cry softly. Margaux remained stone-faced, as cold as a marble statue.

Luis is going to have to move fast, Vittorio thought.

Margaux could feel the perspiration sliding down from her armpits.

"Now, now, Zee. I didn't mean to make you cry. But listen to me, all of you." They immediately quieted down although Xenia continued to weep.

"This afternoon I received a cable from my doctor telling me it was all a mistake and I can live to be a *hundred.*" Toro threw his fist in the air like Joe Louis did when he knocked out Schmeling and became champion of the world.

Xenia jumped up and threw her arms around Toro's neck. "Daddy, Daddy!" she screamed.

Margaux began to sob.

Toro put his arm around her shoulders. "Just think, honey, we'll have at least another ten years together...maybe more. I am one lucky son-of-a-bitch," he said, raising his fist in the air again. "Waiter, more champagne. We need more champagne!"

Vito whispered to Nick, "I'm gonna be a fuckin' old man by the time...Jesus."

"You ain't alone, buddy," Nick answered sullenly.

Margaux was lying in her luxurious bed, staring up at the ceiling, when she heard Zee and Nick bring Toro to their cabin.

"Where's Margaux, where's my bee-yu-ti-ful wife? I want to have another glass of champagne with my bee-yu-ti-ful wife."

"Shhh, Daddy. Margaux is asleep. She said she's not feeling well. And you've had enough champagne. Let's just get you into bed and we can celebrate again tomorrow."

"No, no. I want one more drink with Margaux," Toro said, pulling away from Zee and flopping down on the couch in the stateroom.

"Did you see her sobbing when she thought I was going to die? When she heard the good news she just couldn't stop crying."

"Nick, did you bring that bottle of champagne like I told you? C'mon guys, don't be party poopers, it's early yet and...and...." Toro eased back on the soft leather couch and began to snore.

"Problem solved," Zee giggled, and covered her father with a blanket and turned off the lights.

Margaux buried her head in her pillow, pounded on the mattress and continued to sob quietly until she finally fell asleep.

When the ship docked at the pier in Tahiti, Margaux was one of the first passengers to disembark. She left a note for Toro:

Toro, I've gone shopping. I'll meet you and the rest of the gang for drinks and dinner.

It was exactly noon when Margaux walked into the Dockside Cafe in Papeete, the principal city on the exotic island of Tahiti. She had agreed to meet Luis Ramiriz for lunch and selected a table with a spectacular view of the nearby island of Moorea.

She hadn't quite figured Luis out. She assumed his initial interest in her to be solely physical and she was pleased that an attractive younger man was flirting with her, even though there were many unattached women on board the big ship who had paired up to share a cabin for their vacations. She decided that at least as long as the cruise lasted, he could help take her mind off the disaster of being married to Toro.

Gary and Lucie had filled the void of her unfulfilled sex life with Toro, and although that was yesterday and this was today, Gary was constantly on her mind. In any case, Luis' interest in her was a welcome antidote to the blue funk that had begun when she learned that her husband's death was no longer imminent. She knew that all she had to do was give Luis a high sign and they would be headed to bed. If it weren't for the penalty she would pay if she got caught, she would probably be inclined to let the game play out just for the hell of it.

"*Bonjour, madame. Voulez-vous quelque chose à boire?*" the waiter said. When Margaux looked totally perplexed, he added, "Would you like something to drink? I'm sorry *madame*, I thought I recognized you as a French actress I saw on television."

Margaux looked up at the handsome young Tahitian waiter with a wide friendly grin and a very slim butt. *Oh, God*, she thought, *if I were free, I'd love to spend a few months on this island paradise.*

"Do you know what a cosmopolitan is?"

"But of course, *madame*. This is a small island, but I speak French, Tahitian and English and "cosmopolitan" is the same in all three languages. Are you alone?"

He is so fresh, she thought. "Actually, my lover will be joining me shortly," she said.

"What a lucky man," the waiter replied, grinning.

Glancing briefly at his youthful body as he headed to the bar to get her drink, Margaux said to herself, *It's comforting to know that men are the same all over the world, including this tiny island in the middle of nowhere.* She briefly thought of Toro, overweight, wrinkled, uncouth, totally unsophisticated, with no redeeming qualities except a magnificent head of silver hair and a very large bank account.

Luis caught sight of her and hurried over to her table.

Luis Ramiriz had a problem. What had seemed like a lark when he agreed to set up Margaux had turned out to be quite different from what he had anticipated. Nick had convinced him that he would be doing his thing with a colossal old bitch who was married to his father, but he couldn't believe his eyes when Vito sent him to the bar on board ship the first day of the cruise. He thought she was a knockout, and in fact, ever since he met her, he couldn't think about anything else. He didn't understand it. He knew he was attractive to women, and in fact he had never met a woman he didn't believe he could "take" if he wanted to. He thought they were all so transparent. They would do anything if they could see the $5,000 engagement ring, the wedding with all their buddies marching ahead of them down the aisle, and being able to quit their boring jobs and live happily ever after in the suburbs...a winter vacation in Hawaii or the Caribbean...maybe belonging to a country club and learning how to play golf.

But then, Luis thought, *Vito comes along with this crazy proposition where I get a free cruise vacation and maybe make $50,000. I mean them ain't peanuts as they say, so I agree to the deal. I figure it'll be a hoot, and there's no way I can lose, and then this old bitch Vito has been talkin' about turns out not to be so old and if she's a bitch, I ain't seen it yet. But then, when I start to make a move on her, she just smiles and turns away. She lets me know I'm being a jerk, without actually saying it. She is one classy lady...I mean, what is this shit?*

During lunch, Luis reached across the table and fondled the gold and diamond pendant Margaux was wearing. Then he took her hand and turned it palm-side up. He studied it carefully, placed it gently back on the table and smiled mischievously.

"What was that all about?" she demanded.

"I appraise diamonds and I read palms."

"So what do my necklace and my palm tell you?"

"The diamond is real and is worth somewhere between twenty and twenty-five thousand dollars."

Margaux put her finger to her nose and raised her eyebrows. "I must say I'm impressed with your knowledge of jewelry. Okay, so what does my palm tell you about my future?"

"It's just as I thought," he replied, smugly.

Margaux laughed. "You are so full of baloney, but I'll bite. What did you see?"

He leaned closer to her and spoke just above a whisper. "Before you return to the ship today, you are going to make mad, passionate love with a mysterious young man."

Margaux looked carefully around the dining room: every table was occupied. "Almost all of the men here look mysterious. Can you give me a more detailed description?" she whispered.

He picked up her hand again and caressed her palm lightly with his forefinger. "Yes, yes, I see him clearly. He's quite young, I'd say late twenties, nice-looking in a rugged sort of way. I'm going to guess he is Latino, six feet tall and weighs about 175 pounds. He's muscular. You can tell he works out because his upper body strength shows and he holds a karate black belt." Luis sat back in his chair and casually hunched his shoulders forward and flexed his biceps; Margaux covered her mouth to keep from laughing aloud.

Luis smiled and continued. "He's not too well educated, but he's very, very smart, and he believes that it is inevitable that very soon you and he will make love."

Gazing around the room more slowly this time, Margaux said, "Well, I don't see anyone in the room who fits that description, but even if there were someone, I'm sorry to say it's not going to happen, Luis."

"Why not, sweetheart? You've gotta give me a reason."

"I don't *gotta* do any such thing, my friend," she said, "but in order to avoid any misunderstanding, and perhaps disappointment, I'll *tell* you why. First, I must say I think you are a very attractive young man and should have no trouble finding yourself a young woman your own age. I've seen dozens of them on board the ship. I'm at least five years older than you," she said. *More like ten*, she thought.

"That's no reason at all. I don't care how old you are. It makes no difference to me. That's really stupid, Margaux. I'm serious. I'm not talking kid stuff here. I said, 'making *love*.' I'm falling in love with you, Margaux."

"Luis, Luis, don't say such a silly thing. You're on a romantic cruise. This beautiful island oozes sensuality. A prince can fall in love with a frog under Polynesian skies. I think we had best call for the check. I really don't want to continue this conversation."

"Wait, listen to me, I'm prepared to do whatever I have to do. I may be young in your eyes, but I'm not inexperienced in the ways of the world, or of women, for that matter."

"Oh, I'm sure of that!" Margaux laughed.

"No, no, I didn't mean it that way. Don't you understand, I'm not kidding around—I want to marry you, and I'll do anything to make it happen!"

"My God, Luis, I'm a married woman."

"I know, I know, I'm not blind. I see that rock on the fourth finger of your left hand and the wedding band. I've seen you strolling on deck with that short old guy mauling you. I know, I know. But I don't care. You can get a divorce, you can—"

Margaux stood up. "Goodbye, Luis. Thanks for the lunch."

On the evening they left Tahiti headed for the picture-postcard perfect island of Bora Bora, Vito, Nick and Luis were huddled around a tiny table in a men's-only bar under the fantail.

"So, what's the score, Luis? How we makin' out?" Vito demanded.

"I got what you wanted," Luis answered.

"You're shittin' us, right?" said Nick. "Lemme see."

Luis reached in his pocket and threw an envelope on the table. Vito picked it up and removed a handful of photographs. He and Nick quickly appraised them.

"You can't see her face, Luis. All you can see is her ass, for Christ sake. She'll just deny it's her. You gotta do better'n this, man. I mean I never seen her in action, but it don't look like her to me. Are you tryin' to con us, buddy boy?" Vito demanded.

"It's her, I'm tellin' you. I'll swear to it," Luis countered.

"And she'll deny it with *them* stupid pictures, asshole," Vito cursed.

"Hey, wait a fuckin' minute here." Luis pushed his chair back and stood up. His face was flushed. He was getting hot. "You jerks give me that piece a shit gas station security camera instead of the kind the narcs use. The sucker was at least ten years old. You get what you pay for, asshole." He and Vito were glaring at each other as Vito eased up and out of his chair. The bartender, who had his eye on the trio as the argument heated up, quickly slipped from behind the bar. "Is there a problem here, gentlemen? I've got security on the line, but I don't want to call them in unless we need to."

"Naw," Nick spoke up. "We're okay, just a little disagreement among friends. We'll be leavin' in a couple minutes."

Luis and Vito sat back down at the table. "We'll figure it out tomorrow," Nick said. When the bartender left them and returned to the bar, Nick continued, "Listen, buddy, there ain't no hurry no more, 'cause my old man ain't gonna die right away like he was supposed to. It was a stupid idea anyhow."

"Why not just wipe *her* out? She loses, we win two million bucks guaranteed. Quick 'n easy, eh?" Vito said.

"Don't look at me, guys," Luis warned. "That's not in my contract. Hey, what's this two million bucks thing, anyway? Nobody told me nothin' about two million bucks."

"It's got nothin' to do with you, Luis," Nick said.

"Okay, I get it now. I do the dirty work, you give me a cruise ticket that costs you maybe fifteen hundred bucks, and after I boff her, you guys collect two million. Is that it? Sounds like a real sweetheart deal you give me," Luis sneered.

"That ain't it, Luis. We was gonna cut you in when we got the payoff." Vito explained.

"When's that supposed to happen?" Luis asked.

Nick and Luis both turned to Vito. He ignored them, ordered another round of drinks and pulled a cheroot out of his jacket pocket. No one said anything while he lit it. He took a few puffs and pointed the cigar at Luis.

"I got another idea." He lowered his voice and nodded, indicating he wanted them to huddle closer. "How about this. The old man gave the Bitch that necklace thing which he claims he paid twenty-five grand for. On top of that he's been loading her with expensive jewelry since he met her. Ten to one she brought every diamond he give her on this trip to show off and I figure that diamond necklace alone has got to be worth half of what the old man paid for it, like maybe ten, twelve grand; the whole stash could bring, say, fifty, sixty thousand."

"I figure it's worth twice that," Nick said.

"Great," Luis sneered. You the one that's gonna sell it, Nicky?"

"What could you get for it, Luis?"

"The thing is, you can't sell that stuff all at once," Luis replied. "See, most of what I've seen of hers has to be cut up. It's too easy to identify as it is, so maybe everything, after you pay the jeweler to cut it and give the fence his thirty percent, I guess you might get forty or fifty grand out of it."

"Okay," Vito said, "You snatch it and sell it, Lu, keep ten thousand and Nick and me split the balance. That way we get our investment back plus a little bit. What do you think?"

"I think it stinks. I take the risk of being caught during the snatch, getting it through customs and dumping it when we get back to Brooklyn, and you guys get the big cut. No way."

"Okay, so we split it three ways. We're talking peanuts here, anyway," Vito offered.

"No," Luis said. "I've got a deal for you guys. This is what we're going to do. You and Nick snatch it, I mean if either of you gets caught in her bedroom, you're family. You can make up an excuse why you're there. I got no excuse. One of you grabs the jewelry, you bring it to me I'll get rid of it and we split fifty-fifty."

No one said anything for a few minutes. Finally Vito said, "Okay, here's the deal. Whoever steals the jewelry takes fifty percent of the pot. We'll draw straws to see who gets to make the snatch, and the other two guys split what's left."

Nick and Luis nodded approval.

"I can make a key to get in the room," Luis said, "but the room safe where she probably keeps her jewelry could present a problem."

"I might be able to handle that," Nick said. "A lot of times Carmen goes to the gym with the Bitch back home. She she told me that once she mentioned to the Bitch that sometimes she forgets the combination to her locker and keeps it in her wallet. The Bitch says she's got a foolproof way of remembering her combination. She always uses the last four digits of her cell phone number. I'm bettin' she done the same thing in her stateroom safe. It's worth a try. I've got her number in my cell phone directory."

"That's good thinkin', Nick. Before we do this you should check that out first, okay?" Vito said.

"Not a problem. I got another idea. The time to pull this off is when we're having dinner with the family. That should give whoever gets the short straw at least two hours to make the haul without worrying about being caught because Pop and the Bitch are at the table every night for them two hours. If you or I make the heist, we can always give some excuse for not showin' up for dinner."

"How about pulling this off tomorrow night?" Vito suggested. "We're scheduled to be in Bora Bora and I seen on the bulletin board there's a big show with local dancers after dinner. I'm sure the old man and the Bitch will be going. He loves takin' her to them things."

They shook hands on the deal and Vito went up to the bar and picked up three straws.

CHAPTER FIFTEEN

It was still dark when Hoarai nudged his daughter Tiare awake with his bare foot. She hurried to get dressed for the adventure with her father.

He walked down to the water's edge and gazed out at the massive American luxury liner that had just entered the Bay of Povaii in Bora Bora. A few circles of yellow light shone through the portholes of the honeycomb of cabins lining each of her five decks. As the early morning sky began to turn pearl gray, Hoarai stood mesmerized by the marvel of the huge cruise ship. The harbormaster had informed him one day that the ship carried 1,500 passengers and a crew of 500. "*E aha*, how can it be?" he marveled.

Hoarai was a large man. His straight black hair fell to his shoulders. Much of his honey-brown body was covered with tattoos. Tiare met him at the door of their shack with a cup of steaming coffee and a piece of *straua*, the Polynesian coarse grain bread she had warmed over the grill. She smiled at him, eager and excited about the prospect of their day fishing together.

They pushed off in the pirogue, their long smooth strokes barely causing a ripple as the paddles whispered through the calm sea.

As soon as they reached deep water they each threw over a line. The sun was now fully up above the horizon. They could feel its warmth on their backs as they slowly drifted toward the coral reef. Suddenly, Tiare felt a powerful strike on her line.

"Papa, help," she cried. "It is so big. I'm afraid of it."

Hoarai grunted as he tugged on the line. After a few moments when there was no movement, he chuckled and said, "I'm afraid you are just hooked onto the reef, my child."

"No, no, Papa, I felt him pulling the line."

"Then you must have frightened him to death, little one," Hoarai said, laughing. When he began to pull in the line, Tiare was the first to see what she had caught. She screamed, "Papa, it's a man!"

When they pulled the dead body alongside the canoe, Hoarai discovered that there was something clutched in the drowned man's fist that gleamed in the midmorning sun's rays. He studied it for a moment and then slipped it deep into his pocket.

"I think we have done enough fishing for today," he said, after lashing the body to the side of the outrigger canoe.

"We go home now," he grunted, heading the little craft back across the bay.

CHAPTER SIXTEEN

Capitaine Aeva Fontein's father was French and her mother was Polynesian. She had inherited the best characteristics of both cultures. Although most young Polynesian women were short, curving and soft, Lieutenant Fontein was tall, curving, and as hard as the rock that was mined from *Te Anuanua* mountain in the center of the island. Her intelligence quotient was off the chart, and her dream was to become an investigator in the French *Sûreté*, stationed in Paris. However, after ten years in the service, when she was promoted to lieutenant in charge of the six male officers on the island of Bora Bora, she realized that she had been politically sandbagged. She was professionally marooned on the exotic island, babysitting the local population. The boredom was slightly reduced by the presence of the resort hotels, but her duties were mostly limited to dealing with Saturday night drunks, petty larcenies and domestic quarrels.

Her intelligence, education, and ambition put her out of reach of most of the young single men residing on the island, and her position as chief of police did not lend itself to romantic encounters with the tourist population that passed briefly through her life.

It was just after nine o'clock in the morning when she received a call from her deputy stationed in the village of Taaroa advising her that a dead male body had been discovered by Hoarai Omanatu near the reefs on the east side of the lagoon opposite the cruise ship, *Seadancer*. The victim was caucasian, wearing a bathrobe and pajamas. *Capitaine* Fontein instructed her deputy how to secure the body according to protocol and advised him she would meet him there as soon as possible. She then commandeered the sole police watercraft and arrived at the scene within twenty minutes.

She was pleased to have her routine administrative duties interrupted by what appeared to be the unnatural death of a foreign national. She looked forward to the intellectual challenge of the investigation and immediately began to record the details of the circumstances presented to her. She learned from Hoarai that his fishing line had caught in the clothing of the deceased, well below the surface of the water, which indicated that death must have occurred less than 72 hours earlier because it took that long for a dead body to develop the gases that would cause it to float to the surface.

Based upon her experience, *Capitaine* Fontein believed that the victim had met his death just a few hours prior to the discovery of the body. There were three possibilities, she decided: accidental death, suicide, or murder.

She checked with the cruise line and learned that the ship had arrived the day before and was scheduled to remain in the harbor for two days. She called her superior officer in Tahiti and was advised that he would send the medical examiner to Bora Bora on the afternoon plane to determine the cause of death.

"Let's hope it's not homicide, Lieutenant Fontein, because I'm going on holiday to France tomorrow morning, *certainement*. I made my reservation six months ago. *Vous comprenez,* Lieutenant? It is you who must take charge, if necessary." Aeva experienced a rush of excitement at the prospect.

"I understand, Major. I will do whatever must be done. You do not forget that I was by your side for many years. You taught me well."

"I always had great confidence in your judgment, Lieutenant. Perhaps the stupid fellow accidentally fell overboard or lost all his money in the casino and decided to throw in the towel?"

"I hope it is as simple as that," Aeva lied. "*Bon voyage.*"

When the medical examiner, Dr. Brulée, was instructed to take the afternoon plane to Bora Bora, he was furious. He was in the middle of the local club's annual golf tournament, and for the first time in his life he was ahead of the pack by two strokes. The match wouldn't end for another two days.

He waited until he was certain the plane would be full before he attempted to make a reservation. He was jubilant when he learned he would not be able to get to Bora Bora for several days. To establish a record, he told his secretary to book him on the first available plane to Bora Bora which turned out to be three days later. Then he left his office immediately and turned off his cell phone in case a cancellation turned up. *After all,* he said to himself, *it's not a life or death situation. The poor fellow can't get any deader.*

Aeva's examination of the deceased revealed multiple bruises, trauma marks around his mouth, bruises on his face and body, and a severe laceration on the back of his head. She was not qualified to determine the cause of death, but the *Seadancer* logo stitched on the pocket of the bathrobe indicated that he was most likely a passenger from the ship. After loading the body on the police boat, she ordered her deputy to drop her off on the *Seadancer* and then take the body to the morgue.

When they arrived at the big cruise ship, she was piped aboard and escorted directly to Captain Warren's quarters.

CHAPTER SEVENTEEN

Roger Warren had played varsity football at the United States Naval Academy. During his years at the Academy he was always a team player, but he enjoyed his time alone more than most. His love of books, keeping of a serious diary and pursuit of his passion for building ancient sailing ship models didn't allow him much time to join in the folly of hanging out with his buddies with no particular purpose in mind except to drink as much as possible without becoming comatose. However, he rarely refused an invitation to quaff a few beers and watch a football game with his comrades.

Young women were attracted to him because he was gentle without being a wimp, self-assured without being macho, and genuinely curious about many of the subjects that interested them, such as theater and the visual arts. He dated whenever the opportunity presented itself, enjoyed casual sex, and shied away from romantic entanglements.

He thoroughly disliked Colonel Wilhelm Von Krupp, who taught military science. One morning, Colonel Von Krupp discovered that his prized vintage Volkswagen was parked on top of the administration building. Most of the members of the faculty were amused, but Von Krupp was furious and demanded that the perpetrators be caught and expelled from the Academy. A small group of known student pranksters were deemed to be the most likely suspects, and Von Krupp insisted that they be prosecuted. As soon as charges were officially made against them, Roger and his friends, the real culprits, stepped forward and acknowledged that they were responsible for committing the dirty deed. The student newspaper, *Eight Bells*, dubbed the miscreants "The Magicians", and ran a photograph of the Volkswagen stranded atop the four-story building. Everybody on campus, including the faculty and administration, chuckled until the national press learned of the event, and then all hell broke loose.

While guilt was established by the confessions of the defendants, punishment for the crime became a controversial issue because although the boys had accomplished the task in one night between midnight and dawn, it had taken the maintenance staff several days to locate a crane capable of removing the vehicle from the roof of the building, and then another few days to get it down on the ground and running again. In the meantime, once the national press picked up the story, every major television news network gave it continuing coverage. *TIME* magazine ran a cover with photos of the eight cadets and the caption "How did they do it?" *The New Yorker* ran an article entitled, "Homeland What?"

When news of the disciplinary hearing leaked out, the media frenzy began all over again. The nation was equally divided between those who wanted the boys to be thrown out of the Academy on the grounds that they didn't want their sons and daughters in the service taking orders from young men who had no respect for the law, and those who thought the incident was a classic example of American ingenuity and applauded the young men. Some decried the possibility of their expulsion and instead called for the resignation of the commandant of the Academy.

The case also struck a chord among America's veterans, who enjoyed seeing the noses of the high and mighty tweaked, but resented the fun that the foreign press was having at the expense of the United States military.

Annapolis, Maryland, the home of the Naval Academy, was soon overflowing with television and print journalists from around the world, but after a few days, during which hundreds of journalists and photographers disrupted the orderly conduct of the Academy's affairs, the commandant of the Academy directed all members of the press to leave the campus. Those who refused were forcibly removed. Thereafter, all members of the press were denied access to the campus until the American Civil Liberties Union got into the act and obtained a court order that allowed for continuing news coverage. The commandant also placed a gag order on the eight cadets, with the threat of summary expulsion if the order was violated. When the president of the United States was asked how he would decide the case he said, "If it were my decision to make, I think I'd punt." It was one of the few amusing remarks the president had made during his term of office. Most people understood that the question was a plant and that one of the speech writers in the White House had given him the answer.

"Ironsides" Collins, a visiting faculty member and retired admiral with a chest full of medals, was appointed chairman of the committee that would hear and determine the fate of the young men. On the day of the hearing, the courtroom was packed with carefully screened faculty and students, curious to learn how the prank could have been accomplished without detection.

Admiral Collins called the court-martial to order. After the charges were read, and the signed confessions were introduced in evidence against the defendants, Admiral Collins addressed the eight young men.

"Gentlemen, first I'm interested to know which one of you was the leader of this group of imbeciles who put their military careers in jeopardy for a few moments of glory in the press?"

Roger stood up. "I'm Cadet Roger Warren. It was my idea, sir," he said solemnly.

"Mr. Warren," the admiral asked, "would you be good enough to share with us why you decided to engage in such childish behavior that has brought ridicule upon this revered institution?"

"I considered, but did not anticipate its consequences. It was a stupid mistake that I deeply regret."

The admiral shuffled through the folders on his desk until he found the one labeled "Roger Warren." The boy's academic record was outstanding, except for a failing mark in military science taught by the owner of the celebrated Volkswagen. He glanced at the heading, EXTRACURRICULAR ACTIVITIES...Football Team Captain, Player of the Year award for performance in the Army-Navy game.

The admiral had seen that game. The teams were tied 21–21 with a few minutes left to play. Army had the ball on Navy's forty-yard line. The Army quarterback threw a Hail Mary pass that was intercepted by the Navy cornerback, Roger Warren, on his own eight-yard line. He ran the ball back ninety-two yards to win the game for Navy. The admiral, seated next to the commandant on the fifty-yard line, had stood up and cheered as loud and as long as the rest of the 30,000 hometown fans in the stadium, and hundreds of thousands of Navy men around the world.

A myriad of thoughts were racing through the admiral's mind. From a personal point of view the whole situation was ludicrous, but politically it was volatile. During some light-hearted banter within the past year, he had been asked by one of the Republican kingmakers if he might consider a run for the presidency. He hadn't taken the suggestion seriously. Nevertheless....

"I've heard enough," the admiral said. "Anyone else have any questions?" Before any other members of the court had a chance to think about what questions they might ask, the admiral continued, "If not, court's adjourned."

When they reconvened to make their decision, Admiral Collins opened the discussion.

"The way I see it, we've got some fine young men here who planned and carried out an extremely difficult mission without a flaw. It was a stupid prank that any one of us might have gotten mixed up in when we were their age, except what they did was brilliantly executed. My recommendation is that we meet three or four times over the next few months so that no one can accuse us of not taking the matter seriously. Then we make the following decision: First, we let the lads stew a bit and make them all take an extra semester before they can graduate. During that last semester the Warren kid must repeat and pass military science before he can graduate.

They'll all be required to take and pass the most difficult courses we teach here during their last semester. I want to see their butts dragging.

"Finally, if I'm not mistaken, my decision will allow Cadet Warren to play on the Navy team for an extra season." The Admiral leaned forward with his elbows on the table and his jaw thrust forward ever so slightly. "Does anyone have a problem with that?" he said, looking directly at each of the other members of the court.

There was complete silence. No one chose to challenge Old Ironsides Collins. And besides, they wanted to win next year's Army-Navy game just as much as the admiral did.

On the way out of the courtroom, one of the junior officers whispered to another, "I guess that's how you get to be an admiral in the U.S. Navy."

When Roger graduated from the Academy in 1993, with an "A" in military science, he signed up for a four-year hitch as an ensign in the Navy. He was assigned to the U.S.S. Constitution based in Hawaii. During that first hitch, he became familiar with every square mile of the Pacific Ocean and all the major islands within it. By 2001, he had been promoted to first lieutenant, and decided to make a career in the Navy. His ship was ordered to the Mediterranean in the beginning of the Iraq War. It was his first wartime experience, and he enthusiastically embraced his duties. However, he became disillusioned when it appeared that his commander-in-chief, President George W. Bush, knew, or should have known, that the reasons he gave to the American people for going to war in Iraq were flawed. What he found most disturbing was his president's unwillingness to acknowledge that a grave error had been made and that the young men and women in the military, as well as countless other innocent people in Iraq, were being killed for no purpose. Finally, he was distressed by President Bush's statement that he believed his decisions on behalf of the nation were being made with divine guidance. God Bless America!

By October, 2005, Roger had decided that although he loved his country and hated the international terrorists with as a great a passion as any man alive, he would be unable to carry out an order that could cause the death of innocent people. After sixteen years in the Navy (twenty years and six months if you counted his time at the Naval Academy) he resigned his commission.

Within one month he was hired by the Pacific Pearl Cruise Lines as first mate on the *Seadancer*, a mega-ton luxury liner carrying 1500 passengers throughout the South Pacific.

On April 12, 2008, the ship left Hawaii headed for Tahiti. When it was 100 kilometers from Papeete, the seaport in Tahiti, the captain of the *Seadancer* collapsed with a fatal heart attack and Roger was given command of the ship. The cruise company ordered Roger to complete the cruise with visits to several South Pacific islands, including a two-day stopover in Bora Bora.

"I'm sorry to interrupt you, sir," the first mate said, "but Lieutenant Fontein, the police chief from Bora Bora, advises me she has a matter of great urgency to discuss with you."

When Lieutenant Fontein was ushered into Captain Warren's spacious cabin, he was awed by the demeanor of the tall, attractive young woman who was introduced to him by his first mate. He stood up and extended his hand to her.

"Welcome aboard the *Seadancer*, Lieutenant. What stroke of good fortune brings you aboard my ship on this beautiful day in paradise?"

Aeva stepped forward, took Roger's hand briefly and bowed her head ever so slightly. "*Enchantée*, Captain. But I regret to tell you I come with very unhappy news. I believe one of your male passengers has been involved in a fatal accident—or worse, perhaps. A man has been found dead in our lagoon near your ship. We must determine the identity of the deceased and the circumstances regarding the cause of death."

"That's terrible!" Roger exclaimed, distressed by the news. Well, of course we will cooperate with you in every way possible."

Aeva sat stiffly on the chair offered to her and carefully recited what she had learned.

When she finished, Roger said, "So at this point I guess the first step is to try and find out who this unfortunate fellow is, if indeed he *is* one of my passengers."

Aeva bristled. "It is the most reasonable assumption at this point. The man was pulled out of the water near your ship wearing a *Seadancer* bathrobe. What more do you need, sir?"

"You never know," Roger said, smiling. Please, sit down. How about a cup of coffee?" *She is an excitable Frenchwoman with a little power and no brains,* he decided.

"I don't drink coffee, but I would like a cup of tea, if you don't mind." *He's a stupid, arrogant, macho American male,* she thought. "But if you don't have tea, a glass of ice water would be fine." She offered him her most engaging smile.

What is it with this lady? Roger asked himself. *One minute she's Dracula's Daughter and the next she's Madame Sugarbun.*

"You shall have both." Roger picked up the phone and gave the order to his personal steward. "Now, where were we?" he asked, settling back behind his desk.

"You must give me a list of your passengers and crew. I know that you require all passengers to be photographed before they come on board and at the same time you copy all pertinent information such as date of birth, residence and so forth from their passports. You will give me those photographs and the personal data for each passenger and crew member, forthwith. Then, you will arrange a roll call this afternoon so that we can ascertain if any one has "*jumped the ship*" as you call it. If our medical examiner finds that the cause of death involved foul play—in other words, if we have a murder on our hands—you must quarantine the ship until we can begin to sort things out. Now, with respect to—"

"Hold it, just hold it right there, Lieutenant This is an American ship under my command. You don't give the orders here, I do."

"*Mais non, monsieur Capitaine.* It is you who lack understanding of the situation here. First of all, you say this is an American ship, but she's flying a Panamanian flag. Next, this ship is in the waters of my country, and I'm the one who's in command here. If our medical examiner determines we have a homicide, and my investigation indicates that the murderer is most likely a passenger or crew member of this ship, we can not allow the *Seadancer* to leave our harbor until we complete our investigation and either arrest the perpetrator or determine that he or she is not on board this vessel."

Roger felt his gut begin to churn. "What the devil do you mean you won't *allow* the *Seadancer* to leave the harbor until your investigation is completed? Let me make my position perfectly clear, ma'am: We're scheduled to depart here in two days, at eight o'clock in the evening, and that's what we are going to do. I've got 1,500 guests on my ship who are scheduled to arrive in Hawaii at seven a.m. next Sunday morning in time to catch their planes back to America, or wherever, and I have another 1,500 people waiting to come aboard this ship within a few hours after we arrive, and there is nothing and no one who is going to stop us. So, Lieutenant Fontein, you have..." Roger glanced at his watch and made a quick calculation, "exactly fifty-three hours and seven minutes to identify your dead man and do whatever you have to do, but at 8:01 p.m. on the day after tomorrow, we are moving out! Now, if you will excuse me, I have a ton of work to do. I'll have my mate escort you off-ship."

Aeva stood up. "You're not going anywhere until we say so, Captain Warren." Aeva pulled her cell phone out of her pocket, and dialed her headquarters on shore.

"Who the hell do you think is going to stop us?"

"The French Navy, if need be," Aeva spit out the words, and then turned her back on Roger and walked to the far side of the room. "Sergeant Marera," she said, loudly and clearly, "send all officers who are presently on duty to the *Seadancer* immediately. *Le Capitaine ici est foux. Prennez-vous les armes.*"

"I am not *foux*...crazy...as you have just advised your subordinate, Lieutenant. Now, may I suggest that before we declare war, we sit down and rationally discuss how we might resolve this problem?" Roger said, with considerably more equanimity than he felt.

Aeva hesitated, realizing that perhaps she had been carried away by her personal need to be taken seriously and to be satisfied that the ship's captain was not resisting her commands because she was a woman. She took a few steps to the chair opposite Roger's desk, hesitated, and then sat down.

"What do you have in mind, Captain?"

Roger sighed inwardly.

CHAPTER EIGHTEEN

Aeva was born in a hovel in the town of Mahina on the north coast of Tahiti, a quarter of a mile from Matavai Bay where Captain Cook and the renowned *Bounty's* Captain Bligh landed. Her mother, Vaiora, danced in a folkloric show presented at the Tahiti Beachcomber Hotel every Saturday night. She was the star of the show and was paid five dollars for each performance.

Jacques Fontein, an aggressive young Frenchman who had a degree in hotel management from the University of Lausanne in Switzerland, joined the Beachcomber Hotel staff in 1968. He was taller than most men and held his own in a game of rugby. He was also strong-willed and ambitious, but he melted like sherbet in the sun at the first sight of Vaiora, and within a few months they became lovers.

A child was born on July 19, 1969, the day the first man landed on the moon. "She is our moon-child!" Vaiora exclaimed. In the language of Polynesia, the word for moon is *avae* and the word for child is *tamarii*. Vaiora took some letters from each and named her daughter Aevamari, but soon everyone just called her Aeva.

With her father's blue eyes and her mother's almond complexion she stole the hearts of all, including her taciturn father. Although Jacques acknowledged Aeva as his child, and gave her his name, as the passion between Avea's mother and Jacques began to diminish, the differences in their educational and cultural experiences became more and more problematic.

When Jacques returned to Tahiti after spending three months in Paris and learned that Vaiora was two months pregnant, their fragile romantic relationship ended. However, Jacques continued to maintain an interest in Aeva's welfare until he left Tahiti to become the manager of a small resort hotel in Fiji. Although he sent money to Vaiora to support the child, he began to ease both of them out of his life.

Jacques expected Fiji to be a duplication of his professional and social life in Tahiti. He quickly discovered that the cultural, social and business dynamics of the two islands were totally different. He was challenged by the differences and excited about the responsibilities he assumed as general manager of the small, upscale resort, and was certain he had made the right career move.

It was perhaps four months after he had left Tahiti that he felt something was missing, but he couldn't quite put his finger on the problem.

One evening, after all the guests had settled into their rooms and the hotel facilities had shut down for the night, he picked up a half-full bottle of French red wine, stuffed a wine glass in his pocket and took a stroll along the beach in the small cove where the hotel was located. He climbed up on a rock ledge and settled in. The dark sky was awash with a billion points of light, and as he pondered the infinitesimal role humans play in the drama of the universe, he tried again to determine the cause of his malaise.

I'm making more money than I could have imagined at this stage of my career, he thought. *The people here are delightful. My work is particularly rewarding, and there seems to be an endless supply of interesting, attractive women available in all sizes, shapes and colors. What in God's name is wrong with me?* At that moment a falling star streaked across the sky and he knew, he absolutely knew, the cause of his depression. He missed being a part of his daughter's life. It was as simple as that. He toasted his newfound wisdom and headed back to the hotel.

By the time Jacques approached Vaiora with the idea of having Aeva come and live with him in Fiji, she was again pregnant with her third child, and offered no objection to the plan. Aeva was five years old when her father enrolled her in the first grade of the English-speaking Fiji public school system.

Aeva was at the perfect age to acquire a third language, and excelled in her new school environment. Although she thoroughly enjoyed the easygoing lifestyle during the summer vacations she spent each year with her mother in Tahiti, by the time September rolled around she looked forward to the more structured, disciplined life that her father provided.

By the time she was thirteen, Jacques had purchased an ownership interest in the hotel he managed in Fiji and acquired an attractive young *parisienne* bride. Aeva had considerable difficulty in accepting Jacques' new wife, Simone, who was too young to understand how to deal with becoming the overnight mother of a teen-aged stepdaughter. The situation soon became intolerable for all of them. Jacques was devastated by the turn of events but was unable to find a solution for the problem. Teenagers are complex to begin with, and introducing into Aeva's life a competitive, self-absorbed, somewhat immature, attractive young Frenchwoman—who was only ten years older than Aeva herself—created a hostile and volatile domestic environment.

Finally, Aeva took the initiative and demanded that she be returned to her mother. Faced with a no-win situation, Jacques made arrangements for Aeva to fly back to Tahiti. They corresponded for a while but the letters became fewer and more formal, until finally they just ceased. In place of love, Jacques gave Aeva financial security and educational opportunities that satisfied both Aeva and her mother.

When Aeva completed college in Tahiti, which is comparable to high school in the United States, she enrolled in a two-year criminal justice program at the Lycée in Montpellier in southern France, and upon graduation she was immediately accepted as a law enforcement trainee in Tahiti.

She was bright, ambitious and aggressive—three character traits that quickly put her on a collision course with her male colleagues.

On her twenty-first birthday, the chief investigative officer in Papeete, the capital of French Polynesia, called her into his office.

"Come in, Aeva. Please sit down. Coffee?" he asked.

"Oui, merci." When the ritual was completed, he sat back and looked hard at the attractive young woman who was the cause of so much dissention among his men. *I don't understand it,* he said to himself. *Why won't she make it easy on herself by not excelling in everything? Why must she continually rub their male noses in their own stupidity?*

"I'm going to send you back to Paris, Aeva. You have performed exceptionally well as my assistant during the past two years. More than that, you have demonstrated courage and leadership qualities beyond my expectations. Ordinarily, I would have no problem in recommending that you be promoted to the rank of lieutenant, but if I were to pass over a number of your male colleagues who are either Tahitian or French, and have served many years longer than you have here in Tahiti, I would have a mutiny on my hands. The times are changing, which is as it should be, and I intend to make certain you are treated fairly. Therefore, you will receive further training in Paris as an investigator, and attain the rank of lieutenant in France before you return to Tahiti."

Aeva and Roger sat locked in each other's gaze. The seriousness of the situation on both sides had finally registered with each of them. When Roger didn't immediately reply, Aeva repeated the question.

"What did you have in mind, Captain?"

Roger started to speak, hesitated, stood up, and began to pace silently back and forth. Aeva remained immobile. She followed his movements out of the corner of her eye. Roger returned to his chair, picked up the silver letter opener on his desk, glanced briefly at Aeva, placed the letter opener carefully again on his desk, leaned back in his high-backed leather chair, stared at Aeva and said, "You see, Lieutenant, at first I honestly thought you were just trying to throw your weight around. And having spent sixteen years as an officer in the United States Navy, where occasionally, abuse of authority has been known to occur at all levels up to—and including, in my opinion, our commander-in-chief—I wasn't looking at the situation objectively. As a consequence, I sort of got off on the wrong foot." He hesitated. Aeva leaned forward, ever so slightly. She spoke slowly, deliberately, cautiously.

"I agree, and acknowledge that I am equally to blame. Initially I thought you were another arrogant American. By the time I realized I was mistaken about that, I had gotten myself in so deep, I didn't know how to gracefully withdraw. I am grateful for the opportunity to seek a reasonable solution to the dilemma we face, and I welcome your suggestions as to how we might go forward together."

My God, Roger thought. *This is not only an attractive lady, she's….*

Before Roger had collected his thoughts sufficiently to respond to Aeva's surprising candor, there was a knock on the door and his second-in-command burst into his quarters. "I beg your leave, Captain, but there are a half-dozen local police with pistols at the ready demanding to see the lieutenant. I swear they're acting as if they're prepared to blow up the ship if we don't produce her immediately."

Roger turned to Aeva. "Unfortunately it doesn't look as if I have time to tell you what I have in mind. Please trust me. It's your call, Lieutenant."

Aeva immediately stood up and marched out of the cabin.

While she was gone, Roger's first mate said, "Incidentally, Captain, I don't know everything that's going on, but shortly before the SWAT team arrived, a passenger by the name of Mrs. Margaux Santoros reported to us that she can't locate her husband on the ship. Apparently he wasn't feeling well during dinner and returned to his cabin. He usually leaves their cabin early every morning before his wife awakens, but they always meet for lunch. However today, he didn't show up for lunch and she hasn't been able to find him in his usual haunts.

"She's in her early thirties, I'd say, and I wasn't really paying careful attention to what she was saying, until I asked her to describe her husband, and she told me he's seventy-six years old, around five-foot five, weighs about 180 pounds, brown eyes, and silver hair. I figured I should report to you right away because it sure looks like we know who fell overboard last night. I was on my way up to see you when the Bora Bora Commandos showed up."

"Thanks, Kip. Here's a photo of the deceased that Lieutenant Fontein gave me. Check it out with Mrs. Santoros and call me immediately, one way or the other." At that moment, Aeva knocked. The officer excused himself and ushered her back into Roger's quarters.

When she and Roger were alone once again, she smiled apologetically and said, "The troops are under control. I must say, it was gratifying to know that my men were apparently prepared to protect me with their lives. I will never, ever forget this day. It has been both the most rewarding and the most humbling day of my life."

"You know what, Lieutenant? I know it's against your rules and mine to have a drink on duty, but I have a bottle of champagne that I've been saving for a special occasion and damned if I don't think there could never be a more appropriate occasion than avoiding the commencement of World War Three. Besides, it's French champagne…the very best." He stepped over to a wall cabinet, retrieved the bottle, opened it with a pop and a flourish, poured two glasses over ice and pronounced, "I offer a toast to reason and mutual respect."

Aeva picked up her glass, touched its rim to Roger's glass and pretended to take a sip. She would not destroy the solemnity of the occasion, nor did she intend to violate her commitment to refrain from consuming alcohol on duty. Roger had no such compunctions.

"Now, Lieutenant, let me offer my plan for your consideration. With 1500 passengers and approximately 500 crew members, there is no way in hell you can conduct a meaningful investigation in the short period of time available before we must depart this beautiful harbor. However, in order to prevent doing incalculable emotional and financial injury to my present passengers and the passengers waiting to come aboard in Hawaii, I absolutely must depart two days from now."

"I do understand the problem, Captain."

"On the other hand you have every legal right and obligation to protect the innocent and bring the guilty to justice. Soooo…here's my proposal. We have five days left on this cruise. I hereby invite you to travel with us and then fly back to Bora Bora from Hawaii at my company's expense if you haven't solved the problem before we leave here."

Aeva immediately thought of all of the reasons why she must reject the plan. She was about to protest when her inner voice said, *Wait, Aeva—don't jump so quickly. Hear him out. It's not such a crazy idea.*

Before Aeva had a chance to respond to Roger's offer he said that he would immediately make available to her the passports of every person on the vessel. Within twenty-four hours, she should have information from Interpol with respect to the criminal records of all the passengers and crew members aboard the *Seadancer*.

He told her that she could count on his cooperation to assist her in every way possible in the conduct of her investigation.

"Also, I believe we've discovered the identity of the victim based upon the photograph you gave me, and—as you assumed—he was indeed a passenger on my ship. I'm expecting confirmation momentarily.

"Finally," he said, "our next port of call is Fiji. After that we sail to Samoa, then return to Hawaii. We're scheduled to arrive in Fiji three days from now. Without a court order we have no legal right to prevent anyone from disembarking at that port; however, we'll honor your jurisdiction while we're moored here in French Polynesia." Aeva did not immediately reply.

"So what do you think of my proposal?" Roger asked.

Aeva hesitated. *Fiji. I haven't seen my father in so many years.* She felt that she was in the center of a maelstrom. She had no immediate superior with whom she could confer to obtain approval of this bizarre proposal. She could try to reach the attorney general for all of French Polynesia but to do so she would be required to reveal the fact that her superior, mentor, benefactor and dear friend was inappropriately incommunicado, in all probability in Paris visiting his mistress.

She was about to reply when the phone rang.

"Yes, Kip. So you have a positive identification. Do what you have to do for Mrs. Santoros. I'll check back with you later." Roger hung up the phone and turned back to Aeva. "We've positively identified the victim. He was a passenger on our ship, as you suggested," he smiled. "That information should make your task a little easier. So what do you say about joining us?"

"*Capitaine* Warren, I accept your thoughtful and generous offer."

"Good. Then it's settled. However there is one condition I must impose in order for our pact to take effect."

Aeva was startled. "What is your condition?" she asked warily.

"You will join me for dinner in my cabin this evening, and if it turns out that a homicide has indeed been committed on my ship, I'll personally help you find the culprit in whatever way I can."

"Culprit?"

"*Un homme mauvais.* The guilty man."

"Or—*la femme,* perhaps," Aeva laughed.

"*Oui, oui. Cherchez la femme.*" Roger smiled and poured himself another glass of champagne.

CHAPTER NINETEEN

By the time the *Seadancer* arrived in Fiji, Aeva had been able to obtain background information through Interpol for everyone on board the ship who had a criminal record, including Captain Roger Warren, who had pled guilty to disorderly conduct while attending the United States Naval Academy. Regrettably, the medical examiner stationed in Tahiti had not yet arrived on Bora Bora, but the local physician, a young Polynesian, had offered the opinion that until an autopsy was performed it would be impossible to determine the cause of death, although asphyxiation from drowning seemed to be the most likely finding. He reported that the victim had suffered a severe blow to his mouth. There were broken and missing teeth, and a metal dental bridge was bent out of shape from the blow. He had suffered a severe laceration to the back of his head that could have been caused by a fall, or perhaps he was struck by a heavy object.

"So what do we do now, Sherlock?" Roger asked Aeva, as they pored over the records that had been sent to her from Interpol.

"Sherlock? Who is Sherlock? A Shakespeare character—am I not correct?" Aeva asked.

"No, that's Shylock, the money lender. Sherlock Holmes is a famous literary detective."

"But of course. I am so stupid. I know about Sherlock Holmes. So if I am Sherlock, you must be Dr. Watson. That means you are my assistant and must do everything I say."

"As long as it doesn't have anything to do with running my ship, I guess I can handle that...for a while anyway," Roger smiled.

Roger arranged for Aeva to work in a small office adjacent to his quarters. Whenever his work schedule permitted it, they dined together briefly in the evening, and occasionally Roger would stop by her station where she would fill him in on her progress. She put in eighteen-hour days, interviewing possible witnesses and spending countless hours checking and cross-checking the data in the Interpol report, searching for suspects.

Shortly after midnight, as they approached the island of Fiji, Roger noticed the light spilling out under her office door and invited her into his cabin for a nightcap.

He eased back in his big leather chair and said, "Now, let's hear what you've been up to."

By the time she finished giving him her report, he had nodded off.

"Captain?" she said softly. He immediately opened one eye.

"I'm sorry, Lieutenant, I can't keep my eyes open."

"Are you growing old, Captain?" Aeva teased. He immediately sat up straight.

"Not a bit," he said. "Look at that spectacular moon peeking up over the horizon." Indeed, the moon had bathed the massive ship in silver shadows. He reached over and pulled Aeva to her feet.

"It's time to take a stroll around the deck of my mistress. Take our minds off sleuthing and enjoy each other's company for a bit before we turn in. By the way, have you ever seen Fiji before? The islands are beautiful, but we'll only hang there for a single day. There's not much to do but relax and enjoy the leisurely pace of the people and the island."

"I was hoping to take a few hours off tomorrow," Aeva said. "I have some personal business I would like to attend to while I'm there."

"Of course. Perhaps I could take you to lunch ashore. I know a lovely little restaurant where they serve the most delicious crab cakes you'll ever find, anywhere in the world."

"Do you mean, Cocina's?"

"That's exactly the place I mean. How do you know about Cocina's?"

"The fact is, I spent a number of my growing-up years on Fiji, and Cocina's is my father's restaurant," Aeva smiled.

"Damn! You're always surprising me. Why didn't you tell me about this before? You let me ramble on like a tour guide when you're the one who'll be guiding me. C'mon, let's amble around my ship so that I can act important while you fill me in on all the juicy tales of life on that fantasy island."

It was after one o'clock in the morning by the time they had completed their tour and Aeva had explained how it had come about that she had lived with her father on the island. When she came to the part about losing her father to another woman, she sighed.

"If only I had been a bit more mature," she said. "I haven't seen him in ten years. Can you believe how foolish that is? I still love him and I know he loves me, but...." she touched the corner of her eyes with her handkerchief. "Forgive me, please, I'm being so silly, but I just can't help it."

Roger put his arm around her shoulders and pulled her close. She looked up at him and smiled. "Thank you for being my friend, Captain," she said, squeezing his arm ever so gently.

CHAPTER TWENTY

When Aeva entered Cocina's shortly after it opened for the dinner crowd, she vacillated between joy and apprehension at the prospect of seeing her father for the first time in more than ten years. Roger followed behind her, standing quietly in the shadows. The dining room, constructed of bamboo beams and thatched roof, was wide open to receive the soft trade winds. Guests were beginning to trickle in as the late afternoon sun began to fade. Aeva approached the maitre d'. "Is Mr. Jacques Fontein at the restaurant this evening?" she asked.

"Yes, he is. Ordinarily, he doesn't come in until much later, but I saw him in the kitchen just a few moments ago. Who shall I say is asking for him?"

"Please tell him an old girlfriend wishes to say hello," she said, mischievously.

"That should bring him out in a hurry," the maitre d' laughed.

Aeva put on her sun glasses, adjusted her dress nervously, turned and smiled at Roger, who gave her a thumbs-up sign. A few minutes later, a balding, grey-haired gentleman approached Aeva. He was grinning when he reached out to take the hand she offered him.

"I'm Jacques Fontein. Frederique is playing a joke on me," he said. "I never in my life had such a beautiful young girlfriend. I am so sorry you have made a mistake, but may I treat you to a drink at the bar?"

"Of course. It is your daughter Aeva who told me to introduce myself that way and she was certain you would offer to buy me a drink," she laughed. She turned to Roger. "This is my friend Roger Warren. He is the captain of the *Seadancer*."

"Welcome, sir, it's an honor to have you as a guest at Cocina's. Please follow me." He took Aeva's arm and guided them to a secluded table with a view of the setting sun. He took the drink orders and said, "I want to hear everything about Aeva," and then he hurried off to the bar.

"How long do you intend to continue this charade?" Roger whispered.

"Don't you dare give me away," Aeva warned him. When Jacques returned with the drinks he pulled up a chair, held his drink aloft and said, "To Aeva."

"I'll drink to that," Aeva said. Roger raised his glass and smiled.

"Now tell me, young lady, how long have you known my daughter? How did you meet her? How is she? Please tell me first, how is she? I haven't seen her in five, no, it must be ten years."

"Shame on you," Aeva said. "She told me to tell you that she misses you and loves you very much."

Aeva's father looked away, took off his glasses and wiped his eyes with the back of his hand. Aeva put her hand lightly on her father's arm. "Daddy," she said softly. Her father immediately put his glasses back on, took her hand and turned it palm-side up. The small scar was still visible from the time the fishhook got caught in her hand when she was ten years old.

"Oh, my God," he gasped, throwing his arms around her and smothering her with kisses. "Aeva, Aeva, my darling Aeva," he cried.

It was almost midnight when they parted with a promise to have lunch together on board the *Seadancer* before the ship departed for Samoa. They solemnly vowed to never lose touch with each other again. Aeva's stepmother, Simone, joined them for lunch and she and Aeva discovered that it was perfectly reasonable for two women to love the same man. It also helped that Simone sported a few wrinkles, was a bit overweight and wasn't nearly as beautiful as Aeva remembered her.

CHAPTER TWENTY-ONE

Tiare, the daughter of Hoarai, was the best student in her class. Her teacher told her parents that one way or another, she must continue her education in France or the United States.

Tiare had awakened before anyone else in the family. It was her birthday—she would officially be a teenager. In her great-grandmother's time, you became eligible for marriage when you turned thirteen. Her family celebrated all the children's birthdays with a feast including real ice cream. Her mother would always fabricate a new tie-died *pareau* for the girls and a shirt for the boys. Hoarai, a gardener at one of the luxury hotels on the island, was well known for his wood carvings, and never forgot to carve something special for his children's birthdays—for the girls, a wooden comb, perhaps. *I already have three combs,* she thought, as she dreamed about the ice cream.

Hoarai had a small workshop behind the family's modest home and had carved a jewelry box for Tiare. He had to repair the pendant he had taken from the drowned man's hand, intending to put it in the box. First, he carefully repaired the broken chain by connecting the undamaged links. Then he meticulously removed the large diamond from the face of the pendant and replaced it with a wood carving he had made with Tiare's initials.

When Tiare had finished the last scoop of ice cream, Hoarai handed her his hand-carved jewelry box. "Happy Birthday" he said, softly.

"It is beautiful, Papa," she cried, throwing her arms around his neck and kissing him. "It will be my treasure box. I will lock it up so my ugly sister cannot steal all my jewels."

Everyone laughed, not only because Tiare didn't possess any jewels but also because her sister was acknowledged to be one of the most attractive young women on the island.

"So, open it up," Hoarai demanded.

Tiare fumbled with the box, but she couldn't remove the top. "It is stuck, Papa," she said, disappointment in her voice. She handed it gently to her father.

"*E aha*. Open, Aladdin," and in a flash he held the box up in the air in one hand and the lid in the other, for all to see. Then he put the two parts together and cried, "Close, Aladdin" and gave the box back to Tiare.

She took it carefully, "*E aha.* Open, Aladdin," she intoned, but she couldn't open the box.

Everyone laughed except Tiare. When Hoarai saw Tiare's face flush and realized she was about to cry, he pulled her onto his lap and whispered something in her ear. She held the box up in the air.

"*E aha.* Open, Aladdin," she said shyly. She removed the top held it up for everyone to see and then immediately closed the box again. Everyone in the family applauded. "Let us see," they begged. The box was passed all around but no one could open the box. They all laughed when the baby in the family marched around screaming "*E aha Din Din.*"

"Thank you Papa," Tiare beamed. "Now, no one can steal all my money because they can't open the box."

Donai, the oldest boy, said, "I will steal the whole box and open it with a hammer."

"You will have to hit me with the hammer first," Tiare answered, holding the box tightly to her chest.

Finally, when everyone including the baby had quieted down, Hoarai said to Tiare, "Why don't you look inside the box?"

"I did, Papa, the box is empty."

"Is that true?" Hoarai said, perplexed. "Let me see that wicked box." He opened the box and held it upside down, but nothing came out. "I told you so, Papa," Tiare laughed. Hoarai held the box up in the air again and shouted, "*E aha.* Where is the gift for Tiare, Aladdin?" He shrugged his shoulders and handed the box back to Tiare. She looked inside again and discovered a tiny package wrapped in tissue paper. "Papa, Papa, look," she screamed. The whole family craned forward to see as Tiare unwrapped the tissue paper. She gasped as she removed the exquisite gold chain and pendant with the letter "T" hand-carved in wood on the face of the pendant.

The next morning Tiare approached her father and asked him if he would walk with her down to the quiet cove below their home.

"But you are so serious, my child," he laughed. "Why are you so mysterious?" She just shrugged her shoulders until they had reached a spot where they couldn't be seen or heard. Then she invited him to sit beside her on a large rock overlooking the sea.

"Look, Papa," she said, handing him the gold pendant he had given her. "You see the initials engraved on the back? *MS/DS* engraved inside a heart. What does that mean?"

"Oh, ho," he smiled. "This is a very old pendant. It is what we call an antique and it is very valuable because it is so old, and now it has my darling Tiare's initial engraved on the front. Hoarai turned the pendant over in his hand. "See, on the back here are the initials of the lovers who owned it, maybe one hundred years ago—who knows? maybe more."

"But Papa, I know where you got it. I saw you take it from the hand of that old man who drowned in the bay." Hoarai looked to see if anyone could have heard what the child said. His face was flushed when he stammered, "That is true, my child, but if I had not caught it, it would have fallen to the bottom of the sea. I immediately thought of you and your birthday coming up and decided that it must be a gift from the gods, just for you, so I carved your initial in wood from the *Marumaru* tree and put it on the pendant and now it belongs to you. Don't you like it?"

"I love it, Papa, but it belongs to that man we caught."

"Tiare, my dear, that man is dead. I rescued it, and now it belongs to my darling daughter."

"No, it belongs to the man's daughter. You must give it back," Tiare begged, trying to hold back her tears.

"But I don't know who she is and if I ask the *gendarmes* they will question me and want to know why I didn't bring it to them sooner and then they will take it and sell it and keep the money!" Hoarai became angry.

"I'm sorry, Papa," Tiare wept. Hoarai picked her up.

"Now, now, Ma Petite" he said, rocking her back and forth in his arms.

"But it is so beautiful, Papa, and I love it, but…but…you always taught us that we must never take anything that doesn't belong to us, and…I'm so sorry, and now you hate me." She started to sob again. "No, no," he said, holding her tight and kissing her wet cheeks. "I am the one who is sorry. I was wrong and you are right. I must try to find who it belongs to."

Hoarai carried the pendant around in his pocket for several days, worrying about what he should do. He knew he must keep his promise to Tiare and return the pendant to its owner. *But who is the rightful owner of the diamond I removed?* he asked himself over and over. *I took it from the sea, like a fish, or perhaps more like an oyster that lives in the sea. When a man takes an oyster from the sea and finds a pearl inside the oyster, the pearl belongs to the man who found the oyster. Doesn't it follow that if I catch a man in the sea what he has in his hand belongs to me?* Hoarai asked the Goddess of Right and Wrong if that were not so.

Not so, cried the Goddess. *A man and an oyster are not the same. And an oyster shell and a gold pendant are not the same. And a diamond and a pearl are not the same.*

That is of course true, Hoarai said, and continued to try and solve the moral dilemma. After many hours of thought, Hoarai cried out, "*E aha*, I have found the answer."

The gods have created all things in the world and therefore all such things belong to all men. However, whatever a man makes with his own hands belongs to the man who makes it. A stone is only a stone until a man carves it into an arrowhead, and then it becomes his arrowhead. So it must be that since I did not make the gold chain and pendant they belong to the man who died in the sea, but the diamond was created by the gods and belongs to the man who finds it. Therefore I must remove from the pendant the carving I made with my own hands and return the gold chain and pendant to the man's family, but I am entitled to keep my carving and the diamond and sell the diamond so my Tiare may study in Paris.

Hoarai sang a happy song as he carried the gold chain and pendant to the office of the *gendarmerie*.

CHAPTER TWENTY-TWO

Roger wasn't able to join Aeva in her work until early evening when the *Seadancer* was well under way and headed back to Hawaii. They were again seated on opposite sides of Roger's desk. Aeva had narrowed the list of suspects down to four passengers and two crew members, all of whom had criminal records. Among the passengers, Luis Ramiriz was from Brooklyn, New York with a record for stealing jewelry, and the other three suspects were related to the victim, Toro Santoros.

"Let me see what you've got on my crew members," Roger asked, disturbed by the idea that any of his five hundred employees had serious criminal records.

"Yes, yes," he said, "as it happens I know both these boys, Rodriguez and Subente. They work in the officers' mess in the kitchen. They're very hard workers. I like them both. I think you can eliminate them immediately. Besides, you see, they were arrested but they weren't convicted. It's not fair, you know, just because—"

Aeva interrupted him, "*Mais oui, Capitaine*, I agree." She smiled. "I like it when you get upset because you care about your workers. That is a good thing, and I share your view that being charged with a crime should not be evidence of anything. Unfortunately, when we are faced with the task of finding a murderer, and we have no clues at all, we must begin with the basics. There are 1,500 passengers and 500 crew members to consider. We have to start somewhere."

"Of course you're right, and I suppose if I didn't happen to know them personally...." he sighed. "Incidentally, I'm afraid I don't understand why you've included members of Santoros' family among your initial suspects."

"That's also pretty basic police work," Aeva said, shuffling through the mass of documents that she had received from Interpol and the French Police Bureau, headquartered in Paris. "In France, about seventy-five percent of all homicides are committed by family members. The percentages are much different in the United States where it seems every citizen feels he must exercise his right to own a gun, including your bandits and gangsters who seem to insist on killing innocent people every day."

"Now, just a minute, Lieutenant, you have no right to...to...." Roger began to splutter, and Aeva laughed out loud.

"You are such a funny man, Captain. Are you sure you don't have any French forebears?"

"As a matter of fact, my grandmother's maiden name was Michelle Bessou," Roger chuckled.

Aeva clapped her hands. "Aha, I knew it," she smiled. "Now look at this." She handed Roger three documents identified with the Interpol logo. He studied them carefully as Aeva sat quietly, watching his reaction.

"Unbelievable. I mean...my God! Margaux McBride Santoros...grand larceny...the old man's son, Nicholas, alias Nicky Santoros, drugs and assault...and did you see this? The son-in-law, Del Renzo, is wanted in Sicily for attempted murder. What more do you need?"

"A lot more, Captain, but let me share with you what I learned from the victim's daughter, Xenia Del Renzo. She is the only member of this happy family group that wasn't celebrating the demise of Toro Santoros, who booked this cruise for his family when he thought he had only a short time to live. As it turned out he was right about that, but not in the way he expected. This is a tragic story, Roger, and I've got some interesting theories I want to pass by you. For instance, do you think $2,000,000 could motivate someone to kill an old man?"

"Are you kidding? In some parts of the world the price for murder is as little as $100. So who paid somebody $2,000,000 to murder old man Santoros?"

Aeva stood up and stared out the large window of Roger's luxurious cabin at the dark night sky. "Of course, Captain, if I knew the answer to that question, my quest would be over. But I believe I'm closing in on the—what did you call him? The culprit, no?"

"The culprit, yes." Roger replied, leaning forward, eager to hear Aeva's assessment of the situation.

She turned back to him, picked up a single piece of paper, and handed it to him. "Read this," she said. Roger took the document from her and held it up to the light. It was written in French. He turned to Aeva.

"My dear Lieutenant," he laughed, "I'm flattered that because I've memorized a few words like *bonjour, merci and voulez-vous* something with me, you believe that I'm able to read French. Unfortunately such is not the case. Would you care to translate it for me?"

Aeva retrieved the letter, studied it for a moment and answered. "This is a supplemental report I received this morning from Dr. René Bauvier. He is the head of the forensic laboratory in Paris. I think he was looking for an excuse to spend a few days on our beautiful island of Bora Bora to personally examine the body of the victim.

"His report indicates that he is uncertain about the cause of death because the victim's lungs were only partially filled with sea water. He explains that if Santoros had died from drowning they should have been totally filled with water. Or if he was dead before being tossed overboard, there wouldn't be any physiological mechanism to suck any water into the lungs because when the heart stops pumping blood, all muscles stop working including the lung action to suction in air and expel carbon dioxide. In other words there wouldn't be any process by which any sea water should have been introduced into the lungs.

"He is flying to Tahiti to conduct a more detailed examination and has asked me to have the body transported there as soon as possible."

There was a discreet knock on the door and the ship's steward entered the cabin. "Excuse me, sir," he said. "A cable marked 'URGENT' just arrived for Lieutenant Fontein."

"Thank you, Mr. McClellen, come right in." The steward crossed the room, gave the message to Aeva, and departed. Roger sat silently while Aeva read the cable to herself.

"No bad personal news, I trust?" Roger asked, when Aeva had finished reading the lengthy message.

"No," she smiled, "but a very interesting bit of evidence has just surfaced. Apparently, the local fisherman who discovered Santoros' body floating in the bay has delivered to my associate in Bora Bora a very valuable gold pendant that he found clenched in Santoros' hand when he pulled him into his boat. My man tells me the initials *MS* and *DS*, entwined within a heart, are engraved on the back of the pendant. He also tells me that a local jeweler has estimated the value of the chain and pendant at upwards of $5,000."

Roger whistled. "Five thousand dollars! The plot thickens, eh? But of course," he added, "whoever owned the pendant is the killer."

Aeva laughed. "You won't be offended if I suggest that you are a lovely man and a fine ship's captain, but your sleuthing skills need some sharpening up?"

"I'm not offended at all. I'm enjoying myself immensely since I have no responsibility in the matter whatsoever."

"You can't be too sure about that, my friend. How about a claim by the heirs of the deceased Mr. Santoros that your ship didn't provide adequate security to prevent one of your passengers from being pushed overboard while taking a leisurely stroll around the deck?"

"Ouch," Roger winced. "I know there are a number of lawyers among the passengers on board. They're all probably just waiting for us to enter American waters in Hawaii so that they can serve me with legal papers."

"Not to worry, sir, I am willing to personally testify as to the high standards of your security forces. Incidentally, Captain, you did instruct your staff to examine the luggage of all your passengers for hidden weapons, did you not?"

"Absolutely," Roger said. "Right now, I think I had best take a turn around the ship to make certain everything is running smoothly. Call me if there are any new developments."

Aeva started to laugh, but Roger was actually striding toward the cabin door. "*Arrête*. Stop," She commanded. "You can't leave me now. We arrive in Hawaii"—she glanced at her watch—"in less than twenty-four hours. You can't abandon me when we are so close to identifying the killer."

"I told you already whoever owned the gold chain is the culprit, but you won't listen to me. Obviously the old man tore the pendant from the neck of its owner as he was being strangled to death, thereby identifying his killer. Men don't usually wear $5,000 pendants, or carry them around in their hands just before they drown in the sea. Therefore, I suggest that you arrest Mrs. Santoros since she is the only female suspect. By the way, whose initials are engraved on the pendant?"

"Please come back and sit down, Captain. Although your powers of deduction are flawed, I find you to be extremely good company. Besides, we only have a few more hours before we reach our destination, and I would really like to spend them with you."

"My dear Lieutenant...Aeva...I do believe you are blushing, and as for me, I would be pleased beyond measure to spend the next twenty-four hours, and then some, in your company." Roger retraced his steps. Aeva stood up. They embraced.

Margaux couldn't bear being alone in her cabin where reminders of Toro pervaded their living quarters. She had last seen him when she had been escorted to a local hotel where his body was being preserved in the freezer because there wasn't a morgue on the island. The local custom was to bury the dead within twenty-four hours of death. She was asked to identify her husband as the man who had fallen overboard and drowned in the Bay of Povai. His face was bloated, his skin mottled and gray. His closed eyelids were swollen and puffy. She was now a multi millionaire, she was free, and all she could think about was Gary Samson thousands of miles away.

She had found a secluded corner on the upper deck where she was able to hide from Nick and Vittorio, who had accused her of causing Toro to commit suicide. She closed her eyes as she sat on the deck with her knees drawn up and her head resting on her arms. She dozed off and dreamed of Gary. When she awakened, she sent a cable back to America.

CHAPTER TWENTY-THREE

Gary's secretary knocked gently on his door. "Come in," he answered.

"Sorry to disturb you, Mr. Samson, but this cable just arrived and I thought it might be important."

"Thanks, Evelyn." Gary turned away from his computer, ripped open the envelope and began to read the message.

> *Dearest Gary, I am on the cruise ship,* Seadancer. *My husband Toro died two days ago. Our next stop is Fiji and then back to Hawaii and home. I have been dreaming about you ever since our meeting at the Bear Mountain Bridge and wishing I had handled the situation differently. I love you and want us to be together as soon as possible, but in my new life I must put my own needs aside and consider the great sadness that the death of my husband brings to his daughter Xenia. While I, too, am sad about Toro's passing, all I do is think about you and miss you. Can we meet three months from now and celebrate the Fourth of July together?*
>
> *If your answer is yes, I will be in the lobby of the Palmer House in Chicago at noon, July 4, 2008. Please e-mail me at SEADANCER@PEARLCRUISE.COM, Attention Margo McBride Santoros.*
>
> *Just send me a one word message, Yes or No.*
> *Love me Gary, please love me... Always,*
> *The girl from the Palmer House*

"Oh Lord," Gary rejoiced, giving a thumbs-up sign. "Evelyn, book me on an early morning flight to Chicago on July fourth and reserve the Executive Suite at the Palmer House for the Fourth of July."

When Evelyn left his office, he swiveled his chair back to the computer and sent an e-mail to Margaux on the *Seadancer.*

My Dear Margaux,
YES YES YES YES YES YES YES YES YES YES

CHAPTER TWENTY-FOUR

Roger and Aeva were seated at the captain's table in the main dining room on the *Seadancer*. It was the first time they had appeared together in a social situation on board the ship. Roger was wearing his dress blues.

Aeva was wearing an evening gown she had purchased at the ship's exclusive French dress shop. She had chosen an ivory, iridescent silk, off-the-shoulder reproduction of a gown designed by Ralph Lauren. It was in perfect contrast to her beige Tahitian skin and ink-black bobbed hair style. Just the appropriate amount of cleavage gave testimony to the exquisite body that was hidden beneath the gown. Roger stared in awe at her caterpiller-to-butterfly transformation. As the dinner guests passed by their table, neither of them escaped the inquisitive and appreciative eyes of both males and females. Their nods of approval were unanimous. Roger laughed quietly.

"Do you care to share whatever it is that you find so amusing?" Aeva asked, not without a bit of concern that she might be the cause. "Did I do a *faux pas*?"

"My dear, in English you don't *do* a foolish mistake, a *faux pas*, you *make* one. However, I assure you that you did neither. I was smiling because I guarantee that the gossip among the diners includes the riddle of where I've been hiding my Polynesian princess until the last day of the voyage. But I'm also positive that they'll sleep better than ever tonight because they'll deduce that if I've been smart enough to capture your affection, I must be smart enough to guide the *Seadancer* safely back to Hawaii."

"Do you realize, my dear Captain," Aeva responded, "that you have just delivered the longest speech you've made this whole week? Furthermore, as far as *do* or *make* a *faux pas* is concerned, in French the verb is "*faire*": *Je fais*—I do,—I make. If you Americans aren't able to communicate with each other without requiring two verbs where we who speak French are quite capable of understanding each other with the single verb *faire*, I say "*tant pis*", the meaning of which is *tough fooking bananas*."

Roger exploded with laughter to the delight of everyone in the dining room.

As dinner came to a close with the second cappuccino, Roger said quietly, "I have a proposition for you."

"That sounds naughty in French *and* English," Aeva quipped.

"Whatever has gotten into you tonight?" Roger teased.

"Can't you guess? I'm out of uniform. I am a half-French, half-Polynesian sex-starved unattached woman who believes that she is falling in love with a handsome, witty, very bright, kind, stodgy, old American." Aeva blushed...profusely.

Roger was speechless. He had been dreaming about making love to Aeva from the moment they had signed their truce. The thing that had stopped him was the fear of rejection. She had not given a word or sign of encouragement to indicate that she might welcome his attention.

At first he was stunned by her admission that she was attracted to him, as he was to her, and then in a flash of insight, he realized that she wasn't inviting him to be her guest for a one-night stand. She was offering something much more meaningful—a loving relationship. He knew that such a relationship was fraught with danger as well as incredible joy. He was ten years older than she; they were born and raised in two different cultures; they both considered their respective careers as an extremely important element in their lives; he was an agnostic, she was probably Catholic. And children...What about children? Her mother had been promiscuous; her father had put his love of a woman above his love of his child. Love demanded commitment. He had only known her for one week. How could she expect him to declare himself with so little evidence that what they felt was more than infatuation that could collapse when they re-entered the real world and discovered their incompatibility because of politics or religion or alcohol or drugs or physical abuse or stubbornness or bitchiness or deceit or money—God yes, money...and possessions and, and, and....

Aeva sat silently, instinctively realizing that Roger was taking her "call to love" seriously, and also understanding that if he politely declined her offer of a serious relationship she would be devastated. But she had already considered that possibility before she extended the invitation and she knew she was emotionally strong enough to deal with the consequences.

"My dearest Aeva," he began, "We have less than twenty-four hours before we each must go our separate ways. My schedule doesn't allow me to return to Bora Bora until three months from now. When I depart from Hawaii in two days, I take my ship through the Panama Canal to New York, and.... Anyway my proposition, got lost in the hurricane of my own thoughts born of the same kind of feelings you have expressed; but as you suggest, I am stodgy and conservative and fearful of being hurt. All of that is evidenced, I suppose, by the fact that I'm almost forty years old and I've never fallen in love before.

May I suggest, in keeping with my old-fashioned way of looking at life, that I take some of my vacation time and spend three days with you when *Seadancer* returns to Bora Bora in three months? I could have my first mate take over for those three days and we could escape to wherever you choose, just you and me. We would walk and talk and swim and drink and eat and make love—"

Aeva interrupted, "Must it be in that order?"

"No, you tease. We can…I don't know how you say it in French, but in English we say we can fook each other's brains out and not eat at all as far as I'm concerned."

Aeva said, "Sounds good to me, no matter what language we say it in. So I'll withdraw my invitation temporarily, and—"

"No, no, no. There's no way in hell I'll allow you to do that," Roger countered.

"Actually," Aeva replied, I think your way is better, because doing it your way I'm guaranteed three days alone with you. But—*three months?* My God, dear Roger, that sounds like an eternity. On the other hand if we go my way, it could be tonight and then I might never see you again."

"Nonsense, darling. I offer you a compromise. We'll go with your plan tonight and I swear, I swear, I swear, that I'll show up on your doorstep within one hour after the *Seadancer* enters the Bay of Povai ninety days from now."

Aeva held out her hand, "Shake," she said, "You've got yourself a deal, Captain. I'll meet you in your cabin in exactly two hours."

"Two hours?" Roger grumbled. "It's ten minutes past nine, now."

"So?" Aeva asked with eyebrows raised.

"So, nothing," Roger laughed. "I'll see you at eleven."

"Or thereabouts," she answered, then she slipped out of her chair and was gone.

When Aeva returned to her quarters the next morning, she quickly pulled out all of her worksheets and the memoranda that she had been exchanging with the FBI office in Hawaii. She had narrowed down the prospects from six to three. She then called Marty O'Rourke, the lead FBI investigator in Honolulu, and told him that she didn't know how to solve her major problem.

"Which is?" he asked.

"I don't have sufficient evidence to confirm my suspicions, and I don't have the time or the means to acquire it before we reach Hawaii. The suspects—Margaux Santoros, Nicholas Santoros, and Vittorio Del Renzo— should be arrested and held for questioning, which we can do under our law, but I understand from speaking with your assistant that in the U.S. you can't do that, even if I convince you that my suspicions are reasonable."

"Yeah, Tex explained all that to me, but I can tell you, Lieutenant, under our law there's more than one way to skin a cat."

"Skin a cat, sir?"

"To skin a cat is an American colloquialism."

"Colloquialism? I don't understand. *Merde.*"

"*I* understand *merde*, Lieutenant," O'Rourke laughed. "Let me start over. I've studied the file carefully and I must say you've done a superb job in the short time you had to consider 2,000 suspects. I'm also inclined to agree with your suspicions. Okay, here's the scenario—"

"I'm sorry, sir, "scenario?" Aeva asked.

"The picture...the story...my thoughts on how to solve the problem, okay?"

"Okay, I'm with you, now." Aeva said.

"Number one, they all live in Brooklyn, New York, and Margaux Santoros and Nicholas Santoros are on probation. We can arrest Nicholas Santoros for violation of probation because he didn't get permission from his probation officer to leave New York State. Vittorio Del Renzo is an illegal alien wanted in Sicily for attempted murder, so we can pick him up anytime we want and in our view, Margaux Santoros is the least likely to skip and the easiest to monitor."

"Now, the trick here is not to let these guys know they're suspects until they arrive in New York. We don't want to have to pay to have them transported back east, but we don't want them to escape either. I guarantee you that within twenty-four hours of the time they arrive back in Brooklyn, we'll have the two guys locked up, and we'll keep close tabs on the lady all the way. After that, the U.S. Attorney for the Southern District of New York will take over the case. What I'm telling you is...fuhgeddaboudit."

CHAPTER TWENTY-FIVE

Roger joined his first mate on the bridge, checked the chart, plotted his position and calculated they could expect to arrive in Hawaii at the end of the day.

When he had made a lunch date with Aeva she had promised to fill him in on the progress she was making in her investigation. Although they had only been apart since eight a.m., when he left her sleeping in his private quarters, he was excited about joining her at noon.

I know it's crazy, he said to himself, *but somehow I can't keep from smiling whenever I think about her, which seems to be most of the time.*

Having satisfied himself that all was as it should be, he left the bridge and headed back to his quarters where he arranged a special luncheon menu for himself and Aeva. Within moments after his arrival, Aeva knocked on his door.

"Come in, come in," he said. He shut the door and took her in his arms.

"I feel like a silly teenager," she said, laughing, as Roger led her over to the table set with an elegance normally reserved for royalty.

"There are all these important things I must do in the next two days," she said, "but I'm not able to concentrate on anything except the memory of what has happened to me in the last few days."

"You know, Aeva, I've read hundreds of accounts of what being *madly in love* is supposed to feel like, and as the years rolled by I concluded that it was all plain old malarkey, figments of the imagination of men and women authors skilled at telling tales that we all wanted to believe in. But Aeva, my dear, it's not a myth. I can personally attest to the fact that it exists and it's the most wonderful, beautiful experience of my life."

"Oh, my Captain, I'm so happy, I can't stop laughing...or, or crying." She pulled a handkerchief from her pocket, dabbed at her eyes and blew her nose. "*Mon Dieu,*" she wailed, "I am a basket case. Officers in the French Polynesian *gendarmerie* are not allowed to cry."

"To hell with the French police. We're in international waters and as long as I'm captain of this ship you laugh and cry whenever you damn well feel like it, and I'm overwhelmingly joyful to be the object of your laughter, but not your tears. Now you must sit down and celebrate our good fortune with me." Roger opened a bottle of champagne that was chilling in a silver bucket on the table, poured a glass and handed it to her.

She pushed his hand away. "I can't. I'm on duty."

"It seems to me we've been down this road before, Lieutenant. However, since I hold a superior rank, I command you to put aside your scruples and join me in celebration of our love."

"Aye, aye, sir, you leave me no choice."

When they finished lunch, Roger leaned back in his chair and said, "Now, you promised to tell me absolutely everything that's been happening behind my back with your investigation."

"Well, I have quite a bit more confusing information. Perhaps you will be able to see something in it that has escaped me. So, here goes....

"I realized that I had never identified the actual scene of the crime. I had been thinking all along that this is such a vast ship, I assumed it would be impossible to pinpoint the spot where Santoros was thrown into the sea, but then I thought, *If Santoros was wearing a bathrobe when he was thrown into the sea, isn't it logical that he would not have been wandering around the ship, but rather he would most likely have been in his cabin and I should immediately inspect the Santoros staterooms?*"

"That makes sense to me," Roger said.

"But I can't do that without a court order. Where am I going to find a judge to issue a search warrant?"

"Aeva my dear, on this ship, I am the law. If you want a search warrant you've got it. I'll sign whatever you need. The law all over the world is the same. The captain of a ship has the power and the duty to maintain law and order on his ship."

"Wonderful," Aeva exclaimed. "Why didn't I think of that earlier? But of course, up until now, I hadn't seriously considered that he might have been dumped over the rail from his private balcony."

"There you are. I told you all along his wife did it," Roger said, grinning triumphantly.

"Oh, my dear Captain, I must insist that you stick to steering this boat. Your powers of deduction are seriously flawed."

"How so?" he asked.

"Mr. Santoros weighed around 180 pounds. The balcony railing is three feet high. I would judge that Mrs. Santoros doesn't weigh more than 120 pounds maximum. It would be impossible."

"Hrumphh," he replied. "Nothing is impossible."

"Okay, improbable. Also, the housekeeper who serviced the Santoros suite told me that on the morning of Santoros' death she noticed that one of the chairs on the balcony was missing.

"And listen to this. Mrs. Santoros tells me that all of her jewelry has been stolen. She couldn't say exactly when because she says she was so upset by her husband's death she wasn't thinking about her jewelry until several days later. When she reported the theft to your security officer she told him it had to be one of the ship's employees who did it because her jewelry had been taken from her room safe, which was locked. She claims that altogether the value of her jewelry was in the neighborhood of seventy-five to one-hundred thousand dollars. What do you think of that?"

"I think she probably has insurance and has exaggerated her claim. What kind of a lady is she, anyhow?"

"She's extremely attractive, quite charming, and very bright."

"Hmmm, interesting."

"Actually, I understand she is a lawyer," Aeva said.

"That does it. Book her, I say."

When Aeva returned to Bora Bora, she personally interviewed the fisherman who had discovered Santoros' body. He told her that when he found the gold pendant clutched in Santoros' hand, he slipped it into his pocket and forgot about it, but later, when he showed it to his daughter, she suggested he should bring it to the police so they could return it to its rightful owner.

Aeva commended him and had him sign a detailed statement concerning the circumstances of his discovery. He said the tiny heart-shaped latch on the chain was locked when he removed it from the dead man's hand.

After writing up her report, she wrapped the chain and pendant securely and sent them to the forensic laboratory of the *Gendarmarie Nationale* in Paris.

CHAPTER TWENTY-SIX

Devon MacDonald entered his office on the morning of April 12, 2008, turned on his computer and checked his e-mail. The first message was from his buddy Marty O'Rourke, one of his classmates from Notre Dame the same years Devon had played tight end. O'Rourke had written to ask if Devon could use an ace investigator from May to October—the only months, he said, he would consider leaving his island paradise.

Devon made a note in his daily calendar to call Marty that afternoon. When they finally connected, Marty explained the situation in the Santoros matter.

"It's a weird case, Dev," he said. "There's a lot of circumstantial evidence, and applying the old MOM rule, Motivation, Opportunity and Means, we've got $2,000,000 of *motivation,* and plenty of *opportunity,* but the *means and* the cause of death is a puzzler."

"How so?" Devon asked.

"The wife of the victim, Dimitri Santoros, is included in the list of suspects, because she also gains big bucks as a result of her husband's death. That's where the $2,000,000 comes into play, but I really can't see the guy's wife overpowering her husband who was built like a bull. On the other hand, Mrs. Santoros is a disbarred lawyer. She was involved in some nasty business in your town about three or four years ago. Her maiden name was McBride."

"Not Margaux McBride?"

"Yeah, that's her name, spelled *M-a-r-g-a-u-x*. She spent a year in Richford Hills state prison, and then she married Dimitri Santoros shortly after she got out."

"I can't believe this. I was with the county D.A.'s office in, let me see…it must have been '04 or '05 when she was tried for grand larceny. I sat second chair through the whole trial. She's a piece of work, I'll tell you, but murder—I don't see it."

"I kind of figured it that way myself, Dev, but this lady investigator from Tahiti believed that she might have had something to do with it, since she gets two million bucks as a result of her husband's death," Marty said.

"Well, I guess my opinion is, that although she couldn't or wouldn't do it herself she could be mixed up in it somehow, and we should keep an eye on her."

CHAPTER TWENTY-SEVEN

Lieutenant William Garvey snapped the leash onto the collar of his son Dane's golden retriever. Garvey had given the honey-colored, three month-old puppy to his boy on his ninth birthday. Upon learning that the fancy, gaily colored dessert served at the birthday party was called "tortoni," that's the name the boy chose for his dog.

Every Sunday morning at eight-thirty, Lieutenant Garvey and Dane would take Tortoni to the park for an hour's run. On the way, Garvey would stop and pick up the Sunday paper, buy a box of dog treats for Tortoni and a surprise treat for Dane—maybe a kite or a comic book, or if he were feeling particularly magnanimous, a new baseball cap or an airplane kit. Despite the fact that the pressures of Garvey's job did not give him a great deal of time with his son, or perhaps *because* of it, the time they spent together was especially meaningful and rewarding to both of them. Except for dire emergencies, Garvey would not let anything interfere with their Sunday routine.

On this beautiful spring morning, Dane wanted to try out the new baseball glove he had also received for his birthday. At this time of year, their loyalties to the last vestiges of basketball began to give way to the excitement of the approaching professional baseball season. Garvey and his son were avid baseball fans and immersed themselves every Sunday in the adventures of the New York Yankees and the Mets. After their session in the park, they would return home to a feast of blueberry pancakes, sausage, and lots of Vermont maple syrup.

"Sit still, damn it," Garvey grumbled. He tried in vain to calm the dog, who was keyed up by the excitement of the outing.

At that moment, the phone rang, and Dane picked it up from the hall table. "Hello?" There was a moment's silence, and then Dane said forlornly, "It's for you, Dad."

"Who is it?"

"I'm not sure, but it sounds like Sergeant Schwartz."

"It better not be. He knows better than to call me on a Sunday morning," Garvey said, irritated. He handed the leash to the boy, picked up the phone and said gruffly, "Hello."

"Lieutenant? Sergeant Schwarz here."

"What the hell is it?" Garvey demanded impatiently. "Did someone shoot the Police Commissioner? Because it better not be anything less than that."

"Somebody killed somebody all right, Lieutenant, and that's why I'm calling you. The victim was a guy by the name of Dimitri Santoros. He's from Brooklyn. Have you ever heard of him?"

Garvey carried the phone over to the easy chair just inside the hall, and sat down. "If it's Toro Santoros, the Garbage King, I have. Give me the story."

"The U.S. Attorney's office just sent down a massive file involving a homicide that took place in Bora Bora."

"Is that in the South Bronx?"

"Not exactly, sir, it's an island near Tahiti, in the South Pacific."

"What the hell has that got to do with us?"

"Apparently the Santoros family was on a cruise ship near Bora Bora and Santoros got himself murdered."

"That sounds like the South Bronx to me," Garvey quipped.

"Anyway, Santoros' son and son-in-law are the principal suspects. The U.S. Attorney says he doesn't have enough evidence to hold them for the grand jury, but the son is in violation of his probation, and apparently the son-in-law is an illegal alien. He wants to keep them under lock and key until they can put the homicide case together."

"And it couldn't wait until Monday morning?"

"The thing is, Lieutenant, the suspects are expected to arrive on American Airlines at JFK tonight and he's concerned if they find out they're under investigation they might try to skip."

"Okay, pick them up at the airport."

"Yes, sir, I just wanted your okay. You've got the silver bars on your collar and I've only got stripes on my sleeve."

"You won't have them long, if you call me again on a Sunday morning, that's for sure."

"Gotcha, Lieutenant."

On Sunday evening when American Airlines Flight 986 from Los Angeles arrived at John F. Kennedy Airport in New York, Sergeant Schwartz and three deputies were waiting. The pilot had been alerted to have the flight attendant obtain physical descriptions of Vito and Nick. The pilot then relayed the information to the U.S. Attorney's office. Sergeant Schwartz matched that information against the passport photos on file for Nick and Vito. They were spotted easily as they exited from the plane. Each of them was turned aside by the deputies and handcuffed. The sergeant explained the situation to Xenia and Carmen, advising them that both men would be arraigned on Monday in the federal courthouse at Foley Square in Manhattan.

CHAPTER TWENTY-EIGHT

"Hello, pretty woman," Gary said, when Margaux rushed into his arms in the lobby of the Palmer House Hotel. After checking in at the front desk, Gary arranged to have their luggage sent up to their rooms. Then he returned to where Margaux was waiting in the lobby. When they entered the elevator, Gary put his arm around Margaux's shoulder and casually turned her back to the lighted sign above the door indicating the floor numbers. They were alone. She snuggled against him; he kissed her on the forehead and the tip of her nose. "My darling, my darling," she whispered. When the elevator stopped and the doors slid open, Margaux turned and gasped. "The penthouse! You crazy, wonderful man!"

Once the luggage was delivered, Gary went behind the ornate bar in the living room and opened a bottle of champagne. "We've got some important things to discuss," he said, as he poured the sparkling wine.

"Like what?" Margaux kicked off her shoes and curled up on the plush suede leather sofa. Gary handed her a glass of champagne. They clinked glasses.

Gary pulled up a chair opposite her, took a sip of his drink and looked directly at her, thoughtfully, and finally said, "I'm not insensitive to the fact that you've been a widow for only three months. Where do we go from here, sweetheart? It's your call."

"First, I want us to walk through the park like we did the last time we were here. Then I want to stroll again beside the lake with your arm around my shoulders, and we can smile at the people along the way who will recognize that we're lovers, and they'll smile back at us. I know that in the minds of many people—maybe all people—it's too soon after Toro's death for me to be seen in public with you, and to feel joyful, but I don't care what people think. I only care what you think."

"So, how do we deal with your husband's death? Do you believe that he accidentally fell overboard in the middle of the night?"

"The only other possibility I see is that somebody intentionally killed him. Since he had just received news that he had many healthy years ahead of him, there was no reason for him to take his own life. Do you think I'm shameless, insensitive, lacking in remorse?" she asked. "I wonder about such feelings myself…I—"

"Hold on," Gary interrupted. "It sounds as if you're about to embark on a guilt trip. Compassion should be reserved for the living and respect for the dead if they've earned it. I assume you'll continue to grieve for some period of time, that's as it should be and I'm sure you have memories that you'll always cherish but when there's nothing more to be done for someone you've loved and lost. You must move on."

CHAPTER TWENTY-NINE

On the morning following the arrest of Nicky and Vittorio, Xenia made an appointment to meet with Barney Rifkin.

"Xenia Santoros...excuse me, Del Renzo, is here to see you, Mr. Rifkin," Barney's secretary called over the intercom.

"Send her right in," Barney answered.

"Hello, Mr. Rifkin," Xenia said shyly, when she was ushered into his private office.

"Zee, please, come in, sit down. I haven't seen you in such a long time. I'm so sorry about your dad. We were friends since before you were born, and now, here you are, the mother of a little boy—Dimitri, Junior. Am I right?"

"Yes, sir, he'll be three years old next week and we call him Tri. It's spelled <u>t</u>-<u>r</u>-<u>i</u>, but pronounced *tree*."

"How can it be? I remember when Toro brought *you* into my office to show you off. I swear you couldn't have been more than a few months old. Of course he thought you were the most beautiful baby ever born. And here you are one of the most beautiful young women in Brooklyn," he laughed.

"I don't feel beautiful, Mr. Rifkin. I feel so terribly sad about my father, and now I'm facing this awful business of my brother and my husband in jail, suspects in his murder."

Barney put his arm around her shoulders and gave her his handkerchief. When she finally gained control of herself, Barney was shocked to see that her makeup had been wiped away with her tears. There were deep shadows under both eyes, but her left eye and cheek had obviously been badly bruised.

"My dear Xenia, whatever happened to you? Please tell me. I promised your father that if anything ever happened to him, I'd take care of you."

Between sobs, Xenia blurted out the whole depressing story: Vito's gambling, his messing with other women and his physical abuse. When her father discovered that she was borrowing money from him to pay for Vito's extravagances, he refused to give her any more money. That was when Vito started to steal from her, including all the jewelry she had inherited from her mother.

"We've mortgaged the home that Daddy gave us free and clear. My marriage is a disaster. I can't stand the sight of Vito, and now, if it's true what they say—that Nick and Vito are somehow involved in the death of my father—I hope they both go to the electric chair."

"Now, now, Zee. Don't jump to conclusions so quickly, unless you know something I don't know, and if you do…" Barney said, pulling a yellow legal pad out of the top drawer of his desk, "I want you to tell me everything you know. I talked to both of them in jail less than an hour ago as you asked, and they both absolutely deny that they were involved in your father's death in any way. Besides…" Barney hesitated a moment and looked at Xenia, who continued to stare at the floor. "I just realized that I may not be able to represent either one of them." Xenia immediately looked up.

"Why not? I mean if they're innocent, like you said, why wouldn't you defend them? Is it because they don't have any money? I mean, even though I hate Vito, he *is* the father of my child, and since I'm inheriting part of Daddy's estate, I would pay you to defend him."

"No, no, dear, it doesn't have anything to do with money. It's a pretty complicated business. You see, there's a conflict of interest problem that prevents me from—"

Barney's secretary interrupted him. "Mr. MacDonald is on line two, Mr. Rifkin. He says it's very important."

Barney immediately picked up the phone.

"Yes, Mac, what's up?"

"On this Santoros case. I've decided not to present anything to Judge Kershner on Wednesday."

Barney smiled and nodded to Xenia. "I figured you didn't have anything much or you would have taken it directly to the grand jury. I couldn't understand why you arrested them in the first place."

"I didn't realize until I had a chance to review the file this morning that Santoros is on probation and is in violation for leaving the state without the permission of his probation officer, and Del Renzo, or I guess his real name is Calfano—Luigi Calfano—is an illegal alien. So I'm withdrawing the charges involving the death of Toro Santoros and holding young Santoros for violating probation, and Immigration and Customs Enforcement has issued a warrant against Del Renzo or Calfano, whatever his name is, so neither one of them is going anywhere for the time being. They won't be released until those matters are resolved. Maybe you and I can sort things out before then. I just thought I'd clue you in so you wouldn't have to burn the midnight oil preparing for a preliminary hearing on the murder charge."

"Yeah, thanks, Mac." Barney's expression was that of a man who had just swallowed a bite of apple and discovered only half a worm in the remaining part. When he placed the receiver back in its cradle, Xenia looked at him, perplexed. Barney pushed the button on his intercom.

"Hold all my calls," he said to his secretary. "Xenia and I have a lot to talk about."

Lieutenant Bill Garvey and Sergeant Schwartz had been summoned to the United States Attorney's office at Foley Square in Manhattan.

When they entered the car, Garvey directed the young officer who was chauffeuring them "to the federal courthouse—the Moynihan Building, downtown—500 Pearl Street."

"So how come we have the honor of meeting with the goody-goody Mr. MacDonald, the illustrious U.S. Attorney for the Southern District of New York?" Sergeant Schwartz asked.

"Hey, shmuck, knock off the wise-ass remarks. Devon's a first-class guy, and a damn good prosecuting attorney. He told me to bring my best investigator along, but since she wasn't available, I decided to bring you instead."

"You're a funny man, Chief, but I must tell you that I'll be taking over MacDonald's office as soon as I graduate from law school. I can't wait to be able to summon you to my office whenever I want to, Lieutenant."

"God help us all if that should ever happen. But if by some miracle you pass the bar exam, and by an even bigger miracle you get hired by the U.S. Attorney's office, you can bet your sweet ass I would resign from the force before I would allow such an injustice to occur. Anyway, I'm due to retire in nine years and you'll probably still be in law school."

"I don't think you understand, Lieutenant. I joined the NYPD when I received my Associate's degree in criminal justice in 1988 from CCNY. I started out as a patrolman. You offered me a better job with higher pay and better benefits a couple years ago. And I'm going to graduate next year from NYU Law School after attending night school for almost six years. My wife, the city of New York, the federal government, the state government, an NYU scholarship and a student loan will be paying for my last year in law school. I'm thirty-three years old and I'm planning to be number one in my class this year. All the big law firms are going to be bidding for me, but I intend to work for peanuts and serve my country instead of going to work on Wall Street with a starting salary of $150,000 a year."

Garvey leaned forward and spoke to the driver. "I hope you haven't been listening to the bull crap Schwartz has been throwing around back here. You've only been with us for a few months and I don't want you to be corrupted by the Sergeant."

"Oh no, sir," the young officer said. "I've heard a lot about Sergeant Schwartz already."

"I'll bet you have." Garvey said.

The Daniel Patrick Moynihan United States Courthouse was named in honor or the beloved senator from New York who was born in 1927 and died in 2003 after a distinguished career in the United States Senate.

George F. Will, a conservative columnist, once commented that Moynihan wrote nineteen books, which was more than most senators have read.

"Of course, you realize, Schwartz, that Senator Moynihan and I are both Irish."

"My mother is Irish," Schwartz responded.

"That doesn't count," Garvey countered.

"Do you know what the senator said when he learned of President Kennedy's assassination?" Schwartz asked.

"This better not be a joke, Sergeant."

"He said, 'I don't think there's any point in being Irish if you don't know that the world is going to break your heart eventually.' Senator Moynihan is one of my heroes."

"Well, we finally agree on something," Garvey said as their car pulled up to the curb in front of the magnificent courthouse building. Vying for the last word, Schwartz replied, "I'd bet my life that if Moynihan were alive today he'd be supporting Obama for president." The young officer stifled his laugh when he looked in the rear view mirror and saw Lieutenant Garvey's reaction.

When Garvey and Schwartz were ushered into Devon MacDonald's huge office, Schwartz whistled softly.

"Good morning." MacDonald remained seated behind his massive desk, but smiled and held out his hand to the two officers. "Good to meet you Sergeant...Schwartz is it?"

"Yes sir, Isadore Schwartz. But I never much liked the nickname 'Izzy', so when I attained the rank of sergeant I insisted that my subordinates just call me 'Sarge'. You can call me whatever you like, sir." MacDonald laughed. "That reminds me of something my father always said: 'Call me whatever you want but don't forget to call me to dinner.'" Lieutenant Garvey's chuckle was obligatory.

"Take a seat, gentlemen, and we'll get this show on the road."

Schwartz glanced discreetly around the office with its spectacular view of the Manhattan skyline. A portrait of President George W. Bush hung on the wall behind MacDonald's desk. It seemed to Schwartz that Bush was staring at him. He turned his chair away and looked again. Bush was still staring at him.

MacDonald had a stack of files on his desk. He riffled through them and selected one from the pile. "Santoros" was printed in bold letters on the outside of the file.

"My buddy, Marty O'Rourke, sent me this one. There are a number of fascinating legal issues that need to be addressed, beginning with which court has jurisdiction of the case.

"Marty is the lead investigator in the FBI office in Honolulu. He's been in touch with the chief of police for the island of Bora Bora, a lady by the name of Fontein, who appears to have done a remarkable job. Marty has also been working directly with the forensic lab people in Paris because Bora Bora is one of the islands of French Polynesia."

He handed each of them copies of the massive file and suggested they move into the conference room next to his office.

When MacDonald stood up, Schwartz marveled to himself, *Holy shit! he's got to be at least six-foot two. And he's got it all. He's tall, distinguished-looking, personable, probably went to Harvard or Yale. I'm sure he lives in Westchester County, has a gorgeous wife and three kids, and plays golf on the weekends at the country club. Since he spells his name MacDonald and not McDonald, I'm sure he's Scotch and not Irish, attends the Episcopal church every Sunday morning and will be running for Congress one of these days soon.*

Now, take my situation. I'm going to get a law degree ten years after everybody else, I live in the Bronx and I'm short, fat, and Jewish. It just ain't fair.

After they had seated themselves around the highly polished mahogany table in their plush swivel chairs, MacDonald said, "Let's start with page 236, right on top, there." MacDonald spread the contents of the file neatly on the table and picked up a large tabbed portfolio. "Here's the way I see it. The Bora Bora lady narrowed the primary suspects down to the two palookas you picked up at the airport, Nick Santoros and Luigi Calfano, alias Vittorio Del Renzo.

"There's another new piece of information from Lieutenant Fontein that I see here in the front of her report, that just arrived. Are you ready, guys? Here's the kicker. She learned a few days ago that the fisherman who found the body recently turned a valuable gold chain and pendant in to the police claiming it was clutched in Santoros' hand when he dragged the body into his boat AND…now get this!…the necklace belonged to Santoros' wife."

"Holy shhh," Schwartz exclaimed.

"But," MacDonald continued, "the chain wasn't broken."

"Now you're putting us on, right?" Schwartz chuckled.

"And," MacDonald laughed, "Lieutenant Fontein immediately

rushed the pendant and chain to Paris, and they were able to lift a fingerprint off the back of the pendant and it's not Margaux Santoros', and it's not Nick Santoros', and it's not Del Renzo's. We know that because we have all of their prints in our data bank."

"Mr. MacDonald," Schwartz, asked, "are you sure you didn't steal this scenario from one of those crime shows on TV?"

"I haven't finished yet, Sergeant Schwartz. The fingerprint may belong to a convicted Cuban jewel thief by the name of Luis Ramiriz, who was also a passenger on board the ship along with the victim." MacDonald smiled.

"Unbelievable," Garvey said.

"You gotta be shittin' me." Sergeant Schwartz said, so softly no one could hear him.

"Now, I understand that a detailed autopsy and forensic report will be forthcoming from the French, but like all of us in this business, they are overworked and they tell me that it could take some time to complete it. Until we've got sufficient evidence to convince a grand jury to indict one or more of these yahoos, the ball is in your court, Bill," MacDonald smiled benignly at Bill Garvey.

This is one of those rare occasions when I'm glad I'm only a sergeant, Schwartz thought.

Carmen Santoros sat across from Nick in the visitors' cubicle at the Twenty-ninth Street federal prison in Brooklyn, New York. They could see each other through the glass partition but they couldn't touch, and they had to lean up close to the perforations in the glass to be able to communicate. Carmen had tried her best not to cry when Nick came into the cubicle wearing a prisoner's orange jumpsuit.

Before she had a chance to say a word, Nick growled, "You gotta get me out of here, Carmen. It's no big deal. The judge has set bail at fifty thousand dollars because Rifkin tells me they figure there's no way I can raise that kind of money. They don't know that with the old man dead I'm entitled to fifty percent of the estate, which is gotta be worth a couple of million, after the Bitch's one-third interest is deducted."

Carmen put her hand up against the glass, instinctively trying to touch her husband. "What do you want me to do, Honey? I don't even have money to buy food for me and the kids. You never told me anything. You never shared anything with me about money and—"

"Jesus Christ, Carm, stop bitchin' and help get me out of here. Listen to me." Nick put his lips up to the glass and whispered. "There's about five thousand bucks under my shorts in my gym bag in the bedroom closet. That'll take care of you and the kids for a while, but you gotta go see Rifkin right away and find out how to get my inheritance so I can get the fuck out of here. They ain't got nothin' on me except leavin' the country without my probation officer's permission. They're just stallin' to try and pin Pop's murder on me, which is bullshit!"

Nick and Carmen talked as long as they were allowed. When she left the prison, she understood clearly that Barney Rifkin had to do whatever was necessary in order to get Nick released on bail. It took almost a week before Barney could meet with her. He told her that Toro's will was in his safe, and he wanted to meet with her and Xenia to discuss the administration of the estate.

Carmen had never been to Barney Rifkin's office before. She was concerned about how she should dress, and finally decided she would wear one of the dresses she usually wore to Mass. She was disappointed when his reception area turned out to look like her dentist's waiting room. When Zee arrived, she stood up to greet her. Toro and Zee were always more kind to her than her own husband. She knew Toro had made Nick marry her when she got pregnant. And she was certain that Toro had cared more for her kids than Nick did.

"Mr. Rifkin can see you now, ladies," the receptionist said, and led them back to the attorney's office. Barney's office was more in keeping with what Carmen had expected: dark mahogany furniture, heavy velvet burgundy drapes, bookshelves crammed with leather-bound law books and a genuine oriental rug on the floor. "Good afternoon, Xenia...Mrs. Santoros. Please come in. Here," he said, indicating two leather chairs facing his antique desk. Would either of you care for a cup of tea?"

"Sounds good to me," Zee said.

"Me too," Carmen seconded.

When the ritual was completed, Barney went to an old-fashioned safe, fiddled with the dial and withdrew a large manila folder. He returned to his desk, placed it in front of him and ceremoniously withdrew an envelope with the words, LAST WILL AND TESTAMENT OF DIMITRI SANTOROS embossed on its face. He picked up a silver letter opener and carefully slit it open. He glanced briefly at the contents of the multi-paged document, placed it back on his desk and looked up at Zee and Carmen.

"Ordinarily, of course, we'd arrange the reading of the will when all the members of the family could be present, but I understand that Nick wants us to proceed without him. Is that right, Mrs. Santoros?"

Carmen nodded and said "Yeah, he asked me to sort of represent him so's things can move along as fast as possible."

"Good," Barney continued, "and Margaux knows that all of her rights are described in the prenuptial agreement that she and Toro made prior to their marriage, so when I checked with her she acknowledged there isn't any reason for her to be here, either. I'll make copies of the will and the agreement for each of you to study at your leisure, but for now, in view of the length of the document, I thought I might just share with you the highlights and answer your questions—perhaps explain how the probate of the will and the administration of the estate process works.

"To probate a will means to offer it to the judge of the surrogate court for his approval. Not as to its contents, of course," he said, "but the judge must be satisfied that it is indeed Toro's last will and testament, and that anyone who would have an interest in his estate if there were no will has been properly notified about his rights and so forth."

Good Lord, Carmen thought, *Isn't the old pooper ever going to get around to telling us what the damn will says?*

"The law jealously guards the wishes of the deceased, so everything must go by the book. In this case, Xenia, you've been named executor of your father's will. That means he's entrusted to you the obligation of carrying out its terms and conditions, paying the expenses and so forth. You must sign a petition asking the surrogate judge to issue an order authorizing you to proceed with the administration of the estate. He has also directed that you engage my services as attorney for his estate. As you know, your dand and I go back a long way together with mutual affection and respect."

Now, Mrs. Santoros, Nick must sign a *waiver and consent* document indicating that he waives his right to object to the authenticity of the will and he consents to its probate. Ordinarily, it would also require a consent from Margaux, but, as I said, since she signed that prenuptial agreement, she waived all of her rights as the surviving spouse in exchange for a lump sum payment."

"How much?" Carmen demanded.

"In round numbers I'd say about $2,000,000." Barney said.

"Holy sheeee. Two million bucks to the Bbb...to Margaux?" Carmen exclaimed. "What about Nicky? What's he going to get?"

"It's pretty complicated, Carmen—may I call you Carmen? I'm trying to simplify it as best I can. As I was saying—"

Carmen interrupted him again. "All I want to know, Mr. Rifkin—I guess I should say, all that Nicky wants to know is how much is he going to get, and how soon is he going to get it? That seems like a simple question to me."

Barney pushed his horn-rimmed glasses down to the end of his bulbous nose, propped his elbows on his desk and cupped his double chin in both hands. He looked directly at Carmen over the top of his glasses and growled, "If you want a simple answer to that question,

Mrs. Santoros, the answer is that Nicholas isn't going to receive a penny under his father's will. Toro put everything in trust for the benefit of you and your children and for the benefit of Zee and her child. Does that answer your question?"

"How can that be? Nicky told me that he's entitled to half of the estate. He and Zee are supposed to split the estate fifty-fifty."

For a moment, Barney realized he was in danger of losing his temper, which he knew could only make matters worse. He leaned back in his high leather-backed chair, took a deep breath and said, "I'm sure it will be a great disappointment to your husband, Carmen, but you must remember that Nicholas was a bit of a disappointment to his father."

"But Nicky is his son, he's entitled...."

"No, Mrs. Santoros, Nicholas isn't *entitled* to anything. Toro had every legal right to do whatever he wished with his money. He could have given it all to the Salvation Army, if he chose. What he actually did was to provide for you and your children in a most generous way. He's directed that one third of his net estate—which I estimate should amount to about $2,000,000—be placed in trust for you and your children no matter what Nicholas says or does. He can live with you and the children in a house owned by the trustee and he can share the food you buy and put on the table. I'm also sure the trustee will be willing to buy a car for you that your husband can drive, but not sell. Do you understand, Carmen?"

"If Nicky were here he wouldn't put up with this shit," Carmen cursed under her breath.

"What did you say?" Barney demanded.

Carmen looked straight at him. "Nothing," she replied. "So what's next?"

"First of all," Barney began again, pronouncing each word slowly and distinctly, "the will directs the executor—" he paused and looked up at Xenia, "that's you, Zee—to pay all of the funeral expenses and so forth." Barney noticed Carmen looking at her watch. "To make a long story short, in addition to the gifts I just mentioned, Toro created two trusts: one for you and your children, Mrs. Santoros, as I explained earlier, and the same for you and your son, Zee. I think you told me the other day that he's three years old. Am I correct?"

"He'll be three years old in November, and would you believe, I began my sophomore year at Columbia University last month."

"Congratulations, Xenia. Toro was very proud of your accomplishments, you know. He told me on more than one occasion that he knew how difficult it was for you to be a mother and at the same time get the grades at the University that—"

"My boy Nick Jr. is two and the baby is six months," Carmen interrupted. And I know all about Zee's kid. What I want to know, Mr. Attorney, is when can we get the $2,000,000?"

Zee exclaimed, "I can't even imagine how much money that is."

Carmen spoke up. "Nicky said his father told him that his estate was worth around $10,000,000. Where did the rest of the money go?"

Barney was seething, but had regained control of his anger. He picked up the estate portfolio from the top of his desk, flipped though a number of pages and said, "I'll make a copy of all this for you and Nicholas, Mrs. Santoros. As you'll see, in general terms, the gross estate has an estimated value of around $7,000,000, but then, of course, the estate has to pay off its debts, taxes and other obligations first."

"Seven million? How can that be if Toro told my husband it was worth ten million?"

"Well, it probably *was* worth that amount at one time. In fact until a few months ago it could have been worth more than that, but shortly after he married Margaux, Toro decided to put a substantial amount of his investment portfolio into stock. It seemed like the right thing to do at the time, because while Margaux was managing his affairs, she had doubled the value of his investments, and I would say that six months before his death the value of the estate could easily have been as much as $10,000,000 or more; however, as I'm sure you both know, the stock market began to go to hell in a hand basket a month ago, and it's still declining as we sit here today. That's why it's so important that we get this will probated as soon as possible, so we can try to stop the bleeding. You see, until Zee is appointed executor, there isn't anyone who's authorized to sell the stocks that keep diminishing in value every day, it seems. Right now, one third of the estate might be even less than $2,000,000."

"Oh no," Carmen exclaimed. "But wait a minute. You say there's $7,000,000 in the estate, now. I'm no mathematical genius, but one third of seven is more, not less than $2,000,000."

Barney picked up his accounting report and began to punch numbers into the calculator on his desk. "As I said, first we must pay the estate taxes and administration expenses. That leaves us with $6,000,000 and after Margaux is paid her one-third, that leaves $4,000,000 to be divided between you and Zee."

"Why can't you break that agreement with the...Margaux?" Carmen demanded. "Nicky says she's not supposed to get a penny if she committed, like, adultery, and Nicky says he's sure that she's been screwing around. I mean even me and Zee seen her hangin' around with some guy by the name of Luis we met at a bar on the ship. We was all together. Me and Zee was right there in the bar and seen it all. Ain't that right, Zee?" Carmen didn't wait for Zee's answer. She continued, "I seen her with him a couple more times after that. I even seen them two eatin' lunch together in Tahiti."

"Nicholas told me about that when I went to see him in jail, but I must tell you, Carmen, suspicions and proof are two different things. Of course, if there is evidence that Margaux committed adultery before Toro died, she isn't entitled to anything."

"Nicky told me you'd say something like that, but he wants to know how come they can hold *him* in jail but they can't hold the Bitch—sorry, Mr. Rifkin, but them is Nicky's words, not mine. How come?"

"One thing at a time, please, Carmen."

"Just let me make sure I've got this straight, Mr. Rifkin. If the executor of the estate—that's you, Zee...if you refuse to pay Margaux there'll be an extra two million dollars to split between you and me. Just don't pay her, Zee. Make her prove she wasn't screwin' around."

"Actually, Carmen, you raise a very interesting legal point about who has the burden of proof in the matter. Does the executor have to prove Margaux committed adultery or does Margaux have to prove she didn't?" Barney smiled. "Let me see exactly what the prenuptial agreement says." He rummaged through his file and extracted a copy of the agreement. "Okay, here's what it says: '*In the event the husband shall predecease the wife...the estate...shall pay to the wife the sum of $2,000,000 in full settlement of all spousal claims...HOWEVER, in the event the wife shall commit adultery at any time during the first four years of the marriage of the parties, the wife shall be paid $100 in full settlement of all claims against Dimitri Santoros or his estate.*'"

"So what's the answer, Mr. Rifkin?" Zee asked. "What am I supposed to do?"

Barney leaned back in his massive high-backed chair and closed his eyes; after a few moments of total silence, he said, "The way I see it, the agreement uses the word '*shall*'...'*the estate...shall pay...$2,000,000...*' Now, in the law, the word, shall is mandatory, that is to say, she must be paid. The question arises with the word, '*However*'. Does that create a condition precedent or a condition subsequent?"

Carmen sighed audibly. "Mr. Rifkin, Nicky don't give a rat's...uh...damn about all this legal mumbo-jumbo. I mean, the guy is sitting in jail waiting to get bailed out and he figures he's got millions of dollars coming to him, and when I tell him Margaux is going to get paid two million dollars and there's nothing for him, and some old trustee guy is going to tell him where we're going to live and what we're going to eat...he's gonna go berserk. By the way, who is this old trustee guy you keep talking about?" Carmen demanded.

"Me," Barney replied, smiling benignly.

"Oh, God," Carmen wailed, "He's gonna kill me."

CHAPTER THIRTY

Aldo Sanchez, the private eye Toro had hired to follow Margaux to find out if she was committing adultery with Gary Samson, settled back into the depths of his leather Barcalounger and opened the local newspaper. He skimmed through the news and was headed to the sports section when his eye happened to catch a brief announcement on the obituary page.

> *Dimitri Santoros, 76, died on April 19, 2008 while vacationing on the cruise ship* Seadancer. *The luxury liner was anchored in the Bay of Povai in Bora Bora, French Polynesia at the time. He is survived by his loving wife, Margaux Santoros, his son Nicholas Santoros and his daughter Xenia Santoros-Del Renzo.*
> *Mr. Santoros was a former president of the Brooklyn Greek-American Club....*

Aldo took the paper into his den and cut out the article. Then he entered the date on his desk calendar, flipped over the page and made a note to call Mrs. Santoros and express his regrets. He also planned to check with the surrogate's court to see if Toro's will had been offered for probate.

It was several weeks before he received word that the will had been filed. When he checked with the court clerk the following morning he learned that the will directed Toro's executor to pay his wife, Margaux M. Santoros, in accordance with their prenuptial agreement.

Aldo hurried down to surrogate's court to try and find out the value of Margaux's claim. He discovered that a copy of the prenuptial agreement was also on file with the surrogate. When he read it over and discovered that the estimated net value of the estate was $6,000,000, and that Margaux was entitled to one third of it, *provided* she had not committed adultery during the marriage, he could hardly keep from screaming out loud, *You conniving little bitch. You made me betray Dimitri for a few pieces of silver.*

And then he thought, *I wonder if Mrs. Margaux Santoros might be interested in buying the copy of the videotape I've got sitting in my safe. The one where she and the green Jaguar convertible guy were dancing nude in that cabin in Vermont. That ought to be worth something to her...or to somebody....*

When Aldo called the telephone number for Toro's residence he learned that the number had been disconnected. There was no listing in the phone book or on the web for Margaux Santoros, and the phone company information service informed him that she had an unlisted number. It took Aldo a month working with his investigative sources to wheedle the number from a disgruntled cook who had been fired by Margaux. When he finally got through to her and suggested they have a little chat, she told him it would take a while to settle the estate and she would get back to him.

She never did. Of course, they both knew that as a matter of law, the contract they had made was unenforceable.

Carmen had read the situation perfectly. When she handed Nick all the legal papers Barney had given her and told him that Margaux was going to be paid $2,000,000 and he wasn't entitled to anything—he did go berserk. As soon as he started screaming at Carmen, the prison guard forcibly removed him from the visiting chamber. A week later when she nervously revisited him, she initially couldn't believe it. He was smiling and in high spirits. He told her he had met an inmate by the name of Peter O'Shaunessey, a brilliant lawyer who had been disbarred for attempting to run over his wife with the family station wagon. The court had considered releasing him on bail pending his appeal, but he had made the mistake of telling his prison bunkmate that his only regret was that her injuries were limited to two fractured legs, and if he had it to do over again she would be pushing up daisies. His bunkmate squealed on him in exchange for early release from prison, a new identity, and a ticket to Venezuela. The lawyer would have to serve his fifteen years in prison.

Nick had shown him his legal papers. When Nick had explained to him that his wife and kids were entitled to the income from a $2,000,000 trust fund, O'Shaunessey agreed that he and his former law partner would take the case on a one-third contingency fee basis.

The lawyer had since spent every available moment working on Nick's case on the computer in the prison library. His former law partner was a successful trial lawyer in Manhattan, and between them they had developed a legal strategy that they thought could prevent the executor of the estate, Xenia Del Renzo, from paying any money to Margaux until a full-blown hearing was held in surrogate's court. He indicated, however, that in order to be successful in the court hearing Carmen would have to use some of her trust funds to hire a private investigator to locate Luis

181

Ramiriz, and hopefully to find additional evidence of Margaux's infidelity.

Carmen checked the note she had made before leaving home in Brooklyn: Williams and Feinberg (formerly Williams, O'Shaunessey and Feinberg), Suite 2200, 975 Third Avenue.

When she exited the elevator on the twenty-second floor she found herself standing in the reception room of the law offices, which occupied the top three floors of the building. She gazed out upon the East River and mentally compared it to Barney Rifkin's second floor walk-up office in Brooklyn. *This is more like it,* she thought. She studied the plaque on the wall beside the elevator that listed the names of over one hundred lawyers whose offices occupied the three floors. She glanced at her memo again for the name of the lawyer she was supposed to see: Carl Brown. The receptionist escorted her back to the lawyer's office, which turned out to be just slightly larger than the back seat of her Volkswagen.

"Hi, Mrs. Santoros, I'm Carl Brown. Sorry about the accommodations here, but all the conference rooms are booked and I didn't want to delay taking action on your husband's case until next week." He knew her name and all about the case, and he wanted to take action as soon as possible. He even had a bunch of papers all ready for her to sign. Carmen was hooked.

"Here's what we're going to do. Our private investigator has already done some preliminary work, which reminds me, I'm supposed to pick up a check from you to cover his costs." Carmen fished in her purse for the $5,000 check Nick told her to bring with her. She had borrowed the money from Zee, and in turn Nick had signed all the papers that would enable Zee to have her father's will probated and Zee herself appointed as executor.

"Thanks," he said, throwing the check into his file without looking at it. "Here's the deal, Mrs. Santoros. Judge Bartley has signed my order to show cause seeking an injunction to prevent your sister-in-law from giving any money to this lady, Margaux, until he's heard proof on all the issues. As I'm sure you know, there's really only one question: 'Did she or didn't she?' The thing is, we've got to stall this case until our investigator has a chance to do his job.

"I spoke with your husband yesterday and he gave us some leads on how to track down this Ramiriz character. We also put a tail on Margaux, and we think we may have hit pay dirt. She's been meeting regularly with a guy who lives out on Long Island. A place called Sea Cliff. She spent the night there last night. Of course that doesn't help the case directly because what she does after your father-in-law's death isn't evidence of what she did before his death, you know, but messing with this guy only three months after your father-in-law died tells us something about the lady.

"We figure if she's gotten that cozy with this man just a short while after Mr. Santoros' death, it's reasonable to assume she probably knew the guy before he died. At least it's a start. Any questions?" Before she could collect her thoughts enough to ask a question, he said, "Okay then, I'll be in touch with you as soon as we hear anything." He stood up and offered Carmen his hand, then steered her back to the elevator. The next thing she knew, she was back on the sidewalk, trying to remember everything Mr. Brown had told her so she could report it all to Nick.

As trustee, Barney agreed to make an advance payment to Carmen so that she could put up the bail money for Nick. When Barney met him in jail and arranged to have him released, he told Nick that although he would represent him in the violation of probation matter, he could not help in the controversy between the estate and Margaux because of a conflict of interest.

"Hey, Rifkin," Nick demanded, "whose side are you on, anyway?"

"That's the point, Nicholas, I'm the attorney and trustee for the estate. I'm not permitted to be on anybody's side, as you put it."

When Margaux was served with a copy of the court order preventing Zee from issuing a check to her, she called Barney Rifkin immediately.

"Barney, what's going on? You told me as soon as Zee was appointed executor you would ask her to cut me a check. I need that money. I'm broke. I used all the available cash I had to pay all the household expenses that had accumulated while we were on the cruise. I'm holding about ten thousand dollars in travelers checks, but I can't even cash them because they're in Toro's name."

"Zee can cash those checks," Barney said, "but the money has to be deposited to the estate account, I'm afraid."

"What about all those charges the family ran up on the ship? Toro was planning to pay all that stuff, but I had to take care of it with my own money and all I've got left is a few thousand dollars cash that Toro had squirreled away in his desk."

"Bring me the receipts. That's a legitimate estate expense. Zee can reimburse you for that. Anything else?"

"Yeah, who is this Williams and Feinberg law firm?"

"I've run into them a couple of times. It's a very aggressive outfit. They were one of the first offices in Manhattan to start advertising big-time on television. I knew Pete O'Shaunessey, one of the senior partners, pretty well. He got himself a new young wife and went bonkers. Tried to kill her when he caught her messing around, I guess. He's doing fifteen years in state prison."

"I don't care about their dirty laundry. I just want you to get them off my back."

"You know I can't help you, Margaux. I'm representing Toro's estate. He appointed me trustee for his kids. I shouldn't even be talking to you, except I guess if you're representing yourself in the controversy I can speak to your lawyer," he chuckled.

"Hey, Barney, it's not funny."

"You're right, Margaux, I'm sorry."

"I thought you were my friend. We've been through a lot together, you know."

"I know, but I have an obligation to protect the assets of the estate, and they're claiming you cheated on Toro and have forfeited your rights. I can't talk to you about it, Margaux. I suggest you hire a good attorney and follow his advice."

"I am a good attorney," she replied.

"I'm sorry, Margaux," he said, and hung up.

"You old bastard!" she cursed, and slammed down the phone. She went into the kitchen and made herself a vodka martini, although it was only eleven o'clock in the morning. Then she called Gary. She asked him to meet her for lunch at the Algonquin. He said he was committed for lunch, but she told him she had to see him as soon as possible and suggested he come to dinner at her place. He agreed to meet her there at seven.

CHAPTER THIRTY-ONE

It was the first time Gary had ever been to her home. He didn't pay any attention to the nondescript car parked on the street, or notice the driver who secretly videotaped him exiting from his green Jaguar, walking up the front steps of Margaux's home and kissing her when she opened the door. A bit later the private investigator ambled over to Gary's automobile and took a picture of it, its license plate and location.

After Margaux showed Gary around the house, they settled down with their drinks on the glassed-in porch facing the harbor.

"Read this and tell me what you think." Margaux handed him the thick packet of legal documents.

He read them carefully. When he finished, he said, "Looks like you've got yourself a problem, sweetheart. Who is Luis Ramiriz? I don't remember you ever telling me about him." Margaux stood up, stared out across the bay, turned and leaned against a marble column.

"He's a lying little bastard, that's who he is. I don't know how these shyster lawyers ever dug him up, but I swear to you, Gary, I never, never slept with him, as he claims in that affidavit. I met him casually on the cruise ship and he tried every which way to get me into bed, but it never happened. He's a very smooth, good-looking young kid, but that's all he is—a young punk from Brooklyn who thinks he's irresistible to women. When I brushed him off, like the crumb he is, he became belligerent. I guess he figures by making up that pack of lies that he'll be getting even with me for bruising his male ego." She picked up the legal documents that Gary had dropped on the floor and stood in front of him.

"Now, please give me your thoughts on what I must do about this damn lawsuit," she said.

"I'm not interested in the lawsuit at the moment. I'm interested in taking you to bed. All this talk about sex with you standing there with those lush boobs and spectacular legs and that tight ass has got me all hot and bothered. Come here," he said, taking off his jacket and starting to remove his tie.

"Not now, Gary, just help me decide what to do and then...." She turned her back on him and wiggled her bottom.

"Damn," Gary said, and slumped back on the couch. "Okay, so what's the question again?"

"Now don't start pouting. If you'll just pay attention to me, we'll get this over with much faster," she said, holding the papers in front of him.

"All right already, what's the problem?"

"I've got to find a way to discredit Ramiriz' testimony, otherwise it'll just be his word against mine."

"So, what do you know about him?"

"Actually," Margaux answered, "I don't know a damn thing about him. Like I said, we had a couple of drinks together on board the ship, and then I met him accidentally in a restaurant in Tahiti. He started hitting on me. I told him to get lost. He became obnoxious, and I got up and left the restaurant. I never saw him again."

"Are you sure there isn't more to it than that? Let's think it through." Gary stood up and started to pace the room. "Tell me, if the trustee doesn't pay you, who gets that money?"

"Zee and her sister-in-law."

"How do they fit into this whole picture? What can you tell me about them? You've never told me anything about the Santoros family."

"Zee is a sweetheart, and she's got a cute little kid, but she's married to a colossal creep. Of course, she's only a kid herself, really. I think she just turned twenty or twenty-one, as a matter of fact."

"And her brother?"

"He's a bad actor. Right now, he's in jail for violating probation. He and Zee's husband are both in jail. I don't know what the deal with Zee's husband is. Something to do with immigration, I heard."

"Did you ever see either of them with this Ramiriz fellow?"

"Well, yeah. A couple of times I saw the three of them drinking in one of the bars and hanging out together in the casino."

"Now we're getting somewhere, but—it doesn't matter. The really serious problem here is the lawsuit itself."

"What do you mean by that?" she demanded. "If I can't stop the hearing from going forward, it's going to be his word against mine. That's why we've got to get as much dirt on this jerk as possible. A jury isn't going to believe that little scum bag."

"That's not the point. Don't you see, love, the only way you can deny their claim is to take the stand and testify that you didn't commit adultery during your marriage. Am I right?"

"Of course, but I don't get it. Don't you think the jury will believe me?"

"You're missing the point. Look, so you take the stand and deny everything he says. Fine, I agree—the jury will be on your side, but then what happens? What do you do when their lawyer cross-examines you and asks the sixty-four dollar question?"

"What's that?" Margaux asked.

"How about this: 'Tell me, Mrs. Santoros, and remember you are under oath and have sworn to tell the truth. Please answer this simple question *At any time during your marriage to Dimitri Santoros did you ever commit adultery?*'"

"I still don't get it. I told you I never slept with that kid!"

"What about me? Remember me? Remember the Palmer House? Remember our afternoon in Sea Cliff? Remember Lucie's apartment and the cabin in Vermont?"

"But, Gary, no one but you and I know anything about that. What's the problem?"

"The problem is you would be lying under oath. My marriage busted up because the woman I thought I loved turned out to be a consummate liar. I've got a slew of character faults, but I just can't handle lying. And from my way of thinking it doesn't matter that it's under oath—the ugly fact is that you seem to be prepared to avoid telling the truth for financial gain."

"Wait a minute, Gary, Have you forgotten there's $2,000,000 in the kitty here? That's two million United States dollars, sweetheart. Have you thought about what we could do with $2,000,000?"

"God damn it, Margaux, money's got nothing to do with it. Can't you see that?"

"Don't be stupid, for God's sake. Money's got *everything* to do with it."

Gary shook his head and slowly eased himself back in his chair. "I'm sorry, Margaux, but we've been down this road before, and it's no less painful the second time around."

"What the hell is that supposed to mean?" she hissed.

"Have you forgotten that road we traveled when we met at the bar next to the Bear Mountain Bridge? You asked me to promise to marry you at the end of eighteen months. Why couldn't you have told me the truth—that you were counting on your husband dying by that time so you could have me *and* the two million dollars? And what were you planning to do with me if he didn't conveniently die as you anticipated?"

"I prayed every night that my husband would die within a year, as his doctor told him he would."

"But, Margaux, can't you see how awful that is? That you would pray—to whom I can't imagine—that a man you must have loved at one time...would die?"

"Don't you understand, I never loved *him*, I loved *you*. Don't you get it? What's wrong with that?"

"Everything. If you fall out of love with me, I guess you'll start praying *I* get hit by a truck."

"Don't be such an ass."

"Okay, pretty woman. I give up. I guess the only thing I can do to insure against my early demise is to promise to go to Shanghai just before your trial begins so they can't subpoena me."

"That's not funny," she said, turning her back on him.

"It wasn't intended to be. I just wanted to make sure you realize I won't lie for you." He hesitated for a moment. He didn't know what more to say or do. He didn't want to leave with such jagged feelings between them. But when he looked back at her, she stood staring fiercely at him, her lips curled down, her lower jaw thrust forward and her arms crossed over her chest. He stood up, put on his jacket and walked slowly toward the front door.

"Please don't leave," Margaux said, so softly he barely heard her. Gary turned around. She reached out to him and in seconds they were back in each other's arms.

Margaux opened a bottle of champagne and Gary cooked bacon and scrambled eggs. They went out onto the patio and ate silently, with an enormous moon bathing the Statue of Liberty in a silver mist.

Finally, Gary broke the silence. "I love you, darling, but I just don't know how to deal with this problem between us." He picked up her hand and pressed his lips into her palm.

"And I love you, and I'm begging you to *understand* the situation," she said.

"The problem between us hasn't been created because I lack understanding. What we're talking about here is simply telling the truth."

"You're being naive," she answered.

"Not at all. It's just a matter of what's right and what's wrong."

"Why can't you see my side of it just once? Why is your opinion about what's right or wrong any better than my opinion?" she demanded.

"Because we're not discussing a matter that is susceptible to opinion," he replied.

"There you go again. That's your opinion. You're not God, you know."

"That's your opinion." He laughed.

"Everything is a joke with you, Gary. But this is no joke."

"I agree. I was just trying to lighten things up a bit. For instance, turn around and look out that window. The poet Emma Lazarus wrote the poem that's etched in bronze on the base of that beautiful Lady of Liberty you see standing so tall in the harbor, there."

"So what does that have to do with anything?"

"The title of her poem is *The New Colossus*. I believe it's in the first line where she speaks of the old colossus, the brazen giant of ancient Greece, a mighty conquerer, a symbol of 'might makes right' and then she stacks him up against our Statue of Liberty which stands for freedom and the 'rule of reason.'"

"And your point is?"

"Might doesn't make right, and neither does money. Let's change the subject, okay? How about another glass of champagne?" He scooped up some of the dirty dishes, and then waited for her answer.

"I don't want anything." she sulked.

"Whatever," he said. He took his time washing the dishes, trying to find a way out of the impasse. When he finished, he found Margaux sitting on the couch in the living room, reading a magazine. She didn't look up when he entered the room. He sat down on the edge of the chair across from her, head bowed, shoulders sagging, emotionally drained.

"I give up, sweetheart," he said. "Most times, when an irresistible force engages an immovable object, the only solution is for the irresistible force to go around the immovable object; but in this case that's impossible. What you're proposing to do is gut-wrenchingly wrong."

Margaux stood up and sauntered over to her writing desk, pulled open the top drawer and took out a pack of cigarettes. She knew Gary hated her smoking. After lighting up, she took a deep drag and blew the smoke in his direction. "I take it that means unless I see things your way, we're all through. Is that it?" she said.

"No, dear Margaux, it has nothing to do with my way or your way. It has to do with truth. Can't you see that, for God's sake?"

"Come off it, Gary," she said, pointing the lighted cigarette at him. "Was it wrong for you to bed me down when I was married?"

"I didn't know you were married. You lied about that."

"How about your stalking me, when I was begging you to leave me alone—when *I* was trying to do the right thing by honoring my marriage vows? Where's your honesty and integrity in that little maneuver? It's all bullshit."

"Again, I didn't know you were married. Besides, I believe the truth is that you weren't trying to preserve your marriage as you claim, you were just trying to protect your fucking $2,000,000." He started toward the door again, and then stopped and said, "The dilemma you face now is crystal clear. You can follow your heart and come with me or you can pick up your bag of fucking gold and go dance with the devil."

Margaux stepped in front of him. "You're a rotten son-of-a-bitch, Samson."

"And you're a whore, Santoros."

She slapped him in the face as hard as she could.

He instinctively clenched his fist and started to take a swing at her, but instead, he turned and walked away. His nose was bleeding. He was pretty sure it was broken. He pulled the front door closed behind him. Margaux picked up the crystal cocktail pitcher and smashed it against the wall.

The man sitting in the shadows filmed Gary shuffling along the sidewalk with his head down, like an old man.

Gary sat with his hands on the steering wheel, staring blankly ahead for several minutes before turning on the engine. Then he wiped away the blood from his nose and drove cautiously back home.

CHAPTER THIRTY-TWO

Work on other cases took Lieutenant Garvey and Sergeant Schwartz away from the Santoros case for a few days until they received a report from the FBI fingerprint laboratory in Washington, D.C. They were unable to make a 100% positive identification because the pendant had been submerged in sea water for several hours before it was recovered, but fortunately the oil from Ramiriz' skin and the sea water didn't mix, so the FBI fingerprint expert was prepared to testify that in his opinion it was Mr. Ramiriz' right thumbprint on the back of the pendant.

Garvey ordered Schwartz to take a hard look at Ramiriz and report back to him. Luis' rap sheet included several convictions for jewelry theft, but Schwartz couldn't make any connection to the Santoros family until he came across a note in the file that Margaux Santoros had reported a theft of jewelry to the security officer on the *Seadancer*. When he obtained a copy of the report and the claim she had filed with her insurance company—with a detailed description of a stolen necklace—he was satisfied that the pendant turned in to the police in Bora Bora and the stolen pendant were one and the same, with one major difference: Mrs. Santoros claimed her stolen pendant was valued at $25,000, five times greater than the pendant the fingerprint lab was holding in Washington...unless, of course, Mrs. Santoros had lied to her insurance company about its value.

When Garvey read Schwartz' report, he immediately suspected that Margaux had filed a fraudulent insurance claim, and instructed Schwartz to follow it up with the company. "Remember, that lady spent a year in state prison for grand larceny. It looks like she's up to her old tricks," Garvey reminded his associate.

Schwartz was able to track down the jewelry store where Toro had purchased the pendant and confirmed that he had paid $25,000 for it. The jeweler suggested that it may have been devalued because Toro had insisted on having it engraved, which diminished its value as an antique. "I told him not to do that. In fact I refused to deface that beautiful piece, but he wouldn't listen to me. Obviously some other jeweler was willing to make a few bucks and did what the customer asked him to do. Still, the diamond alone that was inlaid in the face of the piece should be worth around $15,000 or more."

When Schwartz called the FBI lab to clear up the mystery, the agent in charge said, "I'm looking right at it as we speak, Sergeant Schwartz, and I'm telling you there are only a few diamond chips on this pendant. There's sort of an indentation on the face of it that looks as if there may have been an inlay at some time, but it's gone now, sir. No doubt about that."

Lieutenant Garvey and Sergeant Schwartz were huddled in Garvey's office.

"Okay, Sherlock, the college graduate, what's your take on the whole situation?" Garvey demanded.

"I'm not ready to commit yet. I have to fine-tune my ideas first."

"So who we got left? Del Renzo? Margaux Santoros? Nick Santoros?... and I told you to check out the guy with the fingerprint on the pendant—Louie Rodriguez or whatever."

"Not Rodriguez, Chief...his name is Luis Ramiriz."

"I don't want any of your lip, Schwartz. Just give me the facts, like that guy used to say on TV."

"Okay, okay. I checked him out just like you told me. But he's got an explanation, and the widow, your girlfriend Margaux Santoros, confirms it."

"Cut out the wise-guy crap, Schwartz. Just show me what you've got."

Schwartz opened his briefcase. It had seen better days, but his wife had given it to him on their first anniversary and he wouldn't part with it. He removed the notes of his meeting with Luis.

"Like I said, Boss, Margaux has explained how Ramiriz' fingerprint could have ended up on the back of her fancy necklace. She confirms what Ramiriz claims. He says they were having lunch together in a restaurant in Tahiti. He thought the large diamond pendant she was wearing was very valuable. He sort of fondled it and turned it over to see if the initials of the artist who made it were on the back. That's when his fingerprint must have gotten on it, he says, and that's what she says. Of course they could be in cahoots together and both be lying."

"Sure, they could have done the job together. She's got the brains. Does he have the muscle?"

"You know, boss, you might have something there. He's a real well-built dude. By the way, did you know Margaux Santoros is suing her husband's estate for $2,000,000?"

"You're kidding me, right?"

"No bull. I was talking to Sanchez the other day when he stopped in the precinct. He told me he's making more money than you and me combined. Do you suppose that's true?"

"Knowing Aldo, it wouldn't surprise me. We give him information because he's a good old guy and then he sells the info for thousands of dollars. Not bad, eh? Where did I go wrong, Sergeant?"

"I'm sure as hell not going to go there, Chief, but what the hell—it's only money, right? I don't begrudge him a little extra cash in his old age. He spent thirty years trying to put the bad hombres in jail.

"He tells me he's pissed off at Margaux because apparently he did some work for her and she didn't pay him."

"By the way," said Garvey, "Attorney MacDonald wants us to meet with him tomorrow morning. He says he's received an interesting report from France that he wants to share with us."

CHAPTER THIRTY-THREE

The French National Police, known as the *Gendarmerie Nationale*, employs over 100,000 people to attend to France's domestic security needs. Its forensic laboratory, dedicated to assisting in the investigation of homicides committed within France's territories—including French Polynesia—is located in a highly secure building in the heart of Paris.

Xavier Renard was one of its bright young scientists, specializing in the newest branch of investigative science: DNA. He was assigned to the suspected murder of Dimitri Santoros, an American national visiting the island of Bora Bora in French Polynesia. The history that had been meticulously documented indicated that the victim, a seventy-six year-old American tourist, had been assaulted and dumped overboard from a cruise ship moored in the Bay of Povai.

Renard's superior, Dr. Bauvier, had flown to Bora Bora and then on to Tahiti, intending only to examine the body there and make a finding as to the cause of death. But he quickly discovered that there were so many legal and scientific issues involved in the case that the body would need to be transported to his laboratory in Paris where the most sophisticated forensic equipment was available in order to determine the cause of death and to assist in the prosecution of the accused. Until a prime suspect could be identified, however, the jurisdictional issue and the associated costs could not be resolved.

Dr. Bauvier had communicated with Lieutenant Aeva Fontein in Polynesia, and subsequently Renard had been in touch with U.S. Assistant District Attorney MacDonald, in New York, who was awaiting his final report before proceeding against several suspects who had been identified by Lieutenant Fontein.

On October 13, 2008, Renard entered his lab and settled down in his tiny cubicle office to finalize his report. He pulled a standard form up on his computer and began to insert the information that had been accumulated by various other members of the forensic team. He was particularly interested in the autopsy report that concluded that in the opinion of the physician who had examined the body, the victim had sustained multiple facial injuries including several broken teeth and damage to dental bridgework, in all probability caused either by a severe blow to the face or by contact with the coral reef in the bay. Also, the victim had sustained a deep laceration, a concussion, and a fractured skull, presumably caused by a blow to the back of his head. Further, the victim had been thrown from a great height into the sea and drowned. The body had been discovered in less than eight hours by a local fisherman.

Besides the injury to the back of the head, there were multiple contusions and abrasions on the body, which might be attributed to an assault, or to the trauma to the body when it struck the water and later washed against the coral reef. He also noted that the only possible physical evidence connecting one of the suspects to the crime was a fingerprint on the back of a pendant that was discovered clutched in the hand of the victim.

They're going to need a lot more than that to get a conviction, Renard thought as he laboriously continued to fill in the blanks on the form.

Although it was a very unpleasant job, given the time that had elapsed between the occurrence and the transfer of the body to the morgue in Paris, he decided to examine the corpse himself.

By the time Toro's body had been wheeled into the chamber with its ceramic tile walls and floor, Renard's olfactory organs had adjusted to the foul odor. An orderly turned on the bright florescent lamps for him, and he went to work. He clamped open the jaws and turned on the switch of his battery-operated headlamp, directing its beam deep into the interior of Toro's mouth. He explored the broken teeth and the twisted bridgework with a probe. "Yes, yes," he muttered.

He took a series of photographs of the interior of Toro's mouth, and then selected a pair of long-nosed medical pliers and carefully removed, tagged and deposited several specimens of tissue into a plastic evidence bag.

Even though the autopsy report indicated that the cause of death was asphyxiation by drowning, he wanted to corroborate that assessment himself, and did so by cutting open Toro's lungs and confirming the presence of sea water. If Toro hadn't been alive when his body hit the water, his heart and respiratory system would not have been functioning to suck sea water into his lungs.

Three days later he completed his report and sent it by Federal Express to U.S. Attorney Devon MacDonald in New York. As soon as MacDonald received the report he immediately called Lieutenant Garvey and instructed him to come to his office as soon as possible.

"Bring that clown Sergeant Schwartz along with you. I like the way his mind works."

"Yes, sir," Garvey replied. "Is this on the Santoros case?"

"That's right, Lieutenant. I've got some pretty interesting new information I want to share with you gentlemen."

The appointment was made for that afternoon. Garvey and Schwartz arrived promptly as planned, anxious to find out what MacDonald had learned. When they were again seated at MacDonald's conference table, he handed copies of Renard's report to them and then sat quietly, observing them as they read the report and the narrative that Inspector Renard had sent along with it.

> *I obtained three small foreign objects from the mouth of the victim.*
>
> *Exhibit A was irregular in shape, about the size of a pin head. It was lodged between two upper incisors, and much to my disappointment turned out to be a morsel of beefsteak.*
>
> *Exhibit B was the same. However, when I tested the third exhibit which had been wedged between a tooth and one of the broken stainless steel struts of the dental bridgework, I hit pay dirt, as you Americans say. It was a tiny piece of human flesh big enough to subject to DNA testing. I was well aware of the fact that it might just be from the victim's tongue or the inside of his cheek, but I checked the victim's DNA and it was not a match! The only logical explanation is that it came from the fist of the assailant who had struck Santoros in the mouth and cut his knuckle on the jagged broken steel strut. A tiny piece of his flesh got caught between the wire and the tooth.*
>
> *Hopefully, this information will enable you to identify the assailant, but at the very least, if it doesn't turn out to match one of your suspects, it will prevent you from charging the wrong person.*
>
> *By the way, the neck on the victim is the size of one of your New York Giant linebackers. Also, I noted that one of the suspects is a woman and I must tell you that it's highly unlikely that a woman could have hit the victim with her fist with enough force to cause the damage to the victim's mouth that I observed. Further, I don't see how a normal woman could have sufficient strength to lift 180 pounds of dead weight over the railing into the sea unless she had an accomplice.*
>
> *I guess that's the best I can do for now. Good Luck,*
> *Xavier Renard*
>
> *P.S. I studied at New York University for two years. I love your American football. If you are going to need me to come to New York to testify, please make sure the trial coincides with the Superbowl game and one way or another, reserve me a seat on the fifty-yard line.*
>
> *P.P.S. I checked with our legal staff on the question of legal jurisdiction that you raised. Believe it or not, it took one of our legal*

eagles two days to figure it out. I think you will be amused by the incredible convolutions of the law (as if that's news to any of us hardworking law enforcement guys.) Here's the story:

We've got an American citizen murdered within the territorial limits of French Polynesia, and I am advised that when it comes to questions of jurisdiction, the country where the crime is committed has jurisdiction. The territory is always supreme. No country can impose its laws on another country. So, any normal person would figure that's easy enough, there can be no doubt about the fact that the crime was committed in French Polynesia, and therefore France has jurisdiction of the case, right?...wrong! Now get this: First of all we have to decide whether the crime was committed on board the ship. If it took place on board the ship, the rule in international law is that a ship holds the same status as a national territory. So if Santoros drowned when he was thrown into the Bay of Povai in Bora Bora, Polynesia is the place where the homicide occurred and France has jurisdiction. If he was dead before he was thrown overboard, the territory of the ship has jurisdiction, and since it is an American ship, the United States takes jurisdiction. But our attorney tells us that although the Seadancer was owned and operated by an American company, it flies the flag of the country of Panama (presumably for tax purposes). Since it's our opinion that Santoros was alive when he was thrown overboard, it would seem that French Polynesia has jurisdiction of the homicide and the U.S. or Panama has jurisdiction of the assault. Hold on, hold on! Before September 11, 2001, the U.S. refused to accept the rule of international law known as the "Passive Personality Principle" that permitted a foreign country to assume jurisdiction over an American citizen who is charged with committing a crime pursuant to the foreign nation's law within the foreign nation's territorial limits. After 9/11 the United States reversed itself and passed the "We Gotcha Bin Laden Act" thereby now enabling America to prosecute members of Al Qaeda in the United States for crimes perpetrated against American citizens outside the U.S.

Until you fellows decide who the murderer is, we can't tell which court has jurisdiction to try the case, but our legal staff says to tell you whoever it is, you can have him, we don't want him, but our General Counsel says he would be pleased to assist you in prosecuting him if you will pay for his airfare and put him up in a nice hotel in New York.

P.P.P.S. Are the New York Giants going to win the Superbowl again in 2010 ????

Schwartz finished reading the report first, but he waited for Garvey to speak.

"Sounds like a helluva guy, don't he, Mr. MacDonald? But I'm afraid I got lost during his discussion about who has jurisdiction in this here case," Garvey said.

"My guess is that a New York judge will decide it however he damn well feels like it," MacDonald replied with a smile.

Schwartz added, "If we decide to prosecute Ramiriz in this country, we better get this trial scheduled the week before Superbowl Sunday, wouldn't you say, Lieutenant?"

"Absolutely," Garvey laughed, "but that means we've got to move on it right away. I'd say we now have enough to get an indictment against Ramiriz, don't you agree, Mr. MacDonald?"

"No, not yet, Bill, but there's plenty of time to figure that out."

"What about Del Renzo and young Santoros?" Garvey asked. "Maybe they got tired of waiting for the old man to kick the bucket so they could inherit a big bunch of money, and decided to hire Ramiriz to move things along a little faster. I remember reading somewhere in Lieutenant Fontein's report that the three of them were seen together on the ship."

"What do you think, Sergeant?" MacDonald asked.

"Well, sir, I was just wondering. Ramiriz acknowledges having some expertise when it comes to jewelry, and he's got a record as a jewel thief. Suppose when he sees that gold pendant Mrs. Santoros was wearing when they were having lunch together, he can tell that big diamond is for real…worth a big bunch of money. So, early in the evening when most of the passengers are away from their rooms having dinner or enjoying the entertainment, he sneaks into Mrs. Santoros' stateroom looking for the gold pendant, and Mr. Santoros catches him there with the necklace in his hand. He grabs it away from Ramiriz who doesn't resist because he's just looking to get away without being identified. If the old guy had left it at that and let Ramiriz escape he'd probably still be alive, but Santoros is a tough old bird and wants to subdue the thief. He underestimates Ramiriz' strength, and gets himself knocked unconscious when Ramiriz strikes him in the face.

"Now Ramiriz has to make a decision. If he lets the old man live, he won't be able to escape off the boat without being identified as the thief, so he throws Santoros overboard. But he panics and throws the baby out with the bathwater, in other words when he threw Santoros overboard the old guy was still hanging on to the necklace."

"Sergeant Schwartz, that's a pretty good story if you're writing a novel, but I can't take that scenario to the grand jury without solid proof that there is a DNA match between the morsel of flesh that that French fellow, Xavier Reynard, found In Santoros' mouth and the suspect Ramiriz. In other words, that it was Ramiriz' fist in Santoros' mouth," MacDonald said.

"I'm coming to that sir. How about this: You'll remember that when the jeweler and Margaux Santoros described the stolen pendant, there was a large, valuable diamond on its face. By the time it got to the lab in Paris, the diamond had disappeared. Ramiriz, the jewel thief, could have easily removed the diamond before old man Santoros caught him, and that's why Ramiriz didn't bother to try and grab the necklace back from him."

"Good try, Sergeant, but not good enough. You're piling conjecture on top of conjecture. It's worth another chapter in your book, or next week's episode on a television drama, but it won't fly in a court of law. If you don't have anything more, please call me when you do." The attorney started to gather up his papers and arrange them in his briefcase.

"As a matter of fact, I do, sir, but it's a bit tricky. Could you just give me a few more minutes?"

MacDonald checked his watch, settled back in his chair and said, "I'm listening. What more have you got, Bill?"

"Don't ask me, sir, whatever Schwartz has it will be news to me."

"Okay, Sergeant, let's get on with it," the attorney said.

Schwartz decided he had to lighten things up a bit because he thought he might be on dangerous ground. "I think I've had a bit of me Irish luck," he said.

"Schwartz? Irish?" MacDonald laughed.

"Begorra, it's true, sir. The Lieutenant here won't believe me, but it was me great-grandmother, Liz Duffy was her name, and she started it all. When she was fifteen years old she ran away from Dublin to America with a young pots and pans peddler by the name of Sammy Schwartz. They ended up in Brooklyn and produced two sons. Would you believe those two boys married Irish Catholic girls? Now I guess it's a family tradition. My mother's name was Katie McDougal and my wife's maiden name was Maureen Delaney. I apologize for the detour here, but you threw down the gauntlet, and I couldn't let it pass. Besides, as you may recall, Ireland's president from 1959 to 1973 was Jewish, which I consider a remarkable feat for a country agonizingly divided by the Green and the Orange."

"Being of Scottish heritage, I always wondered about that," MacDonald said.

"It's because the Irish are united in the joy of life, the power of song, dance and laughter, and the curse of whiskey."

"I agree with the whiskey part," Garvey quipped.

"So, tell me about this bit of Irish good luck of yours, Sergeant," the attorney urged.

"Well, sir, it's like this. Lieutenant Garvey ordered me to track down the Ramiriz fellow, and I caught him one evening in his flat. Actually he lives in a Cuban enclave in Canarsie. I told him about the fingerprint we found on the pendant. I believe I caught him off guard but he immediately came up with that story about having lunch with Mrs. Santoros. At that time I thought he was making it up. He's a mighty smooth talker, you know, but to get to the part about the good luck. While I was in his place, I used his bathroom so I could snoop a little, and I grabbed some hair out of his hairbrush. I took it over to our lab and they tell me it's a perfect DNA match with the piece of flesh the Frenchman found in Santoros' mouth."

"You didn't tell me about that, Schwartz," Garvey grumbled.

"I figured it was an illegal search and seizure. I was planning to recommend we get a search warrant but then...."

"It's okay, Schwartz," said MacDonald, "You did the right thing. I'll get the search and seizure warrant, you can get a legal sample to give to the lab for DNA testing, and I'll make the presentation to the grand jury.

"By the way, Sergeant, I wouldn't call it all Irish luck, I'd say it was also good Jewish thinking." They all laughed, each in his own way confirming that America's diversity is its greatest strength.

"Now let's see where we're going with this case. Just a sec." MacDonald checked his appointment book, shuffled some pages back and forth and said, "I've got an opening in November. I could present the case to the grand jury then and set it down for trial next February. How about that, Bill?"

Garvey hesitated and then looked over at Schwartz.

"What do you think, Schwartz? Does that give us enough time to put the case together?"

"I think that's doable. The evidence against Ramiriz for assaulting old man Santoros is solid and should surely get us an indictment and conviction for assault in the second degree, but unless we can prove that he was the person who threw the old man overboard that's all we've got against Ramiriz because that French fella claims the cause of death was asphyxiation by drowning—am I right, Mr. MacDonald?"

"I'm not sure about that, Sergeant."

"I was just thinking, sir...I'm just learning about the felony-murder doctrine in my advanced criminal law class. Could that apply in this case?"

"Probably not, Sergeant. First of all, in order for that doctrine to apply, we'd have to prove more than assault because that isn't one of the felonies listed in the statute that applies In being able to use the doctrine. The idea is that if the miscreant, the bad guy, commits arson and someone dies in the fire, we don't have to prove *intent* to kill. We only have to prove the arson and the death to convict for murder. But wait a minute…you might have something because if we could prove burglary, that *is* one of the predicate felonies listed. However the death has to occur during the commission of the burglary and that may not be the case here. Do you understand?"

"Not totally, sir," Schwartz said.

Garvey thought to himself, *I don't understand any of it.*

"Look at it this way, Sergeant. If it's established that Santoros died by drowning, then there's an intervening cause of death, you see?"

"I do now. I guess that's why you're the attorney and I'm just the investigator," Schwartz laughed.

"I think you've done a fine job, Sergeant. I'll present the assault case against Ramiriz to the grand jury in a couple of weeks, and you gentlemen will continue to try and find out how Santoros ended up swimming in the ocean at five o'clock in the morning.

"Put it all together, Bill, and call me next week for a final run-through. What do you say?"

"Yes, sir." *I think the kid deserves to take over my job,* Garvey said to himself. *I'm damn glad he's leaving here when he finishes law school.*

When Lieutenant Garvey got back to his office, he locked the door and looked up the felony-murder doctrine in his New York State criminal law text. He was familiar with the legal concept, but hadn't thought about it until Schwartz brought it up. He opened the book to the relevant section and learned that the felony-murder doctrine was the brainchild of Sir Malcom Finch and was incorporated into the laws of England in 1823. It became an important prosecutorial tool in the murder cases where the district attorney was having difficulty proving that the defendant *intended* to kill the victim. In order to prove a defendant guilty of murder, the prosecution must prove *intent* to kill beyond a reasonable doubt. Since intent concerns the operation of the mind of the assailant, it can ofttimes be difficult for the prosecutor to overcome the defendant's claim that he didn't mean to kill the victim. However, under the felony-murder doctrine, if the victim is killed in the course of the furtherance of the commission of certain felonies such as arson, burglary and robbery, all the prosecutor has to prove is 1.) the commission of the underlying felony, and 2.) a death that occurred *during the furtherance of committing the felony.* He closed the book, pushed his chair back and put his feet up on his desk.

Okay, he thought, *it's obvious that after knocking the old man unconscious, Ramiriz, a God-damn foreigner, a crook and probably a communist besides, undoubtedly threw the old guy overboard to keep him from squealing on him. Any idiot ought to be able to understand that, but how the hell are we going to prove it? I think I'll leave that up to Schwartz.*

CHAPTER THIRTY-FOUR

The notoriety Margaux had gained during her earlier criminal trial was once again generating headlines in the *National Enquirer*. The story of her $2,000,000 claim against her deceased husband's estate had all the ingredients that the scandal press thrived on—money, sex, beauty…and a murder mystery. "*What more could we possibly ask for?*" one of the editors commented as he blocked the front page on the first day of the trial.

He had pulled up from the archives a photo of Margaux spilling out of a bikini that they had published on the day when she had been convicted of embezzling a quarter of a million dollars from the estate of Katrina Shauffler. Now, once again, she had created a media frenzy with her flamboyance. The death of her husband, Dimitri Santoros, had not surfaced in the press until one of the reporters happened to be in federal court on the day Nicky Santoros and Vittorio Del Renzo were arraigned. Since Toro's death occurred ten thousand miles west of Brooklyn on a tiny Polynesian island, no one had made the connection between the deceased Dimitri Santoros and Toro, the Brooklyn Garbage King, who married Margaux McBride, the disbarred attorney known as the "Barrister Beauty."

In 2002, Margaux had originally been arrested and charged with the murder of Frank Dunn, senior partner of the prestigious Madison Avenue law firm where she was employed. She was cleared of that crime, but in the course of the investigation, the district attorney uncovered evidence that Margaux and Frank Dunn had conspired to steal $250,000 from their client, Katrina Shauffler. Now here she was again, mixed up in a battle with the heirs of Dimitri Santoros' estate. She claimed she was entitled to $2,000,000 under the prenuptial agreement she had made with Toro. The scandal was made all the juicier because Toro's children refused to pay her claim on the grounds that she had committed adultery during her marriage to their father and therefore she wasn't entitled to a penny.

Margaux was the object of a media bidding war for her exclusive story. The American public loved winners. But they were as fickle as a teenage boy in heat.

It was reported on good authority that *Playboy* had entered the fray and Margaux's closest friend, Lucie Alvarez, claimed that a deal with *Penthouse* magazine was in the works.

Margaux was desperate for money. She was paid $5,000 for a twenty-minute appearance on *Coffee Break,* the newest morning talk-show sensation. When the show's host, Mario Blackstone, asked Margaux, on live television, which lawyer she had chosen to represent her in her multi-million dollar lawsuit against her deceased husband's estate, she answered that she would be representing herself. He said, "How do you feel about the old proverb that 'the lawyer who represents himself has a fool for a client?'"

"The fact of the matter is, Mario," she answered, "I can't afford a good trial lawyer. I'm dead broke!"

"C'mon now, Margaux, you've got to be kidding. My people did a little peeking at the records in surrogate's court and your step-daughter, Xenia Santoros, the executor of your husband's estate, has reported that the net assets of the estate are around six million dollars. Now, I asked Bob Woodson, one of the best known matrimonial attorneys in the city about it and he told me that as Toro's widow, in New York State, no matter what his will provided, as his widow you're entitled to the first fifty thousand dollars, and one third of his estate. That sounds like better than two million dollars to me. You're a lawyer, Margaux, are you telling my viewers that's not true?"

"Oh, that's the law, all right, unless the bride signs a prenuptial agreement like I did," she replied, "but let me tell the women out there among those loyal viewers of yours—" Margaux turned to face the camera— "when you're madly in love with a guy you're about to marry, and on the eve of the wedding he asks you to sign a prenuptial agreement, I suggest you call your lawyer."

"But Margaux," he said, laughing, "you *were* a lawyer on the eve of your marriage."

"Of course I was a lawyer, but first, and above all else, I was a woman who was deeply in love with my husband-to-be. You guys don't understand, or come to think about it maybe you do, and that's our problem. Women, no matter who they are, put love above everything else. Look at it this way: less than twelve hours before I was going to walk down the aisle of Saint Patrick's Cathedral to become Mrs. Dimitri Santoros, Toro casually suggested that I sign a simple agreement. My mind was on a zillion other things. I was exhausted from dealing with the wedding arrangements, including the reception for over 250 guests following the ceremony." She smiled at the television host. "By the way, I hope you got my thank-you note for that lovely silver soup bowl and ladle you and Manuela sent me."

"We did, indeed, and I must say it was one of the most fabulous wedding receptions I've ever attended, but don't let me get side-tracked here. You're asking us to believe that even though you were a lawyer yourself, you didn't understand you were giving up all your legal rights of entitlement as a wife? I don't think a jury will buy that, Margaux."

"No, no, no, Mario, you aren't listening to me. Of course I understood it, and I didn't hesitate for a moment when I signed it because I totally trusted Toro; but in my lawsuit against the estate, I'm not making a claim as Toro's widow, I'm only asking that the estate honor the very prenuptial agreement I signed the night before I got married." She turned again to face the camera, "And all I'm trying say to you ladies out there, is that there's nothing wrong with prenuptial agreements. In this day and age where multiple marriages are not uncommon it's perfectly reasonable for a man with children who is marrying for the second time to want to protect his estate for his children. That's only fair. All I'm saying is don't sign it before reading it carefully, seek advice from your attorney so you understand all the legal gobbledygook, and above all, *don't sign it on the eve of your wedding day!"*

Mario Blackstone had his eye on the clock. He had only two minutes before they went off the air. He planned to save the sixty-four dollar question to the very end, and he wanted a yes or no answer without giving Margaux an opportunity to explain her answer.

"That sounds like good advice to me, Margaux, but if I'm not mistaken, the only issue in your claim against your husband's estate is..." he hesitated, holding his audience in the palm of his hand. "Did you or did you not commit adultery during your marriage to Toro?"

You slime ball, Margaux thought, *you promised me you wouldn't ask such a question.*

When she hesitated before giving her answer, Blackstone asked, "Margaux, darling, is there something about the question you don't understand?" He pushed his microphone slightly forward to make certain he and his millions of listeners could hear her answer. Margaux looked at the studio clock, and slowly wrote a note. She smiled sweetly at the camera. "In order to avoid any misunderstanding, my answer to that question, is—" she said, holding the note up in the air, waving it back and forth until there were only five seconds left before the commercial break and then handing it to Blackstone just as the announcer broke in with his pitch for Clean Act Detergent. Off camera, Blackstone read the note to himself: *"Dear Mario, You are a rotten S.O.B. Love, Margaux."*

Within minutes after the program was over, the television station was flooded with telephone calls from attorneys all over the country offering to represent Margaux on a contingency fee basis. She chose a New York attorney who had won a number of high-profile cases. His name was Jonathan Knight and he was reputed to be one of the best trial lawyers in Manhattan.

In the weeks leading up to the trial involving Margaux's claim against Toro's estate, she and Jon Knight spent numerous hours together in preparation. He was very impressed by Margaux's knowledge of the law and her analytical skills. One day he was over two hours late for a scheduled appointment with her. He explained that he was doing double duty because Eric Stewart, his associate who had been responsible for doing the legal research on all of his important cases for many years, had suffered a heart attack shortly after Jon had agreed to represent Margaux and was following his cardiologist's instructions to take a six-month medical leave of absence.

"There's no one else in my office capable of taking over for Eric. I sort of enjoy doing my own research," he said, "but at the moment I'm overwhelmed by a backlog of cases. In retrospect I probably should never have offered to represent you, but the stakes were high and frankly, I was intrigued by the case and by you, not necessarily in that order." He laughed. "So here I am, weary and frazzled, and lacking sleep but no less devoted to your cause...and inexcusably late. I'm terribly sorry."

"I wanted to be very angry with you for making me sit in your waiting room for two hours reading old copies of *National Geographic* and *The New Yorker*, but you've taken the steam right out of my indignation. I'm really grateful to you for the wonderful job you're doing and I truly believe we have a shot at winning my case.

"Incidentally, I found a very recent decision, reported in a slip opinion, that's on all fours with my case. I prepared a brief for you to look at that might be helpful." Margaux handed him the brief and a copy of the opinion that had not yet been printed in the advance sheets. Jonathan Knight reached into the inside pocket of his jacket and removed his tortoise-shell reading glasses. He put then on and studied the documents Margaux had provided. When he finished, he pushed his glasses up on his forehead and looked directly at Margaux. Picking up her brief and pointing it at her, he said, "This is a first class piece of work that just might help us win $2,000,000." Margaux smiled appreciatively and said, "I also spent a year studying criminal law in the Richford Hills Prison library."

"How would you like to come to work for me? You don't need to be licensed to handle my legal research, and if you can do work for my criminal clients with the same professionalism that I see here, we could make a hell of a team. It's first-class research, Margaux."

"When do I start, Boss?"

In the days that followed, they worked together from eight in the morning until dinner time when one or the other would say, "It's Happy Hour."

Jon had introduced her to a tiny bar and restaurant a few blocks from the office where each evening she would order a dry Gray Goose vodka martini and he would order a Dewars and soda. There was a backgammon board inlaid on one of the bar tables in the corner and they would play one or two games to see who would pay for the drinks and after the second round they would part company until the next morning, when their routine would start all over again.

Margaux was more content with her life than she had been in a very long time, but she never forgave Gary for not trying to understand why she couldn't just walk away from two million dollars.

Occasionally she would lie in bed at night and think about him and cry for what might have been, but that happened less often after she began working for Jon. She knew that if she had presented the same question to Jon he would have agreed with her and not made such a big deal out of it the way Gary had.

When Jon won an appeal in a case they had worked on together, and the judge complimented Jon on the trial brief she had prepared, he invited Margaux to celebrate by having dinner with him at Panache, an upscale restaurant located in a brownstone mansion on East 72nd Street. Jon was in his late forties and had been married and divorced twice. He had never said or done anything to indicate he had any interest in Margaux except as a client and a professional colleague, so she concluded that he was probably gay. After a disastrous affair with her first employer/lover that ended with his death and her imprisonment, her *marriage* to Toro, and being "dumped", as she perceived it, by Gary Samson, she had settled into a life dominated by her work and her continuing love affair with Lucie Alvarez.

One night after going to dinner with Lucie, she stopped back at the office to pick up a brief she had forgotten to bring home. She found Jon still working. She joined him in the law office library. They each went about their work until Jon broke the silence.

"Okay, you win," he finally said, smiling. "I've got to know—what brought you back to my cave at ten o'clock on a Friday night when you're supposed to be living it up in the 'Big City'?"

"I forgot to bring home our brief in the Winston case. I wanted to work on it over the weekend. When I saw the light on here in the library, I thought I'd say hello."

"How come you're all gussied up?"

"Gussied up?"

"That's an expression my grandma always used. It means to be all dressed up."

"Oh yes, I do remember that. The answer is that I went out to dinner with my friend Lucie and we were supposed to hit one of the clubs, but she wasn't feeling well, and I never go into those places alone, so here I am."

"How about I take you dancing? A beautiful woman should never get all gussied up with nowhere to go," he said.

On the evening before the trial Jon Knight and Margaux were still battling about whether Margaux would testify. Jon insisted they didn't have a chance of winning if she didn't take the stand. Margaux was adamant that she was not going to give Williams the opportunity to drag up her affair with her former deceased employer and her criminal conviction for stealing a quarter of a million dollars from a client. Neither of those matters could be introduced in evidence if she didn't take the stand. Jon argued that unless the jurors were blind or illiterate or deaf and dumb, there was no way they wouldn't already know all about the "Barrister Beauty's" indiscretions. "So I don't care a damn about that," he said.

"I'm telling you, Margaux, they'll be begging you to just stand up and say, 'I did not commit adultery during my marriage to Toro Santoros.' That's all you have to do and I'm convinced they'll decide this case in your favor."

"I'm sorry Jon, but I can't do it."

"Can't or won't?" he snapped.

"Won't," she snapped back.

Jon picked up the file and threw it against the wall. Its contents spilled all over the library floor. Margaux was shocked. She had never seen Jon lose his temper before. In fact the only thing about him that she found disturbing was that he was always so calm. His personal secretary of many years once commented that in all her years she had never heard Jon raise his voice in anger.

"I'm sorry, Margaux. That was very childish of me," he said, and began to pick up the legal papers that were all scattered about.

"No, it's my fault. I understand why you're upset with me."

I really don't think you do, Jon thought, sadly.

CHAPTER THIRTY-FIVE

It was a cold blustery day in the beginning of November, 2008 when the trial of Margaux's case was scheduled to begin. She and Jon Knight exited from his limo in front of the courthouse. Margaux had a penchant for wearing all-black outfits. She always added an accent of red with a scarf and a belt to match the color of her lipstick. With her alabaster complexion, splashes of red gave her a startling appearance.

Spectators had begun lining up at the courthouse door, vying for the few seats available in the small courtroom usually devoted to estate matters of little interest to the public.

Cameras flashed wildly as Margaux and her attorney climbed the crowded steps and forced their way into the courtroom. Although surrogate court judges had the power to decide both questions of law and fact in estate matters, Judge Joseph Valentino had decided to exercise his discretion and empower a jury to hear and determine all issues of fact in the Santoros case.

Ordinarily, the first order of business in the jury selection process was to consider the applications of those prospective jurors who wished to be excused from jury duty. For the first time in his twenty-three years on the bench, when Judge Valentino addressed the jury panel and asked that those who wished to be excused step forward and give their names to the court clerk, not a single juror stood up. Judge Valentino smiled to himself in anticipation of what might be expected to occur in his court in the days to follow. He directed the clerk to call the first six jurors, and in record time the jury was selected and sworn.

However, the first battle between the titans of the bar—Clarence Williams Esq., representing the Estate of Dimitri Santoros and Jonathan Knight Esq., acting on behalf of Margaux Santoros—began as soon as Judge Valentino addressed the attorneys.

"All right, gentlemen, I guess we're ready to proceed with your opening remarks," he said.

Neither attorney stood up. The judge waited a few moments, then looked down at Attorney Knight, who stared blandly back at the judge who was clearly perplexed by Knight's failure to proceed with his address to the jury.

"Is it your intention to waive your opening, Mr. Knight?"

"Oh no, sir, but since there's no dispute as to the authenticity of the prenuptial agreement, I believe the executor has the burden of proving why she hasn't paid Mrs. Santoros' claim."

"What do you say about that, Mr. Williams?"

"I think it's putting the cart before the horse, sir."

The judge turned to the jury. "Members of the jury, it seems we may have a disagreement on the law here, so I'll ask you folks to step aside for a few moments until I can get things straightened out." When the jury had filed out of the courtroom, Judge Valentino said to Knight, "Now, what's this all about, Jon?"

"Judge, I'm just protecting my client's rights. She has no obligation to prove what she *didn't* do. The executor of the estate has the burden of proving why she hasn't paid my client the $2,000,000 she's entitled to under the terms of the agreement."

"I believe he may have a point there, Clarence. What do you think?" the judge asked.

"Frankly, your honor, I think it's a ridiculous argument. The agreement says Mrs. Santoros only gets paid if she hasn't committed adultery. That's the issue here."

"Jon? How about that?"

"It's pretty simple, Judge. Until the executor tells us who, when, and where, there's nothing we can say or do. You can't prove a negative."

The judge scratched his head and turned his chair around, with his back to the attorneys. Everyone in the room, including the judge's clerk and the court reporter, sat silently, awaiting Judge Valentino's next move.

When he turned back, he smiled and said, "All right, gentlemen, here's my decision. Mr. Williams, you must first tell us your client's reasons for not paying the claim and then Jon will tell us why you should, then we'll adjourn until tomorrow morning, when the executor will offer her evidence that Mrs. Santoros is an adulteress, because that's all this case is about."

The next morning, the headlines in the scandal sheets screamed

BARRISTER BEAUTY WINS ROUND ONE

Knight's investigator had confirmed that it was an all Christian jury;therefore a plain gold cross lay nestled between Margaux's ample breasts when she entered the courtroom. It matched the solitary gold band on the fourth finger of her left hand. The babble of conversation among the spectators stopped immediately when the court crier announced, "All rise. This court is now in session; Honorable Joseph Valentino presiding."

"Please be seated, folks," the judge said. "Are you ready to proceed, Mr. Williams?"

"Yes, sir,"

"Call your first witness, please," the judge ordered. Williams whispered to his young assistant, Carl Brown, who stood up and left the courtroom. The jurors all followed his movements and kept their eyes focused on the carved wooden courtroom doors, anxiously awaiting Brown's return with a young man whom he escorted up to the witness chair.

Knight leaned close to Margaux and asked, "Who is that?" Margaux scrutinized the individual who stopped beside the clerk of the court. "I don't have a clue. I've never seen him before in my life," she replied.

As a result of a court decision handed down in 1999, the oath administered to witnesses testifying in court was modernized in deference to our American diversity of religious beliefs and the constitutional sanctity of the separation of church and state. The age-old words, *Do you swear to tell the truth, the whole truth, and nothing but the truth, so help you God,* were retired. And the witness is no longer required to place his hand on the Bible.

The clerk addressed the witness. "Please state your name for the record."

"Tommy Rollins," the witness answered nervously.

"Do you swear or affirm to tell the truth and nothing but the truth?" the clerk demanded.

"I do," the witness replied, so softly that no one except the clerk could hear his reply.

"Please be seated," the clerk said, and the young man settled into the solid oak chair that was as old as the courthouse built in 1888.

Williams approached the witness box confidently. "Mr. Rollins, as you know, my name is Skip Williams and I represent the estate of Dimitri Santoros. Where do you reside, Mr. Rollins?"

"I live in Chicago, sir."

"How old are you?"

"I'll be nineteen next month."

"Are you acquainted with any member of the Santoros family?"

"Only his daughter, there," he said, pointing to Xenia who sat at the counsel table next to Carl Brown. "You introduced me to her just before we came into court this morning."

"What kind of work do you do, Tommy?"

"I'm a dishwasher and sort of a part-time waiter at the Palmer House hotel in Chicago."

Williams stepped over to the counsel table, picked up a yellow legal pad, flipped over a few pages and then turned back to the witness. "Were you working on the morning of June 23, 2007?"

"Yes, sir, I sure was."

"Why don't you just tell us in your own words what happened that morning, Tommy, and also how you remember the date so clearly." Several of the jurors leaned slightly forward in the jury box in order to hear every word the soft-spoken young man was saying.

"Well, sir," he said, "it was my first day of work at the Palmer House, and my supervisor sent me up to the penthouse suite."

"Oh, God," Margaux gasped under her breath.

The witness continued. "There was an early checkout and I was supposed to pick up the dirty dishes and glassware because we had people checking into the room around noon.

"I took the elevator up to the twenty-third floor, and then used the special key that operates the elevator between the twenty-third floor and the twenty-fourth floor where the penthouse is located. You can't take the elevator up there without that special key because the doors open up right into the suite. I didn't think nothing about it, because I was told the guests was supposed to be checked out by ten a.m. and it was almost eleven." The young man hesitated, shifted in his seat and didn't say anything more.

The attorney looked up at the boy and said, "Don't be afraid, Tom. Tell us what you saw when the elevator doors opened into the suite."

The boy took a deep breath, then continued. "When the elevator doors opened, I seen a lady standin' in the middle of the room with hardly any clothes on, and I seen a fella kinda messing with her and he was naked too, and I says excuse me and I shut my eyes and turned around and hit the 'close' button on the elevator panel. That's it, sir."

Williams walked slowly up to the witness box and asked, "Do you see that lady in the courtroom today, Mr. Rollins?"

The young man glanced nervously around the room and looked down at the floor. "Yes, sir," he said.

The court reporter who was recording the testimony on her stenographic machine said, "Excuse me, sir, I didn't hear your answer."

"Speak up now, Mr. Witness, so these old ears of mine can hear what you've got to say," the judge said in a kindly way. He then turned to the court reporter. "Read the question back, Jeannette."

"Do you see that lady in the courtroom today, Mr. Rollins?" the court reporter repeated.

"Yes, sir," he answered in a strong voice.

"Please point her out to us, Tommy," Williams commanded.

"I do believe it is that lady sitting right there, sir," Rollins said, pointing directly at Margaux.

The jurors sat back in their chairs. There were murmurs among the spectators, and several members of the news media quietly got up and exited the courtroom.

Margaux remained as still as a stone statue, but her face had turned ashen and she inadvertently cast her eyes downward.

"Your witness, Mr. Knight," the attorney for the estate said, attempting to suppress a triumphant smile as best he could.

Knight picked up his notepad and ambled up in front of the witness with more confidence than he felt. The witness's testimony had come as a total surprise to him. Margaux had told him that the only problem they had with the case was the Ramiriz claim, and had assured him that Ramiriz was lying.

"My name is Jon Knight," he said. "I represent Mrs. Santoros in this case and I have a few questions I want to ask you so I can better understand your testimony. First of all, I'm curious to know how you happened to speak with Mr. Williams about this case?"

Before the witness had a chance to answer, Williams was on his feet. "Objection as to relevancy...and besides it's confidential—attorney's work product."

As if they were of one mind, all of the jurors looked up at the judge. They were hoping he would allow the question to be answered because they were curious themselves as to how Williams had made a connection with the witness.

"Objection denied," the judge decided after a few moments' thought. "The question bears on the credibility of the testimony. Mr. Knight has the right to know what interest the witness may have in the case. I'm going to allow it."

"So tell us, Mr. Rollins, how *did* you get involved in the matter before us? Perhaps first, you might tell us *when* you first got involved?"

The young man smiled. "It was when me and my buddies at work was watching television on our coffee break a couple of weeks ago. We watch that program every day during coffee break."

"What show is that?" Knight asked.

"*Coffee Break,* with that crazy guy Mario Blackstone. See, he was talkin' to a lady about this case, and I says to my buddies, 'Man, I think I seen her before in the hotel here and she didn't have no clothes on.'" Rollins started to laugh and then covered his mouth with his hand.

"So what happened next?" Knight and the jurors were all smiling and when Rollins saw they were laughing *with* him and not *at* him, he continued, explaining that they bet if he called the TV show and told crazy old Mario Blackstone what he had seen, he might get to go on television himself, because Mario Blackstone was always saying that if you had a true, interesting story that he could use on the show he would bring you right to New York, pick you up in a limo, put you up in a fancy hotel, and give you some spending money for a night on the town. Rollins said he didn't have the nerve to call but one of his buddies did. Once he was connected to one of Mario Blackstone's assistants, his friend put Rollins himself on the line. He told the woman about having seen the nude lady in the hotel room, then seeing her on Blackstone's morning show. The staff person said she would talk to Mario about the phone call and possibly get back to Rollins.

"A few days later I got a call from Mr. Carl Brown and at first I thought he was part of the *Coffee Break* show. But then I learned that Mr. Brown was a lawyer and we had a long talk. Mr. Brown told me that he couldn't get me on the television show, but I could be an important witness in a famous case, and that his law firm would pay my airfare and put me up in a big hotel. He said he couldn't pay me nothing except a witness fee and for food and such because it would be against the law. I told him I would talk about it with my mom and the next day I called Mr. Brown back and told him my mom decided I should go for it."

He said his boss gave him the week off, and here he was, and everyone was treating him real nice.

"So tell me, Mr. Rollins, what was there about the woman you saw on the *Coffee Break* show that made you think it was the same person you had seen in the penthouse suite more than a year earlier for only a second or two?" Knight knew it was a dangerous question because an elementary rule of cross-examination is that you must never ask a question if you don't know the answer. But he was desperate to defuse the powerful impact of the boy's testimony.

Rollins shook his head and answered carefully. "I guess the reason was that except in a magazine, I ain't never seen such a beautiful woman like that with no clothes on. I mean she had a right nice-lookin' set of, uh, uh, I mean like overall she was real beautiful."

Most of the jurors were having difficulty suppressing their laughter.

"How long did you say you actually saw her, Mr. Rollins?" Knight asked, with his fingers crossed.

"Oh, I shut my eyes real quick, sir."

"What did the man look like?"

"I can't recollect that at all. I mean, I knew there was a mistake a some kind, and I just wanted to get outta there as fast as I could."

"Is it fair to say you weren't there more than a second or two?"

"That's right, sir, a second or two at the most."

"Just one last question, Mr. Rollins. Would you say there's a possibility you are mistaken about it being Mrs. Santoros that you saw in the hotel room?"

Margaux and her attorney each held their breath as Rollins stared at Margaux. She stared back at him blankly, though her heart was crashing in her chest.

The courtroom fell totally silent. A full twenty seconds passed. Rollins closed his eyes and then he said in a most serious tone of voice, "There's only one way I could be certain about that...and that ain't gonna happen so I guess, like I said before, I do believe she is the lady I seen, but I can't be, you know, positive certain."

"Thank you Mr. Rollins," Knight said, "I don't have any further questions."

"When Knight returned to his seat beside Margaux, she whispered to him, "Now I know why they say you're the best. Thank you." She smiled, but Knight did not smile back.

"Be prepared to call your next witness in fifteen minutes, Mr. Williams. We'll take a short recess now, folks," Judge Valentino nodded to the jury.

"All rise," the court crier called out. The judge walked majestically back to his chambers and the jury dutifully returned to the jury room. As soon as the judge and jury left, the babble of voices from the spectators filled the room.

Back in his chambers the judge's clerk asked him, "What did you think of that, Judge?"

The judge smiled and said, "I thought the witness was brilliant. I was wondering what I would do if one of the attorneys demanded that I order Mrs. Santoros to disrobe so that Mr. Rollins could be 'positive certain.'"

"I fantasized about that a little bit myself, Judge," the clerk said with a grin.

Attorney Williams called his next witness. His name was Terrence VanSant.

"Mr. VanSant, can you give us a little bit of your background?" Williams asked.

"I'm a free-lance writer and photographer."

"Are you a resident of the village of Sea Cliff on Long Island?"

"Oh no, I just rented a place there for a few months, a year or so ago."

"Who were your immediate neighbors while you were spending the summer in Sea Cliff?"

"Mr. and Mrs. Tavelli lived on one side and a fellow by the name of Gary Samson lived on the other. Samson had a big spread with a dock and a sailboat—you know, upscale stuff. I just lived in this little summer cottage. He and I didn't hit it off too well, but since I was only going to be there for a few months it didn't matter to me."

"Tell me, Mr. VanSant," Williams asked, "Did a time come during that summer of 2007, while you were living in Sea Cliff, that a bizarre event took place on your neighbor Samson's dock?"

The witness smiled and said, "I wouldn't call it bizarre, I'd call it *outré*, you know," he answered with a look of self-satisfaction that immediately turned off most of the jurors.

Williams picked up on the jurors' reaction and said, "I'm not familiar with that word, Mr. VanSant. What do you mean by that?"

"*Outré*? It's spelled *o-u-t-r-e* with an accent over the letter *e*. It's a French word, and...oh, I don't know...I'd say it refers to behavior that is a bit outrageous."

Clarence Williams was seething. He believed that the jury might discount all of VanSant's testimony because of his arrogance, but now that he had put him in the witness box all the attorney could do was try to control him. "Please tell us what you observed," Williams asked.

Knight stood up, "If the court please, could we have a date established?"

"Yes," the judge turned to Williams. "Let's see if you can't narrow it down to something more precise than the summer of 2007, Mr. Williams," Judge Valentino said.

"I didn't put it in my diary, for goodness sakes," VanSant piped up.

Knight was on his feet again, but before he could speak, the judge interrupted, "You're right, Mr. Knight...Just answer the questions put to you by the attorneys, sir."

"Please, Mr. VanSant, could you give us your best recollection as to the date that the unusual event took place at your neighbor's house?" the attorney urged.

"I guess it was around the second week in July. I was in my back yard, which was on the top of the cliff. You see, the whole west side of the village of Sea Cliff is bounded by Roslyn Harbor and sits on a cliff. Sea...Cliff, get it?" the witness laughed, but no one joined him. "Anyway, I was in my back yard, photographing some red roses, when I saw Samson and a young lady climbing down the steps that lead to Samson's dock. Ordinarily I wouldn't have paid any attention to them, but the lady was wearing a very skimpy bikini and they were acting silly. Frankly, they were cavorting like teenagers. I always thought Samson was sort of a show-off anyway, and then they both ran down and dived off the dock into the water. The next thing I saw was Samson hoisting up a flag on the flagpole at the end his dock. I was trying to figure out what kind of a flag it was, but it was too far away and then I remembered I had a zoom lens in my camera bag. I screwed it onto my camera, and when I looked through the viewfinder, I realized it wasn't a flag after all, it was a woman's bikini top, so I snapped a picture of it, and then the woman climbed up on the dock and she was topless." He smiled and looked at the jury to see their reaction, but they all remained stone-faced. "Well, the next thing I saw was this semi-nude lady embracing my neighbor, Samson. She appeared quite attractive, so I took a close-up picture of her as well." Williams stepped over to the counsel table and his assistant handed him two enlarged photos.

"I show you Exhibits One and Two and ask you if these are the pictures you took that day."

"They are, indeed," VanSant replied.

"Do you see the woman in the photo here in the courtroom?"

The witness scanned the court room and then said, "I told you in your office when you showed me some pictures of a lady you claimed was Mrs. Santoros, that I couldn't be certain it was the same woman, but you suggested that when I saw her in the courtroom I would be able to make a positive identification." The witness then leaned forward and scrutinized Margaux. After a few seconds, he leaned back in the witness chair. "You must admit, sir, the circumstances are quite different," the witness chuckled. "I just can't be sure about it."

Williams said to himself, *Damn! I should have known better.* Addressing the judge, he said, "I offer the photo exhibits in evidence, Your Honor."

"Any objection, Mr. Knight?" the judge asked.

"No, sir."

"Do you choose to cross-examine the witness, Mr. Knight?" the judge asked.

"No, sir," Knight replied without hesitation.

Judge Valentino looked at the clock, and then turned to the jury. "This seems like a good time to adjourn, ladies and gentlemen. Mr. Williams advises me that he may have one more witness that he intends to call Monday morning, and then Mr. Knight will begin his case. So you're all free until then, but remember you are not to discuss the case with anyone, including your fellow jurors, until you have heard all the evidence. Have a nice weekend, then be back here at 9:30 sharp on Monday morning."

Clarence Williams and Carl Brown remained silent during the ride back to their office in the firm's limousine. Williams was dejected. He had hoped that it wouldn't be necessary to call Ramiriz. As he saw the situation, there were serious problems with Ramiriz. Nick Santoros had supplied the information that Ramiriz was prepared to testify that he had slept with Margaux when they were fellow passengers on the cruise ship *Seadancer*. When Nick produced Ramiriz to be interviewed by Attorney Williams, the first thing he asked was how much he was going to be paid for his testimony. When he was told that he could only be paid a modest fee like anyone else who was subpoenaed to testify, he went into a rage.

"Nick tells me you lawyers are being paid mucho bucks," he said, "and you guys are only going to pay me a lousy witness fee of twenty dollars a day to win this case for you? No way, Hoseay."

"If we subpoena you, Mr. Ramiriz, you must tell the truth. That's the law, sir," Carl Brown had told him.

"You know what, Mr. Attorney? I just got amnesia. I don't remember nothing. Margaux Santoros? Never heard of the lady."

The second problem is, Williams worried, *what explanation has Ramiriz got for videotaping the bedroom scene in the first place? No one is going to believe it was done with Mrs. Santoros' consent. I've got an idea about that, but I don't want to know the answer to that question either, and besides I've got my doubts that it really is Mrs. Santoros in the video anyhow. And finally, Ramiriz has convictions for assault and petty larceny. The jury probably won't believe him no matter what he tells them about his supposed sexual adventure with Margaux Santoros.*

Margaux and Knight scrambled out the back entrance of the courthouse, but there were several reporters there hoping to catch a front page photo or a comment from one of them. When one of the reporters asked her what she thought of the testimony so far, she said, "Where's the beef?" The comment appeared in bold print on the front page of one of the New York City papers.

They went directly to Knight's office where they sat without speaking for several minutes. She decided he would have to make the first move.

Finally he said, "Okay, I give up. What's the story here?"

"Story? What story?" she shrugged.

"The God-damn Palmer House scenario and the Sea Cliff bikini bit. Before I agreed to represent you, I asked you one simple question: Were you innocent of the charge against you or weren't you? You sat in the very chair you're sitting in right now, and you swore to me that you were innocent. Is that true or not?"

"They claimed I wasn't entitled to my share of the estate because I slept with Luis Ramiriz. I told you that was untrue. I also told you I would not testify. We had no discussion about anything else. You were eager to represent me, and I agreed. As far as I'm concerned nothing has changed."

"Are you prepared to take the stand and tell it just that way?"

Margaux turned away from her attorney and stared at the painting of Abraham Lincoln that hung on the wall. If she took the stand and subjected herself to cross examination, she would put herself in an impossible situation. First of all, the whole sordid mess of her felony conviction for grand larceny and her imprisonment would all be hashed over again, but she could probably live with that. The major problem, the problem that had destroyed her relationship with Gary Samson, was that when attorney Williams asked her, "Do you swear that you never committed adultery during your marriage to Dimitri Santoros?" she had only two choices. Either commit perjury, or admit she had slept with Gary on a number of occasions, and lose $2,000,000.

Jon waited patiently for her answer.

"For the umpteenth time Jon, I told you, I'm not going to testify."

"God damn it, Margaux, you've got to convince the jury that Ramiriz isn't telling the truth. The jury wants to hear you say that." He slammed his notepad down on his desk.

"Jon, I was up front with you from the beginning. I told you that if we were going to win this case, you would have to do it without my taking the stand. You agreed. You said that as long as I swore to you that Ramiriz was a liar and that I never slept with him, you would represent me and that you thought you could break him on cross examination. In my opinion, so far you have done that magnificently with Rollins and VanSant. You can do the same with Ramiriz. He's a thief and a liar."

"Jesus, how did I get myself into this situation?"

"For the money and for the publicity you've already gotten. I think there are about 25,000 or 30,000 lawyers in Manhattan. Your name has been in the newspaper and on television a dozen times a day for the past week. You could never afford to buy that exposure. You're set for life."

"That's true if we win! But—we must win! I need your testimony to do that. Please, Margaux," he begged.

"No dice, Jon. I'm going to get something to eat. Do you want to join me?"

"No, dammit. Just bring me back a ham and Swiss cheese sandwich on rye, and a Coke," he said gruffly, and started to spread the contents of his file out on the conference room table.

Attorney Williams agonized all weekend about whether or not he should put Ramiriz on the stand. Ultimately he decided he had no choice. Without Ramiriz he didn't have a case. Rollins and Van Sant had both fallen apart on the stand. There was only a bare chance that Judge Valentino would even let the case go to the jury unless Williams offered some additional proof that Margaux had committed adultery. He finally decided to subpoena Ramiriz, have him identify the videotape depicting Ramiriz and a woman Nick Santoros claimed was Margaux Santoros, and let the chips fall where they might.

He was bleary-eyed when he picked up the stack of unread telephone messages that had accumulated on his desk. He flipped through them quickly and was about to push them aside and deal with them later, when a name caught his attention.. His secretary had written, "Aldo Sanchez called. He says you should remember him from the Gilbert case. He claims to have some important information for you in the Santoros matter. Please call him ASAP."

Manhattan received its first snowfall on a day near the end of November when the Santoros case resumed in surrogate's court. The addicted courtroom spectators, made up mostly of retirees and the unemployed looking for a warm place to spend the day, huddled outside the courthouse waiting for the doors to open. Although the Santoros case no longer rated the front page, the trial was being followed religiously by the media. Reckoning from the judge's remarks at the close of court on Friday, the experienced reporters were anticipating that Margaux would probably testify sometime Monday afternoon, depending upon the length of the direct and cross-examination of Attorney Williams' last witness. Since his case, as far as it had gone, seemed to have fallen apart, they were all curious to hear what Williams' main witness would have to say about Margaux Santoros' infidelity.

Carl Brown, Attorney Williams' assistant, was frantic. He had been waiting an hour in the courthouse lobby for Ramiriz to show up. At 9:25, five minutes before the judge would enter the courtroom, he rushed into the ornate chamber and told Attorney Williams that Ramiriz was a no-show.

"That son of a bitch," Williams cursed. "I should have known better."

The jury was eager to watch the upcoming confrontation between Attorney Knight and Williams' last witness.

They were also excited about finally being able to see and hear the infamous Margaux Santoros deny the implications of the testimony of the young waiter, Rollins, from the Palmer House Hotel in Chicago, and Van Sant, the arrogant artist from Sea Cliff, and wondered how she could possibly explain her way out of the videotape that Attorney Williams had promised to produce as an exhibit, depicting Margaux and Luis Ramiriz engaged in acts of "sexual intimacy," as he delicately described them, in his opening remarks at the beginning of the case.

Although at the close of each day in court Judge Valentino had instructed them that they must not talk to anyone about the case, and they were prohibited from reading anything about it in the newspaper, or listening to the radio or watching television, very few jurors ever followed these impossible mandates. Certainly the judge didn't expect them not to discuss the case with their spouses. They would try to honor the judge's admonition not to be influenced by what they might inadvertently hear about the case outside the courtroom, but as one male juror put it, "If I don't tell my wife every gory detail, I'll end up in divorce court myself."

When Ramiriz hadn't shown up by ten o'clock, Judge Valentino called the lawyers into his chamber.

"What's going on, Clarence?" the judge demanded of Attorney Williams, with more than a touch of anger in his voice.

"I'm sorry, Your Honor, I subpoenaed him for nine a.m. just in case he got hung up in traffic. I don't know where the hell he is, Judge. I apologize, sir, I just don't...."

"I'm sure it's not your fault, Skip, but when he does show up I want you to bring him in to my chambers, because I'm going to give him a tongue lashing like he's never had before." The judge called the court clerk and told her to advise the jury that "We've run into some technical difficulties, and will be getting underway as soon as possible."

At eleven o'clock Judge Valentino summoned the attorneys back into his chambers.

"I'm sorry, Skip, but unless you have any more witnesses I'm going to give the jury an early lunch break and resume the case at one o'clock, at which time you will either produce your lost witness or I'll declare the evidence closed. Is that clear?"

"Yes sir. But if I don't produce Ramiriz, I have one more witness and then I'll rest my case."

"Fair enough, Skip. And Jon, I want you to be prepared to go forward as soon as Skip closes his case this afternoon. Do you have a problem with that?"

"No, sir, subject to my right to move to dismiss for failure to prove a prima-facie case. I'm very serious about that motion, Judge, because as the case stands now I don't see that Skip has proved anything to justify not paying my client what's owed to her."

"I hear you, Jon, and I must tell you, Skip, unless you produce something more substantial than what I've heard so far, I'm inclined to grant Jon's motion. In the meantime, I suggest that you fellows might get together during lunch and settle this case."

"I understand, Judge," Williams said. "I don't think that can happen until I close my case, but I'll talk to my clients during the lunch break, and speak with Jon before he begins his case...I'm certainly willing to try to work something out."

"Me too, Judge," Jon said. "But I've got a tough client who absolutely denies any wrongdoing and, frankly, unless Skip has something up his sleeve beside that videotape he mentioned in his opening address, which I'm inclined to believe is a total fraud, I can't blame her for wanting the case to go to the jury."

"All right, gentlemen, we're adjourned until one o'clock."

When Jon emerged from the judge's chambers he said to Margaux, "Let's go back into the witness holding room where we can talk privately." He put his arm around her shoulders and led her back to the tiny bare room where witnesses were kept while they awaited their turn to testify.

As soon as the door was closed behind them, Margaux asked, "What the devil is going on, Jon? What's up with Ramiriz?"

"I think your friend Ramiriz has flown the coop. I don't think they're going to be able to produce him."

"Without his testimony they have no case. We've won, Jon! Ramiriz was their last witness."

"I hope you're right, but Williams says he has another witness beside Ramiriz and it ain't over till the fat lady sings, as they say."

"Are you ready to proceed, Mr. Williams?" Judge Valentino asked, after the jurors filed into the jury box the next morning.

"Yes, Your Honor. I call Margaux Santoros," Williams said, in a loud clear voice.

The print and television reporters in the room immediately became animated. This was NEWS. There was a rumble in the courtroom from the spectators. Judge Valentino rapped his gavel and the room immediately quieted down. Margaux glanced at her attorney. He put his hand gently on her arm.

Margaux appeared to be in a state of shock. "What am I supposed to do, Jon?" she whispered.

"Just tell the truth," he said.

"If I tell the *whole truth* we're going to lose this case," she hissed.

"If you don't tell the *whole* truth, you're going to lose your lawyer," her attorney replied.

"Mrs. Santoros, please take the stand," Judge Valentino said in a kindly tone of voice.

When Margaux stood up and walked majestically to the witness box half the people in the courtroom had a vision of Joan of Arc; the other half had a vision of Marie Antoinette.

As soon as she was sworn in, she stepped into the box and sat down in the witness chair. Attorney Williams strode up to the lectern and said,

"I have just a few questions, Mrs. Santoros." He picked up one of the photo exhibits and said, "I show you Exhibit A received in evidence and ask you if that is your bikini flying from the top of the flag pole on Mr. Gary Samson's dock at his home in Sea Cliff, Long Island, in the late summer of 2007?" He handed the exhibit to the court attendant, who handed it to Margaux. She studied it for a moment and then answered, "It's not my swim suit, it belonged to Mr. Samson's daughter, but I borrowed it that day, and...."

"And what ?" Williams asked.

"And actually it's only the top half, which was several sizes too small for me." Several of the male jurors smiled.

"I show you Exhibit B and ask you if you recognize the man embracing a semi-nude woman in the photo."

"Yes, that's Gary Samson."

"Is he a friend of yours?"

"Yes."

He held up the enlarged close-up of the seminude woman on the dock embracing Gary Samson.

"Do you agree that Exhibit B is a photograph of you, taken in the summer of 2007 while you were married to Dimitri Santoros, Mrs. Santoros?"

"I do."

Attorney Williams stepped back to his counsel table and picked up a large number of eight by ten-inch photographs. He placed them on the lectern and said, "Tell me, Mrs. Santoros, have you ever been to the State of Vermont?"

"Yes," Margaux answered.

"How many times?"

"I can't remember. Many."

"What is your best estimate?"

Margaux thought for a few moments and said, "Perhaps fifteen or twenty, more or less."

"For business or pleasure?"

"They were all pleasure trips."

"Did you ever spend any time on Lake Somerset?"

"I don't recognize the name, but I've visited a number of lakes in Vermont so I can't be certain."

"Well, let me see if I can refresh your recollection."

Margaux's mind was in turmoil. *Somehow they must have gotten to Sanchez...Gary never mentioned the name of the lake...maybe they've got the wrong name...No, no, Sanchez must have included it in his report...*Her thoughts were all scrambled, colliding with each other like atoms in a synchrotron. She felt faint. *Jon...Gary...Lucie...help me!* She held tight to the sturdy arms of the witness chair. *If I let go of this chair I'll fall forward, down the step, and strike my head on the floor...Maybe I'll die. Yes, maybe I'll die and it will be all over. I wonder what it's like to be dead?... Jon...Gary, please. Please, Lucie....*

"Mrs. Santoros, let me show you Exhibit C, marked for identification," Attorney Williams said. The clerk handed the photograph to Margaux. She stared at it. It was the picture of her and Gary dancing nude in the cabin. She stared blankly at Attorney Williams. Her eyes were glazed over. She heard Jon Knight address Judge Valentino.

"Your Honor, under the rules of this court, the witness is not permitted to testify with respect to an exhibit that hasn't been offered into evidence except to identi—" The jurors gasped in unison as Margaux collapsed and started to fall out of the witness chair. Attorney Williams reached out and caught her in his arms. Once again the courtroom was in an uproar. The judge rapped his gavel but no one was paying any attention to him.

Judge Valentino directed Williams to carry Margaux into his chamber, and told the court clerk to call 911 for emergency medical services. He stood up and addressed the spectators: "Is there a physician in the courtroom? Quiet, please. Is there a physician in the courtroom?" An elderly lady responded "I'm an R.N., Your Honor, perhaps I can help until a doctor is found."

"Thank you so much ma'am. Please come with me."

Jon had followed Attorney Williams into the judge's chambers. He was kneeling beside Margaux who was still unconscious, lying on the floor in the judge's private office. The retired nurse immediately took charge and within a few minutes she had revived Margaux and asked for water. Jon handed her a glass of water. The nurse raised Margaux into a sitting position and forced her to drink the cold water. When the judge was satisfied that Margaux appeared to be in good hands he returned to the courtroom and advised the jurors that Mrs. Santoros had regained consciousness, that he was adjourning the case for the present, and that the clerk would call them after he had an opportunity to discuss the matter with the attorneys.

Once the EMS crew arrived and examined Margaux, they determined that although she didn't appear to be in any immediate danger, they would take her to the emergency room of the nearest hospital for a more comprehensive examination.

When the chamber was cleared except for the judge, the clerk and the two attorneys, Judge Valentino told the attorneys that depending upon the results of Margaux's medical examination he had decided to adjourn the case until the following afternoon when they would resume the trial.

"This would be a good time for you gentlemen to see if you can get together and resolve this matter," the judge said, "and in any event, Skip, I want you to show Jon those exhibits you plan to offer into evidence and I want to see both of you in my chambers at 9:30 tomorrow morning."

Jon Knight told Skip Williams that he would go directly to the hospital, get things sorted out with Margaux, and come to Skip's office to discuss how they might proceed.

After he visited with Margaux and was satisfied that with a good night's sleep and the opportunity to relax in the morning she would be able to return to the witness stand, he arranged for her discharge from the hospital and took her home. They spent several hours there discussing the situation during which she advised Jon she could not go back on the witness stand.

"I can't stop him from serving you with a subpoena, Margaux. You either have to testify or agree to a dismissal of your claim," Jon said. When she told him about the photo Attorney Williams had shown her just before she fainted, and confessed to her affair with Gary Samson, he said, "Well, let me see how we can get out of this mess as gracefully as possible. I'll call you later after I've had a chance to speak to Skip."

When Jon was shown into Attorney Williams' office, they shook hands and exchanged pleasantries. Jon chided his colleague, "I knew you were a skilled trial lawyer, Skip, but I didn't know you had the power to cause witnesses to faint under your cross-examination, like they do on television."

"The thing is, Jon, I've never cross-examined such a skilled actress before," Skip responded, and then he laughed and gave Jon an exaggerated wink. "Did you have a chance to talk turkey with her?" he asked, smiling.

"As a matter of fact, I did. I now know you can crucify her on the stand."

"Hey, Jon, if she had lied to me about that nude picture of her on Samson's dock in Sea Cliff, I was prepared to tear her apart. I wasn't going to show her those photos taken in Vermont until *after* she denied that little escapade in the cabin on Lake Coochie Coochie or whatever the name is. As a trial lawyer, can you imagine the fun I'd have had if she denied that weekend with Samson and then I sprang those porno photos on her? But then I remembered Rupert Forgatch."

"Rupert Forgatch. You got me there, buddy. Who the hell is he?"

"Have you forgotten *McShane versus Forgatch*? I haven't."

"McShane against Forgatch? It doesn't ring a bell," Jon replied.

"Let me refresh your recollection, as they say." Skip smiled. "It was back in the early nineties. You and I were hustling, trying to make names for ourselves as up-and-coming barristers. You represented McShane, a cute little redhead, and I represented the father of a child they had conceived without benefit of matrimony. They were battling over custody of the child, each one accusing the other of the most atrocious conduct—you know, physically abusing the child, doing drugs, allowing the child to play with loaded guns.... We were both scared to death that before the hearing was over we'd have a homicide on our hands. Well, you know what it's like down there in family court, the judges are so overworked and the backlog of cases is so bad that you can never introduce more than a day's testimony at a time. Lord, I've got a case right now where the first witness testified almost a year ago and all that's happened during that time is that the judge has adjourned the case three times.... Anyway, you and I tried to get those kids to settle their differences, but it seemed to me they just couldn't stand to be in the same room together for more than five minutes. Boy, was I wrong."

"Wait a minute, is that the case where my client got herself pregnant while we were awaiting the next hearing date and it turned out your guy was the father of the child *in utero*?"

"The very same. Rupert Forgatch was his name. You saved me from making an ass of myself. Before you told me about her second pregnancy by my client, I had intended to argue to the judge how your little redhead had raped my innocent client and had intentionally gotten herself pregnant the first time. When you learned that my client had impregnated her a second time, in the middle of the case involving the custody of their first child, you could have cut off my whatevers, if we had continued the trial. But you told me you didn't think justice would be served if you sprang that bomb on me during the next hearing, whenever that might be, so you shared the information about the second pregnancy with me and we got the case settled. I always figured I owed you one. Maybe this is it, provided of course it doesn't cost my client too much money," he laughed.

"You're a fine lawyer and a good man, Skip. Thanks for remembering."

"One last thing I've got to say, Jon, if you promise not to be offended or tell anyone I said it."

"I promise, man."

"That client of yours has the most beautiful pair of tits I've ever seen."

"All right, gentlemen," Judge Valentino said. "Jon tells me that you might be able to reach some sort of agreement that could end this controversy. Am I right, Jon?"

"Yes Judge. Skip and I talked yesterday and he said he might be able to help us out of the predicament my client and I got ourselves into. She vigorously denies any wrongdoing with Ramiriz and that's why she claims she pursued this business in the first place, but she admits she hasn't been exactly up-front with all of us and wants to do the right thing now. Skip says he has some thoughts about that."

"What say you, Skip?"

"Well, sir, my real client is Xenia Santoros, Dimitri's daughter. She's a very perceptive young lady. I understand why Dimitri appointed her as executor of his estate. Fortunately, she likes Margaux, because except for this adultery thing which she sort of understands because Margaux was so much younger than her father, and besides, Xenia acknowledges she made a pretty big mistake herself in the love department a few years ago.... In any event, she says except for the Samson hiccup, Margaux made her dad very happy during the last years of his life."

"I'm glad to hear that, Skip. There aren't many people these days who would see it that way," the judge offered.

"You know, Judge, I'm not sure you're right about that. This Obama victory has got me thinking that the young people in this country have taught us old coots that it's time to bury some of the old ways, and these kids didn't just talk about it, they went out by the hundreds of thousands and volunteered to work for Obama. I like what I've seen and respect them for helping our country put this stupid business about skin color in the trash can where it belongs."

"Amen, brother," Jon chimed in.

"To get back at the situation at hand, what do you have for us, Skip?" Judge Valentino asked.

"Well, Zee—that's Xenia's nickname, sir—sees it this way. She believes that with the Vermont photos in play, there's no way that the estate can lose the case, and I agree with her one hundred percent. However, she has agreed to pay Margaux $325,000 to put an end to the ugly mess.

"One more thing involving Margaux," Williams added. "The estate had to pay $25,000 dollars for the negatives of the Vermont photos and she expects Margaux to reimburse her."

"What do you think about Skip's offer, Jon?" Judge Valentino asked. "Under the circumstances I think it's exceedingly generous."

"I agree, Judge. I accept the offer on my client's behalf."

"Admirable, admirable. I commend you both for the honorable way this has been accomplished."

When Jon explained it all to her, Margaux smiled and said, "If it hadn't been for you and Zee I'd be getting nothing and be sent to jail for perjury, and never, ever, get my license to practice law restored. I'm deeply indebted to you, Jon."

"Well, all I can say is that if you wish, you can go on working for me as a paralegal until you get your license back and then, if you continue to do good work, I don't see why I wouldn't take you on as a junior partner. How does that sound to you?"

She stepped close to him, kissed him chastely and said, "I think I'm going to faint."

CHAPTER THIRTY-SIX

"Welcome Home!" Everyone in Aeva's office in Bora Bora gathered around her to learn about her adventure on the *Seadancer*. It only took her a few hours to fill them in and answer all their questions. It took considerably longer for her to readjust to island life, where most of the police action centered around the local bars at closing time.

She owned a shack on a small plot of land beside the sea on the north side of the island. It was only accessible by boat, and on her first weekend off after her return to work, she packed food, drink and a change of clothes and set out in her little four-meter skiff with a six-horsepower outboard motor. It took her an hour, putt-putting along at half speed, to reach the cabin. Over a year had passed since she had visited her hideaway, but except for the overgrowth of vegetation it was exactly as she had left it. She had some serious thinking to do, and she had decided that her little vacation shelter was the best possible place to sort out the questions that needed to be addressed.

First she took her machete that was hidden under the front porch and cleared away the vines and undergrowth that had totally hidden the cabin from view from the water. Then she bathed in the sea and floated on her back with only the deep blue sky and an occasional puff or two of white fluffy cloud above her. She thought about how luscious it was to feel the warm salt water caressing every inch of her nude body. *Just the way my ancestors used to bathe before the missionaries came and taught us to be ashamed of our bodies,* she lamented. *Why did we let them do that? Is their One God more real than our God of the sun and the moon and the wind and the sea? Has their God created a more peaceful world? Has their God produced a less selfish, more sensitive and more generous society than my forebears enjoyed? How come my great, great grandparents didn't need a police force? They didn't need orphanages or government to formalize and supervise adoptions. Every child born in these islands was loved and cared for. Today, do fathers treat the mothers of their children with greater respect and offer them more lasting love because their union has been blessed by the church or sanctioned by judicial decree?* She stood up in the sea and marched tall and proud of her Polynesian blood, exhilarated by the gentle sea breeze that caressed her body. After drying off she slipped on the extra-large *Seadancer* T-shirt Roger had given her the first night they made love, opened a bottle of French wine she had slipped into her pack and settled down in a dilapidated old lounge chair on her tiny front porch. She picked up the book she had brought along, and smiled when she read the title again: *Dictionary of American Slang*. She opened it at random and read aloud, "*I like you a lot*"..."*I dig you, Baby.*"

As the sun began to ease into the sea in a swirl of reds and pinks and purples it took her breath away as it always did. When it finally dipped silently below the horizon, and she began to see the faint glitter of stars waiting in the wings to take over the night sky, she felt more at peace with herself than ever before in her life. *Why is that?* she wondered. *I have more questions and fewer answers than ever. Could it be that I am truly in love? I am more than thirty years old and I have never felt this way before. Eh bien! C'est formidable!* she laughed out loud, scaring away a small young bird the Polynesians call a vini-vini that had been sitting comfortably on a lower branch of a jacaranda tree, observing the strange creature the likes of which it had never seen before.

Roger had sent her a constant stream of messages from the *Seadancer*. Each one contained a map indicating the *Seadancer's* location, coming closer and closer to Bora Bora, confirming over and over their pact to spend three days together. *And what will he say when I tell him I want a child? His child! And then he will ask me, How shall we raise this child? and I shall tell him that we shall smother our child with love. And when she or he comes to us one day and asks us, What are we Mommy? What do you mean, my child? I shall reply, and then, he or she will say, In class today the teacher went around the room and asked each of us whether we we were Catholic or Protestant, or some other faith, and when she came to me, I said, I don't know. My Mommy is Polynesian and she still believes in the wonder of life and my Daddy told me that he hasn't figured it all out yet, but, for sure, we're thinking about it.*

"Why didn't I think of it before?" she said aloud. "We shall spend our three days together right here. I have time to create a love nest to challenge the Garden of Eden, and I guarantee I'll do a better job of it than Eve did." She smiled happily. Then she stood up as darkness was fast closing in upon her, threw her arms up to the sky and cried aloud, "Oh Moon God, I am so deliriously happy. Please, please, let our three days be filled with music and laughter and joy and love in every shape and form. I love my man—oh, how I love my man."

A few days after Aeva returned to her headquarters, Corporal Faree asked, "Is there a problem, Lieutenant Fontein?"

Aeva lowered her binoculars and turned to her subordinate. "*Mais non*, why do you ask?"

"I don't know, ma'am. I can't figure it out. All day long you've been looking out across the bay every half hour, but I can't see anything out there except an occasional fisherman."

"You're right, Dedier, I haven't seen anything other than that myself," Aeva replied.

The young corporal took off his hat and scratched his head. "What I don't understand is that I've never before seen you do something without a purpose. So how do you explain that?"

Aeva looked at him and smiled. "I'll take that as a compliment, Corporal, but you must realize I can't share *all* my thoughts with you."

"I know, I know, but I have this feeling that you're up to something mysterious and I'm trying to solve the mystery."

"Did it ever occur to you that it might be something personal?"

"Absolutely not! *Mon Dieu*, Lieutenant! I've never ever seen you do anything personal while you were on duty. That would be against the rules, wouldn't it ma'am?"

Aeva glanced at her watch. "My goodness, Corporal, look what time it is—ten minutes past four. You've been off duty for ten minutes. This is the first time you have ever remained on duty more than thirty seconds after your shift was over. Have a good evening, Dedier," she said, as she raised her field glasses again and swept the bay slowly. Her heart leaped when she saw the dark spot growing larger on the horizon. She remained outwardly calm, but she wanted to scream out with joy. She waved nonchalantly to the corporal as she casually returned to her office. When she was satisfied that he had left the compound for home, she went outside again and focused her binoculars on the *Seadancer* as it headed straight for the mooring in the center of the bay. Within a few minutes from the time the massive ship had been secured at its mooring and an anchor had been released from the stern, she saw the ship's tender being lowered, and she spied the unmistakable silhouette of the captain in stark contrast to *Seadancer's* white gleaming hull. He stood tall in the bow of the tender as it moved swiftly toward the pier. With studied nonchalance, Aeva locked her office door, hopped into her French Jeep and drove off toward the dock. Her vehicle and the tender arrived simultaneously. It took all her willpower to keep from running into his arms. She saw that after stepping quickly off the small craft, he sent it on its way back to the ship, and then stood quite still, nervously scanning the area until he discovered her leaning casually against one of the palms that bordered the pier. He glanced back to satisfy himself that his mate and crew were well underway, and then hurried over to where she was waiting for him. They were both laughing like love-struck teenagers when they embraced. Their kiss was hungry, lingering, drenched in passion. When they finally separated, Roger held up both arms, fists clenched, and yelled, "Yowie, Kazowie, Kazaam," and pulled Aeva back into his arms for a more gentle but no less fervent embrace.

"How are you, Captain?" Aeva asked in her huskiest, most sensuous voice.

"I'm not sure, Lieutenant. All I can say is that I've counted each agonizing day for the last month, thought about you constantly, and walked around the ship singing aloud the lyrics to that wonderful song from *South Pacific*"—He held his arms wide and burst into song—"*I'm in love, I'm in love, I'm in love with a wonderful girl.*" Aeva pirouetted and said, "Ezio had a better voice, but my Captain is more handsome and sweet and generous and, and, and...I love him with all my heart!"

They kissed briefly again and then he asked, "Where to, my darling? It has to be a place with plenty of ice because I've brought along two magnums of the best French champagne created by the hands of the masters. I'm thirsting for you and ice cold champagne—in that order. Over and over again—Aeva—champagne—Aeva—champagne—Aeva—champagne....

CHAPTER THIRTY-SEVEN

Sergeant Schwartz received a copy of Aeva's report concerning her interview with Hoarai, the fisherman who had discovered Santoros' dead body in the bay. She stated that the fisherman told her that when he found the gold pendant clutched in Santoros' hand, he had slipped it into his pocket and forgotten about it, but later, when he showed it to his daughter, she suggested bringing it to the police so they could return it to its rightful owner. He said the tiny heart-shaped latch on the chain was locked when he removed it from the dead man's hand.

After writing up her report, Aeva had wrapped the pendant and chain securely and sent them to the forensic laboratory in Paris.

When Schwartz received the package containing the chain and pendant along with Toro Santoros' effects from the French forensic pathologist, he documented its contents and entered them all in the inventory log book:

BATHROBE: Take to forensic lab for detailed chemical analysis for blood stains, etc. (effect of salt water???)
PAJAMAS: Check for blood stains etc.
GOLD CHAIN AND PENDANT: Make detailed analysis.
DIAMOND RING: Check with France. Any evidence of bruising of ring finger in an attempt to remove it? Why didn't Ramiriz take the ring? It looks valuable.

When he learned that the *Seadancer* was scheduled to dock in New York harbor before embarking on a cruise to the Caribbean, he contacted Captain Roger Warren and requested permission to examine the stateroom suite Dimitri and Margaux Santoros occupied during their cruise to French Polynesia. When he learned that the suite had remained empty since Margaux had checked out, he asked Captain Roger Warren to please seal the rooms until he had a chance to investigate them upon the ship's arrival in New York.

Sergeant Schwartz was escorted immediately to Captain Warren's quarters when the *Seadancer* docked in New York harbor. He was amazed to discover how knowledgeable the captain was with respect to the evidence in the Santoros case. They spent several hours together discussing the case, and the captain seemed especially pleased when Schwartz commented favorably on the quality of Lieutenant Fontein's investigation.

"She's my wife now, you know. If it weren't for Mr. Santoros' tragic death we would never have met."

After Roger personally escorted him to the Santoros staterooms and left with his best wishes, the first thing Schwartz did was to walk out onto the balcony and look down at the water below. He had never been on a modern cruise ship before and was shocked by its size. The people on the pier looked like ants scurrying about. While he stood leaning on the balcony railing, gazing at the sights around him, he felt as if he were standing on the top of a ten story building.

I've got to be a hundred feet up in the air, he said to himself. Then he had a thought that hadn't occurred to him before. He had always been troubled by the uncertainty of the cause of death. He couldn't understand why the pathologists were unable to decide whether Santoros died by drowning or by a traumatic injury to his brain and nervous system. When he saw first-hand the height from which the body had fallen, he realized that there were any number of possibilities.

Wait a minute, he said to himself. *If Santoros were alive when he hit the water, he would have struggled to keep from drowning and wouldn't have held onto the necklace. But suppose his death was caused by the trauma of striking the water after a free-fall of one hundred feet? I think I better put that question on hold for a while.*

He began his methodical inspection of the suite starting from the entrance door. Nothing of interest turned up until he examined the throw rug in the living room. It was a heavy oriental lying on the highly polished mahogany floor. Although he found nothing unusual on the surface of the rug, when he turned it over there were multiple large stains that he identified as blood stains. He took a number of photographs of the stains, rolled up the rug and tagged it.

He found several human hairs lodged in a crack in the top of the wooden coffee table, photographed them, placed them in a plastic bag and secured the bag to the table with heavy-duty plastic tape.

He measured the height of the balcony railing. It was exactly three feet high. The top of the rail was painted a high-gloss white and was scratched in many places. There were two high-backed fiberglass deck chairs on the balcony.

The next several hours were unproductive. After snapping many more pictures of the suite and packing up his brief case, he headed back to the captain's quarters.

"Did you have any luck?" Roger asked, when Sergeant Schwartz was ushered into his office.

"I believe I did, but I won't know what it all means until I sort it out and run a few things through our lab. If you have a minute I'd like to talk to you, because I need your cooperation with regard to two items."

"Of course. How can I help?"

"The first thing is a rug, the second is a coffee table. I need to borrow them for a while, if I may."

"How long is a while?"

Sergeant Schwartz smiled. "I was afraid you might ask that. It could be for as little as three months, but if I'm right about them, it could be as long as two years."

"Good Lord! What's it all about?" Roger asked.

"The items might be needed as exhibits in the case. If the defendant is acquitted, they could be returned at the end of the trial in February. If he's convicted and he appeals, it could well be two years or more. Of course I could subpoena them, but—"

"No, there's no need for that, Sergeant. We're both on the same team in this matter. I'm as anxious as you are to see that justice is done, as they say. The rug and the coffee table are no problem. I'm sure we'll be able to replace them. Is there anything else?"

"No, sir, at least not that I can think of right now. I know you're headed out next week, so if you could seal and lock the suite I'd like to return in a few days equipped to pick up the rug and the table. After that I'll try not to bother you again."

"I don't suppose you can share any information with me, but I'm very interested in how it all plays out. Actually, I told Aeva I had solved the mystery of who had murdered Mr. Santoros, and she kindly suggested that I was a first class ship's captain, but that my sleuthing skills left much to be desired," he chuckled.

CHAPTER THIRTY-EIGHT

A few days later Schwartz told Garvey he was ready to make a PowerPoint presentation to U.S. Attorney MacDonald and wondered if MacDonald would be willing to come down to police headquarters so he wouldn't have to lug all his exhibits up to the attorney's office.

"Call him and ask. All he can do is say no. I think he'll understand. So what have you got?"

Schwartz started to explain, but Garvey looked at his watch and interrupted him.

"Sorry, Schwartz, I forgot I've got to be uptown in a half hour. I've been invited to a lunch for the Mayor. He's announced that he's going to run again and is looking for support from us. One hand washes the other, you know." He read disappointment in Schwartz's face.

"Look, Sergeant, you know I trust you totally. I'll just sit in with MacDonald when you get it arranged."

When MacDonald and Garvey were comfortably settled, MacDonald said, "I'm ready, Sergeant. I've only got an hour, but you have my undivided attention for that long, so lets see what you've got."

"Gentlemen," Schwartz said, "I want to tell you a story." He hitched up his pants, took a sip of water, picked up a lighted baton from the table and switched off the lights.

He began his presentation by showing an image of a poster advertising the *Seadancer* cruise ship.

He thinks he's an attorney already and he's going to give his summation to the jury, Garvey chuckled to himself.

"On April 12, 2008, this beautiful ship you see here left Hawaii headed for Tahiti. All the players in this drama were on board. Dimitri Santoros and his wife Margaux, whom *we* all know as Margaux McBride, occupied a deluxe stateroom suite located on the upper deck of the vessel approximately here." Sergeant Schwartz pointed his baton at a spot on the poster marked with a circle. There was a measurement noted on the poster indicating that the distance from the balcony to the water was eighty-nine feet.

"They were accompanied by the old man's son Nick and Nick's wife Carmen." He pointed his hand-held remote at the projector and Nick and

Carmen's passport photos appeared side by side on the screen.

"Dimitri's daughter Xenia, called Zee, was also a member of the family party and was accompanied by her husband Luigi Calfano alias Vittorio Del Renzo," he said, adding their photos on the screen. "The remaining character involved in the story is Luis Ramiriz, a convicted jewel thief who was born and raised in Cuba." He clicked the remote again leaving only the portraits of Nick Santoros, Del Renzo and Ramiriz on the screen. "To date, these three are the only suspects we have seriously considered. I believe they all knew each other prior to old man Santoros' death because Lieutenant Fontein's report includes a sworn statement from one of the bartenders on board *Seadancer* that he served drinks in his bar to Nick Santoros and two other males during the early evening of April 18, 2008. Lieutenant Fontain attached a copy of the Mastercard receipt signed by Nick Santoros dated 04/18/08 at 19:23 hours. The bartender remembered them well because they got into a heated argument and he told them to cool it or he was going to call security. He gave positive identification of the three of them from their passport photos. Okay, so, in the early morning hours of April 20, 2008, Santoros' dead body was was pulled out of the sea by a local fisherman, and guess what?...Santoros had the gold chain and pendant clutched in his hand.

"Our task is to determine if Santoros' death was accidental. Did he commit suicide? Or was he murdered, and if so, which, if any, of our suspects is the guilty one?"

Like you're telling us something we don't know, Garvey grumbled inwardly.

"Now, here's the thing," Schwartz continued. "The Santoros family customarily met for dinner in the main dining room on board the ship every night around seven-thirty. However, on Saturday, April 19, 2008 young Santoros and Del Renzo didn't show up for dinner, and during the meal Dimitri excused himself because he wasn't feeling well and returned to his stateroom. Margaux had offered to meet him back in the room after dinner, but he urged her to join the others who were planning to attend the Saturday night show. Everything I've told you so far has been documented without controversy."

Then why are you telling us about it? Garvey complained to himself.

I think I'll tell the story to the jury just like this, MacDonald decided.

"Now the curtain goes up on the second act. I'll be presenting facts interspersed with circumstantial evidence to support my conclusions."

"He's such a ham," Garvey whispered to MacDonald.

"I'm enjoying it," the attorney replied.

"Hrumph," Garvey snorted.

Schwartz projected a highlighted page from the pathologist's report up on the screen.

"Our French colleague has established that a morsel of Ramiriz' flesh was found inside the old man's mouth." Schwartz then displayed an enlarged photo of the inside of Toro's mouth that the pathologist had sent along with his report. It showed Santoros' metal bridgework. Schwartz pointed to the piece of flesh lodged between the metal and Dimitri's tooth.

"Now here's a new bit of evidence you gentlemen haven't seen before, that helps explain what I believe happened."

It's about time, Garvey thought.

Schwartz showed the photo of the coffee table and a closeup shot of the hairs wedged in the crack in the top of the coffee table. "This is the actual table," Sergeant Schwartz said, tapping the table with his wand.

"How did you get that table?" MacDonald asked, nervously. "Did you get a search warrant and a seizure order?"

"I figured I didn't need a warrant."

"Of course you needed a search and seizure warrant," MacDonald countered.

"Begging your pardon, sir, I took the table with the permission of the owner, and therefore I didn't need a warrant according to the rule established by the court of appeals in the case of *People v. Nottingham, 239 N.Y. 331*. It's all documented here," Sergeant Schwartz said, handing the attorney a sheaf of papers. "I've included an affidavit signed by the captain of the *Seadancer* confirming that I removed the coffee table with his permission and that the hairs were caught in the table top, and preserved by covering them with clear plastic that I taped to the table top before I removed it from the Santoros suite. I also have a videotape of our lab technician removing the hairs from the clear plastic covering so he could DNA them. His report says it's Dimitri Santoros' hair."

MacDonald eased back in his chair. "Please continue, Sergeant," he said, smiling.

"Mrs. Santoros, whom I shall refer to hereafter as Margaux, reported that at some time during the night of the event, all of her jewelry was stolen from the safe in her bedroom. So now we've got Ramiriz, the jewel thief, in the stateroom and thousands of dollars worth of jewelry turns up missing, and we've probably got Ramiriz' fist in Toro's mouth, and we've got proof that the victim's head was split open when it struck the table top with sufficient force to crack the top of the table. So now we come to exhibit number four." Sergeant Schwartz turned on the lights and carried the rug over and placed it upside down on the conference table. "Please do not touch," he said.

MacDonald glanced at his watch and stood up. "I've heard enough, Sergeant. As far as I'm concerned, you've given me plenty to think about, but I have a plane to catch and I'll be gone for a week. I must say you men are doing an absolutely superb job on this case."

"Thank you, sir," Lieutenant Garvey said.

"Of course I must see the balance of the second act. By the way Sergeant, is there a third act?"

"That would be the trial of the defendant, sir. You're the lead character in the third act."

"In that case, of course, I'm particularly interested in what you have in store for me. Can we arrange that presentation for me in about ten days from now, Bill?" The attorney reached in his pocket and checked his Blackberry. "How about ten days from tomorrow at around three o'clock?"

"Whenever you say, sir," Lieutenant Garvey answered.

Garvey accompanied the attorney to the elevator. When he returned to the offices he glanced briefly into the conference room and saw Schwartz gathering up his exhibits. He was humming a song that Garvey recognized, but he couldn't remember its name. The Lieutenant shook his head, put on his coat and headed home. He hummed the tune in the car all the way back to his apartment. When he found his wife in the kitchen he hummed it for her and asked if she knew the name of the song. She hummed a few bars to herself and said, "Sure, that's the theme song from the TV program where that English actor, what's his name, plays the part of a sergeant in Scotland Yard who's smarter than the lieutenant."

Sergeant Schwartz welcomed the delay because he wasn't happy with the end of the second act of his play. There were too many unanswered questions. He was satisfied that Ramiriz had struck Dimitri when he was caught stealing Margaux's jewelry and had knocked him unconscious. Although he had no proof that Ramiriz had stolen all of Margaux's jewelry and thrown Toro's body into the sea, in his view they were reasonable suppositions. *Do we have proof of murder beyond a reasonable doubt? I don't think so,* he said to himself.

And then there is the problem of the chain and pendant. If Ramiriz knew, as everyone believed he did, that the necklace was worth around $25,000, why would he have left it in Toro's hand when he chucked him overboard? And, since it is conceded that the chain wasn't broken when it was discovered clutched in Toro's fist, how had Toro managed to take the necklace away from Ramiriz without breaking it and then kept it clasped in his fist before, while or after Ramiriz smacked him in the face—causing a severe head injury—and after all that, still hung on to the necklace when he was thrown overboard?

After his presentation to MacDonald and Garvey, Sergeant Schwartz picked up the rug and the table and secured them in the evidence locker room. Before he left his office and headed home, he glanced up at the portrait hanging on his wall. He had enlarged it from a book cover and framed it himself. It had been hanging there since the day he was promoted to first detective and was given his own office. He spoke aloud directly to the artist's rendering of Sherlock Holmes and Dr. Watson engaged in a serious conversation.

"Hey guys, where the hell are you when I really need you?"

On the following day he carefully examined each of his exhibits again for the umpteenth time, desperately hoping to find something he had overlooked. He had arranged for Santoros' hairs that were caught in the table top and the blood stain on the rug to be analyzed. As he suspected, the blood and the hair belonged to Toro, but the puzzling thing was that the lab technicians told him that the stains on the back of the rug had not seeped through from its pile surface. The blood had been originally deposited onto the *back surface* of the rug.

Further, when he studied the back of the rug more carefully by significantly enlarging the photographs, it appeared that there might be a footprint within the bloodstained area.

These new findings promised to be helpful but he wasn't able to make a connection. And then one night when he was lying in bed mulling over all the evidence, just before he nodded off to sleep a concept crept into his thoughts. *What if....*The more he thought about it, the more plausible the idea became. He slept fitfully all night, constantly awakening and glancing at the clock until the hour arrived when he knew he was not going to be able to get back to sleep. He got up and went to his office even though it was only five o'clock in the morning. He decided he had to examine the gold chain once again.

The sun was just creeping over the horizon when he opened the evidence bag containing the gold chain and pendant. He stared at it, caressed it, let the chain slide sensuously through his fingers. Nothing. He lifted it with the tip of his pen at the clasp and let the pendant swing like a pendulum, and then he saw it. He dropped it on his desk-top and counted the links of the chain. "Maybe," he said aloud. *Maybe, but how is it possible?* he wondered.

He called his friend David, the jeweler, every fifteen minutes beginning at eight o'clock. At quarter to nine, David answered the phone and agreed to see him.

"It's a beautiful chain," David said. "What happened to the jewel that belongs here?" He pointed to the face of the pendant.

"It doesn't matter. I'm only interested in the chain."

"What do you want to know?"

"Everything," Schwartz said.

David put a loupe to his eye and examined the chain meticulously. "It's very old. More than a hundred years, I'd say. I believe it's eighteen carat. It's an open link design. The two segments of gold chain are each soldered at one end to the clasp and at the other end to the pendant. I mean, what else can I tell you?"

"How many links do they have?" Sergeant Schwartz asked.

David counted the links on one side from the clasp to the pendant. "Seventy on each side."

"Wrong. There are only sixty-nine on one side. What does that tell us?"

"We've got a missing link." David laughed.

"How come? What do you think?"

"I'd guess the chain was broken, the link was lost or too difficult to repair or reproduce, so the jeweler simply opened one of the links and reconnected the chain. Who would notice?"

"Me," Schwartz laughed. "Now tell me. Is this chain strong?"

"Very! Why?" David asked.

"I want to know what would happen if you and I tried to pull it apart."

"It would probably cut our hands severely before it would break. We would surely give up before that happened. Of course, as we all know, a chain is only as strong as its weakest link."

"That's what I thought. Okay," Sergeant Schwartz said, putting the chain and pendant back in the evidence bag, "We'll be calling you as an expert witness in an important case."

"Am I going to get paid?"

"A little. The government is broke, you know."

"I'm willing to consider a tradeout for cancelled parking tickets for me and my customers."

"I'll take it up with the chief," Sergeant Schwartz said, laughing, as he exited the jewelry store. There was a parking ticket stuck under the windshield wiper of his personal vehicle. "Shit," he said.

Originally, in his first meeting with U.S. Attorney MacDonald, Sergeant Schwartz had only intended to submit a timeline narrative of the case—a list of the witnesses, with brief descriptions of what their testimony was expected to be, and an index chart of the possible exhibits. However, when Lieutenant Garvey told him he was now in sole charge of the Santoro investigation, he had decided to make a PowerPoint scenario that MacDonald might use in his presentation to the grand jury.

Schwartz hadn't been able to make up his mind as to whether after he was admitted to the bar he wanted to become an attorney for the prosecution or for the defense. Either way, he knew for certain that MacDonald could open doors for him in seeking employment. When MacDonald seemed to understand and appreciate what he was doing, and agreed to return so he could see the end of Schwartz' script, he worked feverishly to support it with as much solid evidence as possible.

After his jeweler friend, David, had informed him that it would take considerable force to break Margaux's gold chain, a wild idea he had been nursing for some time seemed more plausible and he became obsessed with finding more evidence to support his theory. He recognized that he might, on the other hand, end up looking like a fool.

Investigator Loret Wilson was new to the force. Until the time Schwartz called her into his office for a meeting, she had only been performing menial but necessary tasks.

"Hi, Loret," Schwartz said when she entered his office. "Sit down here and let me tell you what I have in mind for you. I guess it'll be your first serious task. I told the chief you were up to it and he said it was my decision for better or for worse."

Loret was very bright and, like Sergeant Schwartz himself, she had an Associate's degree from CCNY with a major in criminal justice. She was eager for the opportunity to prove herself and move up in the Department.

"Your bio tells me that you did a minor in photography at college and although the job I have in mind for you may not appeal to your artistic talent, I guarantee it will challenge your investigative skills," Schwartz said.

"It's the Santoros case, right?" Sergeant Schwartz nodded affirmatively. "I'm pretty excited about being involved," she said.

It took Schwartz over an hour to bring Loret up to speed on the case and then he asked, "How good are you in the darkroom?"

"Are we talking about photography or...what?" she laughed.

"I'm talking about developing photographs. I'm a married man with two kids," he sighed.

"Oh, I checked that out before we met, otherwise I would never have said what I just did," she said, blushing.

"Okay, back to business," he said, picking up the rug he had taken from the *Seadancer*, removing it carefully from its clear plastic wrapping, and laying it face down on the floor.

"Loret, I want you to study that large reddish brown stain, there," he said, pointing to the upper portion of the back of the rug. It looked like an inkblot about eighteen inches in diameter. "Tell me what you see in that stained area."

She got down on her hands and knees and stared at the rug for a minute or two, and then said, "Can I borrow your magnifying glass?"

Sergeant Schwartz retrieved the glass from his desk and handed it to her. She studied the rug carefully again for several minutes. "I see it," she announced proudly.

"See what?" he asked with a straight face.

"The print, the footprint. I see it," she answered.

"Right on! Now here's what I want you to do, and you've only got six days to deliver the goods, otherwise you'll be shipped back to the minor leagues...." Sergeant Schwartz said it with a grin, but they both knew he wasn't kidding.

By the end of the fourth day Loret was panicking, but shortly after one o'clock on the fifth day, she discreetly followed Margaux into the Evolution Sports Club. By the time Loret registered for the day and got a locker assigned, Margaux was leaving the locker room.

Loret changed as quickly as she could and hurried into the gymnasium. She spied Margaux working out on an exercycle and stepped up onto the treadmill behind her. She scanned the room to be certain that no one was watching her, and quickly took a series of photos with her tiny camera. For the next hour and a half, there were no further opportunities to take more photos, but when Margaux headed back into the locker room, Loret followed. Margaux opened her locker and pulled out her shoes and street clothes. She hung the clothes on the rack beside her locker and stuffed her gym gear back into the locker along with her purse. She was totally nude as she stepped over to the table where the clean bath towels were stacked, and casually wrapped one around herself and headed to the shower stalls.

God, what I wouldn't give to have a body like that, Loret thought. As soon as Margaux was out of sight she went to work with her state of the art digital camera.

When Sergeant Schwartz saw enlargements of her best photos he beamed. "Good deal! Now can you get me some high-definition pictures of the blood stain on the rug?"

"Absolutely," she said.

"I want blow ups, say twenty by thirty inches, on my desk no later than eight-thirty tomorrow morning."

"You got it, baby," she replied, shaking her butt as she left the room.

"Wise-ass," he said after she closed the door.

CHAPTER THIRTY-NINE

"Okay, Sergeant, I'm ready for the next act of your play, and as you've recommended, I'm prepared to go to the grand jury and ask for an indictment against Ramiriz charging him with assault. As I remember, you were just about to introduce a rug of some kind into evidence. Am I right?"

"Yes, sir. But the delay in my presentation has given me an opportunity to expand some of my ideas, and I'm going to change the order of things a bit. You'll recall that just before you left we had conjectured that Ramiriz was in the Santoros suite. We know that he struck Dimitri in the mouth with sufficient force to knock him down and split his head open on a coffee table, and we also know that all of Margaux's jewelry was stolen.

"Initially, we thought that when Santoros came out of his bedroom and switched on the light, he caught Ramiriz standing in the living room with the gold chain and pendant in his hand. We thought Dimitri grabbed the necklace away from him and Ramiriz threw him overboard, neglecting to retrieve the chain and pendant before doing so. At this point I no longer believe that theory."

"Why not?" Garvey demanded.

"Hear me out, please, Chief. There are two reasons why that idea won't fly."

"I'm with Bill on this one, Sergeant," MacDonald said. "I don't much like switching horses in midstream. I've scheduled a presentation to the grand jury three days from now. My witnesses have all been subpoenaed, and now you're telling me you've changed your mind. I don't like it, Sergeant."

"Bear with me please, sir." Sergeant Schwartz said. He could feel beads of perspiration sliding down from his armpits. "Here's why I've changed my mind, and if I'm right you won't have any trouble getting an indictment for murder." MacDonald looked as if Sergeant Schwartz had stepped in dog poop and was walking across his brand new white living room carpet.

"We now know from the Frenchman's report that Ramiriz knocked Dimitri unconscious," Sergeant Schwartz continued, oblivious to the sour, disapproving expression on the attorney's face. "I believe there is no way in hell a professional jewel thief is going to throw away a $25,000 necklace, but the kicker is that when you read over the family members' statements carefully, you will see that they were all present when Dimitri gave Margaux the necklace and told her she had to wear it every Saturday, because not only was that the day he gave it to her, but he was born on a Saturday and they got married on a Saturday. I'm suggesting that the necklace wasn't in the safe with all her jewelry that night because it was a Saturday and Margaux was wearing it."

"That's pretty skimpy wishful thinking, Sergeant Schwartz," Garvey complained.

"I don't like it either, Schwartz—I think you've been watching too much television," Mac Donald added forcefully.

"Hold on please, gentlemen, I've got more," Sergeant Schwartz said.

"I'm willing to listen, but it better be good," MacDonald warned.

"Yes, sir," Sergeant Schwartz mumbled, and continued, "…so, like I said, Ramiriz steals Margaux's jewelry but doesn't get the gold chain and pendant because Margaux is wearing them. Anyway, Ramiriz grabs the loot and scrams out of the stateroom. When Margaux returns to their suite several hours later, after the show is over, she finds her husband on the floor. She thinks he's dead but when she kneels down to put her ear to his chest to listen for a heartbeat he grabs the gold chain necklace." Sergeant Schwartz propped a twenty by thirty inch photograph up on his easel.

"What's that supposed to be?" Garvey demanded. Sergeant Schwartz was about to explain when the attorney spoke up.

"I see it. It's a close-up photo of the back of a woman's neck and shoulders with a scar running across the back of her neck—am I right, Sergeant?" MacDonald asked.

"Yes, sir."

Garvey said. "Yeah, now I see it, but…?"

MacDonald cut him off. "Of course. It's the back of Margaux's neck that was cut by the gold chain. However did you manage to get that shot, Sergeant?"

"Two final exhibits, sir," Sergeant Schwartz replied, without answering the question. He put another large photograph on the easel. It was an imprint of the sole of a woman's shoe on a deep, dark red background.

"What you see here is the footprint we found on the back side of the rug I took from the Santoros stateroom, and this," he said, placing another photo beside it, "is a print of the sole of Margaux's shoe taken in the locker room of the Evolution Sports Club a few days ago. The shoe prints are an exact match as to length although the pattern on the rubber soles of the shoes is different. I'll address that problem a bit later.

"I claim that someone turned the throw rug over and rolled Dimitri's body and bloody head onto it. Whoever it was used the bloodstained rug to drag the body across the polished mahogany floor out to the balcony, but Margaux left her calling card on the bloodstained rug when she stepped on it.

"I claim that there is no way in hell Margaux would have been able to lift her husband's 180-pound inert body over that three foot high balcony railing without help. She had to have an accomplice. Ramiriz is the most likely candidate. So my thought is that we have solid proof of assault in the first degree against Ramiriz, and therefore you present the case against Ramiriz to the grand jury and get an indictment against him for assault; but we also serve Margaux with a search and seizure warrant to get a look at her shoe wardrobe and if we're lucky we'll find a shoe that exactly matches the footprint on the bloody rug and if we're *really* lucky we'll find some traces of blood on that shoe. Nobody ever throws away their favorite shoes, you know."

MacDonald eased back in his chair and smiled. Lieutenant Garvey was expressionless, stunned, as if in a trance.

"Any questions?" Sergeant Schwartz asked.

When no one said anything, he clicked his remote and the words THIRD ACT appeared on the screen. He clicked it again and the following words appeared: SUPERCEDING INDICTMENT.

"At this point we'll have Ramiriz in jail without bail because he isn't a United States citizen and Immigration will have become involved. We aren't in any hurry now that we have Ramiriz under wraps so after we seize Margaux' shoes, if we hit pay dirt and the incriminating shoe shows up, we obtain a superceding indictment against Ramiriz *and* Margaux for conspiracy to commit murder. Then we offer one of them a deal to testitify against the other with a plea bargain agreement. I know that we can't convict a defendant solely on the testimony of an accomplice, so the shoe is the key." He sat down across the table from the United States Attorney.

"What do you think, Mr. MacDonald?" Sergeant Schwartz asked.

The attorney didn't answer immediately. He pursed his lips, lowered his head and shuffled aimlessly through the stack of papers on the table in front of him. Finally he looked down at Schwartz. He was at least a head taller than the sergeant. He leaned his broad shoulders forward.

"I think I was too quick to criticize. You've done well, Sergeant Schwartz. Extremely well. With regard to the murder case, at this point we've only got circumstantial evidence against either one of them. I don't like trying murder cases on circumstantial evidence. It's too risky, and invariably it invites a costly appeal if we do get a conviction. However if, as you suggest, we can find the incriminating shoe, I'm willing to go to the grand jury with the scar on Margaux's neck and the shoe and let them decide if they think there's enough evidence to make her stand trial for murder.

"Assuming we find the shoe, I'm willing to bet my weekly paycheck that if Ramiriz is offered a deal where we agree to drop the murder charge against him, and let him plead guilty to assault—if he agrees to testify that he helped Margaux throw the old guy over the rail—he'll grab it."

CHAPTER FORTY

After Ramiriz was arrested and jailed, a time came when Barney Rifkin received a telephone call from the wife of a client of his who was incarcerated. She asked for an appointment to discuss an important matter with him. Her husband had been charged with a minor crime, but because of his illegal status he was being held in federal prison. Since he was also a Cuban, when Ramiriz was incarcerated they became friends. Rifkin agreed to meet with the lady.

"Come in, come in, Mrs. Mendez." Barney extended his hand in greeting. "How is Julio doing?"

"Very well, Mr. Rifkin. His papers have come through so he is legal now and he will be released in a few weeks."

"So what can I do for you?"

"Well, we know we still owe you a lot of money. I'm paying whatever I can every month."

"I'm aware of it and I appreciate that you're keeping your promise. But you said you have an important matter to discuss with me."

"Yes, yes. You see, Julio remembered that you represented that famous lady, Margaux McBride, and he learned something from a fellow prisoner that he thought might be helpful to her. He also thought if he helped her she might be willing to help him with the money he still owes you. He doesn't want anything for himself, you understand, but you know...he would leave it up to you what might be fair. Maybe it's nothing, he says, but he thinks it could be important to her."

"I see. Well, I *am* a friend of Margaux. Her name is now Margaux Santoros, you know."

"Yes. I see her name in the newspaper many times."

"Perhaps you can tell me about it and then I'll be able to see what I can do."

"My husband met a guy in prison by the name of Ramiriz. He is Cuban like my husband Julio. This man tells my husband that the prosecuting attorney handling the case against him has offered him a deal...."

When Mrs. Mendez finished telling her story and left his office, Barney immediately called Margaux. He related what he had learned. She thanked him and said she would send him a check for five hundred dollars to be used for Mr. Mendez' benefit in whatever way Barney deemed appropriate.

Margaux thought about the situation for several hours before she called Lucie and asked her to meet for a drink at their favorite bar at five-thirty when Lucie got out of work. "It's possible my phone is bugged and you might be followed, so be careful." she said, and hung up.

When they had settled in their corner booth, Lucie said, "I'm sorry I'm late, but I bought a wig at Macy's, left there through the delivery entrance in the basement, scooted through one hotel as a blonde where I went up and down the elevator several times, changing from a young blonde to a dark-haired woman with a limp, and here I am. It was great fun. So what's up, Crazy Lady?"

"First of all, I want you to rent an inconspicuous car from Hertz or Avis as soon as you can this evening. I've reserved a small suite at the Mariott Marquis in Atlantic City. I'm registered there under the name Cora Lockwood. Call in sick tomorrow, pick me up at 5:30 in the morning and drive me down there. I can explain the whole thing to you then. All I can tell you now is that this isn't a lark. I need your help. Now please don't ask any questions—just meet me in the ladies' room in a few minutes. I'll give you a small purse with $1,000 cash in it before you leave."

The next morning over coffee in the Marriot suite in Atlantic City, Margaux said, "Of course you remember me telling you about that prick Luis Ramiriz, the Cuban guy I met on the cruise to Tahiti, the guy who ended up being arrested for assaulting Toro?"

"Yeah, I sure do. Has he got anything to do do with all this hokey pokey you're into here?"

"You got it, Babe—here's the story, okay? You know my attorney Barney Rifkin. I think you met him with me once, right?"

"Sure, I met him a couple of times. Seemed like a good dude. Treated you right, introduced you to Toro and so forth."

"Right. So, okay, I get a call from him yesterday shortly before I asked you to meet me at the Algonquin. He told me that through a client of his who's in the same lock-up as Ramiriz, he learned that the Feds are offering Ramiriz a deal that if he'll testify that I threw Toro off the balcony of our suite on the ship, they'll ship him back to Cuba and let Castro deal with him. I'm telling you right out, Luce, that son of a bitch would testify his own mother shot the Mayor if he could avoid paying a parking ticket. I swear to God, Luce, it's all bullshit."

"But I don't get what all this spooky stuff is. Driving in the dark and false name and all. You gotta bring me up to speed, honey."

Margaux got up and poured herself another cup of coffee. Then she stepped to the window and gazed out at the Atlantic Ocean. It was a bitter cold, blustery morning. No one was strolling along the Boardwalk. She continued to stare out the window for a few minutes. Lucie sat quietly, waiting for Margaux to respond.

Margaux turned to Lucie. "I can see it's going to be my word against that slimy bastard's, but I've been down that road once before, and you can never be sure what a jury will do. I'm not going to take a chance on spending the rest of my life in prison if I get convicted. I've made up my mind. There's no way I'm going to let them kill me slowly.

"Gary and Toro are gone. You're all I have, dear Lucie. I've decided to leave the States and start a new life. How about coming with me? I'll pay all your expenses."

"I'll do whatever you want," Lucie answered. "I miss the intimacy we had back in Richford Hills. I love you, Margaux." Lucie stood up and took Margaux in her arms. She felt Margaux's tears sliding down her own cheeks. When Margaux had regained her composure, she lit a cigarette and slumped down in an easy chair.

"I've got a choice. I can stay here, blow my money on attorney's fees and take my chances, or…." Margaux picked up her coffee cup and poured in a shot of brandy from their makeshift bar on the dresser.

"If we go to Mexico to live and I manage my money carefully, I think we can make it.

It took more than an hour for Margaux to describe in detail what she had in mind. When she finished, Lucie said, "Count me in. I'm sure we can make it work. Have you ever heard of a place called Zaragoza in Mexico? My family lives in Caramina, a small village about twenty miles from there."

CHAPTER FORTY-ONE

Gary Samson had been involved in the development of Senator Obama's TV advertising campaign, in the battle against Hillary Clinton for the nomination, and then against John McCain for the presidency of the United States. For over a year the Obama marketing team had been his biggest client.

Although his breakup with Margaux had been an emotionally devastating experience, working with the Obama staff and on occasion communicating directly with the senator had been an exhilarating personal adventure. His return to Chicago to be present for Obama's victory speech in Grant Park, where he and Margaux had spent one of the happiest days of his life, was an emotional challenge. However the Obama victory was such a monumental, all-consuming experience for the country as well as himself personally that the last vestiges of melancholy for "what might have been with Margaux" were buried in the city where the affair began. His last thread of hope that one day they might reconcile unraveled when he read in the news that she had actually made claim against her husband's estate for $2,000,000. *She's crazy!* he said to himself, tossing the paper into the waste basket.

The hundreds of thousands of dollars that Gary had earned working for Barack Obama had revitalized the company. The money he had borrowed from Melinda had long since been repaid and he was solvent again—and much wiser and wealthier as well.

After Senator Obama had become President of the United States of America, Gary was offered a job with the government. He was flattered and briefly tempted by the opportunity, but he ultimately decided that he liked being his own boss with the ability to pick and choose his clients.

When his secretary called him on the intercom and advised him that Mr. Wilson Cambridge was on the line, he recognized the name but couldn't remember who he was or how he knew him. He decided to wing it.

"Mr. Cambridge, what can I do for you, sir?"

"We're ready to do it again, Mr. Samson. Although we're all in financial difficulties these days, our company has decided that the time is appropriate for a little creative marketing. When the economy went into a slump we had to cut back on every non-essential expense, but our Board has directed that marketing our product on television belongs in the essential expense column. So here we are again."

If I could only remember what the damn product is that you're selling, Gary agonized.

"Sounds like the right idea to me," he said, praying for a clue in return.

"And we want to use Bridget again. We think that commercial you did for us was a classic. People still remember it, like "Where's the Beef?" he laughed.

Oh God. Bridget Tulane...Wilson Cambridge, Vice President of Marketing and Sales....InterState Airlines. Gary sighed with relief. "You're absolutely right about that, Wilson," he said. "Does Bridget still work for you?"

"She sure does. After the enormous success of that commercial she starred in, we had to give her a bonus and a raise, but at the same time we added a 'non-compete' clause in her contract.

"So when can we meet and discuss this project? My folks are anxious to get it underway as soon as possible in order to include it as an operating expense item when we make application for our share of the government bailout funds. We must be straight-up on this— our company is taking the president seriously about the new direction he's promised to take the country and the government. No more Washington back-room political shenanigans. We want a long term contract with Samson and Delisle to be part of the five-year economic plan we'll be submitting to the government."

"I'm at your disposal, Wilson. What's the theme this time?"

"We've moved our corporate headquarters from Phoenix to Scottsdale, Arizona, and we're seeking a whole new image. We want you to be part of it."

"You name the time and place, sir," Gary said.

"How about next week, right here in Scottsdale? Will that work for you?"

"Let me take a quick look at my calendar...I'll have to move a few things around but if you can hold off until the middle of the week I can make it happen."

"Done deal. We'll talk again tomorrow about the details and then we can meet in my office next Wednesday at nine a.m. Good to talk to you Gary, I'll call you tomorrow."

The next day they spent several hours discussing the script, the time constraints, the budget and Bridget's participation. When they finished, Gary searched in his computer for Bridget's cell phone number. When she answered he said, "May I speak with the lovely Bridget Tulane, television starlet and mother of two beautiful children?"

"Who shall I say is calling?" Bridget replied.

"A very foolish man who got caught in a maelstrom and fell from grace."

"Just a moment please," Bridget said, placing her hand over the mouthpiece while she decided whether or not she should speak to Gary. She was very angry with him for toying with her heart and then dropping her completely. Finally her desire to see him outweighed her desire to tell him to go to hell.

"Hello, stranger," she said.

"Will you forgive me?"

"I don't think so, but my mother always told me to turn the other cheek."

"I'm sorry, Bridget. I truly am very sorry. I made a terrible mistake. Will you have dinner with me next weekend?"

"Where?"

"In Phoenix or Scottsdale or wherever you say."

"How about San Francisco? That's where I'll be. Tacoma Sunday, Denver Monday, San Francisco Tuesday, Detroit Wednesday, Dallas Thursday...."

"I get the picture. You've got me on the ropes but I don't quit, ever! Suppose I could arrange to have you fly in to Scottsdale on Thursday evening and get the rest of the week off with pay, could we have dinner on Friday?"

"Did you buy the airline? I understand it's for sale like all the rest of them."

"Not quite, but they made me a spectacular offer I told them I couldn't accept unless they put you at my disposal for two weeks beginning next week."

"You are such a liar, Samson."

"You are too, so we're even. I checked your flight schedule with your supervisor, who assured me you'd be in Scottsdale Thursday evening and that you had a two day layover there, at home. Her name is Laura Phillips, if you want to check and see who's telling the truth."

"You're also a rat and a conniver and a... a... bamboozler, and I want to hate you, but I can't."

"Everything you've just said is absolutely true. Nevertheless, do we have a date for dinner Friday night?"

Bridget yearned to say yes and was equally determined to say no. After several moments of silence Gary said, "Bridget? Are you still on the line?"

"No," she answered.

"No, what?" he asked

"No, I'm not on the line. I hung up."

"Bridget?" Gary said softly, "May I pick you up at your home on Friday at seven?"

"Maybe. I don't live at the same place, you know."

"Actually, I didn't know that."

"That's strange. I thought I told all my friends, but it's been...let me see...how many months has it been since we talked, Gary?"

"Too many. How long must I be punished?"

"I haven't decided," she replied.

"When can you let me know?"

"Friday night at 6:45. I live in Cave Creek. Go north on Pina Road when you exit the airport in Scottsdale. Keep going north until you hit Carefree Highway."

"Carefree Highway? You're spoofing me, right?"

"Turn left on Carefree until you hit Cave Creek Road," she said, ignoring his question. "Turn right at the intersection...you'll be headed north again for about a mile. I live on Paseo Dolce Drive."

"Does your house have a number?"

"I suppose so but I don't know what it is. I live at the end of the cul de sac, and I have a pink and purple mailbox."

"I know I deserve this, but it's terribly painful."

"I hope so," she said and hung up the phone.

CHAPTER FORTY-TWO

Garvey and Schwartz were summoned to a conference with Attorney MacDonald and the lead attorney in the United States Attorney's office for the Southern District of New York. Garvey had been advised that the subject of the meeting was Margaux McBride Santoros. Garvey wondered if somehow he was going to be blamed for all the bad press the department was getting. Customarily if the prosecuting attorney believes that a suspect will run before an indictment is handed down, the police will make an arrest first and offer just enough evidence to a municipal court to hold the accused in jail or set high bail until the grand jury hands down the indictment. In Margaux's case, they never expected that they would be unable to pick her up any time they wished. When her indictment was reported and the media learned of her escape from under the nose of law enforcement, the story received nonstop press coverage. Although most of the people who lived in the metropolitan area were grateful for police protection, when they learned that Margaux had slipped out of the hands of the police there was a segment of the population that was rooting for her to escape. It was an embarrassment to the police, and the guys in the street loved it. Almost every New Yorker over the age of sixteen came to recognize the name Margaux McBride Santoros.

There were five attorneys seated at the conference table when Garvey and Schwartz entered the room. After introductions, MacDonald said, "What can you tell us, Bill? The press seems to know more about what's going on in this case than we do."

Garvey thought that if and when they ever located her, he would personally strangle her and save the state a lot of money.

"I've put my best men on the case, and we've interviewed everyone we figured might have been in contact with her, but she's just disappeared. I'm sure you gentlemen appreciate that there's probably twenty million people in the city of New York and the suburbs from Westchester County to Long Island, not to mention upstate New York and New Jersey, which is just a short swim across the Hudson River. Unless one of our snitches comes through, the task is impossible."

"I don't know what to tell you, Mr. MacDonald. At this moment my guess is that she could be holed up in one of the 30,000 hotel rooms in Manhattan or a house boat on the Yangtze River. Of course we haven't given up, but there's a limit to the amount of money and human resources we can afford to devote to finding her."

MacDonald turned to Sergeant Schwartz. "What can you tell us, Sergeant? I told my colleagues here that I considered you to be one of the most talented members of our team. What do *you* think?" Everyone in the room stared at Schwartz. He opened his notebook, hesitated for a few moments of embarrassed silence, and then said, "Obviously we've got to think outside the box on this one. All of the standard stuff we've been doing just hasn't worked. I guess you'll have to tell me how important finding her really is. Unfortunately, she's not the only defendant on our books who has jumped bail, but she sure is the highest profile fugitive I've ever had to deal with."

"So what do you suggest, Sergeant?" MacDonald asked.

"Well, sir," Schwartz said, unconsciously stroking his stubble of black beard, "the problem is, she has no ties to the underworld where our snitches dwell. We've checked the airlines, bus and train stations, rental car agencies and put out an all-states alert. So far we continue to be immersed in total darkness, but I've got this crazy idea that if my sole job was to find her, I do believe that with three months' time, about ten thousand dollars in operating funds and a generous travel budget, I could track her down."

MacDonald smiled. Garvey snickered under his breath.

"Done! Good luck, Sergeant. This meeting is adjourned for three months."

CHAPTER FORTY-THREE

Lucie rented a Ford from Hertz, as Margaux had directed. She paid with the cash that Margaux had given her. They headed south as soon as it was dark.

Margaux decided to keep to the large cities where a stranger would not attract attention, and she chose New Orleans as their immediate destination on the way to the village of Caramina in Mexico.

Before leaving New York, Margaux called one of her former inmates at Richford Hills Prison who was living in New Orleans.

During the trip to Louisiana, Margaux asked Lucie if she remembered Michelle Duchamp.

"She was the cute little blonde from New Orleans, right?" Lucie answered.

"That's the one! We bunked together for a couple months before she was released on parole. We became pretty good friends. Not like you and me, Lucie—I've never had a friend like you before.

"I learned a lot about New Orleans from her and I think she's going to be able to help me carry out my plan to create whole new identities for us. When I'm finished, everyone is going to believe that we're sisters."

"Damn!" Lucie said.

"What's the problem?" Margaux asked.

"I was hoping I would get to be a blonde."

"No way, baby. We're going to become as nondescript and forgettable as possible. I'm going to stay natural black just like you—get a short cut, work on a tan in a tanning booth until our skin color is exactly the same, and I'm going to flatten my chest a bit with one of those sports bras."

"It's a shame to mess with those beautiful boobs, Marg, but I get the point," she laughed. "So where's the next stop? I'm getting hungry."

"We'll take a break soon—I just want to get as many miles behind us as fast as I can. New Orleans is about 1300 miles from New York. I think we can make Roanoke, Virginia by around five o'clock in the morning. We'll crash at a motel south of the city and hole up there until tomorrow night, take a couple of detours and hit New Orleans on Tuesday."

At one point in the long drive to New Orleans, Margaux said, "If I had never met Gary, none of this would ever have happened."

"You're not blaming Samson for this mess, are you?"

"No, of course not. I didn't mean it that way. It's just that if I hadn't fallen in love with Gary, I would have kept my end of the bargain with Toro."

"I understand. You started taking orders from your pussy instead of your brain."

"That was part of it, I suppose, but it wasn't just that. The sex with Gary was great—the best I ever had in my life, and as you know I've had my share of sexual encounters."

"I don't want to hear about them again," Lucie sighed.

"Don't worry, I wasn't about to tell you. I acknowledge that no one can live on sex alone."

"I could," Lucie said. They both laughed.

"I think you really believe that," Margaux said.

"I don't believe I could. I know I could. The problem is I never found a man who wasn't a macho, insensitive, abusive, son-of-a-bitch, except for my *almost* husband Harold."

"That's what I'm talking about, Lucie. Gary was tough, but he was also sensitive and thoughtful. He was wonderful in and out of bed. God, I miss him so."

Lucie shrugged her shoulders. "You could have had him, Babe."

"I know, I know. I just couldn't be certain that it would last. My deal with Toro gave me the opportunity to do whatever I wanted for the rest of my life. So what happens, I lose everything."

When they arrived in New Orleans, Margaux called Michelle.

She agreed to meet them after work. Margaux and Lucie hung out at the club where Michelle worked until it closed and then Michelle took them to an all-night joint where Margaux explained in detail what brought them to New Orleans and what they were seeking.

The next morning they slept late, but shortly after noon Margaux climbed the steps to the address that Michelle had given her, located on Frenchman Street in the Faubourg Marigny District. The office was on the second floor, above the *Que Voulez-Vous* restaurant. When she opened the office door, the only light in the room came from a large-screen television set showing a horse race in progress. An enormous creole woman wearing a New Orleans Saints T-shirt and a Zephyrs baseball cap lounged behind the desk. She motioned for Margaux to take a seat in front of the desk, but did not move her eyes from the television screen until the race was completed. "Just a minute," the woman said while she made some notations in a large book. When she finished writing, she looked up at Margaux. "Yes?" she said.

"I'm a friend of Michelle DuChamp. She told me she would call you about my problem. My name is Carla Estrada," Margaux said. "Did Michelle call?" The woman retrieved a piece of paper, studied it for a moment and replied, "Michelle explained the situation to me. We can arrange for what you need, but I won't be able to deliver the merchandise until tomorrow about this time. You brought the money?"

"I brought $5,000. Michelle said she was sure that would be enough."

"Enough for what?" the woman asked.

"I need a Mexican passport and a driver's license for Carla Estrada."

"Don't know nothing about no drivers license, just the passport. You want a drivers license, that's $2,500 more." Margaux nodded in agreement, reached in her purse, counted out an additional $2,500, put it in the envelope and pushed it across the desktop.

She told Lucie to return the rental car to Hertz and gave her money to buy a second-hand Jeep station wagon advertised in the local paper; then they headed to Laredo, Texas.

Margaux correctly guessed that the Immigration authorities in Texas were only interested in the people traveling from Mexico into the U.S.A. The Mexican Border Patrol paid scant attention to the attractive young Mexican woman and her older passenger, Carla Estrada, when they crossed the border into Mexico.

She calculated it would take them twenty-four hours to reach Zaragoza. Margaux had taken two years of Spanish in college and she and Lucie had studied together for a year during their time together in state prison. Margaux insisted that they would only speak Spanish when they left New Orleans. With Lucie's help, by the time they reached the Mexican border Margaux could speak Spanish well enough as long as Lucie did most of the talking. They figured Margaux's natural jet-black hair would allow her to blend into the background in Mexico.

Margaux had been pondering a problem since they left New York. She knew she was exiled from the United States for the balance of her life. And then there was the money problem. After paying all of their travel expenses and purchasing a vehicle she still had well over three hundred thousand dollars left. It was more than enough to support herself and Lucie in an underdeveloped country. *But what kind of life will it be*? she asked herself.

Lucie brought fresh coffee out on the balcony of the hotel room where they had spent the night after entering Mexico. She poured a cup for each of them.

"We're all packed and ready to hit the road, Boss. I'm pretty excited about seeing my family. It's been over three years since I left home."

Margaux sighed. "You've been such a wonderful friend, Lucie. The only true friend I've ever had. But I've been thinking that the fact that I've ruined my life doesn't give me the right to ruin yours."

"You don't hear me complaining, do you? Hell, I'm having a ball."

"But surely," Margaux said, "you'd like to settle down and have kids. That's every woman's dream, right?"

"I don't know about the dream thing. It's true that's what I expected to do in Caramina before I met Harold. Get married, get fat and have a zillion kids. Can you imagine how my life has changed in the last three years? While I was at good old Richford Hills State Prison Resort, before I met you, all I did was eat, sleep, pump iron, and cry. You encouraged me to become fluent in English and get into that college program. You turned my life around. You found that apartment for me so I had a place to live when I was released from prison, and loaned me money for the first couple of months' rent until I found a job. Hey, lady, I'll never be able to repay you for all you done for me...excuse me, *have* done for me. And it's still going on. If and when you run out of money, I'll get a job wherever you decide we're going to live. I'll support both of us, I'll—"

Margaux put her arm around Lucie's shoulder and pulled her close. "Lucie, my darling, I love you so," she whispered, and kissed her tenderly.

"Not now, hon, it's only ten-thirty in the morning and I have a headache." Lucie laughed. "Oh, what the hell...." She pulled Margaux up and led her into the bedroom.

They showered together and as they were toweling each other off, Lucie said, "I was just thinking. Before I went to prison, if anyone had suggested that I could...that I would...you know, love another woman in the way we do, I would have smacked them. But you know what, it's not the sex, it's all the other things that I cherish. It's waking up in the morning and having someone laugh with me, having someone to share the beauty of a sunrise, or the cry of a loon at sunset or living without fear of being beat up, or cursed at, or humiliated, or...I don't know...do you understand what I'm trying to say?"

"Of course I do. I feel exactly the same way. Sex with a sensitive guy you love is still the best, but sex with a woman you love is pretty damn good, and a hell of a lot better than many women experience. You and I are two people who love each other. We just happen to be female and free to express our love for each other in any damn way we please."

"Once in a while though, you know," Lucie said, "I do sort of wonder what God thinks about it, don't you?"

"I believe *She's* too busy to worry about us," Margaux said.

CHAPTER FORTY-FOUR

Sergeant Schwartz sat on a bar stool stroking the stubble of his unshaven beard. He realized he might have made a career-bungling move, but he had thought all that through before he made his audacious offer to find Margaux.

He had personally supervised the search of Margaux's home, looking for the shoe with the rubber sole print that matched the bloody print on the back of the rug. Although she had abandoned over fifty pairs of shoes, the one shoe he sought was not among those that remained. A search of the home from top to bottom indicated clearly that she had packed up her most intimate and essential belongings in a hurry and skedaddled. Shortly before his meeting with MacDonald, Schwartz had received a report from a friend of his who worked at the Richford Hills State Prison for Women. A review of Margaux's personnel record there turned up the names of four inmates she had associated with while she was incarcerated. Two of them were professional women—an advertising agency executive who was convicted of embezzling several hundred thousand dollars from her employer, and a physician's assistant who was performing abortions after hours at her employer's clinic and pocketing the fee. Then there was Michelle Duchamp from New Orleans; and the fourth was a Mexican national convicted of smuggling drugs into the United States.

After taking on the assignment, it only took him a short while to locate the ad exec, who had moved to Florida, and the abortionist who had returned to her husband and children. He was unable to track down the lady from New Orleans; however, he learned that the Mexican drug runner had also vanished about the same time as Margaux. It was a starting point.

Once he turned up Lucie's name it was a simple matter to locate the Hertz rental agency where she had rented the car and to learn that it had been returned to a Hertz agency in New Orleans. He took the first available flight from New York to Louisiana. With the assistance of the Louisiana State Police he turned up a snitch in the underbelly of that multi-cultured city who led him to the office of Madame Lugans where he bought the information he needed concerning the forged passport Margaux had acquired in the name of Carla Estrada. Madame Lugans made money at both ends of the transaction—first by arranging a forged passport and driver's license for Margaux, and then by selling the information to Sergeant Schwartz.

It took Schwartz another day to make the connection between Lucie Alvarez, the Jeep she purchased, and the license plate registered in the name of Carla Estrada.

At the end his long but productive day, he stopped in a local bar to relax and try to figure out where Margaux was headed. His past experience suggested that the safest place for a fugitive to hide was a large metropolitan city in a foreign country. By the time he finished his second Bud Light, he said to himself, *I smell Mexico! Margaux wouldn't give herself a phony Spanish name and run away to China, right?*

He got bogged down in Mexican bureaucracy for a few days but after poring over thousands of names of travelers crossing the border from the United States into Mexico he spied the names Estrada and Alvarez. When he was able to pinpoint the names as having entered Mexico at Laredo, Texas, in a Jeep registered in Carla Estrada's name, with Louisana license plates, he leaped out of his chair and gave himself a high five.

His euphoria was short lived, though. When he studied the map of Mexico, he cursed out loud, "I never thought about how friggin' big it is."

CHAPTER FORTY-FIVE

Gary rang the doorbell at Bridget's home at exactly 6:45, the time she had advised him she would let him know if she would accept his seven o'clock dinner invitation. Bridget let it ring several times before she casually opened the door. She tried to calm her excitement at meeting him again. It had been almost a year since she had last seen him and she had almost, but not quite, put him out of her mind. There had been a long lingering hope that one day he might call again and now that moment had arrived. At the first sight of her, Gary thought, *Oh man, I had forgotten how lovely she is.*

He had dressed in his sharpest cashmere jacket and tie. She was wearing jeans and an Arizona State University oversized sweatshirt.

"Hi. You must be Jonni," Gary said. "My name is Gary Samson. I have a dinner date with your mom."

"Please come in, sir, I'll tell her you're here." Bridget turned and called up the stairs, "Mom, there's a creepy old man here to see you." They laughed together and whatever awkward greeting she was anticipating never materialized.

They stood for a moment appraising each other. Bridget broke the silence. "You look great, Gary. I expected gray hair and a beard to hide the wrinkles. It's been a long time."

"Much too long, but as you see I've dyed my hair and shaved off my beard. The truth is, Bridget, you look smashing."

"On that note," she said, taking his hand and leading him out to her backyard patio, "please come have a drink. You're still drinking Grey Goose vodka, I hope, because that's what I bought for you, but I couldn't remember if it was with orange or tonic so I have both."

Gary surveyed the area with his critical eye. Everything from the fragrance of the flower garden to the patio furniture was a reflection of Bridget: elegant simplicity...clean lines...unpretentious...thoughtful...casual. The absolute antithesis of Miami Beach, the Hamptons, Madison Avenue and Margaux.

"With orange and a wedge of lime, if you have it."

"Oh yes, I forgot the lime, but that's no problem," she said, and picked a lime off the tree in her garden. She smiled when she handed it to Gary. "There's a paring knife on the bar. Will that be all, sir?"

"No, lovely lady, I want you to sit down and tell me all the wonderful things that have been happening to you since I last saw you."

She poured herself a glass of white wine and settled down next to him on the old fashioned glider. "Cheers," she said, touching his glass with hers. "Well, let's see. After my celebrity was firmly in place thanks to your directorial genius, I was swamped with proposals of marriage. Only one of the hundreds of prospective grooms passed my litmus test. Warren courted me for three months, we became engaged and set the wedding date. But one day while I was addressing wedding invitations, I decided I was getting married for the wrong reasons and I broke it off. It was very painful, as you can imagine. He was a very sweet man and I'm sure we could have lived comfortably ever after, but the spark was missing. And how about you? How has life been treating you?" she asked.

Gary stood up, went over to the bar and cut an extra slice of lime, giving himself time to think how much of the past year of his life he was willing to share with Bridget. He sat down across from her in an overstuffed lounge chair, took a sip of his drink and looked at her thoughtfully. *She's so open and honest and refreshing,* he mused.

"Are you trying to decide whether to tell me the truth or a big bunch of lies?" she asked, looking directly into his eyes above the rim of her wineglass.

"As a matter of fact that was exactly what I was doing, but deception has never been one my strong points. What I mean is that whenever I've tried it, it's always been a disaster, so I'll give you the unexpurgated biographical sketch." He loosened his tie, sank back in the chair, and said, "I met Margaux Santoros not too long before you and I did that airlines commercial together."

"You don't mean the Margaux Santoros whose name and seminude body I've been seeing at the supermarket checkout counter for this past month?" she gasped.

"The very same, I'm sad to say."

"My God, she's absolutely gorgeous."

"I guess that's true, but the long and the short of it is that we had some serious disagreements about some of the things that are important in life."

"Wait a minute, I must confess that I got hooked into buying a copy of the *Enquirer* so I pretty much know the story. You weren't one of her, ah, ah...alleged, ah, ah...."

"Let me tell you about another friend of mine who has also been in the news this past week. Her name is Melinda Joy."

"You know her too? I saw her in *Jazz*. I thought she was wonderful, but isn't she a bit young for you?"

"They announced just last week that she's been selected to play the lead in a new film. She's my daughter."

"Oh Gary, that's wonderful! How exciting!"

Gary said, "You and I both understand the joys and the frustrations and the enormous responsibilities we face as working, single parents. I think it's one of the things that makes our friendship special, don't you?" At that moment the front door flew open and two teenagers burst into the house.

"Speaking of which..." Bridget said, shrugging her shoulders. "Perhaps you'll tell me more about your friend, Margaux, later."

"Mom," they shouted in unison, "Where are you? Here we come, ready or not."

"We're out here on the patio. Come join us," Bridget called back. When they arrived Bridget introduced them to Gary. "Michael and Jonni, do you remember my friend Gary? He just told me he's Melinda Joy's dad." Gary stood up and shook hands with Michael, an attractive sixteen year-old and Jonni, Bridget's thirteen year-old daughter. There could be no doubt who Jonni's mother was. They were mirror images of each other.

"That's cool," Jonni said, "About your daughter, I mean. Does she look for real the way she looks in the movies? Mom and I saw *Jazz* together when it first came out and I saw her once on television. I mean, I think she's fab."

"Actually, I think she looks best in real life, because that's how I know her, of course, but I'm prejudiced for sure," Gary commented. "As a matter of fact she looked a lot like you when she was your age, Jonni." Jonni flushed with pleasure. Michael guffawed.

"Shut up, dummy, you're just jealous because—"

"That's enough, Jonni. It's Michael's way of saying he agrees with Gary. So tell me what you guys' plans are for the evening, because Gary and I are about to go out to eat."

"I realize it's a Friday night and a late invitation, but if you don't have dates already, how about joining your mom and me for dinner?" Gary asked.

Jonni piped up immediately, "Michael's got a date to take stuck-up Alice Ransom to the movies, but I'm available. Where are we going?"

Bridget looked at Gary and her daughter. *I don't believe this,* she thought. *Ordinarily Jonni wouldn't be caught dead dining out with me on a Friday night. And secondly, I would have bet the family jewels that Gary would not be willing to spend our first evening together with a thirteen year-old tagging along.*

"So where am I taking my two lovely ladies?" Gary asked.

"We're going to Hank's Fish Fry. Their Friday night specials are out of this world and they have live country music and we can dance. But of course if you want to go to Antoine's, I guarantee the price will be stiffer, there's no music except recorded 'elevator music' and there's no dancing. It's up to you," she said, and smiled sweetly at Gary. He glanced at Jonni who was holding her breath and shaking her head "no".

"I think I'll choose Hank's Fish Fry. On one condition," Gary said.

"What's that?" Bridget and Jonni demanded at the same time.

"That I get to dance the first dance with Jonni." Bridget thought, *You are too much, Samson.* What she said was, "Okay guys, let's get this show on the road."

It was midnight by the time they got back to Bridget's home. Jonni thanked Gary for inviting her to "hang" with them as she put it, and went straight up to bed. Bridget made coffee and brought out a platter of chocolate cookies she had made that afternoon, and they sat at the kitchen table reminiscing about the evening and discussing Gary's plans for the shoot they would be working on beginning on Monday. Just before he left he said, "I want to tell you something, Bridge. I had a great time tonight. Jonni is such a delight. Not only does she resemble Lindy at that age, but she's a really sweet kid in the same way Lindy was. And she's bright and funny too. You have every right to be proud of those youngsters. But most of all, I think *you* are a really special lady. I don't know where the next few weeks or months may take us, but—"

Bridget put her finger up to Gary's lips to stop him from speaking. "Please, Gary, not another word. It's been a memorable night for me as well. I don't want to spoil this glorious evening by either of us saying too much or too little. Now let me kiss you on the cheek and send you on your way. After your third drink at Hank's you made a date with me for brunch, so I'll see you here around eleven tomorrow morning for Bloody Marys and the lightest, fluffiest omelet you've ever tasted. Now go," she commanded.

"I don't know where to go. Honestly. I came here directly from the airport and I foolishly thought...."

"Believe it or not, we have a delightful little hotel in Cave Creek. It's called the Tumbleweed Grand Hotel. Let me call and see if they have a room." Without waiting for an answer, she stepped out of the hallway, called the hotel and booked the room. She gave him directions to the place, which was only a few blocks away, and pushed him out the door. When she peeked through the curtain and watched him walking to his car, she thought she saw him do a little skip dance, and she smiled in a way that she never had during her courtship with the man she almost married.

CHAPTER FORTY-SIX

Before leaving New York, Margaux had bought a new computer. She transferred all the information she had on her old IBM into her new Dell and then smashed the IBM to pieces with a hammer. She knew that with the newest equipment the FBI had at its disposal they could hack into any computer they chose, and have access to anyone's cell phone records as well. To do it legally they had to obtain a court order, but that wasn't a problem because given Margaux's status as a fugitive, a simple application to any federal court judge was all that was necessary.

Margaux spent an evening online, seeking information about Mexico City. The thing that appealed to her most was that it was a truly multinational, multicultural city. She concluded that it would be one of the best places in the Spanish-speaking world to achieve anonymity and still enjoy a near-normal lifestyle.

They spent three days in Caramina resting up and trading the Jeep for a less valuable car with Mexican plates. The new owner of the Jeep couldn't believe his good fortune in making the deal. They even paid him extra when he agreed to leave the Mexican plates on the car. Stupid women.

Margaux met all the members of Lucie's extended family. Her favorite was Lucie's maternal grandmother, who lived alone on a small farm that she tended all by herself at age eighty-four. Once Margaux succeeded in getting her to speak slowly, with Lucie's help she was able to enjoy the old lady's tales of growing up without electricity, automobiles or indoor plumbing. She still didn't have any of those modern conveniences and claimed that except for television, which she enjoyed when she visited her daughter, she lived happily without them.

On the Saturday night before they left Caramina, Margaux and Lucie decided to go to a neighborhood hangout and have a drink or two. They chose an inconspicuous table at the back of the bar where they could watch the action on the tiny dance floor. The first couple of hours passed pleasantly, but shortly after midnight, a young man wearing a tank top and displaying bulging biceps unsteadily approached their table and asked Margaux to dance. She refused politely but when he forcefully attempted to pull her up to dance she resisted and pushed him away. Lucie picked up her purse and said, "Let's get out of here." As they were leaving the fellow grabbed Margaux by the arm.

"Fuck off," she cursed, trying to break free. He just laughed. His comrades gathered around. "*Olé*" they cheered when he swatted her on the behind. "*Bravo!*" they yelled when he reached for her breast. She kneed him in the crotch. "*Oooohhh*" they gasped. By the time her victim caught his breath, Lucie had hustled her out of the bar.

"That was really stupid, Margaux," Lucie said as they trekked back to Lucie's grandmother's farm without further comment from either of them. When Lucie blew out the kerosene lamp and crawled into bed beside Margaux, she said, "We Mexican ladies have ways to handle that kind of a situation. Only a dumb gringo would say and do what you did." Margaux started to say something, changed her mind, rolled over, turned her back to Lucie and eventually fell asleep.

The next morning Lucie said, "You better not pull a trick like that again."

"Let it go, Luce. I know it was a stupid mistake. That pig really pissed me off. Now, just forget about it, okay?"

"I understand, but the problem is that you have to learn how to deal with that shit here in Mexico. Or anywhere else south of the border. By now, everyone in my home town knows about what happened with my gringo friend and *Macho Pancho* last night. All the women will be scandalized on the outside and snickering on the inside. Every guy in town will be thankful that it wasn't him that got his nuts cracked."

Having no leads as to where Lucie and Margaux might have gone in Mexico, Sergeant Schwartz gave Lucie's parole officer a call. Under the terms of her parole, Lucie was not permitted to leave New York State without her parole officer's permission. She had recently requested and received permission to visit her terminally ill mother in Mexico. The parole officer hadn't bothered to ask where her mother was living, but by checking Lucie's background on the computer she was able to tell Schwartz where Lucie was born. As soon as he finished the call he decided to gamble. He checked his map, packed his bag and headed to Zaragoza. On the way he learned from his DEA contact in Mexico City that the Mexican police force was in total disarray and that it was highly unlikely that there would be any police officers in the small village of Caramina. The only name he could get was Captain Juan Salvadore who was stationed in Zaragoza. When Sergeant Schwartz explained his situation to Captain Salvadore, the policeman smiled and said, "No problem, *señor*. How much you pay?"

It took two hours of negotiation before Salvadore agreed to work for Schwartz and to be paid $100 per day for three days. Salvadore's official pay from his government was equal to $300 U.S. per month. Sergeant Schwartz offered to pay him a thousand-dollar bonus if he discovered where Margaux was hiding within that time.

As soon as he received his first day's advance payment Salvadore immediately set out for Caramina. He had suggested that Sergeant Schwartz wait in Zaragoza while he, Salvadore, nosed around the village. It didn't take him long to confirm that Margaux and Lucie had been there. The story of the unfortunate young man who had suffered an embarrassing injury during his encounter with Margaux on the dance floor was known by everyone in the village. When he learned that Lucie Alvarez was traveling with the American fugitive, he went to see Lucie's father. He made a deal with the old man who told him that Margaux and Lucie had left Caramina earlier in the day. He also knew what kind of a car they were driving and where they were planning to spend the night. He was willing to share the information if he was paid $500 if any charges against his daughter Lucie would be dropped. Salvadore agreed to pay him if Margaux was captured within twenty-four hours. But their negotiations reached an impasse because Salvadore was well known in the village, and the old man didn't trust him. He wouldn't give Salvadore the information until he was paid and Salvadore wouldn't agree to pay him until Margaux was captured.

"Let me talk to the American. Maybe he's got an idea how to do this," Salvadore said.

Sergeant Schwartz was nervously awaiting Salvadore's return and was about to give up on him when Salvadore swaggered back to the inn where they had agreed to meet.

"Give me a shot of tequila and a cold beer," he yelled at the bartender, shoving his cap to the back of his head. "*Mi Dios* it's hot," he said when he joined Schwartz at the small table on the sidewalk outside the inn.

"Any luck?" Sergeant Schwartz asked anxiously.

"*Si*. I know where your lady is. We will get her, but we need more money, and we've got a logistical problem."

"What the hell does that mean?" Sergeant Schwartz demanded.

"Old man Alvarez knows where they will be staying tonight but he won't talk until he gets paid one thousand U.S. dollars first. See, *amigo*, he trusts me but he says he doesn't trust *gringo* cops. He's afraid if he gives you the information you'll cheat him on the payment. I think the best idea is to give me the money he wants because he tells me *las señoras* left this morning so we should go after them as soon as possible."

"Do you believe he really knows where they are?" Sergeant Schwartz asked.

"*Si, si, amigo*. Alvarez is a much honest man."

Sergeant Schwartz sat back in his chair and tried to think it through. *I don't trust you for shit, Salvadore. On the other hand if you bring home the bacon, the price is cheap. I could wander around this friggin' country for months by myself, and come up with a goose egg.*

He pulled out his notebook to see how much he had left in his account. After paying for the information about the passport and what he would have to pay Salvadore, he had about six thousand dollars left in the kitty. He decided it was worth taking a chance.

While Sergeant Schwartz was ruminating about the proposal, Salvadore added up what he could make if they pulled it off.

"That's the whole deal, right? No more surprises?" Sergeant Schwartz asked.

"Well, there is one small thing. It won't cost a penny. You must only take the American lady back to the States. The Alvarez woman stays in Mexico. Saves you the cost of transporting her back to New York and, from what you tell me, she didn't hurt nobody. She just come along for the ride."

Sergeant Schwartz quickly considered the idea. *Nobody really cares about Alvarez. She's a drug runner, anyway. We don't need her. Let Mexico keep her.*

"You got a deal, Captain," he said. They shook hands on it and Sergeant Schwartz gave Salvadore the money. As soon as Salvadore turned his back, Sergeant Schwartz looked down at his own hand. He smiled happily when he confirmed that it was still attached to his wrist.

An hour later, after old man Alvarez was paid his $500 and Salvadore pocketed the extra $500, the information was disclosed that Margaux and Lucie had left Caramina nine hours earlier in an old dark gray Ford and were planning to spend the night in Monterrey, and then head out to Mexico City. Salvadore in due course explained to Schwartz that if they left right away they should be able to reach Monterrey by midnight and have about eight hours to locate the car before Margaux and Lucie took off for their destination in the morning.

"Our chances of finding them in Monterrey are a thousand times better than if they get to Mexico City, *señor*," Salvadore said.

Sergeant Schwartz quickly checked Google on his computer and discovered that there were eighty-six hotels in Monterrey. If he and Salvadore split up when they got there, he could hire a driver so they could each check forty-three hotel parking lots in seven or eight hours. *How many old dark gray Ford cars are there in Monterrey?* he wondered. "Let's go," he said.

CHAPTER FORTY-SEVEN

Gary brought the Bloody Mary mix ingredients, including fresh celery stalks, and also a dozen red roses. Bridget brought her two sets of best friends in the world: Vivian Argetsinger and her husband Joe, who came under loud protest because he had to cancel his golf date, and Nellie Young and her husband Blue who came happily for the Bloody Marys and an excuse to avoid doing all the weekend chores Nellie had been saving up for him. Curiosity and loyalty to Bridget brought the women; threats of chastity brought the men.

Gary was a master bartender and his Bloody Marys were deceivingly potent. They went down as smooth as a strawberry milkshake on a scorching fourth of July in Arizona, and after the third round Gary had received a thumbs up from Bridget's friends. Joe was the most reluctant to signify his approval because he wanted Bridget to suffer for ruining his golf plans, but when the Bloody Marys were followed by Bridget's spectacular omelets and a magnum of perfectly chilled Dom Perignon champagne that Gary had kept as a surprise to accompany Bridget's fresh baked biscuits, even he capitulated.

The conversation skipped around the table with wit and charm and occasional thoughtful controversy concerning the economy, health care, and the war in Iraq.

"When I told you all how I felt about Obama I thought for sure I was going to run into flak here in John McCain's home state and ruin Bridget's party," Gary said. "I don't know if any of you happened to catch any of Obama's campaign ads on TV, but if you thought that they were directed to the issues we're facing in America I'll acknowledge that most of them were created in my shop."

Except for Joe, who supported John McCain, there was general agreement that they liked what they had seen and wanted to know everything he could tell them about Obama.

"I must say that Obama's public persona doesn't vary from the private man I saw. He's extremely bright and patently thoughtful in every step he takes. I was very impressed by him. And the other thing is, he seems to have the ability to surround himself with people possessing many of those same character traits."

"Including the man he chose to handle his TV commercials, right?" Blue said, affably.

"Especially him," Bridget said, laughing, with a spark of pride in her voice.

Nellie and Vivian exchanged glances of approval at the way Gary and Bridget seemed so comfortable with each. Later, when they had a few minutes alone, Nellie whispered to her friend, "It scares me, Viv, it all seems just too good to be true. I've never, ever, seen Bridget so animated and deliriously happy. If it doesn't work out for her she's going to be a basket case."

"The thing that worries me, Nell, is that I'd dump my old man in a heartbeat if someone like Gary walked into my life. God, he's cute! Did you happen to notice those Paul Newman eyes? They keep flashing BED-ROOM, BEDROOM."

They began to laugh and couldn't stop until Bridget came by and demanded to know what was so hilarious. Her two friends looked at each other and started to laugh again.

"That's enough," Bridget said. "Fess up, you two."

"Okay, you asked for the truth," Viv said, somberly. "Nell wants to know if you might be willing to swap Gary for Joe. I think she might be willing to throw in one of her kids as a kicker, if you'll consider the deal." Bridget's pleasure was mixed with relief that Gary had been awarded the seal of approval that they had only reluctantly given to Bridget's "almost" husband, Warren Wilcox.

He may break her heart, Nellie thought, *but he'll give her more joy in the process than Warren could have given her in a lifetime.*

In the meantime the three men were shooting horseshoes in the back yard. Joe and Blue were also appraising Gary with a critical eye. Initially they were both a bit skeptical of him. All three of them were about the same age, but Joe was overweight and balding and Blue was skinny with a middle age paunch. They were envious of Gary's full head of thick dark hair, graying at the temples. It was obvious that he worked out at a gym, while Joe's exercise was limited to getting in and out of a golf cart, taking a swing at the ball, ambling over to the bar at the nineteenth hole and drinking too many martinis.

Blue once brought down the house in the early morning hours during a New Year's Eve party when the happy drunks organized a push-up contest. Blue refused to participate, declaring rather pompously that he had already done a push-up...once.

Gary didn't enhance his chances of gaining their approval by beating them both at horseshoes, but when Bridget joined them and she and Joe beat Gary and Blue, the tide began to turn. After the game, the ladies brought out the Monopoly board and its sundry parts, and Blue and Joe felt much better about Gary when he was the first one to go broke. He was finally voted into the "Bridget and her Best Friends Club" as a full fledged member when he got up from the table to open the wine, tripped over the straw rug, and in attempting to keep from falling grabbed a stand-up lamp that crashed to the ground along with him. As soon as he was satisfied that only Gary's pride had been injured, Joe applauded.

Bridget had anticipated that her friends might hang out at her house for dinner and was sufficiently provisioned so that she could invite everyone to stay for a cookout in her back yard. "But the booze is all gone, guys," she lamented.

"Not a problem," Joe said, I'll be back by the time you get the fire going. He drove home and quickly returned with three bottles of California Merlot and a bottle of Riesling.

The conversation turned serious during dinner and when Blue made a derogatory remark about Sarah Palin, Joe complained bitterly that he was all alone among a clutch of empty-headed liberals, including his wife, who supported women's right to choose abortion, gay rights and awarding citizenship to all the illegal Mexican immigrants presently living in Arizona. The discussion about abortion got hot when Nellie claimed that men shouldn't have the right to vote on the abortion issue because it had nothing to do with them. Gary had remained thoughtfully silent through most of the discussion, but at that point he declared, "I agree with Nellie, and I'm totally supportive of women's exclusive right to do or not do whatever they wish with their own bodies. But here's my dilemma.... You see, I'm the bastard son of a seventeen year-old line dancer in a Broadway musical revue. My father was a thirty-five year-old traveling salesman who probably personified all of the traveling salesman jokes. They both abandoned me, but fortunately they didn't throw me in the dumpster. There's no record of my birth. I don't legally exist. I'm one of the unintended. Now, if abortion had been legal at the time my sixteen year-old mother became pregnant, I would probably have ended up in a medical waste disposal container. Furthermore, my beautiful, talented daughter Melinda, whom I love more than life itself, was also one of the unintended.

"While I'm unalterably opposed to government or anyone else dictating what women may do with their bodies, and I'm pro-choice in every sense of what those words mean, I guess I'm still searching for a way that we can protect women's right to choose and at the same time acknowledge the sanctity of life."

Gary was embarrassed by the silence that followed his speech. He shrugged his shoulders, looked at Bridget and smiled sheepishly. "I think I'll have another drink," he said.

Bridget followed him into the kitchen where the bar had been set up. Gary turned to her. She hugged him tight and kissed him tenderly.

"I guess I made a fool of myself in front of your friends. I'm sorry, Bridge."

"There's no reason to be. It's not passion that offends my friends and me. It's the lack of it that turns us off. There's nothing you could ever say from your heart that would disturb any one of us. They like you, Gary, and so do I…a lot." She hugged him again. "I do have a proposition for you, though. How about joining me in a hike up my private mountain tomorrow…just the two of us, no one except you and me."

"You got a date, lovely lady," he said.

After all of the wine bottles were emptied, Gary tried to convince everyone that he was sober enough to drive himself back to the Tumbleweed Grand Hotel, which was only a half mile down the road, but Bridget would have none of it, so he allowed Vivian to drive him there. It wasn't how Gary had hoped the evening might end. Bridget walked out to Vivian's car with him.

"Okay?" she whispered. "I'll pick you up at eleven." He tried, clumsily, to embrace her and caress her, but she laughed and took him by the hand and put him in the care of Vivian, the teetotaller. The last thing he remembered was Bridget saying, "I'll call you in the morning, love."

CHAPTER FORTY-EIGHT

Caramina was situated at the foot of the Sierra Madre mountains adjacent to the Chihuahuan desert. Although they had only traveled at night while driving from Manhattan to Laredo, Margaux's sense of security after leaving the United States, combined with the treacherous mountain roads in Mexico, convinced her it would be safer to travel by daylight to Monterrey, the first leg on their trip to Mexico City. They left Caramina in the morning hoping to arrive in Monterrey before midnight.

Once, when it was Lucie's turn to take over the wheel, she said, "We've been traveling for over eight hours, Babe. You're going to have to keep talking pretty interesting stuff, otherwise I'll sure as hell doze off and wrap us around a tree." After they swapped places and got underway again, Margaux settled back into the passenger seat.

"Okay," she said, "What can I talk about that will keep you awake? With guys it's either women, sports, or cars. Did I ever tell you about my trial where that bitch judge sent me to prison?"

"At least a half dozen times."

"Beggars can't be choosers, Lucie."

"How about giving me the straight poop on what happened in Bora Bora, on that ship. What was it called?"

"*Seadancer.*"

"Yeah. It sounds romantic…which reminds me, what about Ramiriz? Do you think he killed Toro?"

Margaux hesitated before answering.

"I don't really know, Luce. He's the most likely suspect, but as far as I know, there's no proof." Again she hesitated and then she said, "I want to tell you something but you've got to swear on a thousand Bibles never to repeat it and if you ever get subpoenaed to testify, you never heard it. Right?"

"Hey, man, I no speaka da English. I no unnerstan' nothin'."

Margaux started to speak and then she started to cry. Lucie reached over and took her hand. "Let's forget about it," she said, "Let's talk about something else."

"No. Maybe telling you the story will be like going to confession. I've never been to confession. You're Catholic. Does it really help when you get to confess your sins?"

"Yeah, it does. I think it lessens the guilt feelings. When the priest says you're forgiven, you feel as if you've got a clean slate, see what I mean? Of course you never tell the whole truth if you've done something really bad, but yeah, it helps."

"Okay, well, I need all the forgiving you can give me, Father."

"Oh man, I'm wide awake now, that's for sure," she laughed.

Margaux opened her purse, took out a pack of cigarettes, lit one, and rolled down the car window.

"Hey, what's that stupid shit? You told me you gave up those coffin nails," Lucie said.

"I did. Gary made me quit, but he's no longer in my life and I'll never get through this story without a cigarette."

"Then forget the story. I don't want to see you see hooked on that crap again."

"I'm okay," she sniffled. "It all went down the night after Toro told us there had been a mistake in his diagnosis and that his cancer was treatable. He wasn't feeling well, and he decided to skip dinner. I tucked him into bed and turned off the light. He was asleep before I left to meet up with the family in the main dining room. Toro had invited all of us to see the big stage show that night, but Nick and Vito didn't turn up for dinner. By the time we finished our drinks, I started feeling lousy too. I figured I must have picked up the same bug Toro had, and I told the girls I was going to pass on dinner. They walked me back to our suite, but when I got there I had trouble getting the key in the door lock. Carmen took the key from me and unlocked the door. Then they said goodnight and took off. And then, when I opened the door…."

When Margaux stopped talking, Lucie looked over at her. She was sitting up straight like a zombie and the tears were sliding down her cheeks. Lucie handed her the Kleenex box they had stuffed in the console.

"Thanks," Margaux sobbed, clutching the box.

"Hey, Hon, let's leave it for now, we can—"

"No," she sobbed. "Maybe if I tell you the whole story it will put an end to it."

"Whatever you want to do is okay by me, but I hate to see you bawling and—"

"I'm okay now," she said. "Anyway, after they left, I went into our stateroom, shut the door and switched on the light. Toro was lying unconscious on the floor in the middle of the room. There was blood all over the place.

"I knelt down beside him. I remember I put my ear close to his mouth. He was still breathing, but his breath sounds were weak and irregular. For a few minutes I just sat on the floor staring at him, watching his chest rise and fall. His words the previous night, 'I'm gonna live to be a hundred,' kept echoing in my mind. I began to cry. I don't know why, exactly. If Toro died it would solve all my problems…Gary…the money...but then I had this vision in my mind of Toro and me kneeling at the altar in Saint Patrick's Cathedral and my vow 'till death do us part' echoed over and over again in my mind. I stood up intending to call for help, but when I took a step I slipped in the blood on the polished floor and twisted my ankle. The nearest phone was in Toro's bedroom. I limped into his room but when I reached down to pick up the receiver, something knocked me unconscious."

"*Dios!*" Lucie shuddered.

"When I came to, I was lying on the floor in Toro's bedroom totally disoriented. I had a very sore neck and a wicked headache. I staggered into the living room where I had left Toro lying on the floor.... Jesus, Luce, I'll never forget that moment as long as I live. He was gone! I felt faint and went into my bedroom and passed out on the bed until the phone woke me up. I covered my head with my pillow and tried to ignore it, but it kept ringing. It was Zee. She said Toro hadn't shown up for their regular breakfast date and she wondered if he was okay because he hadn't been feeling well the night before. I said I'd check him out, and then I told her that he wasn't in his room and must be out taking a stroll around the deck."

"Why didn't you tell her the truth, for God's sake! You didn't have anything to hide, right?" Lucie asked.

Margaux looked over at Lucie. "I don't really know, Luce. I guess the whole thing was so bizarre I thought that no one would believe me. I just wanted the whole thing to go away. I didn't want to be involved, you understand?"

"Not really, but—"

"I somehow got it into my head that whatever happened I'd get blamed for it. And then Zee called me back and suggested we meet for lunch. I agreed and after she hung up I tried to piece the whole thing together, but I couldn't."

Ramiriz had drawn the short straw and was elected to heist Margaux's jewelry while she and Toro were at dinner on Saturday night. Nicky and Vito were supposed to keep everybody at the dinner table as long as possible, but when Zee told Vito that Toro had invited the girls to go to the Saturday night show directly after dinner, he and Nicky decided that would give Ramiriz plenty of time to do his thing, so they went to the casino instead.

Ramiriz entered the suite about an hour after Margaux left to meet the family in the main dining room. He succeeded in opening the wall safe in Margaux's bedroom, but then Toro was awakened by his need to relieve himself and as he passed Margaux's adjoining bedroom on his way to the bathroom he spied Ramiriz standing in front of the open safe.

"Hey, you son of a—" Toro's curse was cut short when Ramiriz swirled around and smashed him in the face with his fist, knocking him unconscious, and fracturing his skull when the back of his head struck the heavy wooden coffee table. When Ramiriz heard Margaux and the girls having difficulty unlocking the door to the suite, he realized there was no way for him to escape undetected. He slipped into Toro's bedroom and hid himself in the shadows, leaving the door ajar. He watched Margaux as she discovered Toro's prone body. When she limped into Toro's bedroom and reached out to pick up the phone on the bedside table, he knocked her out with a karate chop to the side of her neck. He stuffed her jewelry into his pockets, and as soon as the hallway outside the suite was clear, he made his way back to his own cabin, undetected.

CHAPTER FORTY-NINE

Sergeant Schwartz and Salvadore rode silently side by side in the car Sergeant Schwartz had rented in Zaragoza. Salvadore was driving fast but expertly over the lonely mountain road. They were each deep into their own private worlds—Salvadore fantasizing about how he would spend his money when they captured Margaux, Schwartz wondering whether his adventure in Monterrey would prove him to be a super sleuth or a fool, and how if he brought Margaux back to stand trial before a jury of her peers he would be able to provide the evidence that would satisfy them beyond a reasonable doubt that she was guilty of murdering her husband; and finally, selfishly considering how such a victory or defeat would impact upon his career. From time to time Salvadore would communicate by cell phone with other members of law enforcement. Sometimes he would explain to Sergeant Schwartz whom he was calling and why, but most of the time the one-sided conversation that Sergeant Schwartz heard was spoken so rapidly and interspersed with so many colloquialisms that he was unable to understand what Salvadore was saying. Occasionally his Brooklyn/Bronx/Lower East Side Manhattan/Puerto Rican Spanish allowed him to pick up bits and pieces of the conversation, which seemed to concern itself mostly with *gringos*, *pesos* and U.S. dollars.

When they were only a few hours away from Monterrey, Salvadore explained that he had finally reached Captain Cortez of the Monterrey police department and had been successful in mobilizing the captain and two off-duty officers to begin the search for Margaux's vehicle. Sergeant Schwartz agreed to pay $500 to Captain Cortez and $100 to each of his men if they located the vehicle before he and Salvadore arrived in Monterrey.

Margaux and Lucie checked into the Crowne Plaza Hotel under Margaux's new name, Carla Estrada. They had a couple of drinks, ate dinner at a sidewalk cafe a few blocks away from the hotel and were in bed before ten o'clock, prepared to be on the road by eight a.m.

Margaux lay awake in bed. Occasionally the headlights of a car pulling into the hotel parking lot would send a shaft of light across the bedroom ceiling. As she tried unsuccessfully to get to sleep she thought about

Lucie's remark: *'Of course you never tell the whole truth if you've done something really bad.'* The nightmarish memory that Margaux would not share with Lucie began when she discovered Toro unconscious in their suite. She thought that if she called for help and he regained consciousness, he would probably end up a vegetable, and he really could live to be 100.

I know he wouldn't want to live like that, she mumbled to herself. *I must help him die. It's what he would want me to do.*

She went to the tiny bar in the corner of the living room, mixed herself a double dry martini and took up her vigil. At four o'clock in the morning he was still alive. She decided she must do something. *I've got to get him out of here. Perhaps if I drag him out into the corridor and leave him there, when he's discovered everyone will believe he was mugged.* The idea had merit, she thought, *but first of all, if I get caught hauling him out there, I'm finished. Besides, there's no way I could avoid leaving a trail along the way. On the other hand, maybe I could...yes, that's it. I'll haul him out on the balcony and push him overboard. I'll report him missing tomorrow, and by the time his body is discovered, if it ever is, we'll be thousands of miles away.*

She bent down and took Toro by the upper arms and tried to pull him gently toward the balcony door. His body didn't budge. She pulled as hard as she could but only succeeded in moving him a few inches. She glanced around the room and spied the oriental runner. Turning it over, she slid it on the polished mahogany floor and placed it beside Toro. Then she rolled him onto the rug so that he was lying on his back. She was startled when he groaned softly, but when she checked his breathing it was still about the same. His eyes remained closed but the blood began to flow from the wound in his head and soaked into the back of the rug when she slid it out onto the concrete floor of the balcony. She was able to prop him up with his back resting against the railing, but she was unable lift him up and over the railing.

Suppose I just leave him here on the balcony, close the door, draw the drapes and go to bed. Toro always gets up early and has breakfast with Zee. I'll sleep late as I always do. The housekeepers never clean our cabin until after I leave to meet him for lunch. When they discover him after I've gone, I'll be as shocked and saddened as everyone else when we get the news.

She considered the problem solved but at that moment, Toro groaned again. This time it was louder, more forceful. She checked his breathing and his pulse; they were both stronger. In his unconscious state he was fighting for his life. She realized that somehow she must push him into the sea before dawn.

She went back to the bar, mixed another drink and returned to the balcony. The word *fulcrum* flashed through her mind when a high-back deck chair caught her eye. She wrestled Toro's body up into the chair and leaned it against the railing. The top of the chair was taller than the railing. As she stood facing him in the chair, the rim of the morning sun had just started to peek over the mountains on Bora Bora. She reached down and lifted the front legs of the chair and began to tip it up. She was only seconds away from easing him out of the chair and into the sea when Toro opened his eyes.

"Margaux," he gasped, reaching up and clutching the gold chain that dangled from her neck. As his body slipped over the rail the chain broke when its weakest link failed.

CHAPTER FIFTY

Aside from Gary's modestly troublesome hangover on the morning following his attempt to drink Bridget's friends under the table, he felt absolutely marvelous. *So what's happening here?* he asked himself as he lay in bed, staring out the window at the mountain that began its rise behind the hotel. At that moment the phone rang.

"Are you back among the living?" Bridget purred.

"Now that I have something to live for…absolutely," he answered.

"Are you ready for a hike up the mountain? You promised, but I wasn't certain you knew what you were committing to, and I might have taken advantage of you in a weak moment."

"Of course you did, but honorable men never welsh on a deal. How soon are you going to pick me up?"

"We said eleven—is that still okay?"

Gary glanced at the clock on the bedside table. "Sure. Just bring me a mug of steaming black coffee, okay?"

"You got it, hotshot, I'll be there in thirty minutes. Bye." She rang off.

"I think this is going to take a little getting used to," he mumbled out loud after he hung up the phone.

He hurried into the bathroom to shave and shower, opened his dilapidated ditty bag (a relic of his father's service in the Marines), fished around for his razor, lathered up and faced the increasingly onerous daily task of looking at himself in the mirror. "Not a pretty sight, but it can only get worse," he mumbled.

He always thought that his morning hot shower was one of the best times of each day. He had been wise enough to choose a profession that presented new challenges daily, and he began to plan for them each morning under the soothing spray of hot water. At his home in Sea Cliff, he had installed four shower heads in his oversized shower stall. Sometimes while thinking through a complex problem he would run out of hot water, and yelp when the spray quickly went from calming warm to bone-chilling cold. Somewhere he had read that Paul Newman attributed his age-defying condition to his ritual of immersing his face and hands in ice cold water for extended periods of time. Gary considered it for a short while and decided he would rather accept the wrinkles than suffer the torture of a daily ice-water dip.

His thoughts on this day, however, were consumed totally by his ever-increasing attraction to Bridget. *Is this just a rebound thing or is it for real?* In such a short time after the Margaux fiasco, he was seriously considering the idea of some kind of permanent relationship with Bridget. "What a scary thought that is," he exclaimed as he rubbed himself down.

He dressed just in time to respond to her call from the lobby announcing her arrival precisely twenty-nine minutes from the time of her last call.

After a chaste good morning kiss, she hopped behind the wheel and they headed off to their adventure. Gary thought she looked delectable in her baggy jeans, hiking boots and T-shirt. They chatted amiably during the time it took to reach the mountain.

"Is it really called Serene Mountain?" Gary asked.

"Absolutely. I named it myself," she laughed. "It's my private hideaway...the place I run to when I need to sort things out in my life. It's my serenity mountain."

"Is that what we're going to do today?"

"Could be, who knows?" she answered, handing him a large backpack. "I put all this together, so now you can carry it. I've got bottles of water, lunch, ice, a blanket, two lightweight jackets in case you didn't come equipped to handle the cool temperature at the top of the mountain, and the wine of course."

"Red or white?"

"Both. I prefer white."

"Hey, darlin', I'll drink anything."

"So I've noticed," Bridget said, but she was smiling when she said it. "Okay, big guy, let's get this show on the road."

Bridget led the vigorous climb that took almost two hours. On several occasions Gary was ready to suggest they stop and rest a while, but he wouldn't give her the satisfaction. He was amazed at her stamina as she climbed relentlessly up the mountain. By the time they reached the top they had consumed all their bottled water, but there was a tiny crystal-clear pool just below the peak where they refilled the bottles, splashed water on their faces and on each other, and then soaked their feet in the frigid stream. Gary told her about Paul Newman's routine. She listened thoughtfully, and then said, "I sort of like wrinkles...on other people, that is." She smiled. "But you see, therein lies the problem."

"What's that?" Gary asked.

"We Americans are so obsessed by appearances. It's shameful. Take the story you just told me about Paul Newman. By the way, he just died a few days ago, did you know that?"

"No, I didn't. Damn! He and his wife were so generous, giving all the millions of dollars of profit from his businesses to charity. Lindy told me she met them a couple of times and she said they were two of the most gracious people she had ever known. She was only one of hundreds of young actors they had met over the years, but they told her they had seen *Jazz* together with a few friends in the private screening room in their home, and that they all thought she had performed superbly. Of course, Lindy was thrilled and ecstatic with their praise, but the point is, they were kind and sensitive to her in a way she'll never forget. But I'm afraid I interrupted you, I just wanted to share that little story with you while I had it in my mind," Gary said.

"No, no, it's a lovely story, and it supports what I was going to say. I don't believe for a moment that Paul and Joanne remained married into their eighties because he remained handsome and she remained beautiful. I want to believe they remained together for so long because of more important reasons—and because I'm square and corny," she laughed.

"I agree with that part about you being square and corny, and I want to discuss that subject in detail, but frankly I'm starved to death, and I'm thirsty for something more than ice water. You didn't give me time to eat breakfast this morning and it's now..."—he looked at his watch—"almost two o'clock."

"In order not to spoil this delightful day, I shall not remind you that except for you and Joe, the rest of us had hot sausage and peppers, potato salad and corn on the cob while you guys had a five course Merlot and Riesling dinner. You get no sympathy from me, Mr. Samson."

"Joe told me the sausages were undercooked and greasy, the potato salad was spoiled by too much salt and the corn wasn't ripe," Gary said with a straight face.

"Even if that were true, which it isn't," she answered quickly, "if you three guys had helped prepare it and cook it instead of sitting out there on the patio telling each other bawdy sexist jokes, while the ladies sweated in the kitchen, then maybe...."

"You win, I give up, let's just get this lunch under way," Gary said, spreading the blanket down on a grassy plot overlooking the valley and opening the bottle of Riesling while Bridget opened the lunch boxes. Gary sipped the chilled wine and gazed out at the spectacular view to the west. He had removed his sweat-streaked shirt and let the Arizona sun caress his back and shoulders. He thought about the ice and snow he had left back in New York.

So why do we punish ourselves for four months every year in the North? Are we crazy or stupid or what? he asked himself.

Bridget brought him a paper plate with fried chicken wings, potato chips and an apple.

"Are you deep in private thoughts or can you share them with me?" she asked, handing him the food.

"I was just wondering why we punish ourselves every winter back in New York when we could be down here in Arizona or Florida or southern California, and I think I've figured it out," he said, stuffing his mouth full of chicken.

"So, give. I certainly don't understand it," she replied.

"Comfort stifles creativity. What do you think?"

"I think you're full of beans!" she laughed, and sat down beside him and leaned against his shoulder. Feeling the warmth of her body and her fragrance drove all other thoughts from his mind. He held her tight, kissed her passionately and tried to pull her down on the blanket. She resisted being put into a sexual position. Gary sat up straight, began to chew on the chicken again, and… sulked.

"We have to talk, Gary. Every time I express my feelings for you, you insist on trying to jump my bones. Can't we just move a little slower? I'm a southern girl. Maybe my creativity is stifled."

Gary didn't laugh. "I'm a man, Bridget, don't you get it?"

"Actually, I think I perceive the situation very well. You attempt to justify your demands upon me by claiming you're a man, when in fact you're acting like a teenage boy compelled by his juvenile testosterone to engage in sex without caring about the consequences. I grew up with three older brothers and they taught me well. Once when Josh was nineteen and had too much to drink, he told me, excuse the language please because it's gross, 'When I was sixteen, I could fuck a chair, or a couch or a pillow, or a milk bottle lined with a chunk of raw meat.' But Gary, he was only a kid, and you're a man who has learned that relationships with a woman, in this case me, are built on many things. Granted, sex is one of them, and a damned important one, but if it's on the top of your list of priorities, all the time, we really do need to talk."

Gary was astonished by her frankness and her perspicacity. No woman had ever spoken so honestly with him. He stood up and paced around a bit before answering her. He needed time to think through what was going on between them. *After all,* he thought, *I only knew her for a week, almost a year ago, and now I've come waltzing back and expect her to lie down and…What a jerk I am!* He sat down on a log, took out his penknife and began to whittle a piece of wood, to calm down. Bridget watched him carefully. She understood that the rest of her life might be determined by what happened between them in the ensuing few hours.

Gary walked back to where she was seated on the blanket. He handed her a little figure he had carved.

"What's this?" she asked.

"It's supposed to be a cat...."

"Oh yes, I see it now. It's delightful. Thank you," she smiled.

"Actually it's a peace offering. Here's the problem. They say that sex is ninety-six percent of an unsuccessful marriage and four percent of a successful marriage. From my perspective it doesn't make any sense to spend days or months building an intimate friendship and then discover that we're not compatible sexually. Why not get that primitive business out of the way first, and then take our time working out the really important aspects of developing a meaningful relationship?"

"Is that what you did with Margaux? she asked.

"Margaux?" Gary was stunned. "Who told you about Margaux?"

"You told me last night after your third vodka martini, just before you asked me to marry you." She laughed out loud when Gary looked as if he had just been advised by his physician that he had six months to live.

"I've never been that drunk before in my life," he responded sheepishly. "Did you accept my marriage proposal?"

"I toyed with idea, but decided that would be playing dirty pool and I would wait and see if you would ask me again when you were sober.

"Incidentally, I looked up your friend Margaux on the Internet this morning. I told you I had seen her picture on the front page of the *National Enquirer* and read about the trial. She sure is a beautiful woman, and a lawyer besides. I was a bit jealous of her but then I decided I'm really a lot nicer than she is, what with her stealing $250,000, spending a year in jail, marrying a man forty years older than her who got himself murdered...isn't Google amazing? And besides, my body is as good as hers, any day," she said, sticking out her chest.

Gary burst into whooping laughter. "That's what I've been trying to tell you. If you'll just share that spectacular body with me, and let us get on with this relationship...or do I have to marry you and then maybe discover that it's not working out, and we have to hire lawyers and end up in a waterfall of tears...It doesn't make any sense now, does it?"

"Of course it does. All I ask is that you give me a ring, symbolizing a commitment. And before you get the wrong idea, it doesn't have to be a big diamond. Just a simple ring that signifies that you honestly believe you're in love with me, that one day in the future we'll marry, and my mom will give me away, and Melinda and my daughter Jonni will be my bridesmaids, and your former partner Pierre DeLisle will be your best man, and my son Michael will be one of your ushers, and all of our family members and our best friends will come and help us celebrate and we'll live happily ever after."

Gary took her in his arms, and they kissed. "You've given me a lot to think about," he said. "Let me take a little walk. I need to be alone to work things out in my own mind. Maybe Serene Mountain can do for me what it does for you." He released her and wandered away. Bridget cleaned things up and packed everything away. She didn't know what to think. The fact was that when he had just held her and kissed her she had had an overwhelming wish that he would throw her down on the blanket and get it over with. *Why am I making such a big deal out of it?* she asked herself. *After all, I'm obviously not a virgin. I just don't want to be used, I guess is what I'm thinking, but I suppose there's no reason we can't have sex for the pure joy of it. Why do I have to get it all entwined with love and commitment and rings and...dammit, I'm sick of beating it to death. When he comes back...if he comes back... I'll tell him I'm okay with it if he tells me he loves me. Surely that's a fair compromise.*

Gary sat down and leaned back against a big rock.

He closed his eyes and dozed for a bit. When he awakened he applied himself again to his carving. Then he walked slowly back to where Bridget was waiting for him. She stood up to greet him and started to speak. He put a finger to her lips.

"First of all," he said, "There is absolutely no doubt that I'm falling in love with you. I can't be certain of it until we know lots more about each other, but I'd say I'm almost there. And with this..." he reached into his pocket and pulled out the wooden ring he had carved, "I hereby commit to becoming your significant other, as they say, whenever we're both satisfied that it's what we wish to do. And finally...." He looked around for the wine bottle. "Now, what did you do with what was left of the wine? I need the bottle and the two glasses—this is important," he said, seriously. Bridget didn't say a word; she just opened the backpack, removed the half-full bottle of wine and the two glasses, and handed them to him. He poured the wine into the glasses and gave one to Bridget.

"This is a special toast," he said, "and the ritual is a little tricky. First we have to stand facing each other and then link our drinking arms together like this...careful now, it's important that you don't spill any wine." Bridget was smiling as he hooked his arm through hers and raised his glass to his lips. "Like this," he said, and she did the same. "Now, when we finish the toast, we gaze into each other's eyes over the rims of our glasses, chug-a-lug until our glasses are empty and then we throw our glasses over the cliff. Are you with me?"

"I don't have to hold on to the glass when I throw it over the cliff, do I?" she asked, deadpan. Before he had a chance to answer, she continued, "And, being the liberal you profess to be, would it be environmentally correct to litter the side of the mountain with broken glass? And another thing...."

"I don't think you're taking this whole thing seriously," he scolded.

"But I am, I am," she whispered.

"Okay then, no more talk, just repeat after me:

"Let's be gay while we may..."

"*Let's be gay while we may,*" she repeated.

"Let's fill our lives with laughter..."

"*Let's fill our lives with laughter,*" she followed again.

"For I'll be true...as long as you..."

"*For I'll be true...as long as you...*"

"And not a moment after, " he concluded.

"*And not a moment after!*"

Then they both drank up the wine and hurled their glasses over the cliff.

Then they laughed and kissed and laughed some more. When he finally released her, she turned away and pulled her T-shirt up over her head and began to unbutton her jeans.

"What are you doing?" he said.

"What does it look like I'm doing?" she shrugged her shoulders and her bra fell away. She stepped out of her panties, raised her arms to the cloudless sky and stood like a Greek goddess in the Arizona sun.

As they began their descent down the mountainside, the sun filled the sky with wondrous pinks and purples as it dipped below the horizon. Gary's psyche was in turmoil. The sexual adventure that he had so craved had been a total disaster. Since she had given birth to two children, he anticipated at least a modicum of sexual sophistication. He was mistaken.

Bridget had performed as if she were a life-sized rag doll: a beautiful mannequin in repose, dutifully fulfilling a distasteful task.

He tried desperately to bring her to climax. When he finally gave up and withdrew, she had smiled sweetly, a woman resigned to her gender.

They hiked silently down the trail until they reached their ice-water spring. Bridget kissed Gary tenderly and raised her left hand. "This is more meaningful to me than a diamond, love. God created the tree and you created the ring. It's a beautiful gift from both of you."

That evening Gary tried to mask his colossal disappointment.

Bridget remained radiant and upbeat. She led the conversation in directions that were interesting to both Gary and her children. When the children went up to their rooms to do their homework for Monday's classes, Bridget sat down close to Gary on the sofa, kissed him on the cheek, and whispered, "Thank you for such a beautiful day, darling. The whole idea of falling in love again after so many years is overwhelming to me. I mean, I want to crawl inside your brain so I can read your mind and share your dreams. The fact is, I really don't have a clue as to who you really are and I want to know absolutely everything about you."

"You can find a lot of it on Google or whatever," he said, smiling.

"Oh, I did that right after I met you over a year ago, but I'm not interested in all that financial stuff. I want to know what's made you the man I'm falling in love with. You told us the other night that your mother and father abandoned you, but I want to know what happened next. I mean, who brought you up? Where did you go to school? I just want to know everything. And above all, I want to know which team we're going to root for in the Superbowl game," she laughed.

When he didn't immediately respond, she whispered, "Hello there—Gary?" She tapped his forehead and said, "Is anybody home?"

"Just me, but I was thinking, you know, about what you were asking me. Actually, I wrote a story about the day I left for college when I was seventeen years old. It doesn't get into the messy part of my life like having to get married in my freshman year at NYU because I had unknowingly and irresponsibly put my prom date in a family way, as my grandma delicately described it.

"We were just kids, you know. We didn't have a clue about what marriage really means, or how to deal with a baby.

"When my daughter Melinda was three years old, my wife decided that she had had enough of dirty diapers and no money, and when she met an attractive man who made her an offer she couldn't refuse, we split up. She got to live in a big fancy house in Philadelphia, and I got Melinda. My daughter Lindy and my profession is what my life was all about, until she went off to Hollywood and I met a certain flight attendant who swept me off my feet." Gary raised his arms in submission.

"So when are you going to let me read your story about when you were seventeen? I told you I want to know everything."

"That's easy. I know it's stored in my computer somewhere. I'll e-mail it to you tonight when I go back to the hotel, if you wish. It's just a snapshot, you know."

"Maybe someday you'll add a new chapter entitled, 'Bridget'," she laughed.

"You can be sure I will," he said.

Bridget waited until Gary had time to reach his hotel and then she booted up her computer. His e-mail message was waiting for her.

Hi Bridget. As promised, here is my story of my teen age folly that turned out to be the best thing that ever happened to me, but I won't recommend it to Michael.
Good night, Bridget. Sweet dreams.

JACK'S FEDORA

It was a bright fall day in 1978. My adopted dad Jack took me to the train station when I was leaving for college.

We stood together on the platform, waiting for the train that would take me to New York City, each deep in thought about what the future might bring. Although I was apprehensive about attending college, my fears were not of homesickness, but rather of the possibility of failure, since no one in my family had ever attended college. The trepidations I had, waiting for the Long Island Railroad to transport me into a new life, were overshadowed by the excitement of becoming a first generation college student.

My dad stood beside me, stooped over, almost a foot shorter than me because of his crippled back. He didn't know what advice to give me. He had dropped out of high school when he was sixteen years old to go to work with his father as an apprentice carpenter.

As the train came to a stop and I was about to board, he reached up gently and took my hand in his.

"I don't know anything about this college business, son, just promise me you'll pass," he asked earnestly.

"I'll do my best, Pop," I said, and then I bent down and hugged him, and we held each other for a few seconds. He kissed me clumsily and as he turned away, I saw him wipe the back of his hand across his eyes. In all my growing up years I had never seen him cry.

The porter announced, "All aboard." I grabbed my two heavy bags, clambered up the metal steps and slid into the first open seat so I could wave good-bye to him, but he was no longer on the platform. And then I saw him in the back of the parking lot, standing by our old Buick, waiting for the train to leave.

I struggled to raise the window but it was stuck and I couldn't open it. Although he couldn't see me, my dad continued to stand there, and just before the train disappeared from sight he waved his battered old brown fedora.

How I wish I could relive that day, stand with him again and tell him how much I loved him. At the time I was so young and filled with self, there was no room in my mind or heart to appreciate the depth of his love, the sacrifices he made for me, another man's child—teaching me how to fly a kite, use a hammer and saw, catch a baseball, dig clams with my bare feet, build a camp fire, sail a boat, drive a car...the list is endless. Perhaps one day Melinda will give me a grandchild and I'll have another chance.

CHAPTER FIFTY-ONE

It was four o'clock in the morning by the time Sergeant Schwartz and Captain Salvadore reached the outskirts of Monterrey. Shortly after 5:00 a.m. Cortez reported to Salvadore that they had found a car that fit the description that had been given to them, but he wouldn't reveal its location until he received the $500. They met, the money was paid, and Cortez led them to the parking lot of the Crowne Plaza Hotel.

Margaux's car was parked with its front bumper against a stone wall that surrounded the hotel property. Salvadore pulled his vehicle into the empty space beside it so close that the driver's door of Margaux's car could not be opened, and then he let the air out of both her rear tires. Sergeant Schwartz took up a position where he could observe the car without being seen himself. He sent Salvadore to the hotel's front desk to seek information concerning the owner of the car. It took Salvadore less than twenty minutes to confirm that the owner was Carla Estrada. She was staying on the sixth floor in Room 607. She had ordered a wake-up call for seven a.m. and had only reserved the room for one night.

"It cost me please, twenty-five dollar, señor." Schwartz handed him the money.

"Now find out if there is an available room near their room and book it," Schwartz ordered, reluctantly handing Salvadore his credit card.

Salvadore went back to the front desk, gave the clerk the ten dollars he had promised him for the information, slipped fifteen dollars in his pocket and reserved the surveillance room.

"Any time, Captain," the clerk winked.

When Salvadore returned to the parking lot, Schwartz said," I've been thinking that we could use Captain Cortez if he's interested. Ask him, okay?"

The two officers spoke rapidly to each other.

"How much?" Salvadore asked, raising his hand and stroking his thumb and index fingers together.

"$100," Schwartz answered.

"He says he needs $300. Is dangerous work, he's married, got kids, no insurance."

"I'll pay him $200, that's it. You guys are impossible." Schwartz took out his wallet. Salvadore put his hand on Schwartz's arm.

"You pay me, I pay him." Schwartz started to protest, thought better of it and gave Salvadore two fifties and a hundred dollar bill. Out of the corner of his eye he noticed that only one bill got passed to Cortez. He wondered if it was the hundred dollar bill or one of the fifties.

"Okay," Schwartz said, "I'll wait here for them to come to the car and make the arrest. I want you guys to follow them out of their room. If they split up, Salvadore, you keep Santoros in sight at all times. He opened his briefcase and handed both officers mug shots of Margaux and Lucie taken from the Richford Hills files.

"They look alike. How tall? How much they weigh?" Salvadore demanded.

"I've never seen either of them myself," Schwartz admitted.

"In that case, I think we should take them when they come out of the room, *señor*," Cortez said.

"No, no. Absolutely not," Sergeant Schwartz replied immediately. "There would be too much risk of endangering innocent hotel guests. She's probably armed and dangerous. She killed her husband. One death is enough. We'll take her down here in the parking lot where we can maintain total control of the area."

Captain Cortez signaled to Captain Salvadore. They stepped away from Schwartz.

"What did he say? I couldn't understand him," Cortez whispered.

"He said the fugitive lady is armed and dangerous. She has murdered many peoples in the U.S. He doesn't want to risk injuring hotel guests. If we arrest her inside the hotel she will try to shoot her way out and kill many peoples."

Cortez spit on the ground. "*Stupido gringo*," he muttered.

The room Salvadore had booked was across the hall from Margaux's. The two officers took the elevator up to the sixth floor. Salvadore glanced at his watch as they exited the elevator. It was 6:45 a.m. He quietly opened the door to room 608.

After she and Lucie were dressed in the morning, Margaux suggested that they have coffee in their room, pack up their clothing, and put some miles behind them before breakfast. When they finished their coffee, Margaux said, "Why don't you take the big bag down and get us checked out? I'll finish packing up my things and meet you in the lobby."

"Sounds good to me. See you down there," Lucie said.

When Lucie opened the hotel room door and headed toward the elevator, Salvadore whispered to Cortez. "That's Alvarez, the short-haired one. Go. I'll wait and follow Santoros."

Five minutes later, Margaux left the room. Salvadore followed her to the elevator. There was a family of five waiting there. The mother had a baby in her arms. Margaux smiled at the mother and wiggled her fingers at the baby. When the elevator arrived it was already filled with hotel guests. The father of the family motioned to Margaux. "Go ahead, Miss. We can't all fit in. We'll take the next car."

"Thank you," Margaux said, and squeezed in just as the door was closing. Salvadore tried to keep the door open, but he was too late. Margaux saw his shoulder holster when he tried unsuccessfully to prevent the door from closing. When the door slid open at the next stop, she stepped out and called Lucie on her cell phone.

"Lucie!"

"What's up?"

"A guy with a gun is trying to follow me. Probably a plain clothes cop. Be careful, there could be someone following you as well. I remember seeing restrooms opposite the front desk. Go to the men's room and lock yourself into a stall. Switch your phone to vibrate. Call me when you get there."

Margaux took the next available elevator down to the basement and searched around until she found the laundry room and a pile of soiled uniforms. She snatched one of the uniforms, hid her suitcase behind some crates and stepped into a dark corner where she stuffed her hair under the cap and put the uniform on over her clothes. Then she grabbed an empty maid's cart and threw in a woman's raincoat and beret that were hanging on the coat rack outside the staff locker room. She wheeled the cart over to the freight elevator and pushed the button for the lobby.

After speaking with Margaux, Lucie noticed Cortez in uniform. She moved slowly in the direction of the restrooms and when a large group of tourists heading for the front desk came between them, she slipped into the men's room. There was only one man there, standing at a urinal. He was startled and about to tell her she had made a mistake but before he had a chance she had ducked into an open stall and shut the door. He shrugged his shoulders, zipped up and left the room. She immediately called Margaux. "Where are *you?*" she asked.

"I'm about twenty-five feet from you," Margaux answered. "I'll be right there."

When Salvadore was unable to enter the elevator, he raced down the emergency stairwell to the lobby. Margaux was nowhere in sight.

"Where the hell did that bitch disappear to?" he muttered as he scanned the guests in the lobby. Then he spied Cortez standing in a corner by the front desk. He hurried over to him.

"Where is your woman?" Salvadore demanded.

Cortez hung his head. "I don't know. She checked out at the front desk and was just standing around. I saw her talking on her cell phone, but a group of people came by. They blocked my view and she disappeared.

"I could have taken her down as soon as she came out of the room, like I wanted...Jesus, I had my hands right on her...."

"Never mind. She's not important."

"What about Santoros?" Cortez asked.

"I think she must have left the room before we got up there," Saladore lied so he wouldn't have to admit he had also lost his quarry. "Schwartz has their car covered so let's guard the exits. I'll take the front and you watch the back."

Margaux exited the elevator, bent her head down, affected a slight limp and slowly pushed her cart into the men's room.

There wasn't anyone there.

"Lucie?" she whispered. Lucie opened her stall door. Margaux grabbed the coat and beret and ducked inside the stall.

"Put on this hat and coat," Margaux said. "Take the elevator up to the third floor, and then go down the emergency stairs and meet me in the basement by the freight elevator." She waited a few minutes after Lucie left and then opened the stall door, threw Lucie's bag in the cart and headed out to the nearest stairway where she abandoned the cart and carried Lucie's bag down the stairs to the freight elevator.

They met in the basement undetected, but several housekeeping employees stared at them as they passed by.

"We've got to get out of here," Margaux whispered. "Here's what we'll do." She handed Lucie her suitcase, and retrieved her own bag. "One of us will take the luggage to the car, drive around the block and pick up the other outside the back gate. We'd better change clothes because those housekeepers who saw us made me nervous." Margaux slipped on jeans and a jacket. Lucie pulled on a large sweat shirt and black pants. Margaux put on her shoulder-length black wig.

"Good idea," Lucie said, and pulled out her own shoulder-length black wig and put it on. They scrutinized each other and Margaux said, "That ought to do it. You've got the car key, right?" Lucie reached in her pocket and held it up.

"Do you want to drive the car?" Lucie asked.

"Let's flip for it," Margaux said. She took a coin out of her pocket. "I'll flip, you call."

"Tails."

"Okay, let's go."

They hugged, high-fived, opened the door cautiously and took off in opposite directions.

Cortez had taken up a position next to the loading dock at the back of the hotel. He settled in beside a pickup truck parked by the dock and checked his revolver. He switched off the safety and laid the weapon on top of the truck fender. He pulled a cigarette out of the pack in his jacket pocket and was fishing for a match when he saw a woman walking casually toward the rear gate. Her back was to him; he couldn't see her face. She had long black hair. *There are millions of women in Mexico with long black hair,* he thought. "Hey, *señora*, stop!" he yelled. *Stupid woman keeps walking. Doesn't even look around. She could be Mexican. Doesn't understand English.*

"*ALTO! ALTO!*" He grabbed his revolver, planning to fire at the ground by her feet. A delivery van drove through the gate, heading toward the loading dock. Cortez screamed again, "STOP! *ALTO! SEÑORA, ALTO! ALTO!*" The woman turned around and glanced at him. She started to run. The truck driver thought Cortez was screaming at him and jammed on his brakes, completely blocking Cortez' view of the fleeing woman. Cortez was fifty pounds overweight and had a bad leg. He limped around the truck. The woman had almost reached the open gate between the stone walls. He didn't have time to stop and fire carefully, holding the powerful weapon with both hands as he should. He aimed at her thighs and pulled the trigger. The .44 Magnum kicked up, releasing a burst of bullets that slammed into the woman's head and cervical vertebrae, severing her spinal cord. She fell to the ground, tried to get up on her knees, but her muscles went into spasm and were unable to respond. She began to cough up blood and collapsed into the gutter. The left side of her face was torn away.

Cortez walked slowly over to the gate and stood over the inert body. He called Salvadore.

"Yeah."

"I got one of them. The one with the long hair. She tried to escape but I got her," he bragged.

"Where are you?"

"By the back gate."

"I figured it was you when I heard the gunfire. I'll be right there."

When Salvadore arrived, he turned the body over.

"*Mi Dios!*" He made the sign of the cross on his chest.

Lucie couldn't see the vehicle she was looking for, but she recognized the area and knew about where they had parked. She walked slowly, trying to appear unconcerned, until she heard gunfire. She started to run a zigzag pattern, expecting to be shot any second. Then she recognized the car about 100 feet ahead of her. She cursed when she reached it because she realized that the vehicle parked next to it was so close that she wouldn't be able to open the driver's side door, and she'd have to enter it from the passenger side. She unlocked the passenger's door. As she opened it, Schwartz wrapped his jacket around her head and pushed her into the car. She tried to scream but he put a gloved hand over her mouth, held her in an armlock, and handcuffed her to the steering wheel. Then he called Salvadore. "Hey man, I've got Santoros here at the car. Come as soon as you can. Forget about Alvarez."

"I think maybe you make big mistake, *señor*. I've got the one you're after." Schwartz removed his jacket from Lucie's head. "Oh, shit!" he growled. "Okay, bring her over to the car and I'll make the arrest."

"I'm sorry *señor*, I can't do that. You better come here. I'm at the back gate in the hotel parking lot. You owe me big money, *señor* but is good for you. I save you much *pesos*." Salvadore ended the call.

"Damn Mexican prima donna," Schwartz mumbled into the dead phone. "Money, money, all he thinks about is money."

Schwartz ran to the back gate. By the time he arrived, a crowd of people had gathered around, blocking his view. He pushed his way through to where Salvadore and Cortez were standing.

"So what's going on, Captain? Where's Santoros?" Salvadore and Cortez stepped back and pointed to the ground where a woman's body lay. Cortez pulled back the edge of the blanket to reveal the destroyed face with a blood-soaked wig askew on the head. It was Margaux. Schwartz could not prevent an anguished cry from escaping his lips.

"We just saved you the cost of flying her back to New York. Should be bigger bonus, right, *señor* Schwartz?"

As captain of the local police department, Cortez took control of the situation. After he and Salvadore received the reward Schwartz had promised for the capture of Margaux Santoros, he decided that Mexico and specifically Monterrey was not interested in bearing the expense of the interment of the American fugitive. "Is your problem, señor Schwartz," he pronounced. Schwartz turned to Salvadore.

"Don't look at me, *señor* Schwartz. This is not my jurisdiction. Captain Cortez is in charge here."

When Lucie got over the shock and anguish of Margaux's death, and offered to take charge of Margaux's body and be responsible for the expenses relating to her burial, all three men readily agreed. Salvadore and Cortez evaporated from the scene immediately.

Schwartz explained to her that he must take a series of photographs and fingerprints to confirm Margaux's identity. With regard to her personal effects, he said he would leave them in Lucie's care, except that he would have to confiscate all of Margaux's shoes, including the pair she was wearing at the time of her death. Although Lucie didn't understand the strange demand, she immediately packed all Margaux's footwear in a large plastic bag and turned it over to Sergeant Schwartz.

Schwartz spent the night in room 608 at the Crowne Plaza Hotel. He felt neither joy nor sadness about how the story had played out until around nine o'clock that evening, after he had dined at a sidewalk cafe and returned to his room and opened the plastic bag filled with Margaux's shoes. It didn't take him long to find the pair whose soles exactly matched his photo of the footprint on the back of the oriental rug.

He ordered a bottle of champagne from room service, put it on his expense account, and decided that when he was admitted to practice law in 2011, he would ask United States Attorney Kevin MacDonald if he could use a young, conscientious lawyer in his office.

CHAPTER FIFTY-TWO

At breakfast on the day after Gary and Bridget had climbed to the top of Mount Serene, Bridget said, "Gary, dear, I loved your story, but you've been so pensive this morning. Does it have anything to do with Margaux?"

"Margaux?" Gary replied, startled by the question.

"Margaux Santoros. About what was in last night's paper, I mean."

"I don't know what you're talking about."

"I'm so sorry, love, I thought you knew." She got up and rummaged through the stack of newspapers on the coffee table, found what she was looking for and handed the paper to him. Then she gathered up the dirty dishes and went into the kitchen.

> BARRISTER BEAUTY DIES
> IN MEXICAN SHOOTOUT
>
> *Margaux Santoros, indicted for murdering her husband, Dimitri Santoros, was shot to death yesterday by the chief of police in the city of Monterrey, Mexico. It was reported that after being followed to that city by Sergeant Isadore Schwartz of the New York Police Department, she was gunned down in the parking lot of her hotel while trying to escape....*

Gary dropped the paper back on the table. "Margaux, Margaux," he mumbled. Images of their incredible passion, buried for so many months, exploded in his mind.

And now, my darling Bridget, so kind and decent and...without any passion at all....

He covered his face with his hands.

That evening Bridget recommended that she and Gary have dinner at Consuela's Cozy Corner, a small restaurant on the outskirts of the city. She was relieved when he seemed free of his early morning melancholy. The restaurant's atmosphere was intimate, with a minuscule dance floor and a juke box boasting hundreds of songs to choose from. Gary ordered a bottle of champagne, stepped over to the juke box, and selected a number of songs from the "Golden Oldies" menu.

They chatted easily for a while. Bridget sipped from her glass of champagne. By the time her glass was half empty, Gary had consumed two glasses. She was waiting for him to resume the conversation they had started at breakfast, but he was in a totally different mood. When the juke box began to play the songs that he had selected, Gary asked Bridget to dance. Noting that if she accepted the invitation they would be the only dancers on the floor, she declined. Gary sulked.

Upset, Bridget went to the ladies room. When she returned to their booth Gary was dancing with Consuela. They were both very good dancers. She saw that the bottle of champagne was empty, and decided *enough is enough*. She removed her cell phone from her purse, intending to call a taxi and go home alone. Gary came back to their booth.

"May I have this dance, my dear Bridget?" The words *I don't feel like dancing* raced through her mind. She opened her lips to speak them, but she had no voice. She looked into his wild eyes and thought, *He doesn't even realize I've been gone for twenty minutes.*

Just then, the music began again.

"Have I told you lately how much I love you?" he said, guiding her out onto the dance floor. He caught Consuela's eye and motioned for her to join them.

"Yes, sir?" Consuela said.

There were five other tables occupied in the tiny restaurant. "Please, dear Consuela," Gary said, "pour champagne for all the guests while Bridget and I dance to our special song." He turned to Bridget. "I dedicate this song to you, love," he said, taking her in his arms. They danced alone in the center of the dance floor, swaying to the slow beat. "*It's impossible,*" Elvis crooned. "*If I had you, could I ever ask for more...it's just impossible.*" When the song ended, the people at each of the tables held their glasses of champagne aloft and cheered. Bridget thought, *He's impossible.*

She returned to their booth, but Gary stopped at each of the tables before joining her. Bridget was dazed by the whole scene: the laughter, the spontaneity, the good cheer among total strangers. *This is what Gary is,* she thought...*the entertainer, the clown, the joker. For him it's all make-believe. It's theater; it's fantasy; but marriage isn't a joke or a three-act play. It's for real, with two real people, not a leading man and a leading lady who embrace and part ways when the curtain goes down at the end of the third act and...I know I should join in the fun, but Gary isn't paying any attention to me. Now he's dancing with Consuela again, and chug-a-lugging champagne.*

This time when he came back to their table she said, "It's after eleven o'clock, Gary, and—"

"*And*," he said, interrupting her, I think you are the loveliest woman in the whole world, *and*...I'm prepared to worship at your shrine for the rest of my life, *and*...after this dance, I think we should go home and make whoopee."

He had punched in another selection from the "Golden Oldies" menu on the juke box—"*I can't help falling in love with you.*"

"I've just changed my mind. I've decided that *this* has to be our song," he said, pulling her onto the dance floor and taking her in his arms.

"What am I going to do with you?" she sniffled.

"Love me and live with me happily ever after," he said.

The next morning, Bridget called the clinical psychologist who had helped her cope with the tragic death of her young husband. Doctor Greene agreed to see her later in the day.

When Bridget came into her office and was seated comfortably, Dr. Greene asked, "So, my friend, what's happening?"

"I'm in the middle of another crisis and I need your help," Bridget answered.

"Tell me about it," the psychologist said.

Bridget hesitated. "I don't know where to begin. I... ah, oh, hell, Emma, I've got myself involved with a man, and...."

"Isn't that what you've been hoping for? What's his name? How did you meet him? Fill me in on the story."

Doctor Greene listened as Bridget explained that she thought she had fallen in love and had been happier than she could ever remember, and then it all seemed to fall apart.

"When was that?" the doctor asked.

"Just a few days ago. Gary, that's his name, and I had climbed to the top of my mountain."

"Your mountain? What mountain is that?"

"It's about three miles from Cave Creek. I climb to its peak whenever I want to be totally alone and think about life. Of course it doesn't belong to me, but since it doesn't have a name, I call it Mount Serene. It's so beautiful and peaceful, you know... Maybe someday you might climb it with me."

"Great idea! But you were saying you and your friend Gary had climbed to the top of the mountain and then what happened?"

"We made love. He had been pressuring me to have sex. I had

resisted because I wasn't sure he was serious about *us*—I mean about a relationship."

"What kind of a relationship were you thinking of, Bridget?"

"I thought I was falling in love with him but I didn't want to get hurt. I didn't want to be used, you know what I mean?"

"I think I do, but why don't you tell me?"

"The thing is, Gary seemed to be a perfect mate for me. He seemed to like my kids and my friends, and he's sweet and funny and successful in business and all, but...I don't know. For example, let me tell you what happened last night."

"I'm listening," Dr. Greene said.

"We went to dinner at Consuela's. He ordered a bottle of champagne as soon as we arrived and by the time the food arrived he had finished off the whole bottle. He asked me to dance and when I said no, he asked Consuela to dance, and the next thing I know he's dancing with another lady. I decided that was enough and I was about to call a taxi and go home when he sort of dragged me out on the dance floor and told me we should go home immediately and make whoopee. And that's another thing, when I agreed to, you know, to do it with him on top of the mountain, I thought he would be really happy that I had given in to him, but the moment it was over, he just clammed up and appeared depressed. I couldn't figure it out."

"Did you ask him what the problem was?"

"Not exactly."

"What does that mean, not exactly?"

"I don't know, Emma, I was so happy and then it all fell apart." Bridget turned her head away. Doctor Greene slid the Kleenex box over to her and waited until she regained control of her emotions. Then she said, "Let's go back to the point where you were on the top of the mountain. It sounds to me as if that's the point where things began to go wrong, am I right?"

"I guess so," Bridget said softly.

"Was your lovemaking a joyful event?"

"I gave him what he wanted, if that's what you mean."

"That's not what I mean at all. I want to know how you felt about what was happening."

"We had sex. What else can I tell you?"

"Let me put it this way. When you were nursing your kids, it was a wondrous experience, right?"

Bridget nodded and dabbed at her eyes.

"You felt connected to them, didn't you? I want to know if you felt that same kind of connection with Gary when you made love."

"I don't see how one has anything to do with the other."

"Okay, how about this? Animals don't make love. They only copulate. Humans do both. What did you and Gary do on the mountain?"

"To be totally honest, Emma, I don't see the difference."

Dr. Greene smiled. "My dear Bridget, I do believe I understand the problem…and, hopefully, the solution.

"Do you think your friend Gary might be willing to come see me? And after that, perhaps the three of us could talk."

CHAPTER FIFTY-THREE

Pierre and Louise sat on their porch and watched the moon rise. It was a glorious Caribbean evening. The fragrance of the frangipani and oleander, mixed with the salt sea breeze, was intoxicating.

"Despite all our problems, darling," Pierre said, reaching over and taking her hand in his own, "I've never been happier in my life. Look at that spectacular moon and those millions of stars in that so-dark blue sky and the booming rhythm of the surging sea, and...and...and God, how I adore you, Oh wife of mine."

"You are so full of malarkey, my dear, dear, Pierre, but what a wonderful life we've had together. I regret I've never been able to give us children, but...."

Pierre interrupted her. "We have Gary and Lindy. Certainly I think of them as if they were part of our family. You were the mother Melinda never had. She worships you."

"And you as well, Pierre. It's true, I think of her as our own child. All of which reminds me—If we're going to have an inauguration party for Hotel Orchedia, we must set a date and make certain that Gary and Lindy can come."

"Absolutely," Pierre said. "I don't know why, but Gary has been on my mind tonight. I hope he's okay. I think I'll give him a call tomorrow. He and Lindy lead such busy lives we have to give them plenty of time to make travel plans that will allow them to stay with us for at least a week."

"When do you think we'll be ready to open?" Louise asked.

"I've heard or read somewhere that you're never "ready" to open a hotel. If you waited until everything is the way it's supposed to be before you open a hotel, it would never open. On that basis, I think we should plan to open as soon as we finish furnishing the first three cottages, and that should be in thirty to sixty days."

"In that case," Louise said, "I have something to show you." She went into the house and returned with a lantern and a manila folder. She handed Pierre the folder. When he opened it, it was a beautiful little painting of their hotel beside the sea.

"My idea, depending upon how many guests we intend to invite, is to paint each invitation with a different view of the hotel...you know, perhaps from a different angle or a different time of day. You see? They'll be souvenirs for the guests and then we can make copies of the paintings to serve as our first brochure. We can't take photographs of the hotel yet because it isn't finished, and we want our guests to come just as soon as the cottages are ready. So what do you think?"

"First of all, the painting is wonderful, and if you're up to it, the idea of original paintings as invitations to our first guests is marvelous. Let me see…We'll need six invitations. There will be Gary, Melinda and two paying couples. It's a deal, sweetheart! I promise to have three units all trimmed out. You'll get them all furnished and we'll send out the invitations to Gary and Melinda immediately for our opening in March."

Almost two months went by before Gary was able to arrange his schedule so that he could revisit Bridget in Scottsdale, although in the interim they had connected twice for an overnight when their work schedules permitted.

They had talked on their cell phones almost every evening no matter where Bridget's flight schedule took her. Their conversations increasingly involved Bridget seeking Gary's male input with regard to Michael or how Gary had handled problems with Melinda when she was the same age as Jonni. He had a vivid recollection of the night she called him to discuss "the pill."

"Jonni is only thirteen, you know," Bridget said. "Actually she'll be fourteen in a few months, but the point is that she's still very young. Now she's sort of befriended a couple of girls in school who are fifteen and sixteen and who told Jonni that they were on the pill. I couldn't believe it when she told me about it." Gary laughed.

"It's not funny, Gary."

"I know, sweetheart. I only laughed because I remember as if it were yesterday when Lindy asked me if she could "go on the pill." She was seventeen at the time, but I was shocked that she asked me. Neither of my parents ever talked to me about sex. But the times have changed dramatically in this generation. Some friends of mine who have a fourteen year-old daughter told me they have a problem with the kids having oral sex in the back of the school bus."

"Oh Lordy, I'm thirty-eight years old, and I have a problem with oral sex," Bridget laughed. Gary didn't answer. He just drew in a breath, puffed out his cheeks and sighed.

Although the subject matter of their nightly conversations sounded more and more like that of a married couple, neither of them mentioned the "M" word. Gary believed that the subject of marriage was so sensitive and so important that it had to be discussed face to face. He was also so convinced that everything was going to work out according to *his* plan that he obtained options to purchase a ten acre parcel of land on the west side of Serene mountain that was accessible by a four-wheel drive vehicle. His idea was to build a two story building on the land. The ground level would be a state of the art studio where his television commercials could be filmed, with video conferencing facilities that would enable him to talk face to face with his major clients in their conference rooms, and with his staff in New York. The second floor would be an all-glass penthouse facing west toward the glorious Arizona sunsets.

But while Gary was making elaborate plans, Bridget became more and more concerned about her relationship with him. She called Doctor Greene.

"*This is Doctor Greene. I'm away from my office for the next few days. If this call involves an emergency, you may call me on my cell phone at 279-2749. Otherwise leave me a detailed message concerning your problem and I'll return your call or suggest that we meet in my office at a convenient time for both of us. Either way I promise to get back to you as soon as possible. Thank you.*"

"Emma, this is Bridget. This is definitely not an emergency, but I believe that my future happiness depends on making the right decision. I'm operating on the theory that as my mom always says, an ounce of prevention prevents a pound of regret, or something like that.

"You gave me such wonderful insight when I got hung up on the sex thing with Gary, which by the way has opened the way for spectacular new joyous experiences for me. Sex education in school didn't materialize until after I graduated and I never had the courage to discuss it with my mother. When I went to college I didn't want any of my girlfriends to discover how naive I was. Then I married Robert who apparently didn't know any more than I did. We were both virgins who understood the mechanics of it all, but didn't understand that there was incredible joy for the woman as well as the man just for the asking.

"Now with your help I understand my role in the process, and Gary and I are reaping the benefits of your wisdom, but I've hit another snag in our affair. HELP!

"I can't blame it all on Gary, I mean, I didn't see him for a year, he storms into Scottsdale three month ago, and within a few days we end up screwing on top of a freaking mountain. Now, *I'm* talking about marriage but he just smiles and keeps changing the subject. He sends me a poem that he wrote that he claims is supposed to make me laugh, but I'm not laughing. I'll read it to you and you tell me what *you* think."

Do you promise to adore this woman?
Do you promise to respect this woman?
Do you promise to love this woman?
Above all others?
I do

Do you promise to cherish this man?
Do you promise to honor this man?
Do you promise to love this man?
Above all others?
I do

By the power vested in me by Mother Nature
I now pronounce you Significant Others.

"Now here's the problem, Emma. He keeps insisting he loves me but he absolutely refuses to talk seriously about marriage, which he believes only makes sense if you're going to have kids, which at our age neither of us has any interest whatsoever in doing.

"I really do think I'm in love with him. But how do I know what this love business is all about? I loved my husband—a sweet, naive man who gave me two beautiful children, but he was as dull as mashed potatoes. Gary has made me laugh more in a a few months than Robert did in the three years we were married. But do I want to marry the Court Jester? The answer to that is, "Yes!" He's what I want as a father for Michael and Jonni, and I'll be able to become a full-time mother for them again. I won't have to go on worrying about what's happening with the kids while I'm away from home, or struggle to pay the mortgage and the taxes on the house, or wonder where the money's going to come from to pay for Jonni's orthodontist bill, or Michael and Jonni's college education. Okay, that's it. I'm willing to give a little here and there, but I've decided it's time for me to take charge here. The problem is I'm afraid if I call for a showdown, I'll lose him.

"What should I do, Emma? I want him to marry me in the church where I was baptized, and take me on a honeymoon to Paris, or get out of my life. I want to tell him to forget about this 'Significant Other' baloney."

Bridget picked up Gary from the Scottsdale airport, three months from the very day they climbed her special mountain together. On the way home they kept glancing at each other and smiling. When they arrived, she took his hand and led him out to the covered patio where she had arranged a bar with a bottle of Grey Goose vodka, a pitcher of orange juice, a bucket of ice and two fresh limes.

"How about a cool drink after your long trip?" she asked.

"You're too good to me," he said, taking off his jacket and settling down in the big overstuffed couch under the lazily turning ceiling fan.

"You're absolutely right about that," she said, as she prepared his drink, "but I want you to be in the best mood possible when we undertake this most important conversation that you keep telling me we must have face to face." She handed him the drink, poured herself a glass of ginger ale, and sat down beside him.

He told her about his plan to build the studio/penthouse on the mountainside, and how she must quit her job so that they could all spend the school year as a family in Scottsdale and summer vacations in Sea Cliff. She seemed so pleased with everything he was suggesting that he was certain she would accept his proposal of living together without the cumbersome trappings of marriage.

"Now, I guess I'm coming to the most controversial part, but I'm sure we'll be able to work it out," he said.

"Uh-oh," Bridget exhaled softly.

"Not to worry," Gary added hastily. But you see, darling, there's only one condition that's at the foundation of all my beliefs, and it's critical to the success of my plan...."

When he had finished explaining in exquisite detail, once again, his rationale for providing every financial benefit a wife was entitled to but foregoing a formal marriage commitment, Bridget burst into tears. Gary immediately took her in his arms and tried to comfort her.

"No, no, you don't understand," she sobbed. "We're going to have a baby in October."

"Oh, no," Gary gasped.

"Oh yes," Bridget proclaimed. "And we're going to get married and live happily ever after."

Pierre stood on the dock, anxiously awaiting the arrival of their first guests, who had responded to the website video Gary and Melinda had created. Although they were exhilarated about the opening, they were disappointed that neither Gary nor Melinda would be able to make it because of prior commitments.

Louise was a bit agitated because the electrical system had broken down on the morning before the guests were due to check in, the extra bed linens she had ordered from Miami were sitting in customs in Aruba, and the cook they had hired from Bonaire hadn't shown up as promised so that she and Pierre were going to have to cook breakfast, lunch and dinner for the three couples checking in.

They put complimentary bottles of wine in each bedroom and rounded up candles and a few kerosene lanterns from their island friends, which they hoped would solve the lack of electricity problem.

Pierre and Louise graciously greeted their first guests at the pier upon their arrival—a distinguished, middle-aged couple from upstate New York by the name of Kerrigan.

When the next two couples stepped off the boat, they shouted "SURPRISE!" and Gary and Melinda encircled Pierre and Louise in their arms. Lindy's fiancé and Bridget and her children Michael and Jonni waited on the sidelines to be introduced and then hugs and kisses were exchanged all around.

When everyone was settled into the hotel, Gary opened his extra suitcase—filled with champagne bottles—and the party began.

The next morning, Pierre and Louise cooked up a breakfast feast.

Before dinner the following evening, as they all gathered for cocktails on the terrace by the sea, Bridget and Gary handed out sealed envelopes to Melinda and her fiancé, to Pierre and Louise, to Michael and Jonni, and to Mr. and Mrs. Kerrigan. Printed upon the outside of each envelope was a warning that it should be opened immediately.

Please join us
For a celebration of love and friendship
as
Bridget Mulvaney Tulane
and
Gary James Samson
Join their hands in matrimony
At sunset this evening
Beneath the Divi Divi tree
On the beach at the Hotel Orchedea
Isla Di Oro Island, Caribbean
Champagne and dessert reception to follow

The marriage ceremony was performed by Mr. Kerrigan, who turned out to be a friend of Gary's and, by a happy coincidence, a New York judge authorized by law to conduct such official acts. The question of whether or not his office had jurisdiction outside the State of New York was not raised by any of the participants, nor would it ever be.

After the solemn vows were made by Bridget and Gary, and after the appropriate toasts were offered and congratulations acknowledged, the bride and groom danced the first dance barefoot in the sand.

EPILOGUE

The Cliffonian, Sea Cliff's weekly newsletter, reported that on October 8, 2010, Gary and Bridget Samson, of 312 Harbor Drive, in Sea Cliff, became the proud parents of a baby girl. They named her Serena Mulvaney-Samson.

CPSIA information can be obtained at www.ICGtesting.com
Printed in the USA
LVOW120858051211

257817LV00004B/2/P